D0189993

Anita Burgh was born in Gillingham, Kent, but spent her early years at Lanhydrock House in Cornwall. Returning to the Medway Towns, she attended Chatham Grammar School, and became a student nurse at UCH in London. She gave up nursing upon marrying into the aristocracy. Subsequently divorced, she pursued various careers – secretarial work, as a laboratory technician in cancer research and as an hotelier. She divides her time between Gloucestershire and the Auvergne in France, where she shares her life with her partner, Billy, a Cairn terrier, three mixed-breed dogs, three cats and a bulldog puppy. The visits of a constantly changing mix of her four children, two stepchildren and six grandchildren keep her busy, happy, entertained and poor! Anita Burgh is the author of many bestsellers, including *Distinctions of Class*, which was shortlisted for the Romantic Novel of the Year Award. Visit Anita Burgh at her website: www.anitaburgh.com.

ANITA BURGH

The House At Harcourt

ORION

An Orion paperback

First published in Great Britain in 2002
by Orion
This paperback edition published in 2002
by Orion Books Ltd,
Orion House, 5 Upper St Martin's Lane,
London WC2H 9EA

A CIP catalogue record for this book is
available from the British Library.

ISBN 0 75284 945 X

Typeset by Deltatype Ltd, Birkenhead, Merseyside

Printed and bound in Great Britain by
Clays Ltd, St Ives plc

For my son Patrick Leith with love

Prologue
1860

Such was the tension in the room that Amelia Eliza Forester, at only three and a half years of age, was aware of it even if she did not understand it. She sat on the floor in the furthest corner, half hidden by an ornate screen, certain that they had forgotten she was there.

She watched intently as her mother, for whom she was named, threw her clothes hither and thither in agitation, whispering in an urgent way to Merry, Amelia's nurse. The little girl clutched to her a faded blue baby blanket, which she called her babbit and which Merry constantly tried to take away from her but never succeeded in doing so.

'What was that?' Amelia Victoria Forester paused in her sorting and looked anxiously about her. She was clutching a flower-encrusted bonnet tightly to her, crushing it. 'I heard a horse!'

Merry lumbered noisily across the oak-panelled room, pushed back the heavy brocade curtains and peered out of the mullioned window into the park of Harcourt Barton. 'Why, ma'am, don't you fret. There's nothing and nobody there. Let's get this done quick, shall us? You look all peaky with nerves.'

'Is the child's trunk packed?'

'It is, ma'am. And a right battle we had over which toys were to go, didn't we, my lovely?' She turned but couldn't see the child and began to hunt the room for her. 'There you are! Hiding from Merry, were you? You'll get your new frock dusty sitting on the floor.' She pulled Amelia to her feet and brushed at her skirt with her large, capable hands.

Suddenly the bedroom door was flung open with such force that it swung back and splintered the panelling of the walls.

'So it's true! You whore!' Frederick Forester stood in the doorway, his feet wide apart, rocking back and forth as if he were still astride his horse. Sweat from a hard ride glistened on his face, his boots were coated with mud and there was anger in his eyes. Little Amelia clung tighter to her blanket.

'Freddie! Please!' her mother cried, swayed on her feet and dropped the bonnet. Merry stepped back nimbly, her bulk hiding the angry man from his child.

'I want you out of my house.'

'What have people been saying about me? Freddie, I beg you, listen to me.'

'Why? You'll only tell me more lies. I prefer to speak with my friends, who show me a greater loyalty than you. May you rot in hell!'

Merry gasped, then crossed herself as he spun round to face her. 'You! Out!' He pointed imperiously at the door with his riding whip.

Merry wavered, looking first to her mistress then her master, her skirt swaying back and forth like a giant black bell, shielding the child, delaying the inevitable as best she could.

'Out!'

'Merry, go.'

Still Merry paused.

'And take that bastard with you!' he shouted.

With one swoop Merry scooped the little girl into her arms and made for the door as fast as her size would allow.

'Put me down! You're hurting me!' Amelia was wriggling. On the landing Merry put her back on her feet. 'Why's Papa cross?'

'Never you mind.' Instead of scuttling back to the

nursery, Merry bent low, one ear to the door. And Amelia heard the swish of the whip and the pitiful screams of her mother.

Amelia was in the nursery. She'd had her tea, not that she had wanted to eat. Neither was she playing with the model theatre, which, for the moment, was her favourite toy. She sat, hands in her lap, large tears plopping on to a picture book which she was not looking at. She and Merry could hear the rumble of thunder as an early summer storm began to brew. The air was listless, heavy, as if nature itself were waiting for an outcome. When the door opened her and Merry's hearts missed a beat. But it was her mother, who entered the room stealthily, dressed for travel. 'I am to leave. Immediately.' She stood ashen-faced, her eyes pink-rimmed from weeping. She moved stiffly, as if in pain.

'We're ready.' Merry indicated the two tapestry bags and the large trunk in the middle of the room.

'No, Merry. The master won't let Amelia come with me.'

'Oh, ma'am, no!'

'I've tried all entreaties. Merry . . .' She turned her back on her daughter. 'Oh, Merry, I'm so afraid.' She was whispering but not quietly enough.

'Mama, why are you afraid? You're crying. Did Papa hurt you?' The little girl tugged at Amelia Victoria's skirt.

Her mother knelt down, placed her hands at either side of the child's face and stared at her, intently as if memorising her image. 'Mama has to go away for a little while, but I'll come back to fetch you, I promise.'

'When?'

'As soon as I can. Don't be afraid – you'll be safe here with Merry to care for you.'

'Why should I be afraid? And why are you crying again?'

'I'll write and you can write to me. You will love to get letters, won't you?'

'I can't write.'

'You will soon. You're so clever.' Her voice broke. She bent forward and kissed her daughter.

'I love the smell of you, Mama.' Amelia sniffed appreciatively at the lovely perfume of roses which her mother always used, then put out a small hand and stroked her face, her lovely face. 'Come back soon, Mama.'

Amelia Victoria jumped up abruptly. 'I'll be in touch, Merry. Take good care . . .' Her words trailed off and she rushed from the room.

Amelia stood on the upper landing and watched, through the banisters, as her mother ran across the stone floor of the hall below, in haste to be gone. Her father stood at the front door, holding it wide open as if to facilitate her going. The realisation of what was truly happening galvanised the little girl. She flung herself down the stairs, her feet barely touching them, screaming for her mother.

'Go back to your nursery,' her father shouted.

'I want my mama.'

'*Eliza*, go back to your nurse.'

'My name is Amelia.'

'Not any longer.' He slammed the heavy oak door shut. Amelia ran to it and pounded on the panels with her tiny fists as she heard the sound of horses' hoofs. Her father grabbed her roughly, pulled her away from the door and held her away from him at arm's length. She tried to kick him but his reach was too long. 'Listen to me, child. You're Eliza from now, and for ever, and never again say the name of your mother in my house.'

'I'm Amelia!' the child said defiantly, and her father slapped her hard across the face. 'Amelia! Amelia!' she shouted, and he hit her again. Amelia, now Eliza, sank

4

on to the bottom stair and bit her bottom lip. Defiantly she did not cry.

'Come upstairs, my handsome.' Merry, who was crying, fussed over her.

'No, I shan't. I'm waiting for my mama.'

She had to be carried forcibly back to her nursery, struggling, kicking, scratching all the way. Each day for weeks she would slip away from Merry, sit stoically on the stairs in the great hall, opposite the large front door, and wait.

But her mother never came. Neither did her letters.

Chapter One
1870

I

'What do you think of our house, Miss Chester?' Eliza Forester had purposely brought her new governess to her favourite spot on the estate. High on the side of a steep hill above Harcourt Barton there stood a great gnarled oak, its branches sweeping to the ground. When the wind blew the tree looked to Eliza as if it were dancing.

From here she could see the whole of her world, for she had never been anywhere else. Below were her father's fields, bright, lush, billowing green counter-panes spread on the red Devon earth. Far beyond, in a misty haze, like the purple smudges of fatigue beneath a beautiful woman's eyes, lay the hills that she liked to think guarded her and the estate.

They could see her father's house and most of the formal gardens, in which strutted the peacocks whose call they could clearly hear. Swans glided across the still waters of the lake. To the west lay the walled kitchen garden where the sun glinted on the greenhouses. They could see the stables, but not quite hear the clock chiming three. Beyond, the horses were grazing content-edly in the paddock. Eliza pointed out the young trees in the arboretum her father was creating. And, further away, Great Wood. 'When I was young I was certain the wood went right to the edge of the world. I prefer not to go there, it's a creepy place.'

Further to the west they could see the farm buildings and the estate land, which spread out far below them. Gardeners, ostlers, stable lads scurried about reminding

Eliza, from this height, of busy insects. When she was here she liked to fancy she was seeing the world as a bird would see it.

Fanny Chester, newly arrived at her post, had no idea how honoured she was to have been invited here: Eliza liked to keep this part of the estate to herself. She had never brought any of her previous governesses here. Miss Chester was different, though: she had liked her immediately. She did not know where the idea had come from, but she felt she had met a friend and she wanted to share things with her. 'This oak was mentioned in the Domesday Book.' The girl stroked the tree tenderly.

'As is the house surely? Or so I was told.'

'That too. Not this house, of course. This one was built by my grandfather. But there's always been a dwelling here, probably since time began. Barton means farm, you know. My aunt thinks we should simply call it Harcourt, that it's *infra dig* for it to be thought a farm. That's short for *infra dignitatem*, Latin for "beneath one's dignity".'

'How interesting.'

'But my father likes it as it is. He calls it an amusing conceit. Do you like it?' She leant forward, an anxious expression on her face.

'The house? It's very large,' Fanny answered cautiously. Years of genteel poverty and reliance on others for the means to survive had taught her, as many other governesses, that to have an opinion was a luxury for the independent.

'Most people love it, but there are some strange people who don't. I think it's the most wonderful place on earth,' Eliza told her.

'As you should.'

They looked down at the vast house where towers and turrets, battlements and buttresses proliferated. From this vantage-point it looked, with its myriad chimneys and glinting windows, more like a village than a single house.

'Can't you just imagine King Arthur riding from here to find his Guinevere?'

'Undoubtedly.'

Eliza threw herself down on the grass and lay flat on her back, peering up at the sky through the oak leaves. She had taken off her rice straw hat and thrown it to the side. 'Mind your dress,' Fanny said. Eliza was wearing a beautiful pale blue silk with a darker underskirt, the sides caught up with pale pink roses that matched the sash at her waist.

'I've marked my boots already.' Eliza stuck them in the air: they were streaked with grass stains. 'Merry will have the vapours.'

'Perhaps I can clean them before she sees them.'

'Would you? That would be kind.' Eliza couldn't imagine Miss Greene, her last governess, volunteering for such a menial task.

Now Fanny lay down beside her, clutching at her own billowing skirts. 'Have you noticed that if you lie on your back and stare at the sky for long enough it's as if the whole world is revolving?' she said.

Eliza sat bolt upright. 'You're the only other person I've met who's noticed that. Merry always says I'm imagining it, or making it up. I can never make up my mind which is worst.'

'Some people forget how wonderful it is to be a child.'

'And you haven't?'

'I try not to.'

Eliza lay back again. When Miss Greene had left she had been a tiny bit upset: she had liked her. It was the abruptness of her dismissal, which had come without warning, that had bothered her the most and, as usual, no one would tell her why she had gone. But now she wondered if it wasn't a good thing she had and this new one had come in her place. She sneaked a sly look at her. They were usually plain poor things, they never had curls as she had, and they always wore such dismal colours, governess colours, greys and fawn.

Miss Chester was wearing grey, but quite a pretty dove colour, and her hair was neatly pulled back, which was a shame – Eliza stroked her own fat ringlet – but she had a pretty nose and lovely grey eyes. And, what was more, she was younger than Eliza's governesses usually were. 'I was worried that I wouldn't like you but I do.'

'I'm glad.' Fanny smiled at her.

'But, then, perhaps I shouldn't in case you go away.'

'I don't understand.'

'Everyone I like goes away sooner or later.'

'Do they?'

'Oh, yes. I've had lots of nursery-maids and governesses but they all leave.'

'Perhaps because you're so naughty.'

'But I'm not, I promise. I try to be good.'

'I'm sure you do. But Merry tells me she's been with you since you were a baby.'

'Yes, but she's the only one. Well, that's not quite true – there's her, Mr Densham, the butler, and the housekeeper and the coachman and four gardeners, and lots of the housemaids and—'

'Everybody else?' Fanny laughed.

'Yes, nearly everybody else.' Eliza giggled.

'Perhaps the others did something wrong.'

'Perhaps, but I don't think Miss Greene would have – she prayed *four* times a day. Do you?'

'Not as often as Miss Greene, just morning and night.'

'Good. I think four times is selfish, bothering God all the time. I'm sure He has lots of other people to listen to.'

'I'm sure He always has time for our prayers. But certainly Miss Greene must have been a paragon.'

'What's that?'

'Someone who is a model of virtue and good character.'

'That was Miss Greene. And does it mean boring too?'

'Eliza! Really!'

Eliza sat up and looked down at her governess. 'You didn't say what you *really* thought about my house. Just vague things.'

From all Fanny had been told about Harcourt Barton by her brother she had been prepared to dislike it but she didn't. Quite the opposite. It was rather ornate and embellished, but charmingly so. 'I do like it – and you're right, one might indeed expect to see knights riding up to it on their white chargers.'

'I'm so glad you do. It would have been difficult to like you otherwise.' Eliza jumped to her feet. 'I shall make you a daisy chain.'

Fanny watched her with an indulgent smile. She appeared bright if somewhat younger than her age. But from what Fanny had gathered Eliza lived here with few companions of her own age or class. No doubt the staff indulged her, which kept her childish. And was that a bad thing? There was plenty of time for her to grow up and take on the problems of adulthood. And how fortunate she was to live in a place such as this. Fanny's brother, Peter, whom she had visited in Richmond on her way here, had been damning of the house and its occupants. 'Harcourt Barton? Please tell me I misheard. Please tell me you're not going there!' Her brother had stopped dead in his tracks as they walked through the park. 'How could you?'

'It's a good position.'

'Don't you ever listen to anything I tell you?' Fanny had been alarmed at his angry expression. 'How could you live under the same roof as those people?'

'I don't understand, Peter, why are you so cross with me?'

'That fiendish family caused the death of our father.'

'But it was the bank that demanded he repay his loan to them when his invention failed, you know that.'

'And his bank was owned by the Foresters of Harcourt Barton.'

'I had no idea of this when I applied to them.'

'They killed him!'

'But the Mr Forester who is employing me must have been a young man at the time. You can't blame him.'

'I can and I do.'

'Father couldn't honour his debt to them. No one killed him,' she had said gently. She and Peter rarely talked about their father's death. It had been many years after the event that she had learnt he had killed himself – such an end was too shameful to discuss. She had been a small child of five when it had happened and had few memories of their father but Peter had been twelve and remembered everything.

'They ruin everything they touch. Even their house,' he went on.

'But I saw an engraving. It looked beautiful.'

'It is as false as they are. They pretend, with their great estate, to be gentlemen when they were spawned by ostlers.'

'To better oneself is not a sin.'

'Usury is. Bankrupting innocents is. They are money-lenders with no heart. They pursue their victims beyond the grave. How could you accept this post?' Peter was swishing his cane back and forth on the gravel of the path.

'Because I did not know. Positions are hard to find, Peter. There are far more women searching than there are places.'

'I don't want you to go there, Fanny. I don't want you tainted by them.'

She had tried to placate him, but he would have none of it. Would she have turned down the Foresters had she known the truth? Honesty made her acknowledge that she probably wouldn't. She needed this position desperately: she had searched for months and her savings had diminished rapidly.

She gazed at the house far below. She understood what Peter had meant about it. The Jacobean house was still there for those with the eye to see it, but hidden now like the kernel of a nut wrapped about with the convoluted stone embellishments added by the Foresters – father and son. To a purist like her brother it would be offensive, but she still liked it.

Was she being disloyal to her father's memory? She had read the Bible but, as she watched Eliza make her daisy chain, she could not believe that the sins of the grandfather had been visited upon her. She hadn't yet met Frederick Forester but had been interviewed by Eliza's aunt, Lady Wickham, and she had gathered he was rarely in residence. There had always been money-lenders, and no doubt they hadn't forced her father to borrow from them. And the Foresters weren't that any way: they were respectable bankers, with a branch in Exeter and another in London. And it hadn't been this Mr Forester who had called in the loan from their father, but his father who had caused the tragedy . . .

'What are you thinking? You have such a sad expression. Is it something I've done?'

Fanny had not noticed Eliza approaching. 'No, Eliza, it is not, and what a lovely chain you've made me.' She smiled.

'Then why are you so sad?'

'I was thinking about my brother, Peter.'

'And he makes you sad?'

'Because I don't see him often and I wish I could.'

'I wish I had a brother or, better still, a sister. But my mama died when I was born so it wasn't meant to be.'

'Perhaps your father will marry again.'

'Do you think so? I wish he would. Then he would be

happy and I could be too. He has lots of lady-friends,' she added proudly.

Fanny stood up. Perhaps this was a conversation she should not pursue. 'We should go, the sun is slipping away and we don't want to catch colds, do we? Put on your bonnet.'

'It's my birthday next week.'

'I must note it in my diary.'

'Will you. It's taken *ages* to come.'

'Your birthday or being fourteen?' Fanny smiled.

'Both!' Eliza called over her shoulder as she began to hurtle down the hill, her bonnet held on only by its ribbons.

'You really shouldn't allow the child to run down the hill in that fashion, Miss Chester. Had her grandmother been here to see her she would be most annoyed with you.' Mrs King looked over her spectacles disapprovingly at Fanny. They were in the housekeeper's comfortable sitting room, at the back of the house, next to the butler's private quarters, enjoying a cup of tea after their dinner. Fanny's duties were over for the night since Merry Greensay would see Eliza to bed.

'I wouldn't dream of letting her do so had Lady Gwendoline been here. I wasn't aware you were watching us.' She smiled sweetly. 'But thank you, Mrs King, for the warning. I shall remember in future.' Fanny had lived in other people's houses long enough to know that she must not make an enemy of the housekeeper, who was a powerful being in any establishment.

'When I set eyes on you I took you to be a sensible young woman and I'm right.'

'Am I?' Fanny laughed.

'Not many like accepting criticism.'

'I didn't take it as such, Mrs King. I thought you were simply advising me.'

'Quite. Do you like the house?'

'It's very impressive.'

'Great barn of a place.' Mrs King stood up and crossed to a magnificent carved Jacobean chest on which stood a tray and a decanter. 'A sherry, Miss Chester?'

'That would be most enjoyable, Mrs King.' Fanny had noticed before that the servants' quarters were often furnished with the most lovely pieces from a previous age, no longer liked by the family since they were not modern enough.

The sherry was poured. Mrs King was already rather flushed and Fanny wondered if it was her first drink that evening.

'Mr Forester never stops building. No sooner do I think it's all over than he's off on another scheme,' Mrs King confided. 'The last one was covering over the inner court, such a lovely place that was to sit, but was he content with it? No. He had to make a conservatory. Have you ever heard of anything more ridiculous?'

'Conservatories are all the rage, I hear.'

'Then that's why he decided on one. He doesn't think of the mess, though, does he? All that mud. He doesn't have to clear it up, does he?'

'Well, no, not exactly.' Fanny took a sip of her sherry. Instinct told her she might be on dangerous ground here. Mud, she was sure, was not a problem: she had already been in the conservatory to admire the plants and all was in immaculate order.

'And what about the smell? The drawing room will reek of musty earth, won't it?'

'But they have put in the vestibule to prevent that happening.' At Mrs King's frown, Fanny added hurriedly, 'I do hope so, for your sake.' It was best not to appear too knowledgeable.

'Then there are the accidents.'

'What accidents?'

'He's replaced all the windows on the stairs and

landings with stained glass. They might look pretty but they're dangerous.'

'I don't understand.'

'They make the place so dark. People are always falling down, cutting and bruising themselves. We've even had a broken limb or two. Well, it all makes for extra work, doesn't it?'

'How terrible for you.' Fanny clucked sympathetically.

'Then he fills the place with all these people – half of them he doesn't even know.'

'Making even more work for you.' Fanny shook her head.

'All and sundry he invites. And some of them aren't who or what they claim to be,' Mrs King said, her voice brimming with disapproval. 'Buying popularity, that's what it is. Showing off. He wants to be one of *them*, you see, but he never will, oh dear me no.' She offered Fanny a plate of biscuits, which she declined. 'I know the genuine article when I see it. I was brought up on Lady Gwendoline's father's estate. Now they really *were*, no pretence there. More sherry?'

'Thank you, no, I haven't finished this yet.'

'You'll see what I mean when Lady Gwendoline arrives tomorrow. Difficult woman but *a swell*.' Mrs King refilled her own glass and sank back into her seat. Then she leant forward and cupped the side of her mouth nearest the door with her hand. 'Of course, she never wanted to marry Charles Forester, but her father, the old Earl, owed the bank too much money, so in return for having the slate wiped clean she agreed to the marriage.'

Fanny did not comment but nodded. It was a story she had heard often enough.

'Same thing with Eliza's mother,' Mrs King went on. 'Pretty little thing she was. Flighty, of course, but they should never have made her marry him. Chalk and cheese, they were, that's what I've always said. And when you think that after all *she*'d been through Lady Gwendoline was behind that match and prepared to let the same thing happen to her niece, why, it doesn't bear thinking about, does it?'

'It's tragic for Eliza that she died so young.'

Strangely, Mrs King laughed inordinately as she poured herself yet more sherry. This time she didn't offer Fanny any.

2

At intervals, the boiler behind the large black range made a screeching, whistling noise. Each time Maggie Bones, who as often as not was called simply 'you', dashed across the room and hit it sharply with a wooden paddle kept beside the cooker for just that purpose. Immediately the noise subsided and Maggie sidled towards the scullery.

'You! Have you finished them potatoes?'

'Half-way through, Mrs Satterly,' she lied, and hauled one of the large saucepans she was still cleaning, from lunchtime, into the sink. Every day she got behind, no matter how hard she tried, even now when they had only Miss Eliza to feed.

Thinking of spoilt *Miss Eliza* made her feel angry. And, temper getting the upper hand of expedience, she banged one of the pans. *Miss Eliza*, indeed. It was stupid to call a slip of a girl 'Miss' and, worse, have to bob to her should she meet her. Fortunately she never had. It was unlikely that the likes of her would deign to visit the kitchens. But she'd seen her, dressed like a doll, Maggie had thought, in her ribbons and lace, and always laughing – but, then, she had a lot to laugh about. Bang went another pot. She scooped another ladle of soda into the washing-up water – it made her hands rough and red, and in winter they bled. *Miss Eliza!*

In the kitchen the boiler bubbled again ominously. Maggie was across the kitchen before Mrs Satterly could screech, 'You!' and whacked the cooker violently.

'Bats and belfries!' Merry Greensay, who was sitting in the kitchen, fanned herself. 'You should have that monster seen to, Mrs Satterly. It might explode and scald us all to death.' She was close to an open door, which led on to the kitchen porch, and she was enjoying a cup of tea with her friend. She had flipped up her skirt and rolled down her stockings, exposing her dimpled white flesh. She spreadeagled her legs and, as she had no truck with drawers, the slight breeze soothed her more intimate parts. Opposite her, Mrs Satterly was perched like a tiny black bird in the centre of a pine and raffia chair.

'It's been done I don't know how many times. I told Mrs King I was off if it wasn't seen to. She sent that bloody oaf Pike to see to it, but he's got less brain than a farting ferret.'

Merry closed her eyes as if to shut out the swear words with which Mrs Satterly peppered her speech. She doubted that the woman knew it offended her – probably she wasn't even aware that she swore. Merry's father had been like that, and quite taken aback when his wife complained.

Merry was not surprised by Mrs Satterly's language: from all her years in service, and from all the cooks she had met, she had learnt that they were precariously balanced people.

'How's the new governess settling in? I spied her when she arrived. Pretty little thing, isn't she? Not like the others. I wonder what the master will make of her.' Mrs Satterly's eyebrows arched meaningfully.

Merry's full, generous mouth disappeared as she sucked her lips into a thin, mean line. 'She's no better than she ought to be, if you asks me.'

'I've never quite understood what that phrase means.

You think about it, Miss Greensay. It makes no sense, no sense at all.' The cook replaced her cup on the butler's tray that stood between them. 'More cake?' she asked, but she was already slicing it. 'So what's this one done?'

'Too full of herself, that's what. Lets our Miss Eliza run wild. I don't know what the master will say.'

'Does he need to know?'

'Well, I shan't be the one doing any telling, that's for sure.'

'I believe that, Miss Greensay,' Mrs Satterly said, with a sly smile.

'And she's filling the child's head with rubbish. Poetry and all that sort of filth. And Rome. Well, it's not right in my book.' Merry poured herself more tea.

'Why Rome?'

'She went there with a family she worked for. Now, why would they want to go somewhere like that when they live in God's own country?'

There was a mighty clatter from the scullery. 'You! What are you doing?'

'Sorry, Mrs Satterly, I dropped a pan.' Maggie's face, its prettiness marred by her frown, peered round the scullery door.

'You been listening?'

'No, Mrs Satterly, that I haven't.'

'You'd better not.'

'That I wouldn't!'

'If you've dented it the repair will come out of your wages. At this rate I'll have your bloody bones in the stockpot.' She laughed loudly.

'What's the joke?' Merry asked.

'Maggie Bones – stockpot. Oh, never mind,' she said, in exasperation. 'And, you, the minute you've done those veg you scrub that table. Ruby! Maud! What are you doing in my kitchen?' she yelled at the two housemaids who had just appeared.

'Going to the laundry, Mrs Satterly . . .'

'. . . to pick up linen, Mrs Satterly.'

'My kitchen isn't a short-cut for all and sundry. Bringing dirt in for my poor Maggie to clean up. In fact, Ruby, you can give her a hand. You scrub that table.'

'But the linen, Mrs Satterly—'

'Maud looks strong enough to do it. You help here.'

Ruby did not argue with the cook – all the servants knew how dangerous that would be. Instead she went to the scullery to collect a bowl and scrubbing brush.

'I tell you, Miss Greensay, you can't get staff like you used to, not like in our day.'

'You never said a truer word, Mrs Satterly,' Merry agreed.

'That Maud's trouble. She needs a close eye on her. I've told Mrs King, but does she listen? Implied the maids were none of my business. But it'll end in tears. She's far too flighty for her own good . . . Cider, Miss Greensay?'

'That would go down a treat, Mrs Satterly.'

In the scullery Ruby giggled. 'Did you hear that, Maggie? What a cheek.'

'All she does is moan.'

'Maggie, have you been crying?'

'No, it's a cold.' Maggie wiped her nose with the back of her hand.

'Don't let her get you down.' Ruby put her arm round the girl's shoulders.

'It's hard not to,' Maggie choked out, and burst into tears. Ruby tried to comfort her while knowing that what she said was pointless: Mrs Satterly was an unkind woman, and she would have hated to work for her.

'Heavens, what's the point in crying? I've so much to do!' Maggie flapped her hands in the air.

'I'll give you a hand with the vegetables when I've done the table.'

'You're so kind to me . . .'

And perhaps she shouldn't have been, Ruby thought, for she was held up again, trying to console Maggie.

Engrossed in their cider and gossip neither Merry nor Mrs Satterly heard the clattering of the large bunch of keys, attached to an ornate silver-plated chatelaine, which bounced noisily against Mrs King's thigh and always heralded her arrival. At the sound of her approach the housemaids scuttled like confetti in the wind. Now she paused in the doorway, an expression of distaste on her face as she saw the two women, red in the face and giggling uncontrollably. She bustled in, a stack of damask napkins in her hands.

'Lawks! It's like market-day in Exeter here this afternoon. To what do I owe this honour?' Mrs Satterly noticed the housekeeper and stood up, smoothing down her white apron.

'Have you seen Maud or Ruby?'

'No,' Mrs Satterly lied.

'Wretched girls! Where can they be? There's so much to do by next week.'

'Organisation, Mrs King, that's what you'll be requiring.'

Mrs King did not react to the slight: all of the servants were accustomed to Mrs Satterly's tongue. 'Should you see them, I'd be obliged if you would send them to me.'

'Of course, Mrs King.'

The housekeeper darted out.

'Why did you say that?' Merry asked.

'Because I don't like the stuck-up bitch. "I'd be obliged!" Who does she think she is? Anyone can be a housekeeper, it don't take no training. I could do her job – but she couldn't do mine. All she does is count linen and scream at the maids. Why does she get paid more than me? That's what I'd like to know.'

'True. She do th[...]
she's a mite too fon[...]

'And what does th[...]

'Nothing. Just think[...]

'Then don't.' Mrs S[...]
angry. 'And she's hard[...]
best, poor little things.[...]
sniffing,' she shouted.

'Are you ready for Mr [...]

'I don't have to be *ready* f[...]
always immaculate. He cou[...]
nothing wrong.' Indignation [...]
rigidly.

'I'd best get back to the nurs[...] [M]iss Eliza will be
looking for her tea,' Merry said, hauled herself to her
feet and lumbered out as Mrs Satterly began to shout at
Ruby.

Once in the servants' passage outside Merry allowed
herself to grin. It was her mentioning Mr Didier that
had caused Mrs Satterly's temper to erupt. The French
chef was due back with the rest of the household. Once
installed he would take over from Mrs Satterly, who did
not take happily to being demoted.

Next week the house would fill. The butler, the
footmen and valets would arrive first – this always sent
a *frisson* through the young female servants. Then the
maids who had been at the London house would arrive,
and more kitchen-maids and women to do the rough
cleaning would come up from the village for the
duration of the visit. For two weeks now the housekeeper and the maids who stayed permanently at
Harcourt Barton had been opening up the main part of
the house. They were all exhausted but excitement was
in the air. They took a pride in ensuring that the house
and gardens looked their best, that everything would go
smoothly, that Mr Forester's guests over the next two
months would find nothing to criticise or belittle.

Merry herself was not involved in the preparations,

in the nursery never varied,
growing up there was less and
That suited Merry: she was quite
in in her sitting room, reading, eating,
umerable cups of tea and hanging out of
ow on the off-chance that Bert Denzle, the
d under-gardener, might just be passing by. He
ad a fine arse on him, to be sure.

3

Eliza was sure that the house must be as excited as she
was: a sense of anticipation pervaded every corner
as the great building was unwrapped. Dust sheets which
had cocooned the furniture were removed, and loose
covers changed from dark winter fabrics to pale
summer chintz. The holland blinds, which had been
closed against the light, that enemy of fine fabrics, were
opened to unveil the beauty of the heavy brocade
curtains and sunshine filled the rooms, banishing the
musty smell of an unused house.

The furniture was buffed until it shone. The silver
was polished until Eliza could see her face mirrored in it
but distorted by the curves of plates and bowls. The
great chandeliers were lowered and the crystal drops
cleaned until they glistened like diamonds. Everywhere
she could hear the sound of tapestries being brushed
and rugs beaten. The air smelt of beeswax, lavender and
the bowls of pot-pourri which Mrs King had placed in
every room. The crack of newly laundered sheets being
folded echoed along the corridors like ships under full
canvas as the maids made up the many beds.

In the grounds the gardeners were tidying, weeding
and repairing. Every day Snuffles, the old cob, was
harnessed to the heavy gardening cart whose wheels
squeaked and groaned as it trundled along behind him.
It was laden with pots of flowers and shrubs, which had

been nurtured, held
behind the kitchen g
height of perfection.
terraces were filled wi
from between the stoi
optimistic root, and t
scrubbed with soda so tha
had been dredged of weec
The gravel paths had been i
which would be redone each
stirred. The lawnmowers cla
the grass until it looked like i
table stretched out before the i

The stables' walls had been w   washed and every
corner scrubbed. The yard was swept and sluiced, then
adorned with pots of geraniums. The feed was checked,
the tack cleaned, and the gleaming horses peered
inquisitively from their stables, pawing the ground with
barely controlled excitement.

At the back of the stables came a loud rumbling as the
furnaces were lit to heat water for the house. Bats,
disturbed from their roost in the boiler-house, swooped
in panic in a mesmerising aerial display watched by
Eliza, who knew where best to position herself to see
them perform.

Everywhere there was bustle and rush.

Eliza was more excited than everyone else that her
father and his friends were coming. It wasn't that she
was unhappy or lonely – there were too many staff in
the house for that. No, each time her father came she
promised herself that this was the visit on which he
would notice her and they would become friends, when
he would be proud of her and, most important of all,
love her and tell her so.

Sometimes Eliza wondered what her life would have
been like if her mother had not died, how different it
might have been. She wished her mother had lived a
little longer, until she was five or six, at least: then she

...t was like to have someone
... se and smother her with kisses.
... d memories.

... other, Lady Gwendoline, noticed her.
... ame she always showed an interest in Eliza
... ed her what she was doing, what she wanted,
... lso told her to sit up straight and eat all the things
... e didn't like. But that was only once a year in August
and each time she arrived, Eliza felt as though she was
meeting a stranger of whom she was more than a little
afraid. Unfortunately as her shyness began to fade each
time Lady Gwendoline's visit ended.

Her father's sister, Aunt Minnie, ignored her unless
she was bullying her. Eliza had once overheard her say
that she could not abide children and wanted none of
her own, so that was probably the reason. Her husband,
Uncle Charles, was another matter: he was interested in
Eliza and she dared sometimes to think he might love
her, not that he had ever said so. He talked to her about
animals and birds, and knew more about trees than
anyone else she had ever met, and the stars and the
planets. He told her snippets of gossip, which he made
her swear not to pass on to a living soul – tittle-tattle
about the lords and ladies he knew and sometimes even
about the Queen. He took an interest in what Eliza
wore and how she did her hair. And he frequently told
her what a beauty she was going to be, how many
hearts she would break, including his own, until she
would blush and giggle. But he didn't always come so
she never allowed herself to look forward to seeing him,
just in case.

Of course Merry hugged her and told her every day
how much she loved her, how pretty she was, but
although that was nice and comforting – and Eliza
knew she loved Merry too – something was missing.
Eliza did not know what it was – how could she? She
just knew that Merry was not enough.

Perhaps, she thought, if she could talk to her father

'True. She do think she's a cut above. And perhaps she's a mite too fond of Mr Densham.' Merry winked.

'And what does that mean?'

'Nothing. Just thinking aloud.'

'Then don't.' Mrs Satterly sat down again looking angry. 'And she's hard on those girls. They do their best, poor little things. Maggie, stop that bloody sniffing,' she shouted.

'Are you ready for Mr Didier?' Merry asked.

'I don't have to be *ready* for Mr Didier. My kitchen is always immaculate. He could walk in now and find nothing wrong.' Indignation made Mrs Satterly sit up rigidly.

'I'd best get back to the nursery. Miss Eliza will be looking for her tea,' Merry said, hauled herself to her feet and lumbered out as Mrs Satterly began to shout at Ruby.

Once in the servants' passage outside Merry allowed herself to grin. It was her mentioning Mr Didier that had caused Mrs Satterly's temper to erupt. The French chef was due back with the rest of the household. Once installed he would take over from Mrs Satterly, who did not take happily to being demoted.

Next week the house would fill. The butler, the footmen and valets would arrive first – this always sent a *frisson* through the young female servants. Then the maids who had been at the London house would arrive, and more kitchen-maids and women to do the rough cleaning would come up from the village for the duration of the visit. For two weeks now the house-keeper and the maids who stayed permanently at Harcourt Barton had been opening up the main part of the house. They were all exhausted but excitement was in the air. They took a pride in ensuring that the house and gardens looked their best, that everything would go smoothly, that Mr Forester's guests over the next two months would find nothing to criticise or belittle.

Merry herself was not involved in the preparations,

much to her relief. Her life in the nursery never varied, but now that Eliza was growing up there was less and less for her to do. That suited Merry: she was quite content to remain in her sitting room, reading, eating, drinking innumerable cups of tea and hanging out of the window on the off-chance that Bert Denzle, the second under-gardener, might just be passing by. He had a fine arse on him, to be sure.

3

Eliza was sure that the house must be as excited as she was: a sense of anticipation pervaded every corner as the great building was unwrapped. Dust sheets which had cocooned the furniture were removed, and loose covers changed from dark winter fabrics to pale summer chintz. The holland blinds, which had been closed against the light, that enemy of fine fabrics, were opened to unveil the beauty of the heavy brocade curtains and sunshine filled the rooms, banishing the musty smell of an unused house.

The furniture was buffed until it shone. The silver was polished until Eliza could see her face mirrored in it but distorted by the curves of plates and bowls. The great chandeliers were lowered and the crystal drops cleaned until they glistened like diamonds. Everywhere she could hear the sound of tapestries being brushed and rugs beaten. The air smelt of beeswax, lavender and the bowls of pot-pourri which Mrs King had placed in every room. The crack of newly laundered sheets being folded echoed along the corridors like ships under full canvas as the maids made up the many beds.

In the grounds the gardeners were tidying, weeding and repairing. Every day Snuffles, the old cob, was harnessed to the heavy gardening cart whose wheels squeaked and groaned as it trundled along behind him. It was laden with pots of flowers and shrubs, which had about her mother it might help. She had mentioned her only once, when she was five . . .

'Papa, why did Mama die?'

'Don't speak of her! What have I told you?' he had roared, leaning towards her with his hand raised as if he were about to strike her. He had frightened her so much that she dropped her doll and wet her knickers. Now she hoped he would forget the incident, but knew she never could.

'Why was Papa so cross, Merry?' she asked, as she ate her bowl of bread in warm milk, which she hated but which Merry insisted she had each night before going to bed.

'I doubt he liked a big girl like you doing her wee-wee on his library rug.' Merry, who was never cross, put on a pretend-cross face.

'But he was angry before I did that. Why?'

'Ferrets and fogles, how could I know that?' Merry stood up and busied herself with folding Eliza's laundry, which she had already done.

'Because you know everything, Merry.'

'Flattery don't work with me and that's a fact. Minx! Geese and goslings, what have you been doing with these stockings?'

'Why, Merry?' When she wanted to know something Eliza always persevered.

Merry turned slowly, clutching the stockings to her ample breasts. 'He can't talk about your dear mama, that's why, so you'd be better off not doing so either.'

'Why?'

The clattering of the miniature milk churn that was delivered each morning and evening to the nursery door distracted Merry. She didn't need to shout for Jenny, the nursery-maid, to go and collect it for Jenny was smitten with Bob, the boot-boy, who had to lug up the shiny churns. Although they were small they were heavy when they were full.

Merry sat down again, a billowing mass of black

bombazine, straightened her lace cap then pulled a notepad towards her and, with a flourish, began to write a letter.

'Why?' Eliza repeated.

'Why what?' Merry said. Eliza stared, unblinking, at her. 'Well . . .' She splayed her hands on the green moquette table cover. 'Well . . . it's hardly surprising, is it, Miss Eliza? Grief! The poor man is consumed with grief. That's why he can't mention your mother's name. Why, he can't bear anyone reminding him.'

'Why have you gone redder, Merry?'

'Have I?'

'Yes. Sort of mottled like the marble on my washstand.'

'Saucepot!'

'Did he love her so much?'

'He lived for her. There wasn't a day when he didn't worship the very shadow of her . . .' That was a sentence from a penny dreadful Mrs Satterly had loaned her. 'The very shadow of her . . .' she repeated.

'If Bumble died I'd want to talk about him all the time.' Eliza looked at her spaniel who, as always, was sitting at her feet in high hopes of a scrap.

'That dog should be in the kennels with the rest. It's not nice having a dog in the room with you,' Merry grumbled.

'If he loved Mama why—'

'And sleeping with you! All them hairs and fleas! If the master ever found out he'd have my guts for garters, that's for sure.'

'Bumble has not got fleas – honestly, Merry, you do exaggerate. In any case, how will Papa find out? I won't tell him. You won't tell him. Nobody knows he sleeps with me but you and Jenny, and she won't tell.'

'Lazy good-for-nothing she is.' Merry had once tried to get rid of Jenny but Eliza had cried so long and so hard that she had been reinstated the next morning.

'Merry, what's a fogle?'

'It's a word that stops me saying something bad, that's what. Now, minx, teeth.' She held out the rag coated with soot from the chimney mixed with salt.

Eliza backed away. 'Must I?' She closed her mouth tightly.

'When you have your coming-out ball do you want shining white teeth or black smelly ones? What would the fine gentlemen think?'

'I hate the taste.'

'No one will marry you with bad teeth. Clean them, there's a good girl.'

As Eliza's grandfather and father had rebuilt the house it was clean and modern and had all the best facilities. In the old house there had been no water – it had been pumped from the well – but now there were three bathrooms and water closets that flushed. When they had guests, though, the maids still scuttled about with jugs of hot water and hip baths to place in front of the bedroom fires: many guests would not give up the old ways and that included Lady Gwendoline, Eliza's grandmother.

Once the kitchens had been dark, gloomy, smelt of burnt fat and soot, and were impossible to keep clean. Now they were spacious with high ceilings and tall windows and the floor was covered with the newly invented linoleum, which made cleaning so much easier. Years ago the dairy had been a separate building across the yard but now it was included in the complex of rooms that led from the main kitchen. There was a still room for making jams and chutneys and bottling fruit, a vegetable store and a game larder. The kitchen-maids had several sinks at which to do the washing-up instead of only one. A new laundry had been built, also in the main house, and opened on to a spacious yard where clothes could be hung to dry in fine weather. It was a marvel: the pipes which carried heat to the house had been diverted into it and wound round the walls to aid in drying the masses of laundry that such a large house generated.

The old kitchens had been such a long way from the dining room that, Eliza's grandmother had told her, their meals had been almost cold when they were served. Now they were linked to the dining room by one corridor and in the servery, which led in to the dining room, there was a large metal warming cupboard so that everything was piping hot.

Eliza lived in the nursery wing with Merry, Jenny and her governess. The school room and day nursery were on the ground floor, stacked with every toy a child could want. They were large, planned for the big family which had once been envisaged.

A staircase led to the floor above. Merry hated it and huffed and puffed her way up it as Eliza raced ahead. At the top was the nursery linen cupboard in which Eliza liked to hide when she wanted to be alone. Merry's, the nursery-maid's and the governess's bedrooms were on this floor, but the night nursery was up two steps and in one of the towers. Everything in the room was, of necessity, curved, including Eliza's canopied bed, which had been built especially for it. Eliza loved this room and often declared that even when she was grown-up she would want it to be hers, high in the tower, overlooking the lovely gardens, with the flock of white doves outside her window who woke her each morning.

The upstairs nursery passage led to the main landing of the house. Suits of armour stood at intervals along it and Eliza was never happy to pass them on her own, convinced that men inside them were watching her. She preferred to use the back stairs, which infuriated Merry who set great store by the fact that she alone of the staff was allowed to use the main ones.

Further along this corridor two large, ornately carved oak doors were kept permanently locked. They led into the suite that had once been occupied by Eliza's mother.

Eliza had never been into it and when she walked past she felt frightened and never knew why. But she liked the scent of tuberoses that hung heavy in the air in this part of the house, as if someone wearing that perfume had just been there.

Eliza was not allowed to enter her father's part of the house when he wasn't there – nor was she welcome when he was. However, this had never stopped her wandering about and exploring – when she could escape Merry.

She loved the huge rooms with their ornate furniture. She spent hours looking at the paintings, the tapestries, imagining herself part of them, in another world. There were many portraits, some of dour, miserable-looking men, some of pretty women, but there was not one of her mother. She knew because she had asked Merry – 'She died, poor dear, before there was time for it to be painted.'

There were so many places in the house to hide, cupboards, secret passages, or heavy curtains behind which, if she heard footsteps, she could stand, as quiet as a mouse, until she was alone again.

Best of all she liked the library and its special smell of leather, books and her father's cigars. She knew it was his favourite room too, and when he was at Harcourt Barton it was where he spent most of his time. When he was away, she felt closer to him in there. She had a dozen hiding places in the library for it contained several tables spread with tapestries that touched the floor. She would select a book and sit in secret to read it. It was in this room that, in a secret drawer of a bureau, she had found a book of photographs. She knew some of the people in them because they had been her father's guests. But there was one woman, with fair hair and a lovely smile, she did not know but to whom she was drawn. She always admired blonde women for that was how she longed to be. Eliza's hair was dark, almost black, but she had blue eyes and was sure that God had made a mistake, having meant her to be fair.

In the back of the album there were a couple of loose photographs, so she took one. 'Merry, who's this pretty lady?' she asked that evening as she slid the picture across the table.

'Hens and hiccups!' Merry exclaimed, and swayed on her chair so dramatically that Eliza was afraid she might topple off. 'Where on earth did you find that?'

'In a drawer,' she replied, and hoped Merry didn't ask where.

'I don't like them there objects.' She threw the card on the table. 'Dangerous they be.'

'Why.'

'All those rays, they can get in your brains. That's why. I've had that many headaches since your father made us all have that image of us taken. Headaches you couldn't imagine . . .'

Eliza knew that Merry was avoiding answering her question. 'Who is she? She's so pretty.'

'I've no idea. Now, you give me that. You might catch something from it.' At the same time they lunged for the photograph, but Eliza reached it first. She raced from the room, along the corridor, down the main staircase, through the drawing room and the ante-room and into the new conservatory. Here, there were whole trees and great bushes and a dozen hidey-holes. She took her handkerchief, wrapped it round the photograph, which was mounted on thin cardboard, and squeezed it into a space in the wall behind a giant yucca. She hid things there that she didn't want the grown-ups to see.

She came often to retrieve the picture and study it. This lady was her friend, she was sure, and she was also sure that once, long ago, she had met her, if only she could remember . . .

Eliza, her arm about Bumble, was sitting on the main staircase, waiting for her grandmother to arrive. It always made Merry cross when she did this because she might make her dress dirty and it was 'unladylike'. But she did it all the same, even though she invariably felt uncomfortable and sad. She had tried sitting on a chair in the hall, even in the drawing room with the door open, but she always ended up on the staircase as if some force tugged her there.

Often she thought that if only she knew why she felt like this she would be able to chase away the sensation, which she experienced in certain other parts of the house too. She had tried to describe it to Merry but her nurse had told her not to be so fanciful and to stop talking like *that* or *they*'d come and *take her away*. She never explained who *they* were or where *they* would take her.

'Here you are! Should you be sitting on the stairs?' Fanny sat down gracefully several stairs above Eliza.

'My grandmother will arrive soon and I always wait for her here.'

Fanny bent forward and tapped her shoulder. 'Eliza, are you crying? What has happened?'

Eliza wiped away the tear with the back of her hand and sniffed. Her governess handed her a wisp of lace-trimmed handkerchief. Eliza shook her head and blew her nose. The hankie smelt of roses, which made her cry even more. Fanny joined her on the lower step and put her arm round her. 'Tell me.'

'I can't.'

'Why not? I will respect your confidence.'

'Merry said I shouldn't.'

'What made her say that?'

'*They*'ll come and take me away.'

'Who will?'

'She didn't say.'

'But I wouldn't let anyone do that to you. I would fight them.' Fanny bunched her small hands into fists, which made Eliza laugh. 'That's better.'

Eliza sighed. At last she said, 'It makes me cry.'

'Sitting here?'

'Yes. I've tried waiting elsewhere but I always come back to my stair, even though I don't want to.'

'Poor you. I know exactly what you mean.'

'Do you?' Eliza was surprised.

'Long after my father died there was a place in our garden and I was always sad if I went there but I kept going to it as if I was drawn by an invisible cord.'

'That's how I feel.' Eliza sat bolt upright, her voice lifting with excitement. 'And—' Abruptly she turned away. 'Please don't tell Merry.'

'I promise.'

'Sometimes I feel there's a muslin curtain across my memory and if I could only blow it away then I would know,' she whispered.

'Or if you could turn round quickly enough you would see.' Fanny crossed her arms and hugged herself, as if what she had said had chilled her.

Eliza thought about this, frowning. 'No, I haven't felt that, ever. But I'm so happy you understand. And you won't let anyone take me.' She paused. 'Listen!' She scrambled to her feet. 'Horses, do you hear them?' She ran towards the library.

'Where are you going?'

'To hide.'

'But aren't you going to welcome your grandmother?'

'She won't want me to.'

'I'm sure she will.'

'She never has before.'

'There's always a first time for everything, Eliza. Come.' Fanny held out her hand to the girl who returned reluctantly and took it.

Densham, the butler, swept importantly into the hall. He stopped in front of the inner glass door, tapping his foot impatiently as he waited for the footman to skid ahead of him and open it – he never deigned to do so himself. Densham walked in a dignified, upright manner, and looked as if he was permanently sneering down his rather large nose. He never missed anything untoward, as many of the footmen and maids could verify, but his posture always made Eliza laugh and today was no exception. 'Ssh,' Fanny said reprovingly, as they followed him out on to the front steps. It was drizzling slightly but that did not bother the pair for they were kept dry by the large stone portico above them.

A coach drew up with a flurry and one of the coachmen jumped down. With a deft flick of his hand he lowered the steps. Mrs King appeared, flustered and smoothing down her skirts. She frowned at the sight of Eliza and her governess, who were standing, unbeknown to them, in the spot where she normally waited to greet her employer and his guests.

Now the coach door was held open and Densham stepped forward, his arm up ready to help.

'I don't need you, Densham, I'm not a cripple yet!' a harsh voice – it always made Eliza think of a rusty gate – called from the interior. And then her grandmother appeared. The short, loose travelling coat she wore was in widow's black, but it was prettily pleated and ruched. Her mourning garb did not extend to her jewellery: there was not a piece of jet to be seen. Instead a vast diamond and sapphire peacock brooch sparkled on her lapel and several ropes of pearls hung round her neck, swinging with her movements. She wore a little straw bonnet with a cockade of black and white feathers, anchored by another sapphire brooch, and two long ribbons that floated down her back, one black and one white. There was nothing sad about her demeanour and although she no longer needed to wear funereal black, she had announced that she would only cast aside her widow's weeds when the Queen did.

'Eliza, what a charming surprise,' she cried, at the sight of her granddaughter, who bobbed a curtsy.

'Welcome, Grandmama.'

'You look so pretty in blue – it matches your eyes.' She bent, proffering her cheek for a kiss. Her grandmother's skin reminded Eliza of the tissue paper in which Merry had wrapped her old baby clothes. 'And who is this?' Lady Gwendoline asked, gesturing towards Fanny.

'My new governess, Grandmama.'

'Manners, manners! I presume your governess has a name, child?'

'Miss Chester.'

'Well, Miss Chester, I trust you are content here at Harcourt Barton. The last woman who taught Eliza was an indescribable bore. Are you?'

'I try not to be, Lady Gwendoline.'

'Trying isn't good enough. I expect you to do better than that. Please be in my sitting room in one hour and I shall judge for myself. Where's Benson?' Lady Gwendoline looked about irritably.

'I'm here, m'lady.' Benson, as old as her mistress but shorter by half, appeared from around the carriage, masked by the boxes and bags she was carrying.

'Tea, Benson. Eliza, come with me.'

Eliza trotted along behind her grandmother, who swept into the house, with Benson, the housekeeper, the butler, two footmen and the boot-boy trailing after them, all laden with boxes, bags and trunks. A flurry of maids appeared to help. Lady Gwendoline's dogs, a gaggle of King Charles spaniels, led the way, yapping and skittering about, noses to the ground, picking up and remembering smells, and adding to the general confusion. Bumble had slunk off to the safety of the nursery: he and the spaniels were not the best of friends.

Although Eliza often took tea with Lady Gwendoline, she was never quite sure if her grandmother enjoyed it. She never asked Eliza a question but barked it at her, quite fiercely, and since she did not always respond to the answers, Eliza could never be sure what she thought. In truth she was rather frightened of her.

'You begin to look civilised at last,' Lady Gwendoline said. She stripped off her gloves and threw them at Benson who, after years of practice, caught them expertly. 'Are you?'

'I . . . am . . .' Eliza had been about to say she was trying to be but thought better of it. 'I like my clothes now.' Which was true. Before, clothes had been a nuisance and she had hated the way Merry always made her put on too many, but lately she had begun to take an interest in how she looked.

'Good. You're becoming a pretty little creature and it's time you did. It's also time you took some responsibility for the household. I enjoyed your welcome.'

'I'm so glad.'

'Your father arrives next week, and I suggest you welcome him and his guests too.'

'Me?'

'Don't be tiresome, child. To whom else could I be referring? Now, what are you learning?'

'Everything, Grandmama.'

'There's a stupid statement! How can you learn everything? No one knows everything. Not even the cleverest of men.' She sat elegantly on a wing chair, perching rather as a bird did, Eliza thought. But unfortunately the bird that sprang to mind was a vulture – she had seen a picture of one in a book about Africa.

'I mean everything I'm supposed to be learning.'

'Such as?'

'Reading, writing, arithmetic, history, biology, physics and chemistry—'

'Physics? Chemistry? Who decided such nonsense? What husband will be interested in you knowing any physics?' Her grandmother's ring-encrusted hands, clasping her ornate silver-topped cane, looked like birds' claws to Eliza. Come to think of it, her nose was beak-like too. 'What are you smirking at?'

'Nothing, Grandmama.'

'Do you know what annoys me more than anything? People who say, "*Nothing*," when asked a perfectly reasonable question. So, what were you grinning for?'

'I can't remember, Grandmama.' Eliza felt herself blush.

'Then you were thinking something rude – probably about me.' Lady Gwendoline ignored Eliza's flustered denials. 'So, you won't tell me and to make matters worse you ignore my questions. What use is chemistry or physics?'

'They are very interesting subjects,' Eliza said quickly.

'What have you learnt?'

'I know how the gas lights the streets in London. I know how to raise water from the well to fill the water tower. I know—'

'A surprising amount. And where are you in history?'

'The repeal of the Corn Laws.'

'That's not history – I remember it happening, so how can it be history? History is kings and queens long dead.' Lady Gwendoline banged her walking-stick on the floor for emphasis.

'Miss Chester says our history is not only our past but our present and our future too.'

'She teaches you riddles, then. What a wonder of the world she is!'

Eliza wondered if she was being laughed at.

'So she's a blue stocking?' Lady Gwendoline continued her interrogation.

'No, she wears white ones.'

This made her grandmother laugh, although Eliza wasn't sure why. 'Benson, the jewel box,' she called.

The maid appeared with a large Moroccan leather case with Lady Gwendoline's crest embossed on the lid, and placed it carefully on a small pâpier-maché table in front of her mistress. 'This is what you need to know.' Her grandmother had unlocked the box with a tiny key and was pulling open one of its narrow trays. It was, Eliza thought, like a tiny leather chest of drawers. '*This* is what a young woman should study and should know about – jewellery and its value. Far more important than gas and water. Now, which is your favourite?'

Eliza liked this game and spent a happy hour learning about the jewels, where they had come from, to whom they had belonged, and when they had been given to her grandmother. How wonderful it must be to have such a treasure chest of one's own. Her own jewel box was very small in comparison and had little in it. This pleasant occupation was interrupted by a soft knock on the door. 'That must be Miss Chester. Now, run along, Eliza, I wish to speak with her alone.'

Eliza stood up obediently, kissed her grandmother, and left the room.

'You're teaching my granddaughter to be an intellectual, Miss Chester,' Lady Gwendoline remarked, a few moments later when the governess had seated herself. She liked what she saw: the girl had an intelligent face and a placid demeanour. This one wouldn't be any trouble, she judged, not like some had – always hopeful her son might notice them.

'She is intelligent and eager to learn.'

'Do you consider that learning will help her in her future life?'

'I hope so, your ladyship.'

'Most of the men of my acquaintance would hate their wives to be too educated.'

'Can one ever be too educated?'

'Possibly.' Lady Gwendoline respected the governess's view, which she herself had shared in her youth: she, too, had longed to learn.

'Then I must teach her to be circumspect in letting anyone be aware of how much she knows.' Fanny looked down at her hands. 'Especially any prospective husbands.'

'Are you being cheeky, Miss Chester?'

'Literal, Lady Gwendoline.'

'Then it is a clever answer. I trust you mean it, and I also trust you succeed. My daughter, Lady Wickham, who interviewed you, tells me you have had a tragic life. For that I am sorry.'

'My parents died. We had no money. Many have far more tragic experiences. I count myself lucky.'

'Parents invariably die, but to have no money is a different matter. Tragedy, of course, can be strengthening for some.'

'Learning has helped me,' Fanny observed. 'I don't know what would have happened to me if my brother hadn't taught me when our father died.'

'But I doubt that Miss Eliza is ever likely to become a governess.'

'I agree, your ladyship.'

'Are you being impertinent, Miss Chester?'

'Merely honest.'

'Hm.' Lady Gwendoline looked away from the governess and out of the window at the view across the park.

'I do not disapprove of learning in a woman. I think that provided, as you suggest, she is prudent and keeps it to herself she may derive much pleasure from knowledge.'

'I'm happy you agree.' Lady Gwendoline saw the girl's face relax, and knew why. Miss Chester spoke her mind, politely, but other employers might not appreciate this characteristic.

'But Eliza leads a solitary life. I should not like her to become so engrossed in her books that she did not learn of the lighter things in life.'

'I will make sure that she strikes an appropriate balance.'

'Sadly, she is dependent on such as you. Her

circumstances have been . . . unfortunate. Too many of her previous governesses have been found wanting and have had to leave.'

'So she told me.'

'I must confess I have often found this strange, Miss Chester. To my mind, many of them were most suitable. However, my son has seen fit . . . Well, my advice to you is not to get too fond of the child, just in case. It's not fair on her, is it?'

'I understand, your ladyship.'

5

Merry had entered into the spirit of the plan for Eliza to meet her father's guests and had taken great care in dressing her. She had chosen pale blue, as she usually did, since the colour complemented Eliza's eyes, and the dress was full-skirted and made of silk, the square-cut neckline decorated with finely pleated Swiss muslin. Round her neck Eliza wore a dark blue velvet ribbon from which hung a pale blue cameo. Her hair was brushed back and the bouncing curls were held in place with matching bows.

'You look good enough to eat,' Fanny reassured her.

'Thank you.' Eliza's smile was strained. 'What if my father is cross with me?'

'I'm sure he won't be. And he will be proud to see you looking so pretty. Every inch the hostess.'

Unfortunately the welcome was not a success.

The cavalcade of coaches, which had been to the railway station to pick up the visitors, pulled up noisily. The grooms were shouting, the horses snorting and whinnying. Dust rose in the air so that they had to shield their eyes. The horses pawed the ground, and shook their heads, aware that they were home. The valets and footmen raced out of the house, pulled down or placed steps, opened doors, proffered arms. Men on horses galloped up. The arrival of such a large group was always a noisy flurry.

Eliza stood straight. As the first woman appeared from a coach she curtsied, as she had been taught, and smiled, but the woman swept past her without a glance, as did the next. They all swished past Eliza, rustling silks and satins, in clouds of heavy scents. The men smelt of sandalwood and tobacco, and a couple smiled at her, while another raised his hat in greeting.

How rude the majority were, Fanny thought. She felt stupid standing a little behind Eliza, bobbing automatically and being ignored. But she felt sorrier for Eliza who had had to force herself to play this role. After five years as a governess, Fanny was accustomed to being ignored. She was used to living in that hinterland inhabited by women like her – above the servants but beneath the family and their friends.

Fanny was aware that Eliza was standing rigid now and that her narrow shoulders were shaking as a lone horseman drew his mount to a stone-scattering halt in front of them. Then the girl sank into a deeper curtsy. The man dismounted, paused for a second, frowned, then swept past her without a second glance.

Fanny saw tears fill her charge's eyes, and rushed to distract her. 'What lovely dresses some of the ladies were wearing,' she said. 'Perhaps they were the latest gowns from Paris.'

'I suppose so.'

'But yours was the prettiest.' Eliza looked intently at the dust on her shoes. 'Shall we go in?'

'They ignored me.'

'Perhaps the ladies were jealous because you look so pretty.'

'Me?' The idea made her smile. 'Most of the gentlemen ignored me too.'

'Then they weren't gentlemen.'

'And my father . . .' Her voice trailed off.

'Was he the last to arrive?' Eliza nodded. 'Perhaps it

was the surprise of seeing you waiting for him when you normally don't.'

'He didn't want to see me.'

'Or perhaps in your finery he didn't recognise you.' Fanny could hear herself prattling and realised that if she were Eliza she wouldn't believe what she was saying either.

'I was hoping . . .' Eliza gazed down the long drive. Then, as it was empty, she turned towards the front door. At that moment they heard the clatter of hoofs. 'Yes!' Eliza clapped her hands and before Fanny could restrain her she was running down the drive where a horseman was cantering towards them.

'Eliza, take care,' Fanny called, but she doubted that the girl had heard. She was running even faster now, waving her arms in the air. The horseman reined in his mount, bent down and scooped her up into the saddle in front of him. They galloped past an astonished Fanny, jumped a fence and disappeared into a nearby meadow.

Fanny stood under the portico, unsure what to do or where to go. Should she tell someone that the child had been abducted? Her anxiety mounted until suddenly they reappeared.

Eliza's face was a picture of joy. Her hair was awry, her cheeks pink, her eyes shining. The horseman jumped down nimbly, threw the reins to a groom and then, with due ceremony, lifted Eliza to the ground. 'There, m'lady. Your beauty astounds me.'

He bowed low and formally, and Eliza giggled, blushed and twirled around. And then, seeing Fanny, she stopped. 'Miss Chester, may I introduce my uncle, Sir Charles Wickham? Uncle Charles, this is my Miss Chester. Did I do that the right way round?'

'You did it beautifully, Eliza.'

Fanny found herself studied intently by a man with fine features. He was not handsome, but he had a kind face. His hair was a nondescript sandy colour and his eyes, she thought, were green, but she did not like to stare. To her astonishment she realised that she hadn't curtsied – but he hadn't forgotten to bow.

'Miss Chester, how gratifying to have such a welcoming committee. But how sad that Eliza refers to you as "my" Miss Chester. Is there no hope for the rest of us?'

Fanny reddened, even as she told herself not to be impressed by such slick compliments.

'Grandmama told me I should wait for the guests,' Eliza put in.

'Then I'm heartbroken.' He laughed. 'I thought you had decided to wait impatiently for your consistently late but favourite uncle.'

'My *only* uncle—'

'Ah, you spoilt it.'

'But still my *favourite*.'

'That's better.' He took Eliza's arm and led her into the hall. Fanny followed, pleased to see her charge so happy and relaxed. And then he was gone, and Fanny felt as if the sun had set.

'I don't think Papa likes me, Miss Chester.'

Eliza and Fanny were back in the schoolroom. They were supposed to be studying India but Fanny knew that today Eliza's heart was not in learning. 'Oh, I'm sure he does,' she replied, while silently agreeing with her. She had seen the expression on her employer's face as he had seen his daughter. He had looked at her with what could only be called loathing. It was fortunate that at that moment Eliza had been looking down.

'I don't think so. He never has.'

'But your uncle evidently does,' Fanny added.

Immediately Eliza brightened. 'And I like him, too, so much. He's a poet and he knows about so many things.'

'Is he your aunt Lady Wickham's husband?'

'Yes . . .' Fanny felt a flicker of disappointment '. . . I

don't like Aunt Minnie—' Eliza slapped her hand over her mouth.

'Too late, Eliza, the words are out,' Fanny said sternly.

'It's the truth, though.'

'Sometimes it's better if we keep the truth to ourselves.'

'But you also said I must never lie.'

'Nor should you. But I didn't ask for your opinion of your aunt so there was no need for you to give it, was there? I didn't see her arrive.'

'I expect she's coming this evening. She's always last. Merry says she likes to make an entrance. But how do you know she isn't here?'

'It was she who interviewed me for this position. If it were not for Lady Wickham I wouldn't be here, and I wouldn't have met you, and that would have been sad.' With that, she hugged Eliza, who hugged her back, which pleased her. Despite Lady Gwendoline's warning she had already warmed to the child – she could not help it: Eliza was so sweet-natured.

And she tended to agree with her about her aunt Minnie. She had undergone many interviews in her life but none as difficult as the one she had endured with Lady Wickham. There had been moments when she had felt like a criminal, so intense and personal had been the questioning. Fanny's references had been inspected with a magnifying-glass, as if they had been forged. Had she not been desperate for the situation she would have walked out in anger, but that was a luxury she could not afford. Fanny had been relieved to realise that as it wasn't Minnie Wickham's child she was to teach she would not have to spend time with the woman.

The schoolroom door burst open and Minnie Wickham stalked in – almost as if she had known she was being discussed. Eliza jumped to her feet and looked guilty. Fanny stood by the table and folded her hands in front of her in case they began to shake. What an odd thing to think, she thought. Why should she be frightened when she had done nothing wrong?

'How are you, child?'

'Well, thank you, Aunt. And you?'

'Do you like your new governess?'

'Very much, Aunt.'

'Well, she might not suit so do not become too fond of her.' She swung round to face Fanny, who felt herself blanch. Had she offended somehow? She swayed. 'Eliza's colour is too high, Miss Chester. You are spending too much time in the sun. You should be guarding her appearance and spending less time filling her head with learning.'

'But I like learning, Aunt, and I like being outside more than inside, especially when the sun shines.'

'I was not aware that I had spoken to you, child.'

'I'm sorry, Aunt.'

'That's better. Now, Miss Chester, her books . . .' She held out a gloved hand as she sat down. Her skirt was so full that it swelled up on all sides of her as if she had been puffed up with air. 'What are you sniggering at, Eliza?'

'Nothing, Aunt. I was stifling a sneeze.'

'This is Eliza's history book, her English, arithmetic . . .' Fanny hurriedly laid the leatherbound blue books on the table.

'Why are you wasting her time with arithmetic?'

'I presumed that one day she will have a home to run so will need to keep accounts and that then it will be useful to her.'

Minnie looked puzzled at this, then scanned the books so quickly that Fanny wondered if she was reading them and, from that, if, in fact, she could read at all.

It was a nervous quarter of an hour and when Lady Wickham finally left they sank into chairs with a heartfelt, 'Phew,' then looked at each other and giggled.

A knock at the door made Fanny's heart sink. Who was it now?

A head appeared round the door. 'Am I disturbing you, ladies?'

'Uncle Charles!' Eliza knocked over her chair in her haste to get across the room and fling herself into the tall man's arms.

'I've come to snoop. Is that all right with you?'

He had the most generous smile, Fanny noted.

'Any chance of a schoolroom tea? Toast we must have and seed cake. Nowhere else in the world can one find cake like Mrs Satterly's.'

'But of course.' Fanny crossed to the bell, and suddenly felt self-conscious. When Jenny appeared she ordered an early tea.

'With scones and cream,' Charles Wickham called.

'And sponge cake,' added Eliza. 'You have the seed cake and I'll have sponge.'

'I'll have both! Thank you, Miss Chester, for allowing this. I enjoy tea here with my niece. It's much more entertaining than in the drawing room.'

'They gossip, you see, Miss Chester, and Uncle Charles hates gossip – don't you?' She turned to him with a cheeky smile.

'That's not strictly true, Eliza. Sometimes I enjoy it, if it's not cruel, but I don't want it as a constant diet. And the talk of clothes . . .' He rolled his eyes heavenward. 'Do you talk of shopping and clothes, Miss Chester?'

'Not really, Sir Charles.'

'That's because she's no money to buy them with.'

'Eliza! What a thing to say!' Fanny knew she was blushing again for her face felt warm.

'Poor Miss Chester—'

The door burst open again and Merry bustled in. 'And what do you mean ordering tea now? It's not even four . . .' Merry was bristling with indignation, but on seeing their visitor she lurched to an abrupt halt. 'Sir

Charles, I never saw you there.' She attempted a curtsy too low for her bulk and but for a chair would have toppled over. Fanny had to look away and frown at Eliza, who was on the verge of laughing.

'All my fault, Merry,' interjected Charles Wickham. 'I begged Miss Chester to order tea for me. And how are you? Well?'

'In fine fettle, sir.'

'Anything to report on Eliza here? Is she rude, impolite, stupid?'

'Why, Sir Charles, none of them things. The light of my life, more like.'

'I'm glad to hear it. So you don't mind us having tea?'

'Of course not, sir, whatever next?' Merry giggled, but instead of leaving the room then, as she normally would, she stood as if waiting for something. Sir Charles turned back to the table and Eliza's books, which he had just begun to look at. When he said no more she turned away with obvious reluctance. She had hoped to be invited to join them, Fanny thought. How odd.

It was the gong, reverberating through the house two hours later, that alerted them.

'Is that the time?' Sir Charles looked at his pocket watch. 'How fast it travels when you are with friends, doesn't it?'

And indeed it had been a congenial time. They had discussed poetry and their love for the works of Lord Tennyson. They had spoken of novels and had marvelled at the inventiveness of Mr Dickens. Sir Charles had recommended several books to Fanny and she felt quite bereft as he took his leave.

'Isn't he wonderful?' Eliza looked up from the drawing on which she had been concentrating for the past hour. 'He doesn't like my aunt either.'

'Eliza, you must not say these things.'

'Why not? He told me.'

'Eliza,' Fanny said warningly.

'It's true. I asked him and he said that sometimes people made mistakes in life and that Aunt Minnie meant well. In other words, he doesn't like her and regrets marrying her.'

'Eliza, you shouldn't jump to such simplistic conclusions.' But Fanny was strangely elated when in truth she should have felt deeply sad for him.

Later that evening, with Eliza in bed and Merry snoozing, Fanny took a bottle of home-made elderberry wine that Merry had given her, and sped like a ghost along the corridor and down the stairs. Laughter and music floated out to her from the main rooms, but she slid past, then across the hall and through the green baize door. A hubbub of another kind of jollity emerged from the servants' hall as she tapped on Mrs King's sitting-room door.

'It is presumptuous of me to disturb you so please tell me to go if it's inconvenient.'

Mrs King had spied the bottle in Fanny's hand. 'No inconvenience at all, Miss Chester.'

'I did wonder if you would be with the others in the servants' hall.'

'My days of enjoying those shenanigans are long over. Mr Densham will oversee them tonight. I shall have to do my stint tomorrow – some of those maids are so flighty. That Maud . . .' She had taken charge of the bottle and was opening it. 'I've just been resting, after such a busy day.'

'I can imagine, Mrs King. These big house parties must be a great trial to you.'

'That they are. And where did you get this wine, Miss Chester?'

'Merry gave it to me.'

'She gave you a bottle of wine?' Mrs King's eyebrows arched dramatically.

'Yes, she wanted my opinion. I don't often get asked for my views on wine but I presumed she had made it and wanted to know what it was like.'

'If you don't mind me saying so, Miss Chester, be careful.'

'I'd no intention of drinking all of it. I don't enjoy alcohol. Just a sip.'

'People aren't always what they seem to be.'

'I don't understand.' Fanny frowned.

'Think. A governess with a bottle of home-made wine – which is often very potent? What if you were found with it? What if Lady Gwendoline got to hear? What if you drank it and became inebriated?'

'But surely . . . No.' She shook her head in puzzlement. 'I'm sure Merry just wanted to share it with me.'

'Did she? Getting on well with Miss Eliza, are you?'

'She's adorable. Such a sweet child and so eager to learn.'

'That's what the last governess found – to her cost. Merry saw to it that she went, didn't she?'

'No one has told me the circumstances of her departure.' Fanny was wary. She knew all about the staff feuds, arguments and jealousies that eddied around below stairs, and had no intention of getting involved in them.

'She was found drunk. She couldn't get out of bed one morning. She was dismissed immediately.'

'As she should have been. How deplorable.'

'Miss Greene was an upright, sober woman.'

'Evidently not.'

'You think so? I disagree. She was meant to become inebriated. It was planned that she should be found in that state.'

'Oh, Mrs King, really! By whom?' But already her heart was thudding, for she knew what the answer would be.

'Merry, that's who. Eliza had become too fond of

Miss Greene, you see. Merry loves the child, I'm not denying that. The problem is she cannot abide the idea of sharing her. So, if you like it here and you like your pupil, you should be vigilant. Meanwhile' – she poured herself a large glass of the elderberry wine – 'sure I can't tempt you?'

Fanny looked at the bottle with horror, as if it contained poison. 'No, thank you, perhaps I'd better not. If you have some barley water that would be lovely.'

Aware of how much Mrs King enjoyed her tipple, Fanny waited as she drank another glass before venturing on the subject that she had come here hoping to discuss. 'Mrs King,' she began, 'in all the houses where I've worked it's usual for my pupils and me at least to put in an appearance in the drawing room, if only for five minutes.'

'You won't at Harcourt, I can assure you, if Mr Forester is here. Unless Lady Gwendoline is on her own . . .'

'That's another thing. I haven't met Mr Forester. He hasn't been to the schoolroom, although his sister and brother-in-law have.'

Mrs King looked disdainful. 'Sir Charles! Bah! A right milksop he is, not nearly good enough for our Miss Minnie. What a fiery woman! What a lovely creature . . .' And she was away, relating anecdotes of Minnie Wickham's youth, which wasn't what Fanny had planned at all.

'But Eliza's father shows no interest in her or her progress.'

By now Mrs King was on her fourth glass of wine: her face had taken on a reddish hue and her speech was so slurred that Fanny had to concentrate hard to understand her. She looked about her as if to check that they were alone. She put her finger, which was shaking, to her lips.

'He thinks she's not his child!'

Fanny sat bolt upright in her chair. 'But that cannot be. She looks so like him, the same colour eyes, the dark hair . . .'

'I agree. But he's decided, and if he's decided there's not much that anyone else can do about it, is there? He thinks she's a' – again, the furtive look to left and right – 'a *bastard*,' she hissed.

6

The skeleton staff which had been left to care for Harcourt Barton had been joined now by those who had been with Mr Forester in London for the past six months. Their reunions were always tinged with excitement, but also with tension. Some of the servants were close friends who had missed each other and were happy to meet again, but others harboured resentments and intended to continue arguments where they had had to leave off. There were new servants, too, for those who had remained in the West Country to meet and decide if they liked. Also, most guests were accompanied by their own valets and maids, but the ladies who came alone were attended by the housemaids at Harcourt Barton. The girls enjoyed this: most of them hoped eventually to be promoted to such a role. Altogether, there were now sixty to be catered for in the servants' hall.

To accommodate such numbers extra servants' rooms were opened up on the top floor. Segregation was strict and the females used one staircase to their landing, while the males used another.

The weeks of entertaining were hard for everyone. The younger servants balanced their indignation at the extra duties with anticipation of the high jinks there would be in the servants' hall. However, the more senior staff, who were no longer interested in flirting, made no secret of their dislike of the added burden. All was made bearable, though, by the thought of the tips that would be shared out at the end of the house-party. But since the butler and the housekeeper divided the funds, many of the others were convinced that they kept the lion's share for themselves.

Over their years in service Densham and Mrs King had made friends with many of the visiting staff, and enjoyed swapping gossip with them. They learnt which families were facing financial problems, or the contents of a will, who was having an affair with whom, and what might be in it for them should their discretion be called upon. Little escaped the servants.

Also at such reunions the Black List was amended. It was maintained by the staff of the great houses and revised as necessary. A cruel, unreasonable or mean employer could not be recommended to someone looking for a new position. The maids and footmen were informed of poor tippers so that their bells were the last to be answered. While the employers thought they were in control, this was far from the truth.

'Did you see that valet who came with the Morton party?' Maud asked Ruby, as they sorted sheets in the linen room.

'He's quite good-looking.'

'Is that all you can say? He's handsome! He looks like a god.'

'I think he agrees with you.' Ruby put a sheet on to a pile for Mrs King to decide if it was worth mending or should be turned into dusters by Betty Potter and her two helpers in the sewing room.

'Hoity-toity!' Maud giggled and stuck out her tongue. 'Jealous, are you? Hasn't he noticed you?'

'No, but I didn't want him to.'

'I don't believe you.'

The sheets finished, Ruby was concentrating on the pillowcases. She had spoken the truth: she wasn't as excited about Alfred Dartagnan as the others since she did not find him attractive – he was too smooth by half. She was certain his name was as false as he was. He was too full of himself and he couldn't walk past a mirror without sneaking a look.

Ruby's life did not revolve entirely around this house, as those of the other girls did. She was fortunate for her family had been tenant farmers on the estate for centuries – long before the Foresters had come here. She could spend her few free hours at home. This enabled her to distance herself from the goings-on at Harcourt Barton. As for sweethearts, at sixteen she felt she had plenty of time for that, which was not to say that she didn't find Henry Morgan, the gamekeeper's son, attractive, but he was twenty-five and he hadn't even noticed her.

'He spoke to me!' Ivy Wilson burst into the linen room, her cheeks flushed with excitement.

'Looks as if he did more than that judging by the angle of your cap,' Maud remarked. 'You'd best straighten it before Mrs King sees you. She'll have your guts for garters. And who do you mean anyway?'

'Alfred.'

Maud stiffened. 'Oh, him!' she said, in a dismissive manner that fooled neither of them. 'What did he say?'

'He said, "Aren't you the pretty one, then?"' Ivy sighed at the memory.

'Well, he was lying, wasn't he?'

'Maud, that's not kind,' Ruby scolded.

'You're jealous because he hasn't spoken to you,' Ivy added. 'You're too fat!'

'Ivy, that's not nice either – and he'll be gone next week. It's hardly worth fighting over him,' Ruby remonstrated.

The door, which was open, swung back and hit Ivy. 'Good heavens, girl, haven't you finished that simple task yet?' They had been so engrossed with their gossip that, for once, none of them had heard the clinking of Mrs King's chatelaine. 'And why's it taking three of you to do it? I recall asking Ruby. Ivy, your cap is a disgrace. Now, shoo, you two, get back to your duties.'

'But, Mrs King, it's easier to deal with the sheets if there are two of us.'

'Don't argue with me, Ruby. You've too much lip on you. Maud, take this pile up to Betty Potter. And you, Ivy, go and sweep the upper men's corridor but don't let me catch you talking to any of them.'

Ivy needed no second bidding since that was where Alfred had been billeted, and ran off, unaware that Mrs King had had the floor cleared of male servants before sending the maids up.

The staff had to eat early for there were forty guests for dinner. Everyone would be overworked this evening. The help from the village had not materialised and so the junior housemaids had been ordered, much to their chagrin, to assist Maggie, who would not be able to deal with the mountain of pots and pans that would ensue.

Visiting valets, much to their annoyance too, were ordered to help the footmen with the washing of the glass, china and silver which would be done in the butler's pantry, which led to the strong room. Densham fretted that silver might be stolen by visiting staff and had hauled in old Brooks, the boiler man, long retired, and sat him in a chair, in the silver store, which managed to insult everyone.

The maids never stopped, all they could do was grab a bite of food and then rush off, always on the run, dresses newly pressed held high in their arms. Water jugs, curling tongs, needles and thread, one borrowed from the other as they dressed and crimped and fussed about their ladies.

Some were lucky and were praised and thanked. Others were not and were shouted at and reduced to tears. They were tired even before their charges grace-fully descended the stairs, and yet the night promised to be a long one and none of them could go to bed until their mistresses did.

7

Eliza knew that if she stayed awake long enough, Merry would soon have had so much cider that she would be fast asleep and the loudest thunderstorm would never wake her. But staying awake was hard. She had not been allowed a light in her bedroom since Merry had found her reading one night at midnight. Tonight she was reciting poetry to herself that she had learnt by heart in an effort to fight off sleep.

She was well into Mr Tennyson's *In Memoriam* when a rumbling from the next room told her Merry was asleep. She slipped out of bed and felt with her toes for her embroidered slippers. She wrapped around her the Paisley shawl her grandmother had given her as a birthday present, and was ready. 'Bumble, stay,' she said, unnecessary since the dog looked at her with the expression of one who had no intention of moving anywhere. She cautiously opened the door.

The landing was pitch dark – it had no window – but she tiptoed along confidently since she knew where every piece of furniture, every ornament was positioned. A sliver of light under her governess's door showed her that Miss Chester was still awake. Eliza knew exactly where the loose floorboard was and moved silently across the landing to the other side.

Once she was on the wide main landing she was at greater risk for it was brightly lit. Most of the ladies didn't return to their rooms until after midnight unless one had a headache, or chose for some other reason to retire early. And the maids might still be turning down beds and tidying. She was certain those she knew wouldn't tell on her but she couldn't be sure of the new ones. So she waited and listened until the coast was clear.

She darted along the landing like a wraith, pausing here and there, hiding beside a suit of armour or ducking down by a large display cabinet if she thought she heard someone approaching. But finally she had reached her objective. She pushed back a heavy brocade curtain, let it fall back behind her, opened a door so narrow that adults could only pass through it sideways and stepped out on to the minstrels' gallery. It overlooked the great hall, the oldest part of the house and the least altered by her grandfather. Here she could crouch in the dark and no one below could see her for, although the hall was bright with candles, the hammer-beamed ceiling was so high that the light did not penetrate this far. She felt for the cushion which she knew was on the bench, and settled down to wait.

About ten minutes later a small orchestra came in, took their seats at the far end by the heavily panelled screen wall and began to tune their instruments. She knew the musicians: her piano teacher was there, and the man who taught her the harp, her singing teacher was playing the violin and the other three she knew from past concerts. Her grandmother complained that they were tone deaf and always out of tune, but Eliza could hear that they weren't. She had learnt that sometimes her grandmother complained for the sake of complaining.

At last two footmen flung open the ornately carved black oak double doors and, first, the ladies in their wonderful dresses swept in. Jewels sparkled at their throats, from their ears and in their hair, as if they had been sprinkled with frost. Many wore fresh flowers too – that was a new fashion, Eliza thought, and, from the bedraggled state of some, not altogether successful. Then the gentlemen sauntered in, wearing high white collars with their tail coats. They seemed taller and even more handsome than she already thought them. It was strange, Eliza thought, how the ladies made such a grand entrance all a-flutter with their skirts swirling and an air of anticipation, and the men looked as if they wished they were somewhere else, yet it was they who made the most impact.

The orchestra struck up and then came the bit Eliza liked best, when each man bowed to the lady of his choice, who sank into a curtsy, her skirt billowing about her. How graceful they were, how elegant, just like the swans on the lake. Eliza knew she would never be able to curtsy like that no matter how hard she practised.

And then they were away, swirling and swooping. Like exotic birds they dipped and swayed. Oh, to be held like that by a handsome man, his white-gloved hand so carefully, protectively placed. Oh, how—

'And what are you doing, young lady?'

Eliza started. 'Miss Chester! You made me jump.'

'What are you thinking of? You should be in bed.'

'Please don't make me go back. Please! I'm not doing any harm. I love to watch the dancing – it's, oh, so lovely,' Eliza begged.

'For five minutes, then.' And Miss Chester sat down beside her. Eliza saw how she gazed down, too, with interest. 'They do look pretty.'

Eliza looked enquiringly at her governess. 'Would you like to be down there with them?'

'Me? Gracious, no. I can't dance.'

'I can. I'll teach you.'

'But I don't think I'd be invited.'

'How sad.'

'Not really. I don't expect to be.'

'When I have my dance, in four years' time, when I put my hair up, I'll invite you.'

'How very kind of you. But you'll be a young woman then and will have no need of me. I shall be elsewhere.'

'Oh, no, Miss Chester, don't say that. I'll never let you go, you and Merry. I want you with me always.'

'Sweet child.' Fanny leant forward and kissed her cheek. Eliza snuggled up to her and, Fanny's arm around her, settled down again to watch the dance below.

A little while later they nearly jumped out of their skins and clutched each other as the door behind them squeaked open.

'I thought you both might like some refreshments,' said a tall figure, carrying a silver tray.

'Uncle Charles!' Eliza giggled with relief.

'I can explain, Sir Charles.' Fanny began to struggle to her feet.

'Please, Miss Chester, don't let me disturb you. What is there to explain? I thought you might like some lemonade, that's all. May I join you?' He was so tall that to sit down he had to fold his long legs, so that his chin was almost resting on his knees.

'Are you comfortable, Sir Charles?' Fanny, in the middle, pressed herself against Eliza.

'Very.' He grinned.

'How did you know we were here, Uncle Charles? I thought no one could see.' Eliza was worried: if she could be seen from below she would no longer be able to watch the dancing.

'If you want to see someone badly enough, you are sure to find them. I sensed you were here, Eliza.'

Eliza was puzzled: although he was talking to her, he was looking at Miss Chester. And when she spoke to him it seemed as though he didn't hear her but her governess. It was as if she had become invisible – she felt uncomfortable and, she realised, a bit hurt to be ignored. She edged towards the carved balustrade and peered down on to the throng as if she didn't mind.

They were dancing a waltz. The local ladies were in full-skirted dresses that swung like giant bells, but the London ladies' skirts were pulled back and bustled, their trains looped over their wrists. Eliza thought them less spectacular than those who still wore their crinolines.

Her grandmother sat to the side of the dancing, in a

high-backed chair, tapping her cane in time to the music. Eliza's father stood beside her, watching, never dancing. How handsome he was, so tall, so upright, by far the most handsome man in the room. Eliza was sure all the ladies were in love with him. How sad that he had eyes for none of them, that he still grieved for her mother. Sometimes she wondered if he would be so cross if she had been born a boy . . .

'No, really! Sir Charles, I – I have to go . . . It is far too late and Eliza should be asleep.'

There was a rustle and Eliza turned to see Miss Chester getting to her feet, looking flushed. Uncle Charles was trying hurriedly to stand too and in the confined space the two were banging into each other, apologising.

'Come, Eliza,' Miss Chester said.

'But they've just started the polka, I've never seen—'

'Eliza!' Miss Chester spoke uncharacteristically firmly, and Eliza stood up.

Her uncle bent so that she could kiss his cheek. 'Let me see if the coast is clear.' He winked at her.

Slowly he opened the door then closed it quickly. He put his finger to his lips. 'Your grandmother,' he mouthed, and stepped out on to the landing.

'Spying, Charles?' Eliza heard her ask.

'You see everything, Lady Gwendoline.'

'Absolutely everything, dear Charles.'

They waited, hearts thumping, for the bustle on the landing to cease. Then his head appeared round the small door. 'It's safe now,' he whispered.

'Quickly, Eliza, and quietly.'

Eliza thought this was totally unnecessary. After all it was her hiding place, and she knew she had to be quiet. But obediently she swept along the corridor, back to the nursery wing. Miss Chester followed Eliza into her bedroom and closed the door behind her. Bumble lifted his head briefly, wagged his tail, then went back to sleep.

'Don't tell anyone about tonight, Eliza.'

'Of course I won't.' She climbed on to her bed and shook off her slippers.

'It's important you don't.' She pulled the covers over Eliza, and straightened them fussily.

'I won't.'

'It would get me into trouble.'

'Me too.' Eliza grinned.

Fanny grabbed hold of Eliza's wrist. 'It's no joking matter, Eliza.'

'I know. But we didn't do anything *really* wrong.'

Fanny relaxed and let go of her hand.

'You like my uncle, don't you?'

'He's very pleasant.' Fanny looked concerned again.

'No, I mean ... I think you'd like to be his sweetheart.'

'Don't be ridiculous. You must not say things like that. If you talk I shall be sent away.'

'I wouldn't let you go.'

'You wouldn't have a choice.'

'I don't mind if you like my uncle—' As quick as a flash, Fanny had hold of her wrist again, and twisted the flesh. 'Please, you're hurting me.' Eliza squealed and began to cry.

Fanny, as if suddenly aware of what she was doing, let go. 'Eliza, I'm so sorry, forgive me.' She tried to take her into her arms but Eliza cringed away.

'Dogs and dungeons! What is going on in here?' The door had burst open and Merry stood on the threshold, her candle held aloft. 'Eliza, what are you doing? Miss Chester?'

Fanny jumped to her feet. 'I thought Eliza was having a nightmare. I came to see if she was all right.' Her voice was high pitched with nerves.

'My poor sweetheart.' Merry lumbered into the room. 'And you were crying.' From a pocket of her dressing-gown she produced a handkerchief and dabbed at Eliza's tears. 'I heard nothing.' She swung round to face Fanny.

'Perhaps you were asleep. I was reading.' There was a fine sheen of perspiration on her face.

'At this time of night? You'll ruin your eyes. Dangerous, all them books.' She returned her attention to Eliza. 'Did you have a bad dream, my poppet?'

Behind Merry, Fanny looked pleadingly at Eliza. 'It was awful, Merry,' she said haltingly, 'I was in this dark wood and this great bear came out of the trees snarling . . .'

'Don't distress yourself by repeating it all, Eliza,' Fanny said, sagging now with relief.

'It's always better to talk the bogeymen away,' Merry contradicted her.

'I don't remember any more.'

'You come and sleep with Merry, my angel.'

'No, thank you.' Eliza pulled the covers closer.

'Are you sure?'

'I'm all right, Merry, it was only a dream.'

'If you're sure.' Merry fussed over her, patting the covers straight, plumping up the pillows. 'My little cabbage.' She kissed Eliza's forehead. 'You should be in your bed too, Miss Chester.' Her voice was stern now.

'You're right, Merry. I'm very tired now.' Fanny, too, bent to kiss Eliza. 'Thank you,' she whispered in her ear.

In the corridor Fanny caught hold of Merry's arm. 'Might I have a word?'

'If you must.' Merry paused by the door to her room.

'It's about Eliza. She seems strangely . . . neglected,' Fanny whispered.

'And what does that mean? I work my fingers to the bone for that little one!' Belligerence poured from Merry in a flood.

'Merry, I'm not talking about you, of course not. She longs for her father to acknowledge her. And I was wondering . . . Well, Mrs King said something that's been bothering me.'

'And what might that be?' Merry had taken an even more aggressive stance.

'It's a very delicate matter . . .'

'Spit it out, woman, I want my bed.'

'She implied . . . Mr Forester thought . . . that Eliza wasn't his child.' Fanny was astonished that she had found the courage to discuss the matter, but she had to know.

'Drunk, was she?' Merry did not seem in the least put out.

'I wouldn't like to say.'

'I would. She's a lush and spiteful with it. Ignore her. If that's all you wanted me for then I'm going to bed.' The door slammed.

Oh dear, thought Fanny. Perhaps she shouldn't have mentioned it after all.

Left alone, Eliza lay in the dark thinking. She lived in such a peculiar world. The adults told her she was never to lie or she would burn in hell yet Miss Chester had just thanked her for doing so. And when she had pointed out that Miss Chester liked her uncle, which was also the truth, she had denied it and that was another sort of lie.

She turned over in bed. Perhaps she should have a little talk with God: she didn't want to go to hell, and perhaps He would understand that it wasn't really her lie but Miss Chester's. She supposed she could confess to Merry, but if she did it would make matters bad for Miss Chester, and Eliza did like her.

That was another worry: whenever she liked someone they always went away. Four governesses and three nursery maids had gone without warning. One day they were there and the next they were gone. It always made Eliza feel so sad.

But she'd been right about her uncle, she was sure.

There had been a look between him and Miss Chester. It was how she looked when she looked at her pony, who she loved more than everything after Bumble.

Now she found she no longer felt hurt because they had ignored her. Instead she was excited for them. How nice that two of her favourite people should like each other – nice for her too because perhaps she would see more of her uncle.

It was a nuisance that Uncle Charles was married. She wondered if when you were married to someone and didn't like them you could somehow become unmarried. That would be the best solution for everyone, she was sure.

8

Ruby woke with a start. She sat up in her bed in the tiny room in the eaves of Harcourt Barton, which she shared with Maud. Something was wrong. She listened intently. 'Maud,' she whispered into the darkness, but there was no reply and no sound of breathing either from across the room. She was alone.

She felt on the bedside table for matches, lit the candle and peered across to Maud's bed. It was pristine – Maud hadn't come to bed yet, that was all. She blew out the candle and lay back again on her pillow.

Then she sat bolt upright. They had come to bed together! It had been two in the morning before they had finished their work downstairs. With only four hours' sleep ahead of her, Ruby had undressed hurriedly, desperate to get into bed.

'Hell's bells! I've forgotten to take the laundry over,' Maud had said, and put her shoes on again.

'You did. I saw you and Ivy.'

'There's a stack of napkins I forgot.'

'Leave it until we get up.'

'And have Mrs King breathing down my neck? They

start at five in the laundry, they'll want to get on with the table linen first.'

'Maud, don't go. You might trip and fall.' But the truth was that, at night, Ruby was frightened by the sighing and creaking of the old house.

'I broke a teacup yesterday. Mrs King put it in the book. I can't afford any more.'

'Miserable old crow.' Wearily Ruby began to get up. The book was a bone of contention for them all: breakages had to be paid for, and they only earned fourteen pounds a year.

'What are you doing?' Maud was pinning on her cap – even at this time of night she was expected to dress properly.

'Coming with you.'

'Don't be silly. There's no point in both of us losing sleep. It's my fault.'

'Everyone's asleep – won't you be scared?'

'Course not. Get back to bed.' And Maud was out of the door, candle held high to light the way. Ruby could hear her dress rustling as she moved along the uncarpeted landing.

Ruby had doubted that she would fall asleep now that she was alone, but exhaustion overcame her.

Now, how many hours had she been asleep? Should she go and search for Maud? Could she have fallen over in the dark and be lying hurt? Or . . . ? No! Maud wouldn't be that stupid. Or would she? Ruby got out of bed, wrapped a shawl round her shoulders and crossed to the window. She pulled aside the curtain and saw that the sky was streaked with the dawn light. It must be near five. 'Oh, Maud,' she said aloud.

'Oh, Maud what?'

Ruby swung round to see her in the doorway, grinning from ear to ear. 'Where have you been? I've been so worried.'

'It took me ages to fold the tablecloths, you know how huge they are.'

Ruby looked at her sharply. Maud had said she was going to sort the napkins. Why was she lying? Unless . . . 'What's his name?'

'What are you talking about?'

'The handsome valet – Albert? Or was it Arthur?'

'Well . . .' Maud giggled coyly, 'Alfred, actually.'

'You didn't, did you?'

'Didn't what?'

'You know what I mean.'

'I just happened to bump into him downstairs. He was sneaking a port, but don't tell. We've been talking, that's all.' She threw herself on to her bed with a long, contented sigh.

'All night?'

'There wasn't much of it left.' Again she giggled.

Ruby poured water into the basin. There was no point in going back to bed now, or in pursuing this conversation. Despite the poor light, she had noticed that Maud's apron was inside out.

She dressed, tying the strings of the plain white apron that they wore for their morning work tight around her waist. Over it she tied a dark blue apron, for she had some brasses to clean.

'Don't go to sleep, Maud. You won't wake up in time. By the way,' she finished pinning her cap in place, 'was your pinny on back to front all last evening? I can't say I noticed.'

Before Maud, who had blushed to the roots of her hair, could answer, she had left the room and was running along the landing then down the stairs to the kitchen.

'No!' Maggie let out an anguished groan as Ruby entered the kitchen. 'It's not that time already!' She looked panic-stricken.

'Don't fret, Maggie. I'm early. It's only ten past five.'

'Do you want a cuppa?'

'Is it your own tea?'

'Mine! I don't get no tea allowance and I certainly can't afford to buy my own, not on what they pay me.'

'But, Maggie, that's thieving.'

'A few tea leaves? What they going to do, lock me up in the nick? No, that's kitchen maid's rights, that's how I see it.' Maggie laughed.

'You look tired.'

'I didn't get to bed until nearly three, and then I hadn't finished everything so I had to get up early.'

'I heard they were getting in extra scullery maids to help you.'

'They couldn't come. The tweenies were told to help me but they buggered off half way through the evening saying it was too hard for them!' Maggie scoffed.

'Didn't Mrs Satterly realise?'

'She said I had to get on with it.'

'She's so hard on you.'

'She could be worse. The cook my cousin works for boxes her ears'.

'What about Mr Didier?'

Maggie perked up. 'He thanked me last night for my hard work.' She smiled proudly.

'And he was right to. You work harder than anyone.'

Maggie beamed with pleasure. 'If I tell you a secret, you won't tell?'

'I promise.'

'I'm hoping he'll want me to go back to London to work in his kitchen there. I hate it here.'

'But wouldn't it be just as hard in London?'

'I could mebbe find a gentlemen to look after me.' Maggie blushed violently.

'You'd have to be careful.' All of them had heard tales of the predatory men and white slavers who preyed on innocent girls in the capital.

'I would be. There's no flies on me.'

But Ruby remained concerned. Unlike many kitchen-maids she'd met, Maggie was pretty and bright.

'If I were there Mr Didier would teach me to cook

and then I could earn lots of money and shout at people,' Maggie went on dreamily.

Ruby laughed. 'You're too nice for that. Anyway, I thought Mrs Satterly was supposed to be teaching you.'

'She did, when I first started. But then I made some pastry and Miss Merry said it was the lightest she'd ever tasted. Mrs Satterly was furious, said it was tough as old boots – reckon she was jealous.'

'Probably.' Ruby smiled.

'Have you ever worked in the kitchens?'

'No, I was lucky. My mother spoke to Lady Gwendoline about me – she'd worked for her, you see, and . . .' *Lucky*, she'd said, but it wasn't how she had felt at the time.

'Did you always want to be in service?' Maggie asked.

'No!' Ruby smiled. 'I wanted to be a milliner, in London, but we didn't have the money to pay for an apprenticeship.'

'I thought all farmers were rich – that's what my dad says.'

'What does he do?'

'He's a farm labourer. Works for a pittance while the farmer gets fatter and richer.'

'Our farm isn't like that. My father was ill for a long time before he died and my brother Jerome was only fifteen when he took over. It was a struggle for my mother not to lose the tenancy. So I had no choice.' She hadn't needed Jerome to tell her it was her duty to get work and help the family's finances.

'Do you want to be a head housemaid?'

'Me?' Ruby laughed. 'No. I'd like to be a lady's maid, and work for someone who travels. I'd like to go abroad.'

'I was listening to that Giselle, Lady Wickham's maid. She said it was an awful life and she can never do anything right.'

'But no one's going to suit Lady W—'

She was interrupted by a loud crash.

'What was that?' Maggie gasped.

Ruby went to the door and opened it gingerly. Ivy was sprawled on the floor in the corridor. 'What on earth . . .'

Ivy tried to stand and yelped. 'I slipped on the stairs and I think I've twisted my ankle.' Tears formed in her eyes. 'Oh, Ruby, what shall I do?'

'I'll get Mrs King.'

Ruby turned towards the housekeeper's room but Ivy grabbed at her hand. 'She'll be livid with me. I'll manage.' Again she tried to stand but fell back.

'Maggie, get some ice, quick!' Ruby took control.

Maggie raced into the back scullery where the lead-lined bin held the ice, which she wrapped in a cloth. She placed it gently on Ivy's ankle, which was swelling rapidly. A couple more maids had arrived and crowded round Ivy, who was now sobbing uncontrollably.

'And where's our breakfast?' Giselle, petite and French, pouted.

'Mrs Satterly's tea!' Maggie was appalled.

'And our breakfast?'

'I haven't had time.'

'Then make time, you idle slut.'

'Don't you speak to our Maggie like that,' Ruby snapped. 'She's been helping me with Ivy here. You're going to have to wait.'

'And don't you, an under-housemaid, speak to me like *that*. I shall report you to Lady Wickham.' And Giselle gathered her skirts and stormed back up the stone steps.

'Ruby, you'll be in trouble,' Maggie was twisting her apron in her hands, 'and it's all my fault.'

'Mrs King will stand up for me.' Her bravado didn't fool anyone – they all knew that upsetting the petulant Lady Wickham was a dangerous pastime. 'And we're going to have to get Mrs King.'

'No,' wailed Ivy. 'I'll get the sack, and then what will I do?'

'You can't work like this – you can't even stand. Mary, run and get Mrs King and, Maggie, go and start the staff breakfasts or Mrs Satterly will be after you. Now, Sarah, you take the tea to Mrs Satterly and tell her what's happened.'

'That's not my job, the kitchen maid takes her her tea.'

'Sarah! Do it!' Ruby ordered.

Within five minutes the housekeeper and the cook, still in their dressing-gowns and curling-rags, had appeared and sent Bob, the boot-boy, to summon the doctor.

'You couldn't have chosen a worse week to do this, Ivy. You really are a nuisance, when we're so busy.'

'I'm sorry, Mrs King. I didn't mean to.'

'How are we to manage? Tell me that, girl!'

'Shall I run home and ask my mother if my sister, Ada, could help out, Mrs King?' Ruby suggested.

'Yes, Ruby, and tell her I'd be much obliged. You,' she pointed at the gaggle of gawking maids, 'double up for Ruby while she's gone. Hurry, girl.'

But Ruby didn't move. 'What is it, child?' Mrs King asked impatiently.

'Giselle has gone to report me to her Lady Wickham.'

'And why should she do that?'

'I objected to her calling Maggie a slut when all she was doing was helping me with Ivy.'

Mrs Satterly went bright red with indignation, but before she could speak Mrs King said, ominously, 'I shall speak to Giselle. Now, run along and don't dawdle.'

When she went to fetch her cloak, Ruby found Maud sprawled across her bed, still in last night's uniform, and fast asleep.

'Maud,' she shook her. 'Maud, for heaven's sake wake up. Ivy's twisted her ankle and its bedlam downstairs. Maud!' She yelled into her ear. Maud turned over and looked up at Ruby with a dreamy smile.

'Oh, it's you.' Each word dripped with disappointment.

'You did, didn't you? You fool!' she snapped, but it was more for fear for her friend than crossness.

'I beg your pardon?' Maud sat up. 'Did what?'

'You've compromised yourself with that valet, Dartagnan, haven't you?'

'Of course not.' Maud blustered.

'Don't lie to me, Maud. And get up or you will be in even more trouble. And cover your neck, you've love bites.' She grabbed her cloak and was out of the room before Maud could answer.

At first she ran across from the yard and down the back drive but when she reached the park she slowed down. If she fell and hurt herself where would she be then, afraid of getting the sack just as poor Ivy now feared? It was so unfair, those steps to the kitchen were treacherous. They were slippery, they'd all complained.

As Ruby entered the yard of her family's farm Spot, their collie, came racing towards her, barking hysterically, then rolled on to his back with joy at seeing her.

'Ruby! What's happened?' As she entered the kitchen her mother stood up, clutching her throat.

'It's all right, Mother. Ivy's hurt herself. Could you spare Ada for a couple of days? We've twenty guests and thirty more due for dinner and all the extra staff.'

'Bertie!' Grace Barnard called. Her youngest son, a cheeky-looking ragamuffin, appeared and grinned broadly at his sister. 'Go and get Ada, she's in the dairy.'

'This is good of you, Ma.'

'The extra money will come in handy. Mr Forester's put the rent up again. But I'll need her back in time for harvesting.'

'Ivy should be right as rain by then.' Ruby doubted it but they'd face that problem when it came.

'Have you had your breakfast?' Her mother was already pulling the large, blackened frying-pan towards her.

Ruby helped herself to a chunk of freshly baked bread and spread it thickly with deep yellow butter as her mother put some bacon on a plate, broke two eggs into the pan, then gave her a mug of milk.

'Mother,' Ruby said suddenly, 'I think Maud has done something . . . stupid . . . you know . . . with one of the visiting valets.' This was not an easy subject to discuss but she had to ask advice from someone. 'I don't know what to say to her.'

'Are you sure?'

'Well, she didn't sleep in her bed last night.'

'But what can you say? She will resent your interference.'

'I like Maud and if Mrs King finds out she'll be turned out and I'd miss her.'

'Perhaps it's best if she goes. She doesn't sound the sort of girl you should be friendly with.' If you're right she knows the penalty, it's her problem, not yours.'

'I just think she lost her head.'

Grace Barnard patted her daughter's hand. 'You're a kind girl, Ruby, but you should think of your own situation. If you're seen to be close to Maud and she's rumbled they might begin to regard you in the same light.'

'They wouldn't!'

'They would. Still, what to do about Ivy? She'll be dismissed if her ankle's really bad and her mother's already at her wit's end with eight young ones to feed and her husband disabled.' She stood up decisively. 'Tell Mrs King, she'd best come here until she's better. She'll be annoyed it's me being the good Samaritan.' At which she laughed, which made Ruby curious.

9

The guests had left, and with just the family to look after, the servants had less to do in the evenings. Now there was time for games below stairs – cards, I-spy, charades and spillikins were the favourites. And flirtations between the younger maids and footmen were common, if always under the beady eye of Mr Densham and Mrs King.

This was the best time, thought Ruby as, dinner over and cleared away, she sat on the window-seat in the servants' hall and opened the book that Fanny Chester had lent her. The governess was good to her: once she had known how much Ruby wanted to better herself, she'd taken a real interest in her.

'Hello, Maud.' She shifted, making room for her friend. She felt mildly irritated – she'd been looking forward to being alone with this new book. She laid it down and put her arm around Maud, who hadn't stopped crying since yesterday morning and the departure of Dartagnan, the handsome valet. Ruby had been right that his name was false, she'd overheard Densham saying he was really Alfred Rowbottom. But as she knew, some adopted foreign-sounding names to make them seem more interesting than they were. It would never work with Mr Forester: like so many employers, he chose the names his servants were to be called. All his valets were called Henry, the footmen were James, no matter how many were on duty, and the boot-boy was always Bob. It caused much ill feeling below stairs. The maids were luckier and kept their own names, but Ruby had heard of households where they were all called Mary.

But what worried Ruby most about 'Dartagnan' was that he lied. She had learnt that he wasn't a valet but a junior footman, who was standing in for his employer's regular man. She hadn't told Maud of either of her findings, that would be too unkind.

'I'm leaving.' Maud sniffed and wiped her eyes.

'What do you mean? Where are you going?'

'I can't live without Dartagnan. He's my life,' she said, and tossed her head dramatically.

'Ssh, not so loud. You don't want them to hear – one of them will be sure to tell on you.' Ruby nodded at the other maids who were a little too close for comfort.

'I don't care who hears.'

'Then you should. You can't just pack and go. How would you manage?'

'I'd get a position with the family he works for.'

'With no reference? They wouldn't even consider you.'

'I'll ask Mrs King. I've worked hard here, she won't refuse me. And if she does it won't stop me.'

'It would be an odd sort of household that allowed sweethearts to work under the same roof.'

'We shan't tell them. We'll be careful. No one need know.'

'Careful as you were here? Oh, Maud, within five minutes everyone would be gossiping about you, you know what it's like.' Maud looked sulky. 'Did he ask you to follow him?'

'He did,' she said, but Ruby was sure she was lying. 'We'll get married.'

'Really?' Ruby tried hard not to sound disbelieving. 'Then what would the two of you do? He can't stay in service if he marries you.'

'We can save. He wants to buy an inn. I could do the cooking. We could marry then.'

'But that would take years.'

'No, it won't. Dartagnan gets good tips from guests he's asked to look after. He's a rich man.'

A liar as well as a seducer, Ruby thought.

'You're just jealous,' Maud went on. 'I know – I've watched you making eyes at him.'

'I haven't, Maud.' But her friend was looking as if she didn't believe Ruby now. Her mother had been right,

Ruby thought. She was wasting her breath: Maud was in no mood to listen to reason. But at least recounting her plans had stopped her crying so perhaps tonight Ruby would get some sleep.

'So when will you go?'

'In the autumn. I couldn't leave you all in the lurch, could I? And I thought if I gave my three months' notice Mrs King would be nicer to me about it.'

'Perhaps.' Ruby was doubtful. It was a rare girl who left a good position for the unknown. And Mrs King, fussy and bossy though she was, cared for the maids in her charge. Maud launched into a long paean of praise for her beloved, and Ruby sat patiently, listening, but eventually she stood up. 'Maud, I'm tired. I'm going to bed now.' Maud looked disappointed but Ruby had had enough. She called her sister and they left the room together.

It was late and Eliza should have been in bed but it had been such an exciting evening she didn't want it to end and begged Merry to let her go out into the rose garden to listen to the nightingale singing. She heard it from her bedroom every night but she had wanted to get closer to it. However, she had been disappointed: tonight it hadn't sung a note.

Still, she sat for a while on a stone urn and looked up at the sky. She'd dined with her father! He had spoken to her! She had felt so grown-up, sitting with the adults, trying to keep up with their conversation. She was glad that she had been placed next to Uncle Charles: he had protected her when Aunt Minnie was particularly caustic. And Miss Chester had helped her once or twice when the sentences wouldn't come out as she had intended, from nerves.

Best of all had been when her father had said, 'Good,' when she had sung to them after dinner. Her stomach had been knotted with nerves but she'd managed 'Cherry Ripe' and he'd said, 'No more, you mustn't tire yourself . . .' Which must mean he cared. She realised she was chilled to the bone, pulled her shawl tight around her, got up and skimmed across the lawn towards the house. Now she was looking forward to being warm in her bed.

Inside, the house was dark and quiet and she suddenly felt uneasy. She climbed the main stairs quickly, her slippers making no sound on the bare oak boards. Her disquiet increased and she began to run along the main landing towards the safety of her room.

Ahead of her she saw a shaft of light flooding out from the door of what had been her mother's rooms. She stopped abruptly and her heart began to pound. She tiptoed towards the door which she could see now was partly open. The scent of tuberoses was even stronger than usual. She pulled her wrap tighter, as if it could protect her. She wanted to flee, yet she wanted to see. She paused, indecisive, putting her right foot forward and then bringing it back. Then she took control of herself and peered round the door of the forbidden room.

A candelabrum stood on the dressing-table. A large mirror, ornate with gilded cherubs, reflected the light, which blazed strongly. Clothes and shoes were scattered on the floor, the bed was unmade, the covers dragging on the floor, a tea-tray with a tarnished silver teapot was on a low table, an open trunk stood in front of the carved stone fireplace, as if someone had been interrupted in their packing and had fled the room. The strong scent of tuberoses was coming from two large vases filled with fresh blooms.

Eliza drew back sharply as a shadow loomed across the room. She should have carried on along the corridor but she was rooted to the spot and couldn't move. When no one appeared she felt bold enough to peer.

She feared that the man standing at her mother's dressing-table must have heard her quick intake of breath. She recognised his tall slim figure: it was her father. What was he doing? Why was he there? She was afraid but in front of her were her mother's room and her clothes. It was the closest Eliza had ever been to any contact with her.

There was a strange noise, a rasping, ugly sound. Suddenly her father slumped forward, his hands splayed on the dressing-table top, and his shoulders shaking. Eliza clamped her hand over her mouth. He was crying.

She entered the room silently and moved over the carpet towards him. She waited, close to him, and hesitated. She put out her hand, the palm a couple of inches from his back. He sobbed loudly. She snatched back her hand.

'Amelia . . .' her father said, as softly as a breath. 'Oh, Amelia.' And then he covered his face with his hands.

His misery gave her courage. 'Papa.' Her voice was as quiet as his and he did not hear. 'Papa, don't be sad.' His shoulders shook violently. It was then that she touched him. 'Papa, you have me.'

He spun round, his face streaked with tears, and looked down at her with an expression of disbelief. 'What do you mean? Why are you here? How dare you?' he shouted.

She took a step back. 'The door was open.'

'What right have you to spy on me?'

'Papa, I heard you – I couldn't bear to hear you crying.'

'How dare you say that of me? Get out! I don't want you near me.'

'Papa, it's not my fault that Mama is dead. Please, listen to me. I long for her too—'

The slap was unexpected and her head snapped back. She felt no pain – that was reserved for her soul. 'Papa—' But seeing his hand raised again, she turned on her heel, and ran from the room, her sobs following her like a shadow.

In the corridor she cannoned into her grandmother, nearly knocking her over. 'Eliza! What on earth . . . ?'

'Get out of my sight!' her father yelled from the doorway.

'Freddie?' His mother stepped forward. 'Freddie, why are you shouting like a costermonger? Stop it this instant.'

'The child was spying on me.'

'The door was open! I was curious! Grandmama, I wasn't doing anything wrong.' That was what Eliza said but it was unlikely her grandmother understood, so muffled and incoherent was her speech through her tears.

Alerted by the shouting, both Merry and Miss Chester had appeared and were peering anxiously around the corner of the nursery corridor. 'Why isn't this child in bed? Get her out of my sight,' Frederick bellowed.

Eliza raced for the comfort of Merry's arms. 'She wanted to listen to the nightingale, your ladyship,' Merry said, as she made a cumbersome bob. 'I'm sorry, sir.'

'You have cause.' He glared at Merry.

'Get her to bed now, Merry, give her some hot milk. I'll talk to you in the morning, Eliza,' said Lady Gwendoline.

Eliza bobbed to her grandmother and, still sobbing, allowed Merry to tug her along the corridor. With her nurse and her governess fluttering and fussing about her, Eliza was ushered back to her room.

Lady Gwendoline approached her son. She pointed into the room imperiously with her stick. As though he were once again a small child, Frederick turned, docile now, into the bedroom. 'Just look at this mess. What are you thinking of? And open that window – the scent of those roses is overwhelming.' She waved her hand in an expression of distaste. 'You behave as if the woman were dead and this was a mausoleum.'

'She's dead to me.'

'Then bury her.' With her stick she prodded various items of clothing on the floor. 'It's been ten years. There should be an end to this nonsense. This room should be cleared. We had need of it this past week—'

'You won't touch a thing in here, Mother.' He swung round to face her, his eyes black with anger.

'As you wish. It's your house, as I am fully aware. I've been speaking with Minnie about this unhealthy obsession of yours.'

'How dare you discuss me with others?'

'She's your sister, hardly a stranger. Of course I shall confide my concerns to her. I need to. I don't understand you.'

'I don't ask you to.'

Lady Gwendoline sat down in front of the dressing-table and turned to face her son. 'I don't wish to argue with you, Freddie.'

'Then don't, Mother.'

'You can't continue blaming the child.'

'She's her daughter. Not mine.'

'Freddie, you are not, as far as I'm aware, blind. She *is* your child.'

'Amelia was an adulteress, how can I be certain she is?'

'For the simple reason that she is your double. Her hair, her eyes, her height, she acquired them from you. Amelia was a stupid, vacuous woman but no one can say that of Eliza. She is highly intelligent, as are you – well, about most things.' She put her hand up as if to take one of his, but he backed away and she let it fall on to her lap. 'I agree, Amelia's behaviour was appalling. I could never forgive her for the pain she caused you and that innocent child. You were right to send her away. But I cannot approve of your continual neglect of your daughter. She deserves better.'

'When I see her, I remember. Tonight, at dinner, afterwards when she sang. It was too much for me,

77

Mother. It was as if Amelia had returned to haunt and goad me.'

'Well, she hasn't. That is all poppycock. And as for shutting Eliza away as you do, transferring your hatred for the mother to the child! Your daughter loves you and she wants you to love her. Sometimes when I see the way she looks at you, I feel I could weep.'

'Love! It's all you women think of.'

'Don't be facile, Freddie. I speak of a different love.'

'What if I allowed myself to love her and she hurt me too? What then?'

'My poor son, how deeply wounded you have been. But why should she?'

'Because Amelia was her mother.'

'You must forget the woman ever existed.'

'Perhaps I do not wish to.'

'If that is the case, then, there is no hope for you. I had believed that eventually your common sense and intelligence would come to the fore. But this situation can and should be changed. And if you won't then I shall. I have my duty and obligations too. One day Eliza will have this great inheritance of yours. She must be prepared for that, not shut away with servants. You risk her becoming like them. She should spend more time with us. She runs wild when we're not here. And Merry is hardly a suitable companion for her.'

'She has her governess.'

'It's not enough. Eliza's too childish.'

'Because she *is* a child, Mother.'

'Barely. She's about to become a young woman, with the responsibilities of her position, yet sometimes she seems like a four-year-old.'

'And that's my fault?'

'Yes. She doesn't have enough contact with society. People she can talk to.'

'Mother, you exaggerate—'

'If you will not listen to me, then . . .'

Mother and son argued back and forth, while Eliza cried herself to sleep.

'Sheep and sugar, you're a sleepy-head.' Merry was pulling back her curtains.

Eliza rubbed her eyes. She felt happy until she remembered the scene of the night before and felt sad, so very sad.

'Well, I have a surprise for you.' Merry placed her clothes for the morning on a chair. Eliza could feel her throat tightening, a lump forming in her chest. 'You look down in the dumps, I must say. Misery and marbles, don't you want to know?'

'No.'

'You will.'

'I won't.'

'We're off to London in November. What a surprise.' Merry stood in front of the window, blocking out most of the light.

'We?'

'We are.'

'And Miss Chester?'

'Her too.'

'Why?'

'Your grandmother summoned me this morning. She feels it's time you saw more of the city. And your father has ordered it.'

'My father?'

'What a silly you sound, like a parrot. Yes, that's right, your papa.'

And Eliza smiled, happiness flooding her, all sadness gone – he wanted her with him, at last.

10

Eliza was convinced November would never come. By the last week in September she had packed a box of books and toys. By the first week in October her collection of china animals was wrapped in tissue paper in boxes she had begged from the butler.

'Now what are you up to?' Merry looked cross.

'I'm packing my dolls'-house furniture. I've asked Mr Densham to find me a large wooden box for the house.'

'We're not taking that great lumping thing with us.'

'I love my dolls' house.'

'Don't whine. You can't and that's that.'

'Why?'

'Because Merry says.'

'But—'

'*But* is for butter and goats.' The dismal expression on Eliza's face intensified. 'I expect your father will buy you a grand new one,' Merry allowed.

At this Eliza cheered, imagining herself and her father shopping together, something they had never done before.

Each day she nagged Merry to pack her clothes.

'There'll be time for that.'

'Please!'

'Eliza, be patient, I'm worked off my feet already.' Merry settled back in her easy chair with her penny dreadful, a cup of tea close by.

'*I'll* do it then.'

'You wouldn't know how to. It's a skilled task. Go and find that Miss Chester – she has plenty of time on her hands,' Merry said, with the sniff she used about things and people who did not meet with her approval. Merry didn't like Miss Chester, Eliza knew, but why was a mystery. She wondered what her governess thought of her nurse.

She left Merry to her book and went into the schoolroom. 'May we go for a walk?' she asked.

'Oh!' Miss Chester exclaimed. 'I didn't hear you come in. You made me jump.' Miss Chester spoke quickly while stuffing a letter into her pocket, which she was having difficulty finding. Her face was suddenly very pink.

'It's a lovely day. And Merry won't let me pack.'

'But, my dear Eliza, it's another three weeks before we go. Try to be patient.' She was tying on her bonnet.

'Three weeks is for ever.'

'I know. I'm excited too. But it will pass.'

'It's very strange, Miss Chester. I want to go and yet I'm sad to leave Harcourt.'

'I'm not surprised. It is wonderful here. But it's only for the winter and then we'll be back.'

'Why are *you* excited? I thought you said you liked it here best of anywhere.'

'I do, very much. But while we are in London I shall be able to see my brother.'

'Is that letter from him?'

'Yes.' She flushed even more deeply and busied herself searching for a handkerchief.

'Might I meet him?'

'He will be honoured.'

Eventually the great day arrived. The baggage had gone first in the large unwieldy wagon – including the dolls' house. Eliza didn't know whether to be disappointed or pleased. Next her father had left, driving his phaeton at a spanking pace to the station – which, since his own father had allowed the railway to cross their land, was close by. Eliza watched him go: she had hoped to travel with him – she had never been on a train – but she was dissatisfied to be told that she was to travel with her grandmother by coach and, worse, they would be stopping at the homes of friends along the way. Lady Gwendoline planned to take a month over the journey.

The following day, early in the morning, Lady Gwendoline, with her maid, climbed into the briska, her favourite carriage: it had seats which could be converted into a bed should she tire. It was vast and they left three hours before the others, so slow was its progress. Finally an overexcited Eliza, with Merry, Miss Chester and Bumble, climbed into the barouche. The horses were pawing the ground and snorting their excitement too.

Eliza was sure she would be sick with anticipation but she wasn't. It was Merry who spent the day groaning, moaning, sweating and vomiting. By the time they reached their first destination, Eliza and Miss Chester were relieved to escape the fetid atmosphere, which was making them feel ill too.

The next morning, Eliza was told that both Merry and her grandmother were too ill to travel. It had been arranged that the pair would stay where they were until they were better. Meanwhile she and Miss Chester were to travel straight to London – and, best of all, by train.

It was like a great smoky monster, awesome in its power. Eliza hadn't known such speed was possible as they thundered along at thirty miles an hour.

'It's as well Merry isn't with us. She's convinced going so fast would force her brains back in her skull,' Eliza told Miss Chester with a broad grin. She had no such fears and would have liked nothing better than to hang out of the window, but wasn't allowed, because of the smoke and the risk of cinders in her eyes.

Paddington Station was exactly as it was in the print she had seen of Mr Frith's painting, Eliza thought: there were so many people milling about. The noise of the trains huffing and puffing, of people greeting, laughing and crying was unlike anything she had ever heard before. There was such an air of anticipation, too, just like in the picture.

They found her father's coach, which had been sent to collect them. It was one of the smartest, its paintwork gleaming, the coachmen immaculate, the black horses perfectly matched. Eliza's first impression was that the city was enormous, and so crowded. How the coachmen didn't crash into each other among all the traffic she couldn't imagine. She hung out of the window, ignoring Miss Chester who told her that to do so was unseemly.

*

'So, what do you think of the city?' Aunt Minnie was resting on a *chaise-longue* in her overheated, fussy boudoir. Eliza had been disappointed that she had first to visit her aunt, whose home was just round the corner from her father's, when she had wanted to explore her new suite of rooms high up in the large house in Belgrave Square.

'It's so big and noisy and there are so many people. It's exciting.' Eliza was at the window, unable to take her eyes off the moving throng in the street below. She ached to be down there among it. She watched two nurses with high-wheeled perambulators – Merry would have been shocked to see babies out on a cold day like today. There was a flower-seller on the corner, with buckets of chrysanthemums, banging his hands together to try to keep warm, a news-boy was yelling his headline, and a group of children with hoops ran by – she must ask for a hoop. On the opposite side a man was calling out his wares, piles of shrimps on a wooden shelf slung from his neck, the mugs for measuring them banging and clanking from the front. In competition the muffin man was shouting even louder. A milk cart drew up and kitchen-maids appeared from the houses, clutching their jugs. She saw coal disappear down a hole in the pavement into one house's cellar. There was a constant flow of people, and her aunt had said this was a quiet street! Eliza could barely wait to see a noisy one.

'Child, you will tire yourself at this rate. And you will most certainly fatigue me. Come away from the window.'

Reluctantly she obeyed and sat on a foot-stool beside her aunt. 'Where's Papa?'

'At his club, I expect.'

'What's that?'

'Heavens, child, you ask so many questions. Are you always so inquisitive? You give me a headache.'

'I'm sorry.' Eliza felt tears prick behind her eyes. Her aunt frightened her at the best of times but to be alone with her was awful. 'I don't know what a club is. I apologise.'

'If you don't know there's no point in apologising, is there? I can't stand people who constantly say they are sorry when they aren't.' She flapped her hand with obvious irritation. 'It's where men go.'

'Why?' Eliza ventured.

'To get away from us, no doubt. And certainly you and your incessant questioning.' Her aunt laughed.

Eliza looked out of the window again while she screwed up her courage to make another enquiry. She took a deep breath. 'When will Papa be back?'

'Late, when you're in bed.'

'Oh . . .' Eliza fought the sadness.

At Harcourt Barton no lights shone at the windows and it was swathed in stillness. Even the owls in the garden were silent, the dogs in the kennels slept, the cats had abandoned the hunt. The old horses in the stables stood hushed. It was as if the house and the creatures knew they had been left behind and were adjusting to this new situation.

Maggie was in her small room next to the scullery. She was crying so fiercely that her hard pillow was soaked. Mr Didier hadn't wanted her to go to work for him in London, and she was doomed to stay here with Mrs Satterly for ever . . .

High up in the house, in the little room with the sloping ceiling beneath the eaves, Ruby lay worrying.

'Maud, are you crying?' she said into the chilly darkness.

'No.'

'You are.'

'I'm not.'

Ruby slid out of the bed, pulled the counterpane about her shoulders, and padded across the room. 'What's the matter? You can tell me.'

'Oh, Ruby . . .' Maud flung herself into Ruby's arms and clung to her so hard that she winced with pain, but she didn't complain. She stroked Maud's hair and made soothing noises and waited for the storm to pass.

'Maud, tell me.'

Maud, her head against Ruby's shoulder, spoke, but her voice was so muffled that Ruby couldn't hear her. She waited. 'Well, say something,' Maud shouted, lifting her head.

'I didn't hear what you said.'

'I'm so ashamed. I don't know what to do.'

'Anything can be solved.'

'Not this. Oh, Ruby, what shall I do?' She looked at Ruby with anguish in her eyes. 'I'm going . . .' She looked down at her stomach. 'I'm . . .' She touched it and began to cry again.

'Maud!' Ruby's eyes widened with shock. 'Are you sure?'

'Yes.'

'A baby!'

'It's not likely to be a monkey, is it?' Maud snapped.

'Dartagnan?'

'Who else?'

'Does he know?'

'I wrote to him but he didn't reply.'

'Did you expect him to?'

'Of course I did. Else I wouldn't have written, would I?'

'Did he give you . . .' Ruby, wary of Maud's temper, continued, 'I mean, did you have the right address?'

'Yes, Hindle Hall, Berkshire. I sent it to one of the maids I know who works there and asked her to give it to Dartagnan. And she . . .' She was searching for her handkerchief, found it and blew her nose. Then she collected herself. 'She sent it back. He told her he didn't want to write to me.'

'The fiend!'

'I wondered if perhaps . . .' Maud began to cry again – with reason, thought Ruby.

'You wondered what?'

'You'd never agree, but then I don't know . . . Perhaps if . . .'

'Maud, unless you tell me how can I help you?'

'I wanted to ask if you thought your mother might take pity on me. If I worked for her – and I'd break my back for her – would she take me in?'

'What about your own mother?'

'She's dead and my father'd kill me.'

'And what about afterwards? What will you do? What about the child?'

'I don't know.' The tears threatened again. 'There's the poor-house, and the orphanage.' Now she sobbed bitterly.

'It's a lot to ask my mother . . . She's already looking after Ivy. Times are hard.' Maud looked anguished. Ruby sighed. 'Very well.' She gave in. 'I'll ask her. But don't raise your hopes.'

Then Maud was all over her, kissing her, telling her what a friend she was. Finally Ruby managed to settle her, but she couldn't get back to sleep. Instead, she lay staring into the darkness. What a dreadful thing to have happened. What a wicked, loose girl Maud was. Why should she ask her mother to help her when it was her own fault in the first place? But she knew she would. Was Maud wicked, or just stupid, with her dreams of love with a man she barely knew? And what about *him*? What would happen to him? Nothing. But Maud was ruined: no good house would take her in now. She would be dismissed, without references, the minute her condition became obvious. They all knew that. She'd heard tales of families who were compassionate and helped but she didn't think this one would. No respectable family would consider her.

Respectable! Ruby knew for certain that when the large party had been here in September two of the women had not spent the nights with their husbands. But, then, they were rich and that was where the difference lay.

11

Almost a month later Eliza's grandmother and Merry arrived, just in time for Christmas.

'Whelks and wisdom, I thought I was going to pop off,' Merry explained, after she had hugged Eliza and Fanny had arranged for tea to be sent to the nursery.

'What happened?'

'What didn't happen!' Merry sank gratefully into an armchair, her black skirt billowing about her like the darkest of storm clouds. 'The doctor said he'd never seen aught like it. When you left me, I went to bed. Not wishing to shock but the sweat was flowing off me like a cascade. That was the Tuesday. Next thing I knew it was Sunday – and all those days lost!'

'Poor Merry.' Eliza kissed her cheek.

'How frightening for you.' Fanny handed her a plate of angel cakes.

'Thank you, Miss Chester. Just what I need. Wasting away, I was. Look at me, just bones!' Both Fanny and Eliza turned away to smile.

If anything, Eliza thought, Merry had acquired yet another chin. 'And my grandmother?' she asked.

'She was ill but not nearly as ill as me, you understand. After ten days it was decided we should return to Harcourt Barton until I was fully recovered.'

'And my grandmother?'

'Her too,' Merry admitted, a shade reluctantly. 'Mrs King has been like an angel looking after me, and Mrs Satterly too, tempting my poor appetite. And what have you been up to, my cabbage?'

'We've been to the park every day, unless it was raining. So many people go, you know.' Eliza sensed

87

rather than saw Miss Chester stiffen. As if she would tell that on these walks they frequently met her uncle Charles! 'And we go to the art galleries, and the museums. And I've been to the opera! And we go to the library and sometimes we take tea at—'

'You must rest, Merry,' Fanny interrupted, looking flustered. There she was again, Eliza thought, afraid she would tell that they had taken tea with her uncle in the Alexandra Hotel, watching the riders on Rotten Row.

'That I will, Miss Chester. I'm going to have to build my strength.' Merry settled back comfortably in the chair as a maid entered carrying a lighted taper.

'Merry, you'll be amazed by this. Watch.'

The maid held the taper to the burner on the wall and, with a loud plop, the gas ignited.

'Heaven and heather!'

'It's the new gas lighting Papa has had installed.'

'We'll be killed in our beds!' Merry flapped her handkerchief in front of her face. 'And it smells.' She wrinkled her nose.

'No, Merry, this is progress. We can read in our beds, which is wonderful, isn't it, Miss Chester?'

It took Merry some time to build her strength. It required getting up late, and going to bed early, with a rest in the afternoon and a succession of trays with refreshments being brought up from the kitchen by grumbling maids. Stout was an important part of Merry's convalescent diet with a medicinal brandy to help her sleep.

She was full of news from Harcourt Barton. Mrs Satterly had had the odd turn – self-induced, Merry confided to Fanny, by too much consumption of alcohol. Ivy was still at the Barnards' farm: her ankle hadn't mended and it was likely she'd have a limp for ever more, which would put paid to her days in service.

'That Grace Barnard is a saint, that's to be sure.'

'Is Ada still working with Ruby?'

'That she is, Miss Eliza, and a useless minx she is, and cheeky with it. Mrs King is none too pleased with her.'

'And Ruby?'

'Good as gold but, then, she's her mother's daughter.'

'And Maud?' Eliza liked Ruby and Maud best of all the maids – they were always laughing and joking.

'She's gone.'

'Gone? Where to?'

'I've no idea and I don't want to know. A right scallywag she turned out to be. She deserves her come-down.'

'What did she do?'

'Never you mind.' Merry pursed her lips, which meant, Eliza knew, that she wasn't about to tell her anything. 'In an interesting condition, among other things,' Merry said to Fanny, in an undertone.

'What's interesting?' Eliza asked. 'What do you mean?'

'Never you mind.'

'You're always saying that and I do mind. I like Maud.'

'Poor child,' Fanny said.

'She should have thought, she knew what was what. No better than she ought to be!'

'Why's Maud a "poor child"? What should she have thought? I know, I know, you've no need to say it. *Never you mind*.' Merry lunged to smack her and Eliza rushed from the room, saying she'd never ever speak to her again for the rest of her life. Left alone, Merry beckoned to Fanny. She looked about her as if checking the room was empty. 'Maud's a thief.'

'Maud? Surely not.' She might have been on the flighty side but Fanny had thought her honest enough.

'Some jewellery was taken from the mistress's room, and she'd been sent there to dust by Lady Gwendoline. That's all the evidence I need.'

'The room that was always shut?'

'The very same.'

'Good gracious. I *am* surprised. Was it valuable?'

'Of course! My mistress never had rubbish for jewellery. Mr Forester lavished only the best on her.'

'Was the constable informed?'

'Lady Gwendoline said no one was to know. The shame of it.'

'Surely it's Maud's shame, not theirs.'

'Be that as it may. But if she ever turns up, I wouldn't like to be in her shoes.'

Merry's idleness did not affect Eliza unduly. The month that her nurse hadn't been with her was the first time she had been separated from her and at first she had missed her. But a housemaid had been caring for her instead, she had had her lessons, and it had been great fun to explore London with Miss Chester, who knew so much about the city. And she had to admit that although she had been concerned for Merry, it was nice not to have her nagging as she constantly did.

She had been disappointed with Miss Chester's brother, whom they had met for tea. He looked like a daddy-long-legs in his black trousers and with his great height. His hair was dishevelled and he smelt of dust. Eliza sensed he didn't like her, which puzzled her since he did not know her, but if he spoke to her he did not look at her and once or twice when she had said something he ignored her, which she had found very rude. She wondered if he might be deaf. Miss Chester was edgy with him and when they had finished their tea she had sent Eliza ahead. When Eliza had turned back she had been pretty sure they were arguing.

Though Eliza enjoyed her expeditions, and the sense of excitement the great city generated, life in London had proved a disappointment. The house was so much smaller than Harcourt Barton that she had expected to see more of her father but he was hardly ever there. He left early each morning to go to his bank and when he wasn't there he was at his club, which Eliza didn't understand when he had such a nice house.

However, on some evenings he entertained at home. The sound of chatter, music and laughter filtered up to the nursery tucked away on the top floor. But while at Harcourt Barton she could hide in the minstrels' gallery and watch the fun, here she could see nothing through the banisters.

There were two worlds here, and she could only glimpse a little of the other one. Certainly she was not part of it. The closest she got was her daily visit to her grandmother in her house across the square. Some days she enjoyed herself, others she didn't – it depended on the old lady's mood.

Lady Gwendoline's rooms were always overheated. She liked to play cards and expected Eliza to play with her, and her inability to do so made her grandmother short with her. Sometimes she had to read to her but since she didn't enjoy the books that was no pleasure either. And Lady Gwendoline saw it as her duty to question Eliza on what she was learning. The trouble with that was that the minute she was asked something her mind went blank and she knew her grandmother thought she was stupid. On other days Lady Gwendoline would suggest playing Happy Families or Snap, with which Eliza had no trouble, but best of all were the times she chose to talk about her past and *that* Eliza found enthralling.

Her father's house was newly built and luxuriously furnished – Frederick Forester hadn't stinted on a single thing. Even Merry could find nothing to complain about in their rooms. It was situated in Belgrave Square, not far from the palace where the Queen and all her children lived. It was Eliza's dream to be invited there for tea one day but so far she had had to make do with watching the soldiers and the carriages rushing in and out with important-looking people in them. She was convinced that one must be her father.

12

'Miss Eliza, put your bonnet on, we're going out.' Merry handed her her brand-new navy felt bonnet with a pheasant-feather trim and dark blue satin ribbons for tying beneath her chin.

'But it's raining, you don't like getting wet.'

'Don't you argue with Merry.'

'But it's cold. You hate being cold.'

'Wear your new boots.'

'They pinch.'

From the wardrobe Merry was taking a cloak. 'Do as I say. Put this on, we're late.'

'But you hate rain.'

'Then we'll take my gamp.'

'Where are we going?'

'To meet a friend of mine.'

'Who?'

'Never you mind. And, what's more, I don't want you telling no one about nothing.'

'Why?'

'Especially that there Miss Chester. She's too nosy for her own good.'

'She's not. She's nice.'

'She gossips and she's up to no good, you mark my words.'

'She never does! Why should it be a secret?'

''Cause Merry says. Now, no more of your questions. You're acting like you were four again.'

There was no carriage waiting for them in the square, which was strange since Eliza never went anywhere but the park on foot. Merry took her hand and literally dragged her along the streets to Victoria Station, where they stood in a queue waiting for a horse-bus. This was a great excitement: Eliza had seen the great wagons lumbering along and had longed to ride in one but had never thought she might be allowed to. Now she had her chance. Given Merry's bulk and the large carpet bag she was carrying, boarding the bus was not easy and there was much grumbling from the other passengers as they had to shift along the already crowded bench to make room for her.

Unfortunately, Eliza did not enjoy the ride as she had hoped: the bus rolled alarmingly, the damp clothes of the other passengers gave off a horrible musty, sour smell, and she did not like being squashed up to the woman beside her, whose breath smelt of something nasty she didn't recognise but which Merry told her later was caused by too much 'soapy suds'.

'What's that?' Eliza asked, as they walked along.

'Not a drink for a lady.'

'Do tell.'

'Gin, hot water, lemon and sugar. Soapy suds.'

'Sounds horrible.'

'Tastes lovely,' said Merry, with a dreamy expression.

'I hope none of them had fleas.' Eliza was already scratching.

'Stop that! It's just your imagination.'

They were in a part of London to which Eliza had never been before and was glad she hadn't. The houses were narrow, unlike her own home with its portico and steps, large front door and fan-light, and the brickwork was black and sooty. Once or twice she glimpsed narrow alleyways that looked dark and forbidding and she could see rubbish lying about, uncollected, unswept, which would never have been allowed in Belgrave Square. Unwashed urchins in ragged clothes played in the street and stared rudely at Eliza, who would have stuck out her tongue if she hadn't been so scared of them. Everywhere there was a horrible smell. She was used to the smell of horse dung, which pervaded the whole city, and liked it for it reminded her of the stables at Harcourt Barton and of the old cob Snuffles and her pony, Silver, but these streets smelt of an awful unidentified smell. She asked Merry what it was.

'What should by rights be in them there sewers, that's

what you're sniffing. Thank your stars you live where you do and not here.'

I do, I do, Eliza thought fervently, for she felt as if she had moved into a new city, one that she did not like at all. She found herself walking closer to Merry's comforting bulk and, for the first time in years, felt for her hand.

Eventually they stopped in front of a tall house which looked a mite smarter than the others, but only just. There was a board outside, which proclaimed it as a lodging-house 'For Genteel Folk'. A card in the window announced that there were vacancies. Given the look of the place Eliza wasn't the least surprised, and she was certain that no one of any gentility would wish to reside there. As Merry sallied up the steep steps she lagged behind: she didn't want to enter such a dingy-looking place. Merry rang the bell and gesticulated angrily at her to join her on the top step. When no one came she rang again, almost yanking the bell-pull out of its socket and then, for good measure, banged on the door with the duck-head handle of her umbrella.

'Keep your hair on! Yes?' A sallow-faced and none-too-clean woman opened the door, wiped her hands on her grubby apron and glared at them. Not that Eliza could blame her: she could see a mark in the paint where Merry had been banging.

'There's no need to take that tone with me, my good woman.'

'That I'm not and hope I never shall be.'

'Mrs Orme is expecting us,' Merry said, in her most haughty manner, having chosen apparently to ignore the woman's reply.

'Mrs Greensay, is it? I'm Mrs Nugent.' Her attitude had changed: she was smiling now and she gave a little bob, which made Eliza giggle. No one bobbed to Merry – didn't she know?

'*Miss* Greensay, I'd have you know.'

'A nicer lady than Mrs Orme I've never known, real

quality. And such a dear. And this must be Eliza?' The woman bent to chuck Eliza under the chin, which made her step back sharply in alarm. 'How are you, my dear?'

'That'll be enough.' Merry poked at her with the ever-present umbrella. 'And it's Miss Forester to you, if you don't mind, Mrs Nugget.' Merry straightened to her full four foot eleven, and breathed deeply, which expanded her size considerably. She didn't proffer her hand, as Eliza expected her to, but perhaps once you had stuck your umbrella into someone that wasn't expected.

'It's Nugent.' The woman waited a second, as if expecting Merry to apologise, but when she didn't she held open the door. 'This way, then, Miss Forester and Miss Greensay.'

They were led into what was evidently the parlour. 'Shall I take your capes before I go and tell Mrs Orme you're here?'

'That won't be necessary, Mrs Nugget. We'll be warmer with them on.' Merry looked pointedly at the meagre fire burning in the grate. The curtains at the window were fusty and worn, as was the furniture. If there had been a view it would have been impossible to see it, so dirty were the window-panes. Merry tutted disapprovingly and flicked at a chair with her handkerchief. 'You'll be better off on a wooden one – I don't reckon much to that there upholstery.'

Obediently Eliza sat down, straightening her skirt as she did so. 'This is a horrible house, Merry. It smells of boiled cabbage. Why does your friend live here?'

'Because she hasn't the wherewithal to live elsewhere, more's the shame and pity.' Merry peered at the one picture on the wall. 'Hardly worth hanging,' she said dismissively, as the door burst open and another woman rushed in in a whirl of grey silk, ringleted hair, and a scent that was not very pleasant – it smelt rather over-sweet.

'Merry! Amelia!'

'This is Eliza, ma'am.'

'Of course, how silly of me. I must have been thinking of someone else. Another little girl . . . long, long ago.' She laughed but Eliza thought it sounded odd, as if she didn't really want to and was having to make herself. She sat further back on her chair, as if distancing herself from the scene. 'How wonderful to see you both.' The woman clapped her small hands with their pink and shiny nails, rather as small children did. 'I've dreamt of this day, I never thought it would come . . .' The pretty hands fluttered. 'Let me take a good look at you.' And the stranger pulled Eliza from the chair and was hugging her and, to her consternation, kissing her face, tiny, hungry little kisses. 'So pretty! So lovely,' she said. Eliza stood with her arms rigid at her sides, like a soldier at attention. She was unused to such emotional display.

'Ma'am, I don't think . . .' Merry stepped forward and took the woman's arm.

'I'm sorry, Merry. I was quite taken aback. I'm sorry, Eliza, did I frighten you?'

'No,' Eliza said. It was one of those confusing lies – she knew it was the answer the adults would expect but it was still untrue.

'I knew you a long time ago.'

'Did you?' Eliza said uncertainly.

'Tea! We must have tea and I've made us some cakes,' the woman said, in a rapid change of subject.

'*You*, Mrs Orme – baking? Well I never did!' Merry winked at her.

'I've discovered I'm a good cook.' She was laughing again with the laugh that wasn't. 'But take your cloaks off. Sit down, Eliza – are you tired?' While she talked the woman was in constant movement, and kept touching Eliza, who wished she wouldn't – she felt it rude for a stranger to do so. 'Are you enjoying London, my dear? Your first visit, isn't it?' But she did not wait for Eliza to answer before she was rushing around the room again. 'The tea!' And she tripped towards the door just as Mrs Nugent entered with a tray. 'Ha, Mrs Nugent, how kind.' And she fluttered back and took a seat as the tray, with mismatched cups, was placed on a table beside her. Then she was up again and fussing about napkins and plates. Finally she settled, and began to pour the tea as elegantly as if the teapot were silver and the cups the finest bone china. All the while she never stopped talking.

She was thin, Eliza thought, and her dress was worn though it might have been pretty once, and it looked as if it had been altered, not too expertly, so that at least it owed something to present fashion. She looked more closely at the woman's face. She might have been pretty once too, but now she looked tired, and her face was grey and blotchy, and her hair didn't shine as Eliza's did. And she kept biting her bottom lip, which looked red and sore.

'You must tell me all about yourself.'

'I'm fourteen . . .' Eliza trailed off – there really wasn't much to say.

'Do you like London? Or have I already asked you that? I'm such a silly!'

'No, I like our house in the country more,' Eliza answered, while tending to agree that she was silly in the extreme.

'Ha, Harcourt Barton. A lovely house.'

'You've been there?'

'Yes, but long ago.'

'You must come again,' Eliza said politely.

'How kind of you, sweet child. If only I could,' was the reply. And then the woman seemed to calm down and became able to concentrate on one thing at a time. Little by little she elicited from Eliza what she liked and what she didn't, her preference in music, the books she was reading, colours, how her room was decorated. With each snippet of information she sighed and placed those pretty hands on her chest as if enfolding the information to herself. Eliza told her of her pony, which she loved but which Merry wouldn't let her ride as often as she wanted.

'How wise of you, dear Merry. What if you fell and hurt yourself?' The pale blue eyes filled with tears at the thought.

'But I wouldn't.' Eliza felt uneasy with this woman. She found herself wondering if she really meant the things she said. And how strange this was – grown-ups rarely asked her anything. In fact, they showed little interest in her – apart from Merry, Miss Chester and her grandmother. The more she talked, the more obvious it became that Mrs Orme was educated and had an air of well-to-do about her, but if so, why was she living here in this awful house in the back-streets?

'Do you have a good governess?'

'Oh, yes, I like Miss Chester best of all my governesses. She's clever.'

'And pretty?'

'Very.'

Mrs Orme looked distressed at this information, and searched for the scrap of lace that was her handkerchief.

'She's not pretty!' Merry butted in.

'She is. Merry only says that because she doesn't like her, Mrs Orme.'

'I never said aught—'

'Merry doesn't like any of my governesses.'

'Maybe she wants you all to herself. If I were lucky enough to be your nurse, I would hate to share you with anyone.'

'Would you?' Eliza said, unsure what she was supposed to say. The unease continued: was she nice or was she pretending to be?

'And your father?'

'Ma'am!' Merry interrupted.

'He's well, thank you,' Eliza answered, as she presumed she should. 'Did you know my mother?' she asked, so suddenly that Merry choked on her tea.

'What makes you ask?' The hands fluttered in a very agitated way.

'Because your scent is like the one in my mother's room.' She had finally identified it: it was a cheaper smell, but very similar.

'I once . . .' The hands were virtually semaphoring now. 'I . . .'

'I think, ma'am . . .' Merry got heavily to her feet. 'We'll be missed if . . .'

'Of course, Merry. Of course.' Mrs Orme jumped to her feet, and Eliza wished the woman had answered her question.

'Before we go . . .' Merry began to delve into the large bag she had brought with her, and came up red-faced from the effort. 'I brought you these, ma'am.' She held a large bundle wrapped in a sheet, which, to Eliza, looked like clothes since she could see a peep of pink silk. That was kind of Merry, she thought. 'And this.' Merry handed Mrs Orme a small leather purse. Eliza hoped it contained a lot of money for she seemed in dire need of it. Back into the bag went Merry. 'And this.' She handed over what looked like a flat jewel case.

Mrs Orme snapped it open, then shut it just as quickly. 'Merry, you shouldn't have done this.'

'And why not, pray? It's yours. And, after all, it's nearly Christmas so look on it as a present from me to you.'

'You are so kind, Merry.'

'As you were to me once, ma'am.'

'But now you know where I live you must come more often.'

'That would be very nice.' Eliza was getting good at this polite lying.

'But I can't just let you go . . . Wait a second . . . I'll get my bonnet.'

'But, ma'am, is it . . . ?' Merry looked anxious.

'Just to the crossroads. Just that far, Merry, my dear one.'

And so it was that the three walked down the road, but at the crossroads Mrs Orme could not bear to leave them. They walked much further back to the city. When they reached Holborn, Merry said, 'Ma'am, I don't want to be unkind . . .'

'No, you're right, Merry. We should part.' At which point the woman burst into tears and began to hug Eliza again, just as a coach containing Eliza's Aunt Minnie passed by.

That evening Merry had been summoned to Mr Forester's study, which was unusual. She was gone some time, which was even more unusual. When she finally returned to the nursery she had evidently been weeping but she wouldn't tell Eliza why. The rest of the evening was normal.

'You were crying, Merry?'

'Tears and tadpoles, I wasn't. I'm going down with a cold, that's what.' She tucked the sheets in tight.

'Who was that lady?'

'I told you, a friend.'

'If she's a friend why did you call her "ma'am"?'

'I never did.' Merry sniffed.

'You did, Merry.'

'Then I wasn't thinking straight.'

'And why when you gave her that jewellery box did she say you shouldn't have?'

'None of your business.'

Eliza decided not to pursue that question – she knew Merry: she'd wheedle it out of her eventually.

'Merry, I kept feeling I'd met Mrs Orme somewhere before. Have I?'

'Not that I know of.' Hurriedly Merry bent down to pick something up from the floor.

'That's a horrible place where she lives.'

'It's better than nothing when you've no money.'

'I could give her my money in the blue box.'

At this Merry wailed hugely and hugged her tight.

'That won't be necessary, my darling. I gave her some today.'

'That was kind of you, Merry.'

'It was little enough. But, Miss Eliza, I don't want you talking about her or about today to no one. Do you understand?'

'I won't, Merry. But, you know, I'm not sure I liked her.'

'Miss Eliza, what a thing to say!'

Eliza opened her book. 'Night-night, Merry.'

Merry hiccuped mightily and hugged her again. Really, there had been too much hugging today, Eliza thought, as she emerged from the embrace and gasped for air. 'Remember, Eliza, whatever happens, whatever you are told, Merry loves you more than—'

'Plum duff?' Eliza giggled.

'That's right, my beauty. More than plum duff.' At which, and quickly for one so large, Merry left the room.

In the morning Eliza woke to find that Merry had left in the night. There was nothing, no note, no explanation. Eliza raced around the house searching for her, asking anyone she saw if they had seen her. They all said they hadn't but she didn't believe them. Baldly, her grandmother told her Merry had been dismissed for bad behaviour, though what she had done she would not say.

Eliza cried and sobbed. She refused to eat, she made herself sick. She wanted Merry back but no one would listen to her.

There was no point sitting on the main stairs here – Merry would never have been allowed to use the front door unless she was with Eliza. So Eliza sat on the back stairs waiting for her nurse to return. No one could make her move, threats of punishment were ignored. She had to be carried screaming to her room and the door was locked to prevent her escaping.

Food was brought to her but she refused to eat. A maid came to clean the room but she wouldn't speak. Miss Chester tried to coax her out, but although she spoke to her it was to tell her to leave her alone.

Eliza thought she would never stop crying. But she did eventually. Four days later she heard a tap on her door and the key turn in the lock.

'Go away!' she screamed at the opening door.

'What? When I've come all this way to see you?'

'Ruby!'

Chapter Two
1872

I

Fanny Chester closed the book, which she was having difficulty reading, and looked out of the window instead. From her sitting room, high in the house, she could look down into the pretty town garden. She could see Eliza sitting in the shade of the small summer-house, reading too. At least from her stillness, she was able to concentrate. Fanny placed the book on the window-seat beside her and sighed. It was a heartfelt sigh, matched by the furrow in her brow.

She had been Eliza's governess for nearly two years, a happy time, but now she feared it was drawing to a close. She loved the child, and leaving her would be one of the hardest things she had ever done. Years ago, when she had first become a governess, she had vowed to herself that she must never grow too fond of one of her charges for positions were always tenuous, dismissal was a constant possibility and often for the most trivial reason.

But Eliza was different from any of the other children Fanny had taught. She was not spoilt as so many had been. She enjoyed learning when some had found all lessons dull, no matter how hard Fanny tried to interest them. Eliza was kind, considerate and her sweet disposition, with her looks, would make her a lovely woman and a constant, loyal friend. But most of all she had the vulnerability of those who have lost their mothers at an early age.

The last eighteen months had been momentous. They had travelled to France with Lady Gwendoline and had worn themselves out sightseeing. They had sailed to Norway with Mr Forester and a party of his friends on a grand steam yacht for the salmon fishing. A good sailor, Fanny had enjoyed the voyage, and she knew she would never forget the wondrous scenery, but the guests had been brittle, shrill, gossiping, the so-called cream of society. Why Mr Forester surrounded himself with such people was a mystery to her. During the few conversations she had had with him he had struck her as a thoughtful, well-read man, not someone who would be content with such vacuous companions. Indeed, he avoided them as far as possible – which only deepened the mystery. He was apparently oblivious to the advances made to him by many of the women. But worst of this group was Minnie Wickham, whom Fanny had come to despise. If a sarcastic or cruel remark was made, it was invariably Minnie who voiced it. If anything was mislaid or lost, she would lash out and accuse the servants with no investigation, no enquiry, being made. And for the amount of attention she paid her husband she might just as well not have been married to him.

There were times when Fanny feared for Eliza's future if she was only to meet such shallow people. But she asked herself constantly if she would have felt so strongly had it not been for Charles.

She outlined a large C on the window with her finger, then smiled at herself for the childish action. Her position was becoming impossible. A day when she did not see him was dreary for her. When she knew they were to meet, or even if she glanced at him, her heart beat at an alarming rate. She loved him, she was sure, for why else would she react in this way? She had no idea what he felt for her. He admired her, she thought, and he found her attractive, she hoped, but how could she know? They were never alone, there were always others present, and always Eliza. Apart from a few 'chance' meetings in the parks and galleries, tea taken on a couple of occasions, what had there been? A smile, a gentle touch as a hand accidentally brushed another. But at such times she allowed herself to think he felt the same for her.

At other times she wondered if it wasn't all in her imagination, her wishful thinking, her stupid dreams. How she despised others who wove fantasies that could never be, and yet here she was, just as guilty as the simplest maid.

If Mr Forester had known about her feelings for Charles she wondered how he would have reacted when she had spurned him last Tuesday. Such a mortifying scene! She shuddered to think of it.

On hearing a clatter in the sleeping house, Fanny had gone bravely to investigate. She had found the night-watchman fast asleep, alcohol-induced no doubt, and oblivious to the noise. In the library she had discovered Frederick Forester in much the same condition. He was sprawled on the floor, fully clothed, an asinine grin on his face. She should have left him there but, worried what the servants would think or that he might do himself an injury, she had finally managed to wake him and help him to his feet. He had appeared abashed but she had reassured him that she would say nothing. She began to leave the room but, seeing him sway danger-ously, had returned and held him steady to prevent him falling. He'd thanked her, laughing at his condition. She supported him as they climbed the stairs to the door of his room.

'Will you be all right, now?' she'd asked as she opened his door.

'Of course.' But his knees had buckled even as he spoke.

'Let me . . .' She'd put her arm around his waist again and guided him, his arm about her shoulders, into the room and across it to his bed. He fell back and appeared to go straight to sleep. She had pulled the counterpane over him, then tucked it around him. That had been when he had grabbed her, pulling her down on top of him and mauling her . . .

Even now, remembering it, she had to cover her face with her hands.

'Mr Forester, please, let go of me . . .' She had struggled.

'Don't be a spoilsport. It's Fanny, isn't it?'

'Mr Forester, I must protest!' But he held her tight and pulled her face towards his, covering it with small kisses, which, given the stench of brandy on his breath, made her want to retch. With one mighty push she fell off him, but before she could stand and run he had grabbed her hand.

'Please, Fanny, I love you . . .'

'Don't say such a silly thing. You weren't even sure who I was a minute ago.' She managed to laugh, hoping humour might extricate her from this intolerable situation.

'No, no. It was your Christian name I was not sure of – how could I kiss a Miss Chester?' He grinned drunkenly. 'From the moment you arrived I have admired you. Please, Fanny, help me . . .' To her horror she saw movement in his trousers, which, despite her innocence, she knew could mean only one thing.

'Sir, if you don't let go of my arm I shall scream for help.' And, for good measure, she dug her nails into his hand, hard. He yelped and let go of her wrist. She stood up but the shock of her ordeal made her stumble and within seconds he had her in his grasp again. His eyes were black with lust, his breath coming in short, noisy bursts.

'Sir, unhand me, I love another!'

Her dramatic declaration, like something from a badly written play, had sobered him and he let her go. She had rushed from the room, up the next flight of steps, terror speeding her. Only in the safety of her own bedroom, with a chair wedged beneath the door handle, had she allowed herself to relax.

Ever since, she had been waiting for the summons to his study to be told of her dismissal. It was inevitable. How could he face her day in and day out? How could she face him? How could she remain here, always wary now and on her guard against him?

'Come in,' she said, to the tapping at her door.

'Lady Gwendoline wishes you to call on her immediately,' the maid said, with an unpleasant smirk.

Her stomach lurched. It was late June and hot, but she suddenly felt chilly. She took a shawl from the chest of drawers to wrap around her shoulders and, with a pounding heart, ran down the flights of stairs and out into the street.

'Well, Miss Chester, and what a pretty kettle of fish we have here.' Lady Gwendoline was sitting at her escritoire in the cluttered morning room of her house across the square. 'I am deeply disappointed in you. I had such trust in you.' At this Fanny felt herself blush. 'Then I see from your colour that it is true.'

'I beg your pardon, Lady Gwendoline, but I'm not sure to what you refer.'

'Aren't you?' The old woman looked at her shrewdly. 'My son tells me you have a lover.'

'No, Lady Gwendoline, that is not true.'

'Are you calling my son a liar?'

'No, he misunderstood me. I have no lover.'

'He distinctly said that you told him you loved another.'

Lady Gwendoline was getting agitated, Fanny noted. 'Yes, I said that. I do love someone, but he is not my lover. He is not even aware of my feelings. I would not dream of behaving in such a manner.'

'And who might this man be?'

'I would rather not say.'

'I don't think you have a choice, do you?'

'I most certainly do.'

'Impertinence will not help you, Miss Chester. As I

see it, whether this man is your lover or not is neither here nor there. You are obviously harbouring immoral thoughts. Rubbish more worthy of a scullery-maid than a governess. As such you make yourself unfit to care for my granddaughter. Wouldn't you agree?'

'My thoughts are not immoral. I would never harm Eliza in any way, I would resign if I thought that was so. I admire someone, that is all, from afar.'

At this Lady Gwendoline shuddered as if she had confessed to some dreadful vice. 'I have no alternative, in these circumstances, but to give you a month's notice. I fear that no references will be forthcoming.'

'But, Lady Gwen—'

'You can "but" me all you like, Miss Chester, I shall not change my mind.'

'This is so unfair.' Panic rose inside Fanny. 'With no references how can I find another position? What could I do? Where can I go?

'Perhaps that is something you should have thought of before confessing to my son.'

'I did not confess.'

'It sounds very much as though you did.'

Panic and fear were nudged aside by anger. 'Lady Gwendoline, I was not confessing. I spoke in that manner to stop your son molesting me.'

'Oh, really, Miss Chester – have you lost your senses? As if my son would bother himself with the likes of you!'

'I was shocked and surprised too, but he did. And that was the only way I could think of stopping him doing his worst to me. I'm sorry to shock you, Lady Gwendoline, it is not easy for me to speak of such matters. But that is how it was.'

'Very well. If you insist on making such lewd accusations I shall give you money in lieu.'

'But his own reporting of what I said shows his guilt. Why should I say I loved *another* if it were not because I was rejecting him?'

'You, Miss Chester, are too clever for your own good. This is not a courtroom and I shall not listen to you. I shall be grateful if you would vacate my son's premises by six this evening. You are to have no further contact with Eliza. Is that understood?'

Fanny's shoulders sagged as Lady Gwendoline turned away from her and began to write a note. 'Perfectly.' There seemed no point in arguing. She turned to go. At the door, she paused. 'Lady Gwendoline, I would like you to consider this. Don't you find it odd that your son has asked you to dismiss me? Why? He has never shown any interest in the education of your grand-daughter before, so why should he now? Or did something happen, as I have told you, and is he ashamed to confront me face to face? Perhaps you should ponder on that, and perhaps then you will have the courtesy at least to feel guilty for the treatment you deem fit to mete out to me.'

She did not wait for an answer – she doubted that one would be forthcoming. She knew that the likes of Lady Gwendoline could never admit they were wrong, that they had acted improperly. She raced down the stairs, her vision blurred by her tears, and back across the square. With the weight of grief in her throat like a stone, she hastened to her room and began to throw her few possessions willy-nilly into her trunk.

And then she stopped. She stood still and began to collect her senses. She had done nothing wrong. She had nothing to be ashamed of. It was these people who lied, who used people, who cared not a jot. She had been told not to see Eliza. Why should she simply disappear from the girl's life, like so many others, with no explanation? She looked out of her window to see that Eliza was still sitting in the shade of the summer-house, reading the same book. In the space of ten minutes Fanny's whole life had changed while Eliza's had not – yet.

On her way to the garden she passed several maids,

all of whom giggled. News spread so fast below stairs. Then she met Ruby.

'Miss Chester, tell me it's not true,' Ruby begged.

'That I've been dismissed? Sadly, yes.'

'But why?'

'I'd rather not say, but whatever you hear I assure you it isn't true.' Fanny spoke with dignity but she longed to hurl herself into Ruby's arms and tell her of the unfairness of it all, but she couldn't: the girl had still to work here. 'I'm sorry . . .' She put her hand to her mouth and fled from the kindness in Ruby's face. One word of sympathy and she would not be able to control herself.

'Eliza.' By the time she had reached her charge she had composed herself.

'Miss Chester, I'm so glad you gave me this book, it is so . . . But what's the matter? You've had bad news? Sit down, you look ill . . .'

Eliza's concern was too much and a sob escaped Fanny's lips. 'I'm sorry, Eliza, I have to leave you,' she blurted out. It was not the carefully planned sentence she had composed on the way here.

'No!' Eliza did not say this word but shouted it. She stood up, the book falling to the grass. Instinctively Fanny picked it up and brushed it tenderly. 'You can't go. You mustn't. Who says you are to leave me?' She lunged at Fanny and clung to her, hurting her, as if by cleaving to her she could prevent her going.

'I don't want to go but I have to.'

'Is it your brother? Is something wrong with him? Is it something we can help with? Let me speak to my father.'

'No, it's not that.'

'Then what? You must tell me.'

Fanny led her back to the bench. 'Sometimes, Eliza, things happen that are not fair, that one cannot fight since one doesn't have the power. This is such as that.'

'Please tell me, is it something I've done?'

'No, my darling. I've been happier with you than with any other student. I love you and will think of you always.' She kissed Eliza's cheek, her sadness almost too much to bear. Then she untangled herself from the girl's arms, stood up and walked quickly across the grass.

'Don't leave me!'

At that Fanny quickened her step and virtually ran the rest of the way. In the hall she met the butler. 'Miss Chester, I have a message from Mr Forester. You are to leave immediately since you disobeyed Lady Gwendoline's orders. Your bags will be sent after you.' Poor Densham, she thought, he looked so ashamed at the words he had to deliver. 'And I'm to give you this.' He handed her an envelope.

'Thank you, Mr Densham. I have enjoyed my acquaintance with you.' She held out her hand, which he shook.

'Likewise, Miss Chester. But your bags, where should they be sent?'

'I don't know. I . . .'

'Might I suggest . . .' And he handed her a card. She glanced down at it. 'It's not a grand establishment, as hotels go, but it's clean and respectable, and it's reasonable.'

'Thank you, Mr Densham, you are most kind. If you wouldn't mind sending my belongings there.'

He was already holding her cloak and bonnet – she didn't wonder until much later where he had got them from. Without another word she crossed the hall. He held open the door for her. She felt that her progress was being watched but all she was really conscious of were Eliza's pitiful cries, which floated to her from the garden where she was being restrained.

The footman yelped more with shock than pain when Eliza kicked him: normally such a quiet, gentle creature, she had taken him unawares. He let go of her arm, and she, grabbing the opportunity, fled from the garden into the house. She ran from room to room, screaming her father's name. Her fury and pain at Miss Chester's departure had swamped her fear of him.

'Papa!' she called as, without pausing to knock, she hurled open the door of his bedroom, which normally she never entered. 'Papa!' She stumbled to a halt. Her father was standing in the middle of his room, still in his dressing-gown, looking more surprised than angry. She registered that he looked ill, but that did not stop her. 'Papa. It's Miss Chester. She says she has been dismissed.' This simple sentence emerged as an impassioned wail. '*Why?*'

'Haven't you been taught that it's polite to knock?'

'*Why?*' she shouted, determined not to be sidetracked.

'Because, in my opinion, she is not a fit person to be associated with you.'

'How can you *say* that? How can you even *think* it? She is the sweetest person in the world, the best teacher—'

'For heaven's sake, don't exaggerate. She's a governess, she is not suitable, she has been dismissed. That is all there is to say.'

'Why have you taken her from me?' She held out her hands in supplication.

He sighed loudly. 'I have just explained to you. Now, if you would leave me?' He turned from her, dismissing her. She moved swiftly and took hold of the sleeve of his heavy brocade dressing-gown. 'I beg your pardon?' He looked from her hand to her face with what amounted to appalled disbelief and he shook his arm as if some insect, rather than his daughter, were holding him. But his expression did not have the effect he had no doubt intended.

'Papa, I need an explanation.'

'I don't have to justify anything to you. You are a child.'

'I'm sixteen next month. I am *not* a child.' She stamped her foot with frustration.

'Then stop behaving as if you are.' Now he was laughing at her discomfort as he inspected his face in the shaving mirror on its mahogany stand. She stood ignored, her heart racing, dizzy with emotion. She took a deep breath. 'Father, I'm sorry. I beg to speak with you. Pray give me the courtesy of your attention.'

'That's better. So?' He sat down on the wing chair, upholstered in a velvet of such a deep red as if it had been steeped in wine. 'So?' he repeated.

As she stood in front of him, her legs felt weak and she longed to be seated too. She held her hands in front of her, one clutching the other so that he could not see them shake. She forced herself to breathe deeply and evenly. 'Father, all my life those I have cared for have left me, usually with no reason given to me – governesses, maids, Merry and now Miss Chester. But this time . . .' she spoke quietly, although she lifted her head defiantly '. . . I want to know why!'

'How dare you speak to me, your father, in this arrogant manner.'

'And how dare you make me so unhappy – again!' She stood her ground. She feared he might hit her, but she knew that if she moved, if she looked away, she would have lost all chance of learning anything. He looked at her long and hard, his blue eyes staring into hers. His were cloudy from over-indulgence, hers clear as the summer sky. Then he studied his hands for what, to her, seemed a long time, but when he spoke he looked over her shoulder as if addressing someone behind her. He did not look her in the eye.

'Those people were invariably found drunk and I deemed them unsuitable companions for you.'

'Miss Chester! I don't believe that of her. She would never be drunk. There has to be another reason.'

'She is a woman of loose morals.'

'What nonsense.' She laughed, a cheerless sound.

'Take care, Eliza. I have tolerated your rudeness thus far, but my patience is at an end.'

'And my heart is broken.' She stabbed dramatically at the vicinity of her heart. 'I loved her, she was my friend, and now I am friendless. She cared for me and you don't. I *want* to see her.'

'You may not. She has already left my house. If she returns, if she tries to contact you, or if you try to contact her, then I shall call the police and she will be in serious trouble. Do you understand?'

'I beg you, don't be so cruel. Please tell me where she has gone. I won't try to see her, I promise, but a letter . . . Just a letter.'

In answer he stood up, took her arm and propelled her towards the door, which he opened. 'This interview is at an end,' he said, as he pushed her out and on to the landing.

'Is that how you see it? As if I, too, were an employee? I am your daughter. I want—' But he had slammed the door and though she beat on the panels with her fists there was no response. *I hate him*, she thought. *I hate you*, she wanted to shout. But she couldn't. They were just words, and she knew that, despite everything, deep in her heart she didn't hate him and could not pretend that she did. She turned disconsolately from the door.

In her room she flung herself on to her bed and began to cry, great despondent, uncontrollable sobs. Then, abruptly, she sat up. She searched in her pocket for a handkerchief, blew her nose and wiped the tears from her cheeks with the back of her hand. Crying would not solve anything, would not find Miss Chester. She was wasting her time in weeping and wailing.

Instead she got off the bed and crept along the corridor to Miss Chester's room. Inside two maids were giggling and whispering. She peered through the crack in the door: they were packing a large trunk. One was holding Miss Chester's best grey dress up to her, twirling around and laughing. She wanted to go in and slap them, tell them to treat her possessions with respect. But she thought better of it. Don't even let them know you're here, she thought. That trunk would need to be sent somewhere.

Back in her bedroom she sat waiting patiently. She had on her everyday bonnet and her walking shoes, and she was clutching her purse. When she heard the thump of the trunk and the complaining voices of the two footmen who were carrying it, she crept from her room and followed them. They carried the heavy object, plus two bags, down the back stairs. Eliza took the front ones, skimmed across the hall, opened the glass-panelled inner hall door, closed it quietly then opened the heavy front door. She crossed the road quickly, causing a hackney carriage to swerve, went into the garden in the middle of the square and hid behind a bush.

It was not long before the two sweating footmen appeared from the area steps and she saw them wave to a hansom cab. 'The Belvedere Hotel,' she heard one say loudly, as they loaded the trunk. 'For a Miss Hoity-Toity Chester. Good riddance to bad rubbish.' How horrid of him! What had Miss Chester done to him to make him speak of her like that?

'Don't know, mate. Bloomsbury, I think,' the other said, to the driver's evident enquiry.

She stayed hidden, waiting for the footmen to go back into the house. Then she stole along the street, intending to go to Victoria Station and take a cab there. She was virtually running down Belgrave Place.

'Eliza, what are you doing out on your own?' The

voice almost made her jump out of her skin. She turned to see her uncle Charles, twirling his cane and smiling broadly at her. 'Have I caught you out? Are you off to find an admirer?'

He rocked on his feet as she threw herself at him. 'Oh, Uncle Charles, please help me!'

He looked to left and right, then waved his cane in the air. 'There's my coach.' A smart brougham, pulled by coal-black horses, with his crest brightly painted on the shiny black door, made its way towards them. He helped her into the softly padded interior. 'Now, tell me the problem,' he said, once they were settled.

It did not take her long to explain. 'You will help, won't you? I'm sure she's done no wrong. She couldn't, ever!'

'I'm sure you're right but you running away to find her will only make matters worse for her, won't it? Now I suggest we drive you home before you are missed and the alarm is raised, don't you?'

But it was too late. By the time she returned a hue and cry was in full throttle.

'As if I don't have problems enough to deal with! Where have you been?' demanded her Aunt Minnie, who had been summoned as soon as Eliza was missed and was in the hall – ready to pounce on her the minute she arrived, Eliza was convinced.

'I went for a walk,' she lied.

'Unattended!'

'You look very hot and bothered for one who has merely been walking,' another voice stated.

'It's hot outside, Grandmama.' Until now she hadn't noticed that her grandmother was there too.

'All the more reason to stay indoors.' But she noticed that, in contrast to her aunt, her grandmother was looking at her almost sympathetically.

'You are a foolish child, venturing out on your own. You know full well that you may go only with a maid in attendance. How disobedient you've become. What if you had been seen? What if you were compromised? What are we to do with you? Frederick, she's back.' Aunt Minnie entered his study.

Eliza was fearful of facing her father again, after the way she had spoken to him. But she need not have worried: he was so angry with her that he did not wish to see her.

'If you were my daughter I would beat you black and blue,' her aunt said. 'My brother indulges you too much. Go to your room this instant. You are to return to Harcourt Barton this very afternoon.'

This news would normally have filled her with joy but going back without Miss Chester, to where they had been so happy and such great companions, would make her absence so much harder to bear.

Fanny Chester sat in the room she had taken at the Belvedere Hotel in Bloomsbury. It was hot and stuffy, situated at the back of the hotel overlooking the kitchens. She had asked for the cheapest accommodation but, looking around her, she wondered how they could charge the amount they had asked. She hoped the noise from the yard below, of crates and bins clattering, would lessen by nightfall or it would keep her awake – if she managed to fall asleep in the first place. But it was clean, and a refuge while she calmed down, took stock and decided what next to do. The proprietor, Mr Potts, was a friend of Mr Densham, they had once been in service together, and because of this connection, he had told her, she would pay a most advantageous rate.

Crowded into the tiny room were a bed, a wardrobe, a dressing-table and one chair, which made it impossible to move around. She sat on the bed and tipped out the meagre contents of her purse. She had a few savings, lodged with her father's solicitor, but she was loath to touch them: they were to keep her in her old age. She smiled at that – at this rate if she couldn't find work then she wouldn't even reach her next birthday. She had the cheque for a month's wages, which at least would cover the bill here with some left over. But with no references what was she to do? She would never find employment as a governess, or even in domestic service. Perhaps she could find work in a shop. She tipped out the rest of the contents of her small bag. A brooch in the shape of a flower tumbled out on to the counterpane. It was made of rubies, she'd been told, but she thought they were much more likely to be garnets. She could sell it but it was all she had left of her mother's. And what would she get for it? But could she afford sentimentality? No.

There was her brother, but she must not bother him for he had problems of his own. And, in any case, if a whisper of her predicament got out then his own position as a tutor might be in jeopardy. She picked up the envelope she had been given this morning and opened it. It was packed with crisp white five-pound notes. She tipped them on the bed and began to count them. Ninety pounds. A year's wages. Guilt money! She stuffed it back into the envelope and looked at her hands as if they were contaminated.

On the dressing-table she pulled towards her a leather folder that contained writing materials. She took out an envelope and addressed it to F. P. Forester Esq. Then she scrubbed out the Esq. One had to be a gentleman to be so-called and he wasn't. She needed his money, but she had no intention of accepting it. She hoped he would be ashamed when he saw she had returned it but she doubted it. She did not add a note.

'Yes?' she said, to a discreet tapping at the door.

'Miss Chester, you're wanted.'

'That will be my trunk. Could you have it sent up, please?' she called. She looked about the room. Where was she to put it? She opened the door. 'No, perhaps I had better leave it downstairs. Is there somewhere I can store it?'

The girl who had been sent to fetch her appeared

half-witted and looked at Fanny vacantly. 'Oh, never mind. I'll find out for myself.' She locked the door, having picked up her handbag and the envelope containing Mr Forester's money. She was on the fourth floor and she did not hurry to descend the dark staircase. In the hall, Mr Potts was waiting for her. 'This way, Miss Chester.'

'Would you please make sure this is posted for me?' She handed him the envelope and a coin.

With a sweeping almost obsequious gesture, Mr Potts ushered her into the front parlour. It was dark in the room – heavy brown paper, poor lighting, huge furniture.

'Miss Chester, I had to come. Eliza is distraught.'

'Sir Charles!' she said, and then, for the first time in her life, fainted dead away.

3

When Fanny had partially recovered it was to find Mr and Mrs Potts and Charles Wickham fussing over her. She gagged at the smell of the burning feathers that were being held beneath her nose. So small was the room that, with the four of them, it was even hotter and far too crowded. The sofa on which she lay reeked of mice, and she felt far from well.

'Open the window, Mrs Potts,' Charles ordered. 'She is so pale.'

'But the vapours from the street will harm her.'

'No more than the fetid atmosphere in here.'

'Fetid! I'll have you know—'

'We can argue later, not now, Mr Potts, if you don't mind. The window!' Since he spoke in the voice of one who was used to being obeyed, the proprietor, against his better judgement, opened it forthwith. 'We should call a doctor.'

Fanny struggled into a sitting position. 'No, please, Sir Charles, I don't need a doctor.'

'But . . .'

She could not help but smile at the worried expression on his dear face. 'I hadn't eaten and it had been . . . such a day.' She sat straighter, the breeze from the open window helping her to recover.

'There's nothing you're not telling us?' Mrs Potts stood over her. She was immense and reminded Fanny of Merry, and then of Eliza. She had to fight the longing to be alone and allowed to cry. 'Only we keep a respectable establishment here,' the woman continued, with a fearsomely stern expression.

Charles, who had been kneeling beside the sofa, leapt to his feet. 'That is an insufferable insinuation to make, Mrs Potts. Miss Chester is a person of the highest integrity. How dare you imply otherwise?'

'All I know is that when young women appear on my doorstep in a distressed condition then faint at the drop of a hat, there's usually more to it than hits the eye.'

'This is intolerable!'

'Sarah!' Her husband laid a hand on her, as if by touching her arm he could restrain her tongue.

'What did you say to me less than an hour ago? "That one will need watching," you said. "She'll be here for no good reason." That's what you said and no mistake.' She wagged a podgy finger at Mr Potts.

Fanny began to stand.

'You must rest,' Charles said.

'Not here. I couldn't possibly . . .' She was on her feet, indignation making her feel stronger, but still she swayed.

'Get Miss Chester's possessions from her room. She comes with me. Not a minute longer will I permit her to remain here,' he ordered, and Fanny could cheerfully have fainted again at the mastery in his tone. Mrs Potts flounced from the room, as well as her large form would allow.

'My trunk? It was to be sent on. My books, my papers . . .'

'All are in the hall. Quite safe. Have you a bonnet? A cloak? I don't want you to be chilled.'

She wavered towards him – she did not mean to but the concern and warmth in his voice made her forget herself and long for his arms to go round her, hold her, comfort her.

'A moment, if you don't mind. There's still a bill to be paid. She's used her room.'

'For half an hour.'

'That's all it takes. You pay by the hour here.'

'And I thought you said you ran a *respectable* establishment.' Charles looked at Mr Potts with loathing.

'As we do. You mind your words, sir. There's them as likes to rest if they've travelled far.'

'And beggars might be kings!'

'How much?' Fanny asked wearily, too tired for this argument.

'Let me.' Charles was removing his wallet from an inner pocket.

'Sir Charles, I couldn't possibly allow you to do that. As you so rightly said, I am not what this gentleman evidently thinks I am.' From her purse she removed a handful of coins. The bill was paid, a receipt taken. Then, with all the solicitude of a concerned lover, Charles helped her to his carriage, which looked incongruously smart in the seedy street.

Everything had happened so quickly and in such a whirl that it was several minutes before Fanny could take stock of what was happening. 'Perhaps if you could find another small but respectable hotel for me, I would be most grateful, Sir Charles.'

'My dear Miss Chester, how many times have I asked you to call me Charles?'

'It doesn't seem right for me to do so.'

'Such nonsense! I should so love to call you Fanny.' And he picked up her hand – she had not had time to put on her gloves and sensed, more than felt, his breath on the back. Dare she think it had been a kiss? A charge of excitement raced through her.

'You are very kind . . . Charles.' She stumbled over such informality.

'Those people were unspeakable. Why did you choose that particular hotel?'

'Densham was kind enough to give me the address. They were friends of his and he was sure they would give me a discount, based on that.'

'Far more likely that he was told to send you there.'

'Why should that be?'

'So that my brother-in-law would know where you were, what you were doing, and whom you were seeing. Am I right in presuming that he made an unsuitable advance towards you?'

Fanny blushed and glanced down modestly.

'I thought as much. He is not to be trusted.'

'But how did you know?' With gathering horror she realised that someone must have been tittle-tattling about her.

'The talk at the house was that *you* had made advances to *him*, had gone to his room late at night.'

'Oh, no!' She covered her face with her hands.

'I knew it was balderdash. You, of all people, with him! I didn't believe it for one minute, dear Fanny.'

'But it is partly true.'

It was his turn to look shocked.

'I *did* go to his room. But it's not as they say. I was helping him. He was so intoxicated he could hardly stand and I was afraid he would do himself a mischief. That was when . . . But I'd rather not talk about it.' And she shuddered.

'May I?' he said softly, then gently put his arm round her shoulders to comfort her.

'You do believe me?'

'Of course I do.'

'He was dreadfully drunk.'

'A poor excuse.'

'But I had worked for him for nearly two years and he had never behaved in such a monstrous way before.'

'With Freddie it's only ever a question of time.'

He removed his arm, which she found she regretted. She did not dare look at him in case he saw her longing for him in her eyes and instead looked out of the window. It was then she realised she was in a part of London she did not know. 'Where are we going? There are fields ... I have to be near the centre to find employment.' She was becoming agitated.

'I'm being presumptuous, I know, but I have a friend who lives in St John's Wood with her sister, I thought it might be a good place for you to seek refuge until you decide what to do.'

'That sounds wonderful. But . . .' She turned to face him, the rocking of the carriage making close proximity to him inevitable. 'Will she mind?' she asked, laughing nervously at having been thrown against him, as the driver negotiated a corner, but finding she enjoyed it immeasurably.

'If you are my friend you are automatically Caroline's too.'

'How old is her sister?'

'Seven, I think.'

'Then I could teach her, perhaps? To show my appreciation.'

'A splendid idea. And I would be honoured to pay you for your expertise.'

'But, Sir . . . Charles, I couldn't possibly permit that. Just to have a roof over my head, if only temporary, is all I ask.' The area was becoming prettier by the mile: tree-lined streets on which stood elegant pretty villas that reminded Fanny of dolls' houses, each with its own garden. 'It's lovely here.'

'Isn't it? And in a few years when the gardens are more established it will be even better.'

'You like gardens?' There was so much more to learn about him, she thought. She had never imagined that gardens could possibly be of interest to one so urbane and sophisticated.

'Very much. I once had a beautiful garden in the country.'

'You speak in the past tense.'

'It was my family home, and had been for five hundred years.' He looked so sad she wished she could stroke the expression from his face. 'But I sold it.'

'After so many generations?'

'My wife doesn't care for the country.'

'But she seems to enjoy Harcourt Barton?'

'Yes, but that house is accessible to London. Mine was far away in Northumberland. Too far to travel, you see.' He smiled wistfully and an even greater dislike for Minnie Wickham formed in Fanny's mind.

'There is one thing, and if you think it impertinent of me to ask, please say and I will understand,' she said.

'And what might that be, dear Fanny?'

'If I wrote a note to Eliza, would you give it to her?'

'But of course.'

'I didn't have time to explain fully. I don't want her to think I simply deserted her.'

'Understandably.'

'And I would like to think I could keep in touch with her.'

'And why not, pray?'

'But if her father or grandmother or . . .'

'Her aunt?' He grinned at her.

'Well, yes, if they found out it might make trouble for her.'

'Then they shan't. I shall make sure of that.'

Shortly the carriage came to halt. Before the coachman had dismounted to open the door, Charles was on the pavement, releasing the small steps for Fanny to alight, holding her hand to steady her. He did not let go as they walked up the narrow path between flowering shrubs that needed trimming and brushed at their clothes. He opened the front door with a key he took from his pocket. 'Caroline!' he called. There was a squeal of pleasure and, in a flurry of pink silk and flying blond hair, a young woman scudded into the hall.

'Charlie! I wasn't expecting . . . ' On seeing Fanny she stopped short. 'Oh!' she said, looking contrite, like a little girl who has been caught doing something naughty.

'Caroline, this is Miss Chester. She is a dear friend of mine. I want you to look after her for me. Will you do that?'

'But of *course*, Charlie. Whatever you want.'

'Fanny, this is Mrs Caroline Fraser.'

'How do you do?' Fanny took hold of the proffered hand, which felt as soft and limp as if it had no skeletal structure. And Caroline's smile did not reach her eyes.

'This is most kind of you, Mrs Fraser.'

'Not at all, Miss Chester. Any friend of Sir Charles is a friend of mine.'

'There! Wasn't that exactly what I told you she would say? You see? Your fears were unfounded. You will love each other.' Charles rubbed his hands together with pleasure, but Fanny found that she did not share his confidence.

4

Having been shown to her room, Fanny was surprised, but also alarmed, by how compact the house was. She was astonished that so many possessions could be crowded into such a small space, but worried that such enforced closeness might lead to difficulties if she were to stay here too long.

The drawing room lacked one clear surface: knick-knacks and ornaments spilled off the mantelpiece, spread across the floor, reached the ceiling and swamped the room. The densely patterned wallpaper was barely visible since the walls were covered in prints and paintings, and the ornately ruched and pleated curtain and pelmet let in little light. Double doors – whose panels were painted with swirls and scrolls in pink and green, highlighted with gold – led to the dining room where a highly polished dining-table stood beneath a finely wrought chandelier of pink crystal, with, to one side, a sideboard – far too ornate for Fanny's taste and much too large for the room.

Fanny had few possessions, and had always longed for more, but this house held far too many. There was hardly any room for people and it resembled a bazaar rather than a home.

There had been no maid to show her up the pretty but narrow staircase. The paintings that lined the stairs were seemingly of Bacchanalian rites and out of place with the flowered wallpaper and the fussy, frilly curtains that hung at the window half-way up.

Caroline Fraser tripped ahead of her, skirts swaying, hands gesticulating as if conducting an imaginary orchestra, explaining that on this main landing were her own bedroom, dressing room and bathroom. This information was imparted so proudly that Fanny felt it politic to voice suitable amazement.

She was led through an arch, covered with another heavy brocade curtain, which they pushed aside. Behind was a door leading into a dark corridor, blocked half-way along with her trunk. They had to manoeuvre past it to get to another door at the end of the passageway.

'This will be your room,' said Caroline. 'It's rather small, and has no view, but I presume that someone in your position is used to confined accommodation and better able to adjust to it than I, for whom it would be most difficult.' This sentence, the longest Fanny had heard her utter, was delivered with a sweet smile and the merest hint of a charming lisp so that she was almost ready to believe Caroline was being sweet rather than snide. *Almost.*

'It's charming,' Fanny said politely. It needed only the most cursory glance to take in the bed, dressing-table, chair and small desk, which filled the room to capacity. For a moment she remembered, with longing, the spacious rooms she had enjoyed in Frederick Forester's houses, then berated herself. Wishful thinking was of no use to her whatsoever.

'There isn't room for your trunk, so it will have to remain where it is,' Caroline said, with a frown, as if it would be of the greatest inconvenience to her.

'It's no trouble – for me,' Fanny added hurriedly, as she saw the frown deepen.

'You do realise that you will have to carry your own washing water up here? I can't expect the maid to wait on you.'

'Neither do I.'

'There's only *my* bathroom, you see.' The personal pronoun precluding its use by others, Fanny realised. 'You will, of course, find the usual . . .' A discreet cough acted as punctuation. '. . . *offices* . . . ' Another dainty cough. '. . . in the yard . . .' She fanned herself with her lace handkerchief, as if blowing away her embarrassment at such matters.

'Thank you, you are most kind.'

'We dine late, at nine. Charlie,' – another flustered wave of the handkerchief – 'Sir Charles wishes you to join us.' Which, Fanny presumed, meant Caroline didn't. 'We meet in the drawing room at eight-thirty.'

Now, left alone in her tiny room, she wondered if she should arrange her few books on the rickety-looking shelf that ran along one side of the bed. Or would it be a waste of time? It was evident that Caroline did not like her or want her here. And she had no intention of staying where she was not wanted. But where to go and what to do?

With difficulty she opened the window, which apparently had been closed for some time. She poked her head out to see a small but perfect garden below that reminded her of her father's: it was just as neat, and he, too, had had a weeping willow in the middle of the lawn, beneath which she and her brother had delighted in hiding. Peter! She must write to him. She must let him know she was here and safe, but she would not tell of her predicament: she didn't want to worry him.

The letter written, she looked at her watch and saw that it was still not quite seven. There was water in the jug on the dresser; it was cold but refreshing as she dabbed it on her face and washed her hands. She changed her plain collar and cuffs for Brussels lace ones, rearranged her hair carefully, pinning her chignon in place, and wondered if a fringe might suit her then decided it probably wouldn't: such styles looked better on pretty creatures like Caroline. That done, she looked again at her watch and saw that only fifteen minutes had gone by. Now what to do?

Remembering Caroline's instructions that there would be no maid to care for her, she picked up the jug of water and the bowl. She opened the door and, skirting her trunk, moved quietly along the corridor through the heavy tapestry curtain on to the main landing. She thought she heard voices but, not wishing to appear inquisitive, ran down the stairs into the hall.

There, she found another door hidden behind a heavy curtain. Perhaps Caroline didn't like doors or, more likely, what might lie behind them – her hostess seemed a highly strung woman.

From the end of the rather dingy corridor she heard the noise of crockery being stacked. She had found the kitchens.

'Excuse me . . .'

'Lawks, you frightened me out of my skin!' A young girl stood before her, hand on heart.

'I'm sorry to startle you, but could you help me? I

need to empty this.' She indicated the china she was carrying.

'I'll do that for you.' The maid moved towards her.

'No, I'm happy to take care of myself.'

'But Madam would be cross with me if I didn't.'

And cross with me if you do, Fanny thought.

'Thank you.' She held out the jug and bowl. 'But I know you ... you're ...' She searched for the name, flicking her fingers with frustration. 'Forgive me, this is so rude of me.'

'You're Miss Chester.'

'It's Maud, isn't it? From Harcourt Barton. What a small world!' She was genuinely pleased to see a familiar face, even if the extent of their acquaintance-ship had been seeing each other in the corridors of that great house. 'When did you leave, Maud?'

'Soon after you all came to London. Why, must be a good year or so, now,' the girl answered.

'Longer than that, if you followed us. Why, we've been in London two years this November.'

'How's Miss Eliza?'

'She's well.' She could say no more and turned away her face so that her pain could not be seen.

'You all right, Miss Chester? You look all pale, like.'

'It's the heat. I must say, this is a pleasant surprise.' She meant it, despite what she had been told about Maud and, looking at her pleasant, smiling face, it was hard to believe she was a thief. Any contact with that lovely house was a pleasure for her, especially now that she was never likely to see it again. 'Don't you miss the fun of Harcourt Barton and the big staff?'

'Here does me fine. There's not so much work, although Mrs Fraser is very particular.' This was said with feeling.

'Now, Maud, I wonder if it would be possible for me to get into the garden. It looked so inviting from upstairs.'

'Of course, this way.' Maud began to show her to the

back door. 'There's just one thing, Miss Chester.' She had stopped half-way across the kitchen. 'It's just that if you see anyone . . . you know, from Harcourt, I'd be ever so grateful if you didn't say that you'd seen me. It's . . . well, it's a bit difficult.'

'I understand. I promise I won't. But I am curious. How did you find your way here?'

'Sir Charles. I . . . Well, I might as well be honest with you. I was dismissed.'

'I'm sorry.'

'Not that I did it, take the jewels, I mean. That was all lies. That old . . .' Evidently she was searching for a more polite word than the one she had been about to use, which made Fanny smile. 'That there Merry. She took them, I'm sure. And it was me what got the blame.'

'How awful for you.' She smiled sympathetically. Having herself been wrongly accused, she knew Maud might be speaking the truth. She waited, wondering if the girl was about to tell her the rest of the sorry tale, but she didn't look as if she was, and Fanny could hardly blame her. Had she had a child or had that been servants' gossip? 'Perhaps you don't know but Merry herself has been dismissed.'

'Good! That's made me feel very happy.' Maud laughed. 'What did she do?'

'No one but Lady Gwendoline and Mr Forester knows that.'

'Nicked the silver, most like.'

'We don't know that, Maud. But how nice of Sir Charles to help you find this post.' She had changed the subject neatly, she enjoyed talking about him – anything to do with him. 'And, of course, you can rely on him not to tell a soul you are here.'

'He's lovely. He's my favourite person.'

'He is kind. That's certain.' She waited, but Maud was not forthcoming. 'Still, the garden, if you would be so kind?'

'That way.' Maud showed her the way. 'Mrs Fraser

normally uses that door there.' Once in the garden she pointed towards a half-glazed door Fanny had noticed in the drawing room.

'I didn't want to intrude,' Fanny said.

'Very wise.' And Maud winked, which puzzled Fanny.

'This really is a charming house.'

'So they do say. It's a bit little, though, isn't it? Not what we're used to,' Maud said, dismissively.

'How many staff are there, apart from you?' Fanny asked. It had crossed her mind that as well as dealing with her own slops she might be expected to take on other tasks as well.

'There was a cook but she had to go – too fond of the bottle she was. And then Mrs Fraser said not to bother to replace her since she eats like a bird. If she's entertaining a woman comes in to oblige. I look after Augusta's needs and mine, and then there's a woman comes in and does the rough. And the gardener, of course, not that he lives in, you understand.'

'Augusta?'

'Mrs Fraser's sister . . . so she says.'

'So much for you to do,' Fanny said sympathetically. It was the ploy she used to bring domestic servants round to her. It worked with varying success. Soon she was listening to Maud's tirade of complaints. How naughty Augusta was and how slovenly the cleaning woman, her own measly wages, Mrs Fraser's unfairness.

On the one hand Fanny felt she shouldn't be listening, but on the other, since she sensed there was likely to be trouble with Caroline Fraser, the more she knew the better.

Eventually Maud left her. It was cooler in the garden, especially under the shade of the willow tree whose fronds swept to the lawn like the full skirt of a lady's dress.

It was a pretty place, not large but every part had

been planned with care, which was strange since Caroline had not struck her as the sort of woman who would be interested in gardening but, then, life was full of such surprises.

Across the lawn from the house was a stable block with a cottage attached, which must once have belonged to a much older and larger house. From inside came noises of domesticity – Fanny could hear a woman talking, a child laughing, pots and pans clanging. The garden was walled, the bricks rose-red as if they were much older than the house. A small terrace was covered in pots and urns. Down one side ran a narrow herbaceous border, a riot of colour.

Fanny made straight for the inviting shade of the tree and ducked beneath its swirling branches. Around the trunk was a wrought-iron circular seat. There, she was sure she was hidden from the rest of the garden. She felt as though she was under water and peering through fronds of seaweed. How Eliza would have loved it.

Then she remembered the willow in her father's garden and felt an intense longing for the past, for the security she had once thought would last for ever, and tried to divert her thoughts elsewhere, but the yearning was too strong. She had learnt from experience that sometimes it was easier to allow such feelings to exhaust themselves so she laid her head against the tree trunk and sighed. It was at this point that she felt a presence behind her. She turned her head and saw a little girl watching her, with solemn, rather sad blue eyes. She was improbably fair, her hair more silver than golden. And she had a pert mouth, which looked as if she was kissing the air. She was dressed in a full pink silk dress, with white lace pantaloons, and carried a doll that was dressed identically. 'Are you Augusta?' Fanny asked.

'And who, pray, are you?'

'Miss Chester,' Fanny replied, bemused by the adult way in which the child spoke.

'Have we met?'

'I don't think I've had the honour.' Fanny stood and made a small curtsy. 'How do you do?' She held out her hand. The child turned slightly away from her. 'I'm a guest here,' she added.

'No one told me you were to come.'

'I'm sorry, my visit was arranged hurriedly.' There was no response. 'Am I sitting in your favourite place? If so, I do apologise.' She stood up, smoothing her skirt.

Her tactic took the child by surprise and the petulance was replaced by confusion which was slowly converted into a small smile.

'Not at all. Please, don't let me disturb you.' With all the grace of a hostess in her drawing room, and charming in one so young, she indicated that Fanny should sit down again on the bench.

'My father had such a tree as this in his garden. I loved to sit there on my own,' Fanny said.

'I too.'

'Sometimes I would pretend it was a house, my house, under the sea. When the sun shone through the leaves, such as now, the light turned to such a lovely green.'

'Exactly!' Augusta was sitting up with a lively expression now. 'And when it rains, it doesn't fall through and there is the noise of it pitter-pattering on the leaves, and the wonderful smell of damp earth, and yet I am safe and dry.'

'But I do hope you never sit here when there is a storm, do you?'

'Why not? That's the best of all.'

'But far too dangerous . . .' And Fanny began to explain about lightning and conductors and the attendant dangers. Augusta's eyes grew larger as she listened. Her pretty mouth was open with astonishment. And then, suddenly, she burst into tears. 'Oh, my dear. Don't cry. I didn't mean to frighten you!' Fanny moved along the curved seat and tried to put her arm about the sobbing child's shoulders. But Augusta shrank away from her.

'Miss Chester! Are you making the lovely Augusta cry? What a scandal.'

'Sir Charles!' Flustered, Fanny jumped to her feet. 'I fear that unintentionally I have frightened her.'

'We can't have this, whatever next?' He slid gracefully on to the bench, insisting that Fanny sit too. He put his arm around Augusta's shoulders. At his touch she did not shy away as she had with Fanny. 'Now, tell me all. What has this terrifying woman been doing to you?' He laughed at the absurdity. Augusta managed a wobbly smile and told him. 'Miss Chester was wise in warning you. What would I do if I came here after a storm and found you fried to a cinder?' At this Augusta shivered and moved closer to him. His arm, Fanny could not help but notice, was now around the child's waist. At this she felt an unpleasant surge of jealousy.

'Charles!' a woman called. He put his fingers to his lips, and Augusta tried not to giggle. 'Charles, where are you? Have you found Augusta? Charles!' Through the fronds of the tree they could see a small satin shoe being stamped. This was too much for the child, who let out a snort of laughter.

'There you are! Is this one of your silly games? And remove your arm, Charles, it's unseemly. As for you, Miss Chester, you should be changed for dinner. Still, it's far too late now. You had better eat in the kitchen.' This last was said over her shoulder as she turned back to the house, tripping over the lawn, giving Fanny no time to explain herself.

Charles looked at her and shrugged apologetically. 'Another evening perhaps.'

'I would have liked that but I won't, I fear.'

'Why not?'

'Because I shall not be here.'

'You leave already? But you've only just arrived.'

'I think it better if I go – in the circumstances.'

'What circumstances?'

'I'd rather not say.'

'But I insist.'

'Very well, then. I don't think I am welcome here.'

'Nonsense. Leave it to me. You must dine with us, I insist.'

'I'd rather not, Sir Charles.' Fanny looked determined.

Feeling her skirt tugged she looked down. 'You could have dinner with me, only we call it supper.'

'How kind of you, Augusta, I should enjoy that.' And she smiled broadly. It was true, she *would* be happier dining with the little girl, but all the same it would have been nice if Charles could have joined them.

5

'Sulking isn't going to help any of us!' That was what Ruby, sitting opposite a stony-faced Eliza on the train carrying them back to Devon, wished she could say. 'Would you like something to eat?' she said instead, and sighed at the lack of response. It had been like this for over two weeks now, ever since Miss Chester had disappeared so abruptly from their lives. After Eliza's initial outburst she had not continued to scream and cry as everyone had expected her to. Perhaps it would have been better had she done so – her icy silence was unnerving.

Lady Gwendoline had been so concerned about her granddaughter that their departure had been delayed while doctors were called. Eliza was examined but, since she wouldn't speak to them either, they had left scratching their heads, saying there was nothing wrong with her physically but admitting defeat as to her state of mind. Nothing had worked – threats of beating, promises of treats, shopping, the theatre, the opera: throughout it all Eliza had sat mute.

While initially sympathetic, Ruby was becoming less so. It was lonely having no one to talk to, and it was downright rude of the girl. To her the solution was simple: let her see Miss Chester and all would be well again. Such a suggestion had been put to the family by Sir Charles, she'd heard from the gossip in the servants' hall, but that had been dismissed out of hand. Since it was rumoured that the governess had been trying to seduce Mr Forester, it was hardly surprising – if it were true.

Ruby didn't believe this tittle-tattle for one moment. She knew Miss Chester better than most and could not imagine her, of all people, creeping into Frederick Forester's bedroom in the middle of the night. It was far more likely that he had crept into hers. She'd heard things about him from others. She smiled at her inconsistency: how contrary of her to accept one lot of gossip as the truth, but not the other. However, she was sure they were barking up the wrong tree. If Miss Chester had an interest in anyone it was Sir Charles – her face changed whenever she saw him: she became younger-looking, prettier. There was not a lot in matters of the heart that escaped Ruby's keen eyes, for, like most girls of her age, she took a great interest in romantic matters.

The train thundered through the lush countryside, none of which interested Eliza. 'Look at that fine herd of cows. They're Jerseys – aren't they pretty? What my brother wouldn't give for a herd like that.' She pointed to the cattle, but although Eliza turned her head and looked out of the window Ruby was sure she saw nothing.

'Miss Eliza, I'm sorry for what's happened but, begging your pardon, it's not my fault she went away so why be like this with me?' There, she'd said what she thought and no doubt she'd get the sack now, but she couldn't go on like this. She felt like an object rather than a person.

She began to unpack the picnic basket Mr Didier had prepared for them. It was as well they were alone in the carriage: it would have been embarrassing to have others witness this silent behaviour. She would have felt obliged to explain. But on the other hand, perhaps if other people had been present Eliza wouldn't have behaved in this way.

'That Didier has done us proud. Look, a lovely roast breast of chicken, some little meat pies.' Carefully she unwrapped the napkins enfolding the food. 'Eggs with curry sauce – very nice, I'm sure. And what have we here?' She took the lid off a small silver tureen. 'Well I never! Raspberries and cream. Such a feast!'

A brick wall might have been more interesting to talk to, she thought. The general opinion of everyone else was that the country air might give Eliza back her spirits, though Ruby wasn't optimistic.

She was in a quandary now. She was famished and longed to eat but thought she had better not until Eliza took something. What a to-do! She leant forward and took a deep breath. 'Miss Eliza, I'm hungry. I'm going to have something to eat, even if you're not. One of these beef pies, I think . . . Mind you, I'd have preferred a pork one but in this heat that wouldn't be wise, now, would it? Who'd have thought there'd be such a heat wave in August? In my experience, it usually rains, what with the harvest . . . And what's to drink?'

And Ruby prattled on, more to banish her own loneliness than in the hope that she might help Eliza. She was running out of things to say but the silence was worse.

Without warning, Eliza burst into tears. Ruby was taken by surprise, a forkful of pie half-way to her mouth. What should she do? What could she say?

'Miss Eliza, what do you want me to do?' she asked eventually. 'Is there something I can do?'

'No.' At least she thought that was what the girl had said. Eliza waved a hand vaguely in the air.

'A handkerchief?' Ruby jumped to her feet, meat pie scattering, fork clattering. From the net luggage rack she took down her bag and found a hanky, which she handed to Eliza, relived that at least she was doing something, no matter how small. She sat beside her and put her arm round her. It was only then that it struck her how thin Eliza had become: she could feel her bones through the fine silk of her dress. 'There, there, Miss Eliza, it will be all right. Ruby promises. I'll make it better for you. Honest I will.' And then she decided it was best if she just let her cry.

'I'm sorry, Ruby,' Eliza said, what must have been a good ten minutes later. 'I can't help it.' Ruby waited patiently. 'It was seeing you with the picnic . . . The last time . . . You see, the last time I was . . . The train . . .' Ruby had to wait a while longer for Eliza to compose herself again. 'We . . . That is Miss Chester and I, we had a picnic. And . . . seeing you, reminded me of that time.' She paused. 'Everyone I love goes away eventually.' Her voice sounded harsh, as if she were trying to control more tears.

'I haven't left you.'

'But you will one day. And then what shall I do?'

'I know. I know. Sadness is an awful weighty thing.'

'I feel as if Miss Chester has died.'

'Well, there's a gloomy thought. Of course she hasn't. She's probably got a new job by now. She'll write to you, I bet.'

'And do you think they'll let me have her letters?'

'I expect so . . . Well, maybe . . . Probably . . .'

At this Eliza laughed a little. 'I see you agree with me.'

'Tell you what, Miss Eliza, if we can find out where she is I could send her a letter and she could write to me and I could give it to you.'

'Would you do that? If you were discovered you'd be dismissed and there's nothing I could do to help you. I'm of no importance in the household.'

'Who's to know?' Ruby hadn't thought of the

possible consequences, which were frightening to contemplate. She brightened. 'Tell you what, it would be better if we get her to post the letters to my mother's farm. Then no one will know anything.'

'That would be wonderful. I asked Sir Charles to take a letter to her for me. He was going to try to find out where she had gone. If he succeeded, she'll know I'm back in Devon.'

If he found her and *if* he gave her the letter, thought Ruby. Unlikely. Sir Charles was too dependent on his wife's money to risk upsetting her family. But, then, Eliza wouldn't know about how he'd very little of his own since he'd gambled away the majority, and how he lived off the Foresters. It was the sort of thing servants always knew, but not necessarily the family.

The train rumbled to a halt. 'Heaven forbid! Two more stops and we're home. I'd best begin to sort us out. You all right now, miss?

'Thank you, Ruby, you've given me hope that I'll see her – one day.'

Eliza looked as if she were about to cry again and Ruby distracted her hastily by asking her to help search for her book. From thinking it would be a good idea if she cried, Ruby felt strongly that there had been enough tears for now.

No doubt it was her imagination but the house seemed to smile at Eliza as she entered it. Once inside the main door and in the old hall, with its warm, familiar smell, Eliza felt a sense of security enfold her. She was safe here, she always would be. If people left her, and hurt her in so doing, she always had the house. It was her protection, her sanctuary. She must try to plan her life so that when she was older and had more control over matters, she need never leave here again!

'And how was London, Miss Eliza?'

'Very noisy, Mrs King.' Eliza smiled at the housekeeper, who had come bustling to greet her.

'So you won't be missing it?'

'No, I don't think so.' She began to remove her cloak. 'It was exciting, and I enjoyed many things – the plays, the opera, the exhibitions – but it is wonderful to be home.'

'That's nice, to be sure. Now, I have your room ready. In the circumstances . . .' Mrs King coughed genteelly, she did not want to mention Miss Chester's name. '. . . I hope I acted correctly, I've had all your things removed from the nursery wing, and opened up one of the bedrooms on the main landing for you. Very nice it is too – with its own boudoir and what—'

Eliza was half-way up the stairs but she halted and turned so sharply that she nearly lost her balance. 'I'm sorry, Mrs King, but did I hear you correctly? You've moved my possessions?'

'Yes, I did. As I said, I hoped I'd done right.'

'You most certainly didn't.'

'But you're a young woman now. Soon you'll be going to balls and the like. Courting, no doubt.'

'Mrs King, no doubt you meant well, but I would appreciate your having everything moved back immediately. Meanwhile, I'll take tea in the morning room until it is done.' With which she moved gracefully down the stairs leaving a disgruntled Mrs King to find the maids to do her bidding.

'Right fool she made me look,' Mrs King complained to Mrs Satterly, after dinner that night.

'Perhaps you should have waited.'

'Well, evidently so.'

'It's best not to interfere.'

'I wasn't, I was being considerate. I thought she wouldn't want to be in the nursery wing with all its memories for her. I was only thinking of her. I can assure you it's the last time I do.' Mrs King's colour heightened more with each indignant phrase.

'It was a bit high-handed, to be sure.'

'High-handed! How right you are. A right little madam she's become and no mistake, with her London ways.'

'Miss Eliza? Never! What do you think, Ruby?' the cook asked, as Ruby entered the servants' hall, having finished her work for the day.

'About what, Mrs Satterly?' She helped herself to a cup of coffee.

'That our Miss Eliza's become too high and mighty for her own good,' Mrs King said.

'She's very upset. It was a shock to her to find she'd been moved.'

'What's she got to be upset about?'

'She misses Miss Chester something shocking. Odd, she's been, for days. The family hoped the change of air might help and it seems to be working. She's cheered up since she got here.'

'She didn't seem that cheerful to me. Right old paddywack . . .' Mrs King added a slug of brandy to her coffee but did not offer the bottle to the other two.

Ruby thought it better not to tell her how angry Eliza had been that her possessions had been touched by others, her drawers emptied, her books moved. Ruby had even worried that it might send her peculiar again.

'I've been wondering if either of you knows where Miss Chester's gone – only I've a book of hers I need to return,' she queried, with studied innocence.

'I do, as a matter of fact. She wrote to me. She'd left one or two things here.'

'Could you give me her address, Mrs King?'

'I'll do no such thing. Whatever next? You'd be letting Miss Eliza know.'

'I never would.' She tried to sound indignant.

'Tell you what – I'm parcelling her things up to post them during the next few days. Give me the book and I'll pop it in.'

'That would be kind of you. Then I won't need to write to her, will I?'

'A bit rude of you, isn't it, if you borrowed it?'

'I'd rather not, if you don't mind. I don't want her to think that I was trying to get in touch for Eliza's sake.'

'That's sensible thinking, my girl. Because if you did you'd be looking for a new post very quickly.'

'But, then, maybe you're right. What if I just pop a note in?'

'Perhaps you should. Your Ada's been a good girl – much more willing and civil than she started out.'

'She's not still here? I didn't see her at supper.' Ruby looked puzzled.

'She's gone home to help your mother with the baby. She's to return at Christmas when Mr Forester arrives.'

'The baby? What baby?'

'You don't mean to say you don't know? Why, your mother's had a baby – kept very quiet about it, I can tell you . . . Ashamed, no doubt,' she added, *sotto voce*, to Mrs Satterly.

'I must go and see her.'

'That might be a good idea. Go on your next afternoon off.'

'But, Mrs King, I was thinking I'd go tomorrow.'

'You'll do no such thing. You've far too much to do. Miss Eliza needs some sorting out, if you ask me.'

6

'So it's true!' Ruby said, as she entered her mother's kitchen, four days later. She was upset to see how tired her mother looked as she sat with a child of about fifteen months playing contentedly on her lap.

'Ruby, my sweet, you look pale.'

'Why didn't you tell me about the baby?'

'Isn't she adorable? We call her Alexandra, after the Princess, and Alex for short.'

'Mother, you haven't answered me.'

'I was afraid you'd be cross.'

'Why on earth should I be? These things happen.' The truth was she had been vexed, the shame of discovering her mother had fallen for a baby at her age! And who was the father? But, then, if it was meant to be ... But the thought of another mouth to feed worried Ruby: it would mean she would have to contribute from her meagre wages for ever at this rate. 'She is pretty.' Alex waved a chubby hand at Ruby. 'Can I hold her? Will she come to me?'

Her mother held out the child who, without a hint of shyness, was content to slide on to Ruby's lap and play with her bonnet ribbons.

'I thought of writing, Ruby, but you know me, there's never time – and getting the words right – I always find that difficult. You might have misunderstood. Anyway, you've only sent me four letters in two years.'

'More than you managed to send me.' Ruby smiled. She knew her mother preferred to bake, scrub the scullery floor or weed the vegetable patch than put pen to paper.

'Truth be told, I'd decided it was best not to tell you. I hoped the problem might, with a bit of luck, be sorted out before you came back. You wrote you were going to Austria with the family – or some such place. Did you go? Had I got the dates wrong?'

'No, it was cancelled ... What do you mean, Mother? Sort out what? I've another sister, that's all, and I love her already. Just the smell of her makes me long for one of my own.' She nuzzled her head in the baby's neck.

'Sister? What do you mean? Sister! Alex isn't your sister!' She looked astonished and then laughed so much that she couldn't speak for a minute or two. This made Alex laugh too and clap her chubby hands. 'Heavens above, girl,' she finally managed, 'what on earth have you been thinking? A baby, at my age! Oh, you silly girl. She's Maud's child.'

'Maud Flint?'

'How many other Mauds do you know?'

'But I thought ... I was told it was your baby. Mother, you don't mean you took the child on for her? How could you be so—'

'Stupid? Is that what you were going to say? That's what Jerome says I am.' She sighed. 'No, duped is a better word. Against my better judgement I took Maud in.' At this she looked hard at her daughter.

'Sorry,' said Ruby with a sheepish expression.

'As you know, I said she could stay until the baby was born. She went to her home to find work and I believed her when she said she'd come back to pick up the child.'

'When did she leave?'

'A month after Alex was born. Last June.'

'And you haven't heard from her since?'

'I had one letter.'

'Where is she?'

'I don't know. She didn't give an address – she said she was about to move somewhere near London and would write again, only she hasn't. But if I did know, what could I do about it? I know now she would never care properly for the little one, else she wouldn't have run away in the first place, would she? And I could never put Alex in the foundling home. Just look at her.'

'How could she leave her?' Ruby stroked the baby's fine blond hair and felt doubly protective of her.

'She was going to ask her mother to care for the little one while she found work.'

'She told me her mother was dead and her father would kill her if he knew.'

'Oh, the silly girl! Why couldn't she have been honest with me. I'd have helped her.'

'Perhaps she was afraid you wouldn't. So what will you do?'

They both looked down at Alex, still sitting on Ruby's lap. Aware that she was the centre of attention the baby beamed up at them.

'She's here now,' Ruby said. 'We're just going to have to pull together and help you.'

'I knew you'd be understanding. You're a dear daughter, and Jerome has been such a help, since he got over his annoyance. And Ivy too – she's still with us. I'm sorry it's been such a shock to you. But who told you she was my child? No, let me guess, it was Mavis King, wasn't it? Spiteful old bitch.'

'Mother!' Ruby was unused to hearing her mother use strong language and glanced at her, but she did not respond. A couple of books lay on the dresser. Reading was her mother's greatest pleasure and Jerome tried to save enough money to maintain her subscription to the library. For her birthday they clubbed together to buy her a book to keep.

'Is this one of yours?' She held up a copy of *Pride and Prejudice*.

'You and Jerome gave me that for my last birthday. It's a good story. Do you want to borrow it?'

'Please.'

'Don't lose it.'

'Mother! As if I would!' Ruby put the book carefully on the table. 'Shall I get us a jug of cider? No, not you. You look worn out.'

There was comfort in being back in her home, simple as it was. Ruby often wished a miracle could happen and she would find herself with enough money to make her mother's life easier. She'd have water pumped into the house and buy a fine cooking range just like Mrs Satterly's instead of the open hearth which, if the wind changed, belched smoke into the kitchen. But there was little chance of that. How her mother managed she'd never know. She cooked, cleaned the house, washed the clothes, fed the chickens, milked the goats and cows, made butter and cream, grew vegetables. Ruby filled the jug from the barrel of cider her mother had also made. If her dreams came true and Henry Morgan, the gamekeeper's son, noticed her, she would end up in exactly the same position as her mother.

'How's Jerome?'

'Working too hard as always. He needs a labourer to help but we can't afford one.'

'He's strong – you worry too much.'

'He works from dawn to dusk. And there's the responsibility too. It's hard on one so young. If only your father hadn't died.' She sighed and took a tankard of cider from Ruby. 'We live in fear that Mr Forester won't renew the tenancy when it comes up for renewal.'

'But we've always been here, back to my great-grandfather and beyond. There's never been a problem before.'

'I've heard he thinks Jerome's too young to cope. Though when your father died, he seemed happy enough that I should continue the farm with Jerome's help. No doubt he's someone in mind who suits him better. Loyalty means nothing to that man.'

'Mother, don't worry.'

'I don't see how not to. It's not just the tenancy, he's putting up the rent on the extra fields we use. No doubt that's how he'll get rid of us, charge us so much that we can't pay. Then where would we go and what would we do?'

'Poor Mother.'

'Still, moaning won't solve anything, will it?' She stood up to sort a pile of clean laundry. 'We've a nice new doctor. Did they tell you? I had to call him to see to Alex. Dr Forbes. He's young and kind – I've heard he's even refused his fee when he knows it would cripple people to pay him.'

'What's happened to Dr Whitney?'

'Retired, thank the Lord. I'm sure he killed more people than he ever cured!'

They both burst out laughing.

'What's the joke?' Jerome asked, as he strode into the kitchen.

'Jerome!' Ruby's face lit up with pleasure at sight of her elder brother. She put the baby down and he swept her into his arms, hugging her until she squealed for mercy. She had always loved him, always been proud of him, and as the years went by her pride had grown as he became taller, broader and, to her eyes, even more handsome. 'Let me look at you.' She took a step back to study him. At twenty-one he was well over six feet tall. He was deeply tanned and his hair was bleached from working in the fields in the sun. The muscles built from hard labour looked about to burst out of his tight-fitting shirt. 'You look better every time I see you. I almost wish I wasn't your sister so I could fall in love with you myself.'

'And you're as pretty as a picture too. London life must suit you.' He bent and kissed her cheek. 'But I'd love you even more if you got me a tankard of that cider. I'm parched.' He sat down on one of the kitchen chairs, his muscled legs stretched out in front of him. Little Alex immediately clambered on to one of his legs, and hung on tight as he lifted her up and down on it to her delight. Then he picked her up and wrinkled his nose. 'I'm sorry, Mother, I think she needs a change and a wash.' He held her at arm's length, pulling faces, making her laugh.

'And I thought I'd got her clean. Come here, you monkey.' And scooping the child into her arms Grace Barnard left the kitchen.

'She does too much.' Ruby poured more cider.

'But how can we stop her?'

'And how can we stop *you*? Mother says you work too hard as well.'

'I have to.' He shrugged. 'But I've got Bertie to help – he's nearly fifteen now and as strong as an ox. Without him I'd really struggle. He doesn't want to farm, though. He wants to be an artist.'

'I never knew that.'

'That's what's sad about our lives – you have to work

away from home, so that he's grown up hardly knowing you.'

'If only Father hadn't died.'

'It would have been the same if he'd lived. He was a lazy old sod.'

'Jerome!'

'It's the truth.'

'But you shouldn't speak ill of the dead.'

'Why? He can't hear. I didn't like him when he was alive so why should I pretend I did just because he's dead?'

'I never knew that either.'

'I hated him. He was idle, he beat Mother, you, me and Bertie. I'd have left years ago, but I couldn't – I was afraid of what he would do to Mother.'

'Oh, Jerome, I thought you were happy here.'

'See how little you know? I'm trapped here. There is no escape.'

'Then if Forester doesn't renew it would suit you?' She looked about the kitchen. This had always been her home and she couldn't imagine them living anywhere else.

'No. If we get thrown out of here we've nowhere else to go. But what angers me about the tenancy agreement is why I'm suddenly too young. I was running this farm for years before Father died. I suited then so why not now?'

'Can't you go and see Mr Forester?'

'I intend to, when he comes down from London.'

'What you need is a sweetheart. You'd see everything differently then.'

'I doubt I'll ever afford to get married.'

'I don't know. Love usually finds a way.'

'That's the sort of stupid thing a woman would say!' He pushed her playfully.

A figure passed by the window.

'Was that Ivy?' Ruby asked.

'She's taken over the dairy, which helps Mother, but she's a mixed blessing.' He laughed.

'It's becoming like a foundlings' home here.'

'I told Mother she was mad but I'm proud of her. She's a good woman, the best.'

'And who are you both talking about?' Grace asked, as she bustled back into the kitchen carrying Alex.

'You, Mother. You're too soft-hearted and kind, and we wouldn't change you for the world.'

'But you never know when hard times, really hard times, might strike and *we* need help.'

'Who'd help us?' Jerome snorted with derision.

'You mean, like storing up good deeds in heaven?' Ruby enquired.

'Something like that. There but for the grace of God go we.'

'Rubbish, Mother. You do it because you're a good woman. You just say that to justify yourself.'

'Found out at last!' Grace laughed. 'Now, Ruby, what's your news?'

Ruby told of their time in London, of Merry's dismissal, the scandal over Miss Chester, and Eliza's unhappiness, how she had withdrawn from them, how she wouldn't eat and had only just begun to speak.

'What's she got to be unhappy about? So she loses a servant, there are plenty more where that one came from. And with all that money, wanting for nothing, she sounds like a spoilt child to me. She should know real hardship and then she'd stop whining.'

'Jerome, that's so hard. She can't help it. And she's never aware of the money.'

'For the simple reason she never has to think of it, that's why.'

'Poor child, with no mother. No doubt she fears that she'll lose everyone she cares for.'

'That's exactly what she said. Why, you understand her better than her own family, Mother. I reckon you could help her.'

'If she'd come slumming, that is.'

'Jerome, what has got into you? You're never normally so spiteful.'

'I hate that family. They bleed us dry with their rents, their demands, and their cussed ways. Forester wouldn't let me plough the Copse field – you know, the large one that runs parallel to the drive. He didn't want it to look ugly for his guests.'

'It is his land, so I suppose he can do what he wants with it,' Ruby said lamely.

'But he charges me rent on it even though he won't let me grow crops on it. Is that fair?'

'It's hardly Miss Eliza's fault,' Grace put in. 'You invite her, Ruby, if you think she'd like to come.'

'Make it market day when I won't be here.'

'What a grump you are, Jerome,' Ruby teased. The door opened. 'Ivy, how lovely to see you,' she said, with genuine pleasure. Her friend limped into the kitchen, carrying a bowl of yellow butter. She barely acknowledged Ruby for she had eyes only for Jerome. So that's what he meant by a mixed blessing, Ruby thought.

7

Eliza was restless, unable to settle to anything. Books suddenly held no interest for her. Her skill at painting and sketching had deserted her, and at the piano, she was all thumbs. Ruby could not play croquet or whist and even dominoes was beyond her. She no longer went for walks, because the familiar surroundings reminded her of walks she had taken with Miss Chester.

'If you're going to mooch around like that I shall get flustered,' Ruby admonished her, as Eliza aimlessly moved back and forth across the schoolroom carpet. It had been decided to turn it into a sitting room for Eliza, since she still refused steadfastly to move into the main wing of the house, wanting to remain where she had been happiest. 'I've work to do if you haven't.' There had been a time when Ruby wouldn't have spoken to her in such a familiar way, but she was becoming irritated with her – she had even begun to think that Jerome had been right. 'Look, why not help me sort these books?' she suggested.

With a sigh, as if it were too much effort, Eliza took a pile from her. She sniffed them. 'Ruby, I miss her so! This smell of chalk reminds me . . .'

'I know you do but if you keep talking about her you'll only make matters worse. Surely there's something you can do to amuse yourself.'

'I'm not a child, Ruby! Please don't speak to me as if I were.'

'Of course you're not.' Ruby spoke in the cajoling way she used with children, thinking that Eliza was certainly behaving like one. 'But you should keep occupied. So, if you could decide which books you want to keep,' she wheedled, 'I know exactly what to do with the ones you don't. Betty Potter's sister has been widowed.'

'Who?'

'The woman who does the mending for us. Well, her sister, Maisie Furnell, has come to live with her. She's setting up a dame school for the estate children. I'm sure she'd love to have them.'

'Really?' Eliza said, with a complete lack of interest. The old Eliza would have been excited by such a plan, thought Ruby, and no doubt would have offered all manner of help. It just showed how low she was.

'Everyone's pleased about the school,' Ruby went on, but did not mention that Jerome had told her most people thought such a school should be financed by the Foresters, as happened on other estates. 'But, then, he's not a real gentleman, so he doesn't know he should,' Jerome had said. Ruby had smiled to herself at the way Jerome grabbed any opportunity to snipe at Mr Forester.

Eliza began to sort the books. One pile towered over the other.

'Maisie will be pleased,' Ruby said, and picked up a box to put them in.

'No! Those are the ones I want to keep.'

'All of them?' Ruby's exasperation spilled into her voice. 'But some are for little children.'

'Am I being silly, Ruby?'

'If you want an honest answer, yes. There are children in sore need of these.'

'Take them, then! Take all of them!' Eliza cried dramatically, and flew from the room – probably in tears, thought Ruby. Maybe she shouldn't have said what she had but something had to be done. She had so hoped the move here would pull the girl round, but day by day she was becoming unhappier. And so was Ruby, because she had to deal with her. Even their planned trip to the farm had not materialised, Eliza always finding an excuse not to go.

There was nothing for it, she was going to have to risk her plan. From a drawer she took the copy of *Pride and Prejudice* her mother had loaned her. She opened it, searched for a particular page and in light pencil in the margin, wrote, '*If I should roam please send me home. Barton Farm, Nr Exeter, Devon*'. Then she wrote a note.

Dear Miss Chester,

Thank you so much for the loan of this book which I enjoyed very much. I particularly liked the scenes where Miss B and Mr P meet.

With affectionate greetings,

She signed it but did not seal the note, ensuring that Mrs King would read it. She could only hope that Miss

Chester knew the book and would have the wit to know it was a message. Carefully she wrapped it in tissue paper and hurried to Mrs King's sitting room. 'I hope the parcel for Miss Chester hasn't been posted?'

'Heavens above! I'd forgotten all about it, thank you for reminding me, Ruby. Is this the book you're returning?'

'It is.' Her heart lurched as she handed it over. Mrs King placed it on a side table. 'How is the work on the schoolroom going?'

'Slowly. I don't know what to throw away and what to keep.'

'Doesn't Miss Eliza help you?'

'It's too distressing for her.'

'I'll speak plainly, Ruby. I'm getting tired of all these tantrums.'

'She hasn't thrown any, nothing like that,' she protested loyally. 'She's just sad.'

'You'd have thought she'd lost a relative. Not enough to occupy her mind, that's for sure.'

'My mother has invited her to tea. I had hoped that would entertain her.'

'Tea? At the farm? Hardly! She's a sophisticated young woman, not a yokel.' Mrs King laughed at the very idea.

Ruby chose to ignore the insult. 'We just thought it would be something different for her to do. New surroundings, new faces – she barely knows any of my family.'

'She refused?'

'Not exactly . . . But if she changes her mind it will be all right, won't it?'

'If she does, but I very much doubt she will. But that's enough chattering. Get back to your work, Ruby.'

Ruby was barely in the corridor before Mrs King was inspecting the book and reading her note. Satisfied that it was as Ruby had said, she added it to Fanny

Chester's other possessions, which were waiting to be posted.

Eliza had been for one of her aimless walks. She was hot and tired and angry with herself that, given the beauty of the day and her lovely surroundings, she was still discontented and miserable. But no matter how much she admonished herself the wretchedness wouldn't go away.

She was aware that people's patience with her was wearing thin. She felt sometimes that they thought she was enjoying this. If only they knew! She did not blame them: she herself would have found it difficult to deal with someone as petulant and selfish as she was. She clung to the hope that her unhappiness would pass. That it was like an illness from which she would recover.

One of her favourite places was the stables. At the moment she found it easier to be with animals than humans. She often paused to talk to the horses, especially Silver, with whom, although she did not ride him any more, she could not bear to part. He remained in the stables, getting fatter by the day.

'I have been wondering, Miss Eliza, if you'd have any objection to some of the estate children riding him,' Rodgers, the chief groom, asked. 'It would get some of that weight off him – it can't be good for him to carry so much.'

'Provided they are not cruel.'

'I'd make sure of that, Miss Eliza.'

Eliza decided to take a short-cut through the kitchen yard. Already she was thinking of the iced lemonade she would order once she was back in the house.

'You're a lazy good-for-nothing scut, that you are!' a raucous voice shouted, and Eliza arrived just in time to see Mrs Satterly push a young girl so hard with a broom that she went sprawling on the cobblestones. 'I'll make you yell! You don't know what pain is! I'll show you!' And she slammed the broom down hard on the girl's skull.

'Mrs Satterly, you go too far!' Mrs King came out of the door all a fluster.

'Mind your own sodding business.' The broom was raised again, but Eliza rushed across and caught it as it swished down towards the cowering girl.

'Stop!' she ordered.

'I told you, keep your bloody nose . . .' Mrs Satterly looked at her blearily, her eyes glazed with anger – or was it alcohol? 'Miss Eliza . . . how nice . . .' Mrs Satterly slurred.

'Not nice at all, Mrs Satterly. You are dismissed.'

'I beg your pardon?' She swayed alarmingly, and lurched towards Eliza.

Mrs King flew towards them, looking to left and right for assistance. 'You! Get help!' she shouted at a gaggle of laundry-maids who had ventured out to investigate. 'Miss Eliza, it's all right. I'll deal with this little problem.'

'It is far from all right, Mrs King. And it's hardly a little problem. This woman is inebriated. I want her off the premises by nightfall.'

'What would your father say? Wait until he arrives. Don't do anything precipitate.'

'My father would be in agreement with me. I don't want to keep repeating myself, Mrs King, but—'

'You don't know what the little cow done!' Mrs Satterly shrieked.

'I don't care! You don't beat people in that way, not in my father's house.'

'Oh, no?' Mrs Satterly stood, hands on hips, wobbling on her high-buttoned boots. 'Oh, no? I should ask your father about that, Miss High and Mighty. Quite a little hobby with him, whipping.'

'Eve! Stop it. You go too far,' Mrs King whispered urgently.

'Don't you Eve me, you drunken old shrew. At least I'm open about partaking of a tipple, don't do it in secret like some as I could mention.'

'You evil woman!'

'What did you mean, Mrs Satterly?' Eliza spoke quietly and deliberately.

'Quite a dab hand with the whip, your papa.'

'My father has never used a whip unnecessarily on a horse.'

'Who said anything about horses?' Mrs Satterly looked sly.

'You speak in riddles and I haven't the patience.' Eliza turned her back on the cook and focused her attention on the scullery-maid. She bent down. 'Are you hurt? It's Maggie, isn't it?'

'Yes, miss.' Maggie felt tongue tied with astonishment that she, of all people, should know her name.

'Are you hurt?'

'No, miss.' She didn't want anyone to know she was aching.

'That's good. Ruby often talks about you and how clever you are.'

'Thank you, miss.' Maggie went bright red, and Mrs Satterly snorted in a way that would have done a stallion proud.

'Can you cook?'

'Yes, miss.'

'Then I suggest you go and begin my supper.'

Maggie's mouth dropped open and Eliza turned to continue on her way.

'I never liked it here. Poor working conditions and a low-class household. I've people *begging* me to go and cook for them,' Mrs Satterly shouted after her.

Eliza turned. 'Then go now.'

'You hoity-toity cow!' Mrs Satterly shrieked. 'Want to know what I meant?'

'Eve!' Mrs King tugged at her sleeve.

'Want to know who your father enjoyed beating up?'

'*Eve!*'

'Go and ask your mother! She'll tell you!'

It had been decided that, since Eliza was nearly of an age to leave the schoolroom and enter society, there was little point in replacing her governess.

'She's too interested in learning. It's a danger that should be guarded against if she's to marry well.' Minnie Wickham gestured to the footman to replenish her glass. 'Really, Freddie, you should do something about your servants. They are too lax. That is the second time this evening I have had to indicate that my glass should be refreshed.'

'Maybe you shouldn't drink so fast.'

'You can be so insufferably rude, Freddie. Where's Densham? At least the service is a little better when he's here.'

'I've sent him to Harcourt. I shall follow him within the week.'

'You didn't say.'

'Do I have to report to you *all* my movements?'

'When you go there you normally invite us. You know how Charles and I adore Harcourt.'

'And we all know why,' Frederick said languidly.

'And what does that mean?'

'Whatever you want it to mean, Minnie.'

'Freddie, you go too far.' Once again she swung round to glare at the footman. 'That was most definitely a snort of mirth from you, young man. Freddie, dismiss him!' The young man's complexion paled.

'You always overreact, Minnie.'

'I want him out of here.'

Frederick Forester sighed. 'Very well. James, leave the room. And stop blubbering, I shan't sack you – this time. Send the other James in with the port.' The footman slunk from the room as if walking sideways he could make himself less obvious.

'You needn't think I'm withdrawing because I'm the only woman here,' Minnie said.

'I didn't ask you to. I want to talk to you and Charles.'

'I thought you might,' Charles said, with resignation, and helped himself to some fruit.

'What about?'

'Money. That's the only thing your brother ever wants to talk to us about.'

'Charles, discretion,' she whispered, as the new James entered the room and ceremoniously placed the decanter of port on the table. That done he began to collect dirty glasses and plates.

'Leave that. Come back later,' Frederick ordered.

'Then it's serious,' Charles said, in mock horror.

'Can you never take anything seriously, Charles?'

'Not if I can help it.' He smiled in his usual disarming way but neither of the other two noticed.

'So, what is it, Frederick?'

'Simpson tells me you have overspent your allowance yet again, Minnie. This will not do. This is the fourth quarter in a row.'

'Then he's lying! I never trusted that self-righteous clerk!'

'He's my chief cashier and a great asset to the bank. He's doing his job, that's all.'

'You can be so stuffy, Frederick. So like Father.' Minnie nodded thanks to her husband who was pouring her some port. She downed the glass in one mouthful, then indicated she wished it to be refilled.

'Issues have to be faced. The bank is not a charity.'

'So that is why there are no other guests? I might have known. You feed us, give us too much to drink, then take advantage of us.'

'I'm doing no such thing. You drink too much of your own free will. I don't force you. I'm just telling you it cannot go on like this. I have asked you both time and again to make economies but you won't. This time I insist, or I shall stop your allowance altogether.'

'You can't do that.'

'I can and I will. Father was no fool. He always suspected that Charles would go through his own fortune and made certain that you, Minnie, would not squander ours.'

'I say, Frederick, that's not very friendly of you.' But Charles was grinning as he spoke.

'It's the truth, Charles. By the terms of his will I am entrusted to administer Minnie's allowance as I see fit. I explained it to you both at the time of Father's death.'

'Yes – but I never expected you to implement it! I'm your sister.'

'And that's why I'm acting. I don't want to see you both in Queer Street.'

'I shall tell Mama.'

'I have already discussed this matter with her and she is in full agreement with me.'

'You are a fiend, Frederick! How dare you discuss my business with Mama?'

'Because I knew you would go whining to her the minute I spoke to you. So I told her first.'

'You haven't changed at all, have you? You're just as nasty and sneaky as you were as a child.'

'I hoped for a constructive discussion this evening, Minnie, not insults. I have been through the figures and they make sorry reading. Minnie, I have instructed Simpson to pay your dressmaker's bills up to date and thereafter you are to halve the sums you spend. Exceed that and they will not be paid.'

'You can't!'

'Your allowance, Charles, is to be halved.'

'How will I manage?'

'Stop gambling.'

'I haven't had a wager in six months.'

'Doesn't card-playing count?'

'Hardly. I thought you meant the horses. But, indeed, I've had the odd run of bad luck at écarté.'

'What gentleman doesn't play cards, Frederick? He'd be a laughing-stock at the club if he couldn't.'

'Then stop going to the club.'

'He'd die of boredom, wouldn't you, my love?'

'That's where I make all my useful contacts, Frederick.'

'Useful for what, Charles? Perhaps you should think of working for your living.'

'Working, me?'

'But he's a baronet!' Minnie's voice quivered with indignation.

'I work,' Frederick pointed out.

'But you haven't even got the knighthood you long and entertain for so obsequiously. I wonder why.'

'Minnie . . .' Charles said.

'Perhaps it has something to do with your treatment of your wife. Or because you are a cuckold. You're hardly the right person to kneel before the Queen, now, are you?'

'Minnie!' Charles stood. 'She's speaking without thinking, Frederick. Pay no attention to her.'

'I shall not. In any case her assumption is probably correct. My wife, Amelia, was a curse in more ways than one. However, I suggest to you both that your London house has to go. Either sold or rented, unless that is—'

'No!' Minnie did not give him time to finish.

'I would reconsider this situation if—'

'I say!' Charles stood up, clutching his napkin, then evidently thought better of it and sat down again.

'How dare you turn us into the street like beggars?'

'Don't exaggerate, Minnie, if you would but listen to me—'

'How could you do that to my house?'

'It's *my* house, if you remember. I bought it, you borrow it.'

'Only because Papa was too mean to me! I begged him for money for a house of my own. Would he listen? No!'

'You had a house once.'

'Don't remind me. Frederick, how could you? If only Charles . . .' Minnie tried to cry but weeping was not in her repertoire, so she made sobbing noises instead and dabbed at her tearless eyes with a handkerchief.

'If only I hadn't gone almost bankrupt? Say it, Minnie! And remind me again of what a useless wastrel I am.'

A bellow issued from behind the fluttering handkerchief.

'Minnie, stop that infernal noise – I'm not fooled for a moment,' Frederick said.

'But my home – my life! Think of the shame!'

'If you will only listen to me for one moment I have a proposal. Eliza will have to be introduced into society next year. As you say, if she is to marry she needs a season. Mama says she is far too old for the task. I suggest you both move in here, and you act as her chaperone, Minnie. I will, of course, furnish you with a suitable wardrobe . . .'

'As well as my halved dress allowance?'

Frederick laughed. 'Agreed.'

'All our expenses?'

'To do with Eliza, yes. Gambling and your other activities are your own responsibility.'

'I don't know what you mean.' But Minnie's eyes narrowed with greed as she made rapid calculations in her head and discovered that Frederick had made a good offer. 'The rental from our house? Who gets that?'

'For the next year, you do.'

'Then it's agreed.'

'Don't you want to discuss it with Charles.'

'There's no need. He does as I want.' She stood up. Charles got to his feet out of politeness, but her brother didn't. 'I shall go now. Come, Charles.'

'Minnie . . .'

'I'm taking the carriage.'

'I'm happy to walk.'

They watched her flounce out of the room, and Charles began to follow her.

'Stay and finish this bottle with me,' Frederick said.

'Are you sure you wish me to remain?'

'Would I invite you if I weren't?'

'Probably not.' Charles sat down again.

'How do you stand her?' Frederick asked, once the port had been poured.

'I beg your pardon?' Charles looked belligerent.

'Don't feel you must perform the honourable act with me, Charles. She's my sister, after all.'

'And she's my wife – so I would prefer it, old chap, if you weren't rude about her.'

'She doesn't deserve you.'

'Nonsense. *I* don't deserve *her*. She's been very patient with me over the years. I wasn't much of a catch even at the beginning, was I?'

'She loved you, and you gave her her title.' Frederick refilled the glasses. 'Does she know about the villa at St John's Wood? And Mrs Fraser?'

'She might.' Charles did not bat an eyelid.

'And it doesn't matter?'

'I have no interest in her lovers so why should she in mine?'

'Where's your loyalty now, brother-in-law?'

'*Touché!*' Charles grinned and raised his glass.

'She might not be so happy to know that Fanny Chester is residing there too. Now, there I do congratulate you, Charles. How did you get her to agree to that?'

'I haven't asked her to agree to anything.'

'Not yet, Charles. But you will.' It was Frederick's turn to grin.

Life at Caroline Fraser's house was becoming intoler-able for Fanny. After two weeks the women were hardly speaking to each other. It was not Fanny's fault: she had tried to be civil, but Caroline ignored her.

'Caroline, I have received a note from my brother, Peter. He would like to visit me before leaving for a tour of Italy. Would that be convenient?' *Caroline* – she had been so pleased when the woman had requested that Fanny use her Christian name, but that had been when Charles was present. She was only pleasant when he was there. Fanny had dined with them on several occasions, when she had seen how delightful Caroline could be when it suited her. But when they were alone, what a different story it was! Then Fanny ate with Augusta and Maud, which in any case she preferred.

As was customary, Caroline did not reply. 'May I take your silence as assent?' Fanny enquired.

'He can't eat here.' Caroline flounced out of the room.

A few days later Fanny was waiting for Peter to arrive. She was excited and happy at the prospect of seeing him, but the pleasure of anticipation was marred by the misery she felt at living here. At least Caroline was out, so she could entertain him in the house. Otherwise they would have had to go to the park or a tea-shop, and rain was threatening.

In this past week she had been able to make some decisions, which was an improvement on how she had been: after her hurried dismissal by the Foresters, she had been reeling from shock and unable to think straight. The conclusions she had reached were that once she had seen her brother she would find other accommodation and employment. She could not con-tinue as a governess – she had replied to many advertisements in *The Times*, to no avail.

As she sat in the drawing room waiting for her

brother she picked up a local newspaper. Out of habit she scanned the advertisements. Would she end up as a sales assistant or in a public house? She shuddered at the idea. Then something caught her eye:

Woman of independent means requires teacher/tutor/ governess to discuss the possibility of establishing a small, select, private school. Only those with the highest qualifications, references and interest in female children to apply by letter in the first instance . . .

Fanny read it again. She had the qualifications, she loved children and teaching – especially girls. A school? That was interesting. References? Ha! There lay the problem. But the address given was in this area . . . If she were to ignore the formality of a letter and attend in person . . . whoever had placed the advertisement might like the look of her. Perhaps she could persuade them that she was not a bad woman, merely a wronged one. Anyway, she had nothing to lose.

'Your brother, Miss Chester.' Maud stood in the doorway, giggling.

'Thank you, Maud. But what is so funny?'

'That's what they all say.'

'Who? What?'

'Oh, never mind.' Another burst of giggling. 'I'll show him in, shall I?'

Fanny frowned. Maud was becoming far too familiar. No doubt it was partly her fault, but it was difficult to eat with someone and keep a decorous distance. And there was something open and appealing about Maud.

'Peter!' Fanny manoeuvred her way across the cluttered room, careful not to knock any knick-knacks on to the carpet. 'How wonderful to see you, at last.' She held out her arms in greeting. Peter pecked at her cheek, like a scavenging bird she always thought, and backed away from her embrace.

'Tea, Maud, if you don't mind.' She spoke quite sharply because Maud seemed to be taking too much interest in their meeting.

'Sit down, Peter. Tell me everything. Italy, you said in your letter. How marvellous for you.'

'Yes, my pupil's father is to join the embassy in Rome and the family has kindly asked me to go with them.'

'There was nothing kind about it. You are a teacher of genius. I should know, you taught me everything.'

'Fanny, what is this place?' He sat on the pretty slub silk sofa, among Caroline's collection of pink and red cushions.

'The home of a friend – well, acquaintance might be a more accurate description. But Rome, think of the antiquities you will see, the museums, the art . . . How I envy you. I must give you a list of all the places I visited, the best food to eat, the best wines.' She clapped her hands with joy for him, just as Maud reappeared with the tea-tray, prettily laid with Caroline's best china and silver. She'd be furious if she found out.

Maud smiled pertly at Peter. 'Shall I pour?' she asked.

'No, thank you, Maud. I shall manage.'

'As you wish.' She eyed Peter boldly and sniggered.

'Maud! Thank you.' Fanny sounded stern. They both waited while she tripped from the room.

'Fanny, what are you doing here?'

'I explained in my letter. I decided to leave my last post – Eliza has no need of me any more. This friend is kindly allowing me to stay here until I decide what to do next.' She had practised this in her room and was proud of the pat way it emerged and how reasonable it all sounded.

'You were dismissed?'

She was handing him a cup and saucer which rattled as her hand shook. 'No.'

'Don't lie, Fanny. You never could, you always blush.' He spoke kindly. 'Tell me what happened.

People like us don't leave our positions unless we have to. You know that.'

Fanny looked down at her hands for some time, collecting her thoughts, unable to look her brother in the eye. 'I was wrongly accused and sent away with no references, nothing.' She said this in a rush, wanting to get the words out quickly and be rid of them.

'As I thought. False accusations of stealing?'

'No. Nothing like that.'

'What, then?'

'I'd rather not say.'

'You must. I insist.'

'It's too embarrassing.' She looked up at him tentatively and he smiled at her, which made her feel a little more relaxed. 'I was accused of unseemly behaviour.'

'With whom?'

'It doesn't matter.'

'It matters to me. Was it Frederick Forester Esquire?' he asked, as if speaking the name contaminated him. Fanny could not answer but nodded mutely. Peter roared, 'No!' jumped to his feet and his cup flew across the room, tea spattering the rose-pink carpet.

'Peter, look what you've done! What shall I do?' She was on her knees patting ineffectually at the spreading stain.

'Leave that.'

Roughly he tried to pull her to her feet but she resisted. Just at that moment Maud, with a jug of hot water, opened the door and saw them struggling. 'Begging your pardon.' She laughed and closed the door.

'Who was that?' Peter swung round.

'The maid. Call her and get her to help me mop this stain.'

'Would you stop that and listen to me? You must answer me. And honestly. Did you have a liaison with that blackguard?'

'Peter! How could you ask me such a question? No, I

did not. And I shall never forgive you for asking.' She wrenched her hand away from his.

'How can I be sure?'

She took a deep breath. 'Because I told you, Brother. Because I do not lie. Because I would never compromise myself in such a way.' She sat down again, dignified, despite the hurt. Calmly she began to pour him another cup of tea.

'Fanny, forgive me. I'm sorry.'

'So you should be. I cannot believe . . .' She shook her head. What was the point in continuing the argument? Was it simply his bitter anger at the Forester family that had caused him to think in this way, or did he think she was capable of doing such a thing?

'I apologised.'

'I realise. But some things need time to be rectified. I was so happy to see you yet now I wish you hadn't come.'

'Don't be bitter, Fanny.'

'I shall try not to be, since such an emotion is too destructive if it can warp one's judgement in such a way.' At her sharp tone he looked shamefaced and it was his turn to study his hands. It was then she noticed that his nails were grimy, his cuffs worn and, worse, he was dirty. Had he always looked like this and her love for him had blinded her? If she was now seeing him as he really was did that mean her love had diminished? She did not like this notion, if she did not love him, she had no one to love. Except, of course . . . 'A sandwich?' She held out the plate to him to stem such thoughts.

'You're still cross?'

'Of course. I am interested you thought that while stealing was beyond me an improper relationship was not. It says much about you, Peter.'

'What else am I to think? I don't know what pressures have been placed on you, what new experiences you have encountered. How you have changed in the past three years. Anything could have happened.'

'I am still Fanny. The same sister.'

'If you are, why do you live here? The sister I knew wouldn't have deigned to cross the threshold.'

'I explained. This is the house of a friend of a friend.'

'And who might that be?'

'Why, Sir Charles Wickham. He is Eliza's uncle and has been very kind to me. Mrs Fraser is his friend.'

'Mistress, more like!' He took an angry bite of his sandwich.

Fanny's mouth dropped open with shock. She closed it, then asked, 'What is wrong with you, Peter? You seem full of the most improper thoughts and theories today.'

'This, my dear Fanny, is a house of ill-repute.'

'Don't be so silly! Mrs Fraser is a widow and lives here with her little sister.'

'Even worse. Corruption of the young. You are innocent, Fanny, I realise that. But you must leave here immediately.'

'And how, pray, are you so knowledgeable about such matters? What have *you* been doing in the past few years?' She could feel herself becoming really angry now.

'I am a man. I have heard talk of these places in this area. You, a respectable woman, should not be sitting here.'

'Then where do you suggest I sit instead? I was desperate. I was taken in. No money is asked of me. I've been teaching the little girl but I volunteered, no one coerced me, and I do so for my keep. And I find your attitude despicable.' But it was making her feel uncomfortable too, for if he was right then it would explain much which was strange about this house.

'Look about you, Fanny. You have lived in fine houses too. You know what is acceptable and what isn't, and this room reeks of immorality and perversion.'

'Oh, really, Peter! I must ask you to leave before we begin to say things to each other that we will later regret.' She stood up and so did he. They faced each other and she felt as if she were looking at a stranger.

'Fanny . . .'

'Please leave, Peter. I shall look forward to your letters telling me about Rome.' She walked purposefully to the door and opened it, in time to see Maud scurrying away. Had she been listening? So what? Fanny didn't care.

'It is sad that we should part in this way. I was only trying to protect you.'

'I realise that. I would wish you had done it in a more tactful way. Goodbye, Peter. *Bon voyage.*'

As soon as he had gone she raced to her room, collected her old references, her bonnet, an umbrella and the local newspaper, then sped out of the house. Just as she had feared, it had begun to rain. She was half-way down the street when she remembered the stain on the carpet. She began to turn, then decided it would have to wait.

10

'I'm not sure I can.' The maid was about to shut the front door.

'Please. Just ask.' The maid looked intransigent. 'I need to see her – I'm desperate.' Fanny could hear the pleading in her voice and despised herself.

But perhaps the maid too had been desperate once, for she wavered. 'She might have my guts for garters!'

'Why might I do that? What have you been up to now, Ann?' a husky voice, full of laughter, called from the hall.

'It's this lady here.' Ann turned from Fanny to answer. 'She wants to talk to you about the school and I said as she was to write.'

While the maid's back was turned, Fanny squeezed past her. 'Madam, I was presumptuous enough to come because if I wrote you wouldn't have bothered to see me. I hoped I might talk to you face to face and explain. You see, I know I am ideal for this position.' Fanny spoke in a gulping rush, not daring to pause for breath and give herself time to think of what she was doing.

'You're wet. You'd better come in and dry out, if nothing else.'

A lovely woman was standing in the hall. She was tall, held herself proudly, had a mass of blond hair, which fell in heavy curls about her face, and a mouth with the fullest lips Fanny had ever seen. Her waist was minute and emphasised her breasts, which were half visible in the low-cut dress she wore. She made Fanny think of full-blown roses, or peaches at their ripest. 'Florrie Paddington.' She held out a hand on which several rings flashed in the light from the chandelier, which was too big for the hall . . . which reminded her of Caroline's.

'Fanny Chester,' she replied.

'Come in, then, Fanny Chester, and tell me what's what.' Florrie led her into her drawing room. But here there was no similarity with Caroline's. It was beautifully furnished without one silk cushion in sight. 'Sit down. Ann, get the champagne – it's nearly time,' she said, peering short-sightedly at a diamond-encrusted watch, which she wore on a gold chain around her neck. Everything about her was attractive, especially her voice. She had, Fanny realised, a West Country accent. 'Well, then, tell me what's so different about you that you decided to come and see me rather than write as I requested?'

Though it was a reprimand, it was delivered in such a charming manner that Fanny did not feel intimidated. Quite the contrary.

'My references are out of date. I was dismissed, last month, from my last position, and without papers from my previous employers I knew you wouldn't want to interview me.'

'Thank you for being so honest with me. I like that. Is it permitted to ask why you had to leave?'

'I was accused of trying to seduce my employer.' For the first time since it had happened, Fanny found herself smiling at the absurdity of what she had just said.

'And you were dismissed? What was wrong with the man? He should have been flattered, an attractive young woman such as yourself.' Florrie laughed as if she, too, found it funny.

'But you don't understand. I didn't do as I was accused.'

'Of course not, I *know* that. Had you done so, you would hardly be sitting here talking to me, would you? No doubt you'd have been well set up, if not for life at least for the time being.'

'You comprehend my impossible position.' Fanny sank back on the sofa with relief.

'It's far more common than you think. What was he to do? You spurned him, how could he face you? Was he old and senile?'

'No, youngish and handsome.'

'Then, of course, the next question is, why on earth didn't you?' Again, the bubbling laugh, so that instead of being offended, Fanny found herself joining in, then clapped her hand over her mouth. This would never do, she thought. 'What are you doing now?'

'A member of the family took pity on me and arranged for me to stay with a friend of his, near here.'

'And he, too, I take it, is youngish and handsome? But you feel more disposed to him?' Fanny blushed. 'Then say no more. I shan't pry.' They paused when the maid appeared with the champagne. Florrie opened the bottle with an expert twist. Fanny was impressed. 'I never like my bottles served open – don't want anyone watering the contents, now, do we?' She winked at Fanny as she poured the first glass and the maid, instead of looking insulted, giggled. 'Now, where were we? My school.'

'I have my previous references here.' Fanny undid a small document case and withdrew her precious store of letters, her lifeline, as she thought of them.

Florrie waved them away. 'I know I asked for them but it was just a formality. I don't listen to what others say. I rely on my own judgement, what *I* see and hear. So, tell me about yourself.'

Fanny hated it when someone asked her to do that. She always felt she sounded so dull. She gave a brief résumé of her life, and when she reached the end, Florrie commented, 'You don't seem to have had much fun.'

'I haven't been unhappy. Some positions were better than others.'

'That must be the same in all walks of life.' Florrie smiled a secret smile.

'Of course.'

'You like children?'

'I have to be honest, not all of them. I had one family, well . . . There was a child I could never take to.' Her hand flew to her mouth again as she realised what she was saying.

'Don't worry, I'm not shocked. I am always deeply suspicious of people who say they *love* children. How can you? There are good and bad ones as there are adults. I wouldn't trust anyone who said they *loved* all people, would you?'

'No, I think not. But I do love to teach. I'm happiest when doing that. And, at the risk of sounding conceited, I'm a good teacher.'

Florrie studied Fanny for what seemed a long time as she sipped her champagne. 'You do realise I have been swamped with applicants?' She waved towards a small desk, the top of which was invisible beneath a sea of papers.

'I'm not surprised.'

'But you're the only one who had the initiative to come here in person. I thought I would be annoyed if someone did that but I find I'm not. And I can see that it was hard for you to do so. Now, as you've been honest with me I'll be honest with you. If, when you've heard what I have to say, you want to walk out of the house without a by-your-leave, I'll understand.'

'Yes.' Fanny sounded unsure.

'I am what is known as a kept woman. I am the mistress of a well-known married man.'

'I see,' said Fanny, in a wavering voice.

'Do you want to leave?'

'No.' This one word emerged as a whisper.

'I shall not remain in this position for ever. He will tire of me – he might at any time – and then I will need to find another protector.'

'Yes . . .' Barely audible.

'And then, undoubtedly, another and another. Until, eventually, my looks fade, my figure coarsens and then perhaps I end up where I began my career, at Paddington Station.'

'Really?'

'I was fortunate. I arrived from my home in Devon, seeking my fortune. And I did find it, in a way, but not how I expected. As soon as I alighted from the train, I was approached by a woman. I later learnt that she patrolled the stations looking for suitable young women to introduce to the London brothels.'

'Oh, no! I've heard such tales.'

'Some of the houses are good but most are bad and the girls last a short time before they are worn out, lose their freshness and are thrown out on to the streets. It's a cruel life but what's a girl to do?' Fanny found herself nodding in agreement on a subject about which she knew nothing. 'Anyway, this woman talked to me and I thought she was so kind, offering me a bed for the night and a meal, when a man came up, pushed her away and threatened to call the police. He turned out not only to be my rescuer but my first lover. A dear man.' She paused. 'Do you want me to continue?'

'Why shouldn't I?'

'Because you're a respectable young woman and many would not even walk on the same side of the pavement as me let alone sit here.'

'You knew no better and you had to live. And I would never stand in judgement for there . . .' She was about to say 'but for the grace of God' but it would have been a falsehood for she would rather die than succumb to a man so sinfully. Instead she smiled and hoped she looked friendly rather than disapproving because she wasn't really. How muddling it all was, she thought.

'Quite.' Florrie looked content with her answer. 'Anyhow, I hope not to retrace my footsteps. I am careful with my money, unlike some of my friends. I invest wisely. But nothing in life is certain and I could perhaps lose everything.'

'You could.'

'You are wondering what all this has to do with my idea for a school. Well, I have two daughters. They don't live here – it wouldn't be suitable. They stay in a cottage with an old friend of mine but I see them every day. They are the light of my life.'

'That's nice.'

'But I don't want them to end up like me. They are illegitimate and will always bear the stigma of this so I must give them something for their future. I decided they should be educated. They must learn so that they can find respectable employment in the world. They can gloss over their origins but no one can ignore them if they know things, can they?'

Fanny was touched, but if only it were that simple! 'It would certainly be a help to them.'

'Exactly. They could teach. They could work in shops. They would get better work in service if they could read and write, if they could converse. And then, if the worst comes to the worst and they have to follow in my footsteps, they need not go on the streets. They will know how to entertain men, amuse them. They could get themselves well set up.'

'That's possible.' A degree of doubt had crept into Fanny's voice.

'Originally I had thought to take on a governess and to share the cost with a friend of mine. But the news travelled and so many others came forward that we decided we would club together and we would find someone like you to teach our girls. There are eight in total and their ages run from five to thirteen. The school idea followed and we have found premises. We will pay you a salary of course, and you will also have the use of the school house while in our employ. So, what do you think?'

'You're offering me the position?'

'I don't see anyone else in here.'

'But what about your friends?'

'It was my idea, they left the decision to me. I like you. You're straight as a die, I reckon. And you haven't an ounce of censoriousness in you.'

'But the others?' Fanny waved at the letters of application on the desk.

'That can be your first task. Answer them for me, I hate letter-writing. You can say that the position is filled. That is, if you want it?'

'Oh, yes, please.'

'How very satisfactory. More champagne?'

11

Previously, when she had entered the house, Fanny knew she had done so dejectedly. Not today! Despite the rain, which was falling quite heavily, she tripped along the path with a light step and smiled broadly at Maud when she opened the door to her.

'Someone's happy.'

'Very, Maud. Thank you.' She handed the girl her

umbrella and, humming, ran up the stairs. She was in such high spirits that she forgot to tiptoe past Caroline's room, as she normally did. When she heard a man's voice she was not in the least put out. 'None of my business,' she said to herself.

In her little room she removed her dress and hung it from the picture rail. In her dressing-gown she began to sponge at the hem, which was in a sorry state with dirt from the sodden pavement. This would usually have bothered her and made her fret since she had only two dresses. Not today!

Once the task was completed she sat on her bed and began to plan. It was a good hour later when she decided to write to her brother and to apologise for being so short with him. Not that she thought she had been in the wrong, far from it, but he was her only living relation and she did not want to fall out with him.

In her letter she began to tell him of her new position. She stopped writing, her pen poised over the paper. He would die of shock if she wrote the truth so she would tell him half of it: '. . . *Some good news, dear brother. I have found employ. I am to teach at a small school, near here, called St Mary's.*' There was no need to tell him that Florrie and her friends had decided to call their school after Mary Magdalene, the prostitute whom Christ had forgiven.

What would her father have had to say about all this? She gazed out of the window at the relentless rain. And what did *she* think of it? A fortnight ago she would have been shocked at the idea that she might consort with such women. But this afternoon she had enjoyed her time with Florrie. She was an intelligent woman, honest, warm-hearted. Who was Fanny to judge her? And, come to think of it, how could society, when she was so open about herself?

Men were to blame for the lives led by women like Florrie. If they didn't pay them for their favours, set them up in these houses, use them, they would never fall by the wayside in the first place. How fortunate she was; she had her education, a choice. For these poor women there was no choice.

There was so much hypocrisy in the world. At Harcourt Barton she had heard the gossip about the grand ladies and the goings-on in the night. She'd even heard that Minnie Wickham had had a lover there the last time they had come. She had tried not to listen to such talk but it was hard not to. Such women were not condemned by the society in which they moved so why should Florrie and her friends be thought of differently? And given the style in which Florrie lived, it wouldn't surprise Fanny if her protector wasn't of the same circle in which the Foresters moved. Maybe it was even Frederick! But, then, it couldn't be, since she had said he was a married man. And that was strange too: people often alluded to Frederick's wife as if she were still alive yet said on the other hand how sad it was for Eliza to be motherless.

There was a tap at the door. 'Mrs Fraser wants to see you, sharpish.'

'Thank you, Maud.'

Ten minutes later, in her second-best dress, she entered the drawing room.

'Don't you ever knock?'

'I was taught that, in society, it was not necessary to tap on the drawing-room door.'

'I can't imagine what society you've been keeping but it's most certainly necessary here.'

'Then I apologise. I won't do it again.'

'No, you will not. I did not give you permission to have gentlemen callers.'

'I beg your pardon but I most certainly have not.' She felt quite pink with indignation.

'That's not what I was told.'

'Then you were told wrong. My brother visited me this afternoon and I had asked you, this morning, if you minded. You said you didn't.'

'That was when I thought you spoke the truth.'

'But I did. If anyone else tells you otherwise they lie. My brother came to say farewell to me before leaving for Italy, as I told you. It is monstrous that anyone could say otherwise. I have no wish to continue this conversation.' She began to leave the room.

'Stand still when I speak to you!'

Slowly, Fanny turned to face Caroline Fraser. 'I *beg* your pardon? How dare you speak to me in that manner? I'm not one of your servants.'

'I'll speak to you as I wish, for you are but one step up from them.'

'If you were a lady, Caroline, you would know that servants should be spoken to with respect and courtesy.'

'I don't need you to give me a lesson on how to behave . . .'

'But you do, Caroline. You most certainly do. However, to return to your accusation. I really cannot see what business it is of yours whom I entertain.'

'This is my house. I don't want you here any more. I don't want Augusta corrupted by *you*.'

'And what about your gentleman caller? Is that not corrupting?'

'How dare you?'

'Then how dare *you* speak to *me* as you have just done? But do not worry. I shall be leaving here tomorrow. I thank you for your hospitality to me at a difficult time. And I apologise if my presence has been irksome to you.' As she spoke she moved to the door. Upon opening it she found Maud, bent double, evidently listening at the keyhole. 'So, Maud, was it you who lied to Mrs Fraser? Was it you who told her my brother was not my brother?' Maud backed away, but Fanny followed. 'I demand an answer and I demand an apology from you, in front of your mistress.'

'And what is little Maud here to apologise about?' They swung round to see Charles who, unnoticed, had entered the hall.

'Charlie!' Caroline looked flummoxed. Maud looked scared.

'I forgot my cigar case,' he said, moving towards the drawing room.

'It's here. Silly you . . .' Caroline trilled. Maud made to go into the back part of the house.

'Maud,' Charles called, 'in here.' He shepherded all of the women into the drawing room. 'Now, if someone could tell me what the bother is about. Caroline?' She stood mute. 'Fanny?'

'I would rather not say, Charles.'

'But I would like to know. Has Maud been rude to you? If so, she will go.'

'Not particularly.'

'There's been a dreadful mistake, Charlie darling. Maud told me that Fanny had been entertaining a gentleman. Don't be cross with her, she was only doing what she thought was right,' Caroline said.

Charles stared at Fanny in disbelief. 'Is this true?'

'No, Sir Charles, it is not.' She was hurt that he might think it was and reverted to the formality of the past. 'The gentleman in question was my brother, though Mrs Fraser seems to find this difficult to believe. Mrs Fraser, I said I would be leaving in the morning. I correct that, I shall be leaving now. I will arrange to have my trunk collected.' With head high she walked quickly out of the room.

She collected a few things together in her carpet bag. The rest she scooped up and threw pell-mell into her trunk, which she closed and locked, slipping the key into her purse.

'Miss Chester, I'm sorry. I didn't mean . . .'

'So you should be, Maud. It might have been very difficult for me but, as it is, it's unimportant, I have somewhere else to go.'

'I only meant it as a joke.'

'My reputation is no joking matter.'

'I know, and I'm ever so sorry. Please, Miss Chester,

take me with you. I'll be getting my marching orders here, I reckon.'

Fanny sat back on her bed. 'Oh, Maud, you silly girl. You should think before you act. I'm sorry, you can't come with me. Where I'm going there's already a maid.'

Maud's shoulders slumped with dejection. 'Never mind. Something'll turn up, it usually does,' she said, with a false brightness. 'Lawks, I nearly forgot.' She went out of the room, then returned with a parcel. 'This came for you while you were out. I was ordered to show Mrs Fraser any mail or packages that came for you, especially anything from Devon. But, well, in the circumstances, she can whistle for it, can't she?' And she handed Fanny the bulky parcel.

Fanny spurned Charles's offer to drive her to her new home and marched purposefully down the road, ignoring his carriage, which kept pace with her. The parcel was weighing heavy but there was no way she was going to weaken. She was angry.

'At least tell me where you're going.'

'What will you do?'

'I feel responsible for you . . .'

She ignored him and moved on. With relief she saw the hotel she had noticed before on a walk and, without a backward glance, she ran up the steps. Charles did not follow her.

In the circumstances the room was far more than she could afford. She had so little money and she now regretted returning Frederick Forester's ninety pounds. 'But you were right to,' she said to herself, in the prettily furnished hotel room. Had she been thinking straight she would have gone to Florrie and asked her if she could move in tonight. But it was probably as well that she hadn't. What if her protector was with her? It would not be an ideal time for her to arrive with her drama. She would have an early supper here in her room, then go to bed and the new chapter of her life would begin in the morning.

She picked up the parcel from the chair where she had put it down. Should she open it now, or wait until she was settled?

Five minutes later, curiosity had got the better of her. She undid the string. She knew it was from Mrs King, and hoped there might be a note in it with news of Eliza.

She was sad about the girl. She had sent her three letters care of Charles, but had received no reply. No doubt Eliza had believed the lies told about her. Inside were the odd things she had left at Harcourt Barton and a short note from Mrs King. There was her hairbrushing set, some ribbons and a nightcap. A small china bowl decorated with roses, which, her brother had told her, had sat on her mother's dressing-table. A couple of books. Her water-colours and ... This copy of *Pride and Prejudice* wasn't hers. She opened it and Ruby's letter fell out. She read it, remembered where to find the scene Ruby referred to. How puzzling. Ruby was in London and yet ... She flicked though the pages and her face broke into a big smile. '*If I should roam* ... Clever Ruby.' She hugged the book to her.

She collected paper from her valise and wrote to Eliza, telling her her news and her address, then parcelled up the book. She would post it to Ruby in the morning on her way to see Florrie.

12

'Are you sure you'll be comfortable?' Florrie looked anxiously about the sitting room of Fanny's new accommodation. 'It's very small.'

'It's perfect.'

'A little shabby?'

'It'll suit me well.'

When Fanny had arrived on her doorstep this morning with a valise and an anxious expression Florrie had been so understanding. She was one of those women who, accustomed to dramas in her own life, was expert at dealing with those of others. Within the hour, they had arrived at the house that was to be Fanny's new home.

'We thought this would be ideal as the schoolroom.' Florrie opened a door to the side of the fireplace and they entered a large, light, airy room, of which one side was tall windows that overlooked the garden. Florrie plunged into the room, her skirts swishing across the floor, sending plumes of dust into the air which the shafts of sunlight picked up and played with. She spun round, her dress swirling about her. 'What do you think?'

'It will be wonderful.' Fanny looked about her with approval.

'I *knew* you would like it. The minute I saw it I could imagine the little ones sitting at their desks, their eager faces looking up at you.'

'I hope they *are* eager!'

'Oh, they will be. If they're not I shall smack them!' Florrie laughed and Fanny joined in: the last person capable of hitting a child had to be Florrie. 'See? A fine cupboard for the books.' She opened it with a flourish and it came away in her hand, thudding to the floor. 'Drat. Something else to be mended. And over here, for winter, we have this magnificent stove.' She bore down on it.

'Don't touch it!' Fanny shrieked, and they laughed.

'This is going to be *such* fun!'

'I do hope you're right.'

Florrie swept gracefully across the room and took Fanny's hand. 'Listen, my dear Fanny, the past is behind you. Forget it. This is a new beginning for you, a new life.'

'It's easy to say but so difficult to do. That I could be so wrongly accused – and twice. I can't forget it.'

'But you must. If I carried all the insults and false accusations that have been thrown at me, I'd be *bowed down* with misery. It's best to forget. *You* know you're innocent and you're the person who counts the most. Know that, and you can hold your head high.'

'You too. Your opinion is important to me.'

'Sweetheart!' Florrie planted a soft kiss on her cheek. 'Then all is solved for I would stake my life on your innocence.'

'Florrie . . .'

'No, don't cry. It never helps, it only makes one feel dreadful. And if you start I'll follow and I can't afford to weep – wrinkles, you understand.'

'Oh, Florrie!' Fanny smiled, blew her nose and felt immeasurably better. 'What was this place?' she asked, when normality returned.

'It was an artist's studio, hence the abundance of light. It needs a lick of paint, but I've arranged that. We shall need desks and a big one for you. And a blackboard, and . . . what else?'

'Slates. A bookcase. A globe of the world – that would not be essential, of course, more of a luxury . . . I can't believe this is real and not a dream. My own school!' She opened a door but shut it quickly. Behind it was a very dirty and noxious earth closet, in a privy, attached to the side of the house.

'Well, yes, that has to be renewed, the bottom of the garden would be more suitable, I think. We should make a list. And out here . . .' Florrie opened a half-glazed door which led to a small yard and an overgrown garden. '. . . I thought perhaps a swing – to amuse.'

'Of course. Children need fresh air.'

'It's such a relief to hear you say that. So many people think it dangerous to health. I'm a country girl and I need it too.'

They heard a banging and a hallooing. 'That will be

Sarah, Molly and Chantal – she likes to pretend she's French, but she isn't, says it's good for business. Stupid, I call it. Darlings . . .' Florrie trilled, as the trio entered the house and moved into what was to be Fanny's living area.

With the four of them, in their elaborate dresses, and Fanny, the sitting room was overflowing. She liked two of the other women immediately, and they were soon chatting together. Only Sarah did not join in.

''Ow many children do you sink you will be able to teach?' Chantal asked her, in an excruciating French accent.

'Chantal, it's us dear, you can drop the accent now,' Florrie said kindly.

'So, 'ow many pupils do you fink yer goin' to manage?' she said in Cockney so strong that Fanny found it almost as impenetrable as the 'French'.

'Didn't you say eight, Florrie?'

'I did, but I think Chantal might be thinking of a ninth.'

'Yes, I don't like the mother but the kid can't 'elp 'avin' 'er, can she?'

'Nine? Why not? The more the merrier,' Fanny said.

'And it evens out the expenses more,' Sarah added.

'You know, Miss Chester, we're very grateful to you. It's not everyone would want to be involved with the likes of us,' Molly said quietly.

'Rubbish!' Sarah said harshly. 'Our money's as good as the next person's, is it not, Miss Chester?'

Why was there always one person who threatened to spoil things? 'What you do for a living is up to you. I'm here to teach your children, the rest is irrelevant,' Fanny said.

'See? What did I tell you all?' Florrie looked smug.

'And please, call me Fanny, let's all be friends.'

'I think I'd prefer to call you by your surname, as I expect you to call me Mrs Driver. After all, we are paying you.'

'As you wish.' Fanny coloured at the snub.

'You're a stuck-up cow, Sarah. Don't worry, Fanny. Her protector's an aristocrat, she thinks it makes her a cut above the rest of us.' Florrie laughed.

'It's nothing of the sort. I just think it's more professional. We should begin as we mean to go on.'

'When will you open for the children?' Molly enquired.

'I'm not sure. I have little of my own to unpack. When will the schoolroom be complete.'

'I reckon on a fortnight,' Florrie replied.

'And will Miss Chester be paying rent until that time?' Sarah asked.

'No, she won't.' Florrie, taller by a good six inches and far more imposing than the petite Sarah, looked at the other woman in such a way that her aggression fizzled out like a damp squib.

When they left Fanny felt quite exhausted. She was not used to so much noise and so many people at the same time – or to so much inconsequential chatter. Not that she hadn't enjoyed their company – although Sarah, she felt, was not as wholehearted about this venture as the others were.

Certainly they had been interested in her plans – how she was to proceed, what she hoped for the children to achieve. They were all willing to help but she hoped, for the sake of the children, their curriculum *and* herself, that their enthusiasm would fade a little once the school was open. Otherwise the ensuing interruptions, and disruption, might overwhelm her.

Meanwhile, she had to settle in. Her quarters were in a dear little cottage attached to the studio, and very old. Water had to be drawn from a well in the garden and there was nowhere to wash. She eyed the grate with suspicion – it didn't look as if it had been used in many a year. What would happen when winter came? Would a fire be possible or would it smoke horribly? The sitting room was furnished with a table, two chairs and a sofa, all in need of a good brush and polish. There was also a small bookcase, a corner cabinet and a broken mirror.

Upstairs her bedroom contained a bed with a lumpy mattress, a wardrobe that threatened to topple over on her when she opened the door, and a bedside table. The second bedroom was bare.

The kitchen had a small range, a sink with a bowl, and a storage cupboard that stank. Behind that was the room for the maid, Polly, whom she was yet to meet. It was in an even worse state than her own.

'It's a roof over your head. You're lucky,' she told herself, in a no-nonsense way. She removed her white cuffs, rolled up her sleeves and, half an hour later, smudged with soot, she had a fire in the range, and the kettle on. In the yard she found a broom and set to.

Eliza's dismissal of Mrs Satterly had made everyone at Harcourt Barton sit up and take notice of her. The household was in a state of shock. She had been seen as a child, not as a young woman capable of hiring and dismissing servants. It was a cataclysmic occurrence, for mostly they had felt safe when the rest of the family were away.

On the day of the dismissal, Mrs King had pleaded Mrs Satterly's case.

'She shouldn't have beaten Maggie in that way,' Eliza retorted. 'I would not stand by and see an animal thus treated, let alone the kitchen-maid.'

'She realises that now, Miss Eliza, and is sorry. She doesn't know what made her behave in such a manner.'

'Alcohol, presumably.'

'Oh, Miss Eliza!' As she spoke Mrs King made a bobbing motion as if she were about to curtsy – or trying to ingratiate herself. It was a new experience for Eliza, which she did not enjoy. The housekeeper didn't normally behave in this way.

'Then if she apologises to Maggie she may stay. I would appreciate it if you would tell her so.'

Mrs King looked unsure. 'Yes,' she said, 'I will,' but her words lacked conviction.

'And, Mrs King, one other thing before you go. What did Mrs Satterly mean that I was to "ask my mother"?'

'I've no idea, Miss Eliza.'

'It was most unkind.'

'That it was.'

'Is she mad?'

'She might be. She *is* a cook, after all.'

At the first sign that the interview was over Mrs King rustled off, in her black bombazine, her chatelaine clanking against her thigh. Five minutes later she returned to Eliza's turret room. 'Well, that's done, so maybe we can return to normality.'

'I should like to see Maggie, if you would be so kind, Mrs King.'

'She's working.'

'Then she should stop and come to see me.'

'So, Maggie, I hear that Mrs Satterly has apologised to you. Is that so?' Eliza asked, as Maggie entered her room.

'No, Miss Eliza, she didn't.' Maggie bobbed a curtsy.

'Very well.'

And then it was Mrs Satterly's turn. She arrived looking belligerent, not in the least shamefaced as Mrs King had said she was. 'I have never apologised to a scullery-maid in my life and I have no intention of starting now. I won't hit her again, I'm prepared to vow, but that's as far as I'm prepared to go.'

'Then I'm sorry, Mrs Satterly, we have reached an impasse. Apologise or go.' Eliza looked at her calmly.

'Then I go. But I'm telling your father and your grandmother about this.'

'As you wish.' Eliza turned back to her book, but looked up again before the cook could leave. 'There's just one other matter. What did you mean when you referred to my mother?'

'I've no recollection.' The woman looked shifty.

'It was not very kind of you.'

But Mrs Satterly did not reply. Instead she turned sharply on her high-buttoned boots and stamped out of the room. Eliza could hear her slamming doors as she progressed through the house in a fine temper.

Unknown to Eliza, Mrs King had notified Frederick Forester of the trouble with his cook, by telegraph. The household waited keenly for his response, none more so than Mrs Satterly who had not left but, in anticipation of her immediate reinstatement, was hidden away in her room. When it came, it said, 'Am in full agreement with my daughter stop Forester stop'.

Some below stairs rejoiced but others muttered about the loss of an excellent cook. Yet they need not have worried: Maggie had been watching Mrs Satterly and listening to her and, if anything, her food was even better.

Everyone had learnt a lesson and from then on Eliza was treated with more respect and a touch of wariness, as if she were already an adult and could affect their lives at a whim. Eliza regretted that her old easiness with the servants had gone but now she had power. Dismissing Mrs Satterly and righting a wrong had given her confidence in herself and she felt Miss Chester would have been proud of her.

'Ruby, you know that several weeks ago your mother invited me to visit? Well, I would like to go tomorrow, if that can be arranged.'

'I'll ask Bob, the boots, to nip across and ask,' Ruby replied, wishing Eliza had given her more warning. She knew her mother would want to clean the house from top to bottom with such an important visitor due.

Eliza was entranced by the Barnard farm and the

house, and said so. 'Such a warm and welcoming kitchen, Mrs Barnard.'

'I don't know what got into Ruby, Miss Eliza. You should be in the parlour by rights.'

'But this is perfect. Please, let me stay here.'

'You'll be wanting tea?'

'How kind of you.' She sat at the table and watched as Grace, Ruby, Ada and Ivy scurried back and forth from the parlour with the china, cutlery, napkins and cakes that had already been set out there. Now everything was put on the kitchen table.

'Cake, Miss Eliza?'

'No, thank you.'

'Scones? Cream, jam?'

'I couldn't possibly. I don't wish to appear rude but I have not long had my luncheon.'

Ruby saw the disappointment on her mother's face: she had been baking all day for this.

'Tea?'

'No milk or sugar, thank you.'

At least she was drinking that, thought Ruby. They never normally had tea, these days: it was a luxury they could do without.

'It's so nice here, Mrs Barnard. I can't tell you how happy I am that you're not standing on ceremony for me. I prefer things to be simple.'

Ruby didn't dare look at her mother. The table was covered with her finest tablecloth of drawn threadwork, made by her own mother. The cups and plates were her only set of bone china, which was only ever used on great occasions such as christenings and funerals – as yet her mother hadn't had any weddings to cater for. The room had been burnished and there were even flowers.

Eliza found Mrs Barnard easy to talk to. As she sat at the table, watching her, listening to her, she felt she had met a woman who, in the future, if she needed advice, she might turn to. She wondered if Mrs Barnard would be able to take Merry and Miss Chester's place in her life. And then, to her surprise, she found herself wondering if, after all, she was in need of such a person any more. Over the last few days she had felt quite different and far more in control of her emotions.

That notion did not last long. The door opened and in strode Jerome Barnard. Tall, strong, tanned, handsome. And Eliza found her emotions scattering this way and that.

Chapter Three
1872–4

I

Fanny was in her element. It was a joy to teach a class such as this and she wondered why she hadn't tried before to become a schoolmistress rather than a governess, concentrating on just one or two pupils. This work was far more satisfying: her students wanted to learn – their mothers had impressed on them how important to their futures education would be. All of them, even the youngest, Amy, who was only five, appeared each morning, their faces alert with interest.

She worked hard. With such a diversity of ages to teach it was essential she was well prepared in the mornings so that each group had work to do while she concentrated on another. Her evenings were spent readying herself for the next day's classes.

The big advantage of being busy was that she had little time to think of Charles. Also, she realised, she no longer dreamt of him at night. Was it the work, tiredness, or had sense finally prevailed? She was pleased, for she had been bothered by the unsuitability of her caring for a married man, and one who, she now knew, kept a mistress.

She had improved her shabby rooms beyond measure. She and her maid, Polly, had spent a whole week scouring the house. Polly, thin, with a squint but willing, had been astonished when Fanny had donned an apron to help her. 'If we both set to it will be done faster,' she explained.

Once the dust and filth were removed, she had spent some of her precious savings on fabric for curtains, which brightened her rooms enormously. Polly's brother, an odd-job man who had been employed by Florrie to build what was needed in the schoolroom, had also made her a small bookcase and a cupboard. He whitewashed the walls for her, too, and scrubbed the yard. At a local auction she had bought a small desk and chair and could not resist a pair of colourful vases which had taken her fancy. She had found the auction a heady experience and decided not to go again: it was easy to lose one's head and bid for pretty things one could ill afford.

In the evenings she would sit in her sitting room and marvel at how her life had changed. After years of living with other people's furniture, she now had her own, and even her wardrobe had increased. Florrie had noted that she only had two dresses and one Saturday she and her maid, Ann, appeared with a large trunk packed with clothes she no longer wore. 'I hope you aren't insulted to be offered cast-offs.'

'Never. Such pretty colours.' Fanny peered into the trunk with a degree of trepidation, for her style was not Florrie's and she could not imagine herself dressing in some of these revealing outfits.

'Of course, they need altering. You won't want to look like me, now, will you?' Florrie chuckled. 'But I thought a modesty tuck here, a bit of sewing up there and you'll be right as rain,' she said.

'It's so kind of you.'

'Not at all. Ann here's in a bit of a sulk, aren't you?'

'Of course not, Mrs Paddington.'

'Yes, you are. She usually has my cast-offs and hawks them, don't you? But I said, "Not this time. Miss Chester's need is greater."'

'I'm sorry, Ann. If any don't fit I'll let you have them.' Which, Fanny decided, would be a good way to get rid of any that were irredeemably unsuitable.

Florrie picked up a primrose satin dress and held it up against Fanny. 'There! You see what a spot of colour does for you? Transforms you. You're a pretty woman and you should make more of yourself, stop wearing those mouse colours. Why do you think God went to all that trouble producing lovely shades like this to have people like you dress as if they were trying to disappear?'

'Mistresses don't like their staff to look too nice.'

'You never said a truer word. I'd kill Ann if she dared look too attractive.' She shrieked with laughter. 'But, still, I'm chattering on. To business. You've got another pupil, if you don't mind. It's the one Chantal mentioned. The mother's finally made up her mind and she starts on Monday.'

'Doesn't her mother want to meet me first?'

'Says she hasn't got time. In any case, she claims it's her sister but I take that with a pinch of salt, I must say. Name's Fraser. Not my cup of tea.'

'I know her.' Fanny's heart sank.

'And, judging by your reaction, this is not a happy decision.' Florrie grinned apologetically.

'Caroline Fraser didn't like me at all – I don't know what I did wrong. But I'm amazed she wants to send Augusta here. Or does she know I'm the teacher?'

'She never asked. Perhaps we should say we can't take Augusta.'

'That wouldn't be fair. She's a nice child. It's not her fault who her mother is.'

'It might be fairer to you if we see how she behaves. If she's difficult then we shall ask Mrs Fraser to remove her child.'

Fanny put all thoughts of Caroline out of her head and spent a happy weekend altering a couple of the dresses with Polly's help. She had listened to Florrie about the yellow one and altered that first. She had no full-length mirror to see herself in but she sensed it suited her, and when Polly had squealed in pleasure at the sight of her in it, there was no doubting it. She had also worked on a pale green shantung silk, whose low-cut neck she filled with some lace she had in her baggage. And a fawn one too, which was more her colour of choice, but she would wear the others since she had promised Florrie that she would.

Everything was perfect, except for one thing: Eliza had not replied to her letter. She wondered if she had even received it. Had Ruby's strategy failed in some way? She debated with herself whether to write again then worried that this might make life difficult for Eliza if the first letter had been intercepted. Perhaps it might be better for her if they had no contact, if she backed away, hard as it would be. Then Eliza would be able to forget her and forge on with her future.

On the Monday, despite Florrie's generosity, she put on her old grey serviceable dress. There was much dust and chalk in the schoolroom and she didn't want to ruin her new finery.

'Hello, Augusta. This is a pleasant surprise.'

'Miss Chester!' The child's face lit up in a wide smile.

'You didn't know I was going to be your teacher?'

'No. Caroline just told me that now Maud has gone she needs me out of the way. She said she hadn't time to look after me. And she said school seemed a good idea.' Augusta said all of this without rancour.

'Maud's gone?'

'Yes, the same day as you. She cried, and I cried. It was awful, Miss Chester. She begged Caroline to let her stay. She got on her knees, but it was no good. She left.'

'Poor Maud. Do you know where she's gone?'

'Sir Charles gave her the fare to go back to Devon where she came from. "Good riddance to bad rubbish," Caroline said. But I don't feel like that about her. She told me she didn't mean to be bad, that it had just sort of slipped out . . .'

'Did she tell you what she'd done?'

'No, she said it was best not talked about.'

'I hope she has gone to Devon,' Fanny said anxiously.

Anything might happen to the girl if she stayed in London. Even though Maud had caused her problems she had not held it against her. The girl spoke without thinking, would do and say anything for a laugh. She wasn't malicious – nosy, yes, and thoughtless, but she was young. In any case, if it hadn't been for Maud she wouldn't be here. Maybe she would make some enquiries when she next wrote to Mrs King. 'Now, come and let me introduce you to your classmates . . .'

Like the other children, Augusta settled well, and Fanny was happy to see that the strange formality she had noticed when she first met the child had disappeared. Then one morning Augusta arrived at school with red-rimmed eyes and her old sad expression.

'Augusta, why have you been crying? What's happened?' But her sympathy only made Augusta cry again so Fanny had to wait until she stopped.

'I told Caroline that you were my teacher and she was angry,' she told her. 'She ranted and raged and said if I told anyone, especially Uncle Charles, that you were she'd make me leave. And, Miss Chester, I don't want to. I like it here, I love you . . . Why was she so cross?' And the tears threatened again.

'Good gracious, Augusta, we'll have to find a boat if you continue or we'll drown.' This made the little girl giggle. 'That's better. I'm sorry, Augusta, but I don't know why she should react in such a manner. But it's quite simple, if you don't tell then I won't, and no one need know and you can stay here for ever.' She smiled expansively, but she was worried: Caroline was vindictive enough, she was certain, either to make her own life difficult or to remove the child.

For the rest of the day she worried. She was not unduly surprised when, shortly before the school closed, the door opened and Caroline swept in. Her heart leapt and from the corner of her eye she saw poor Augusta's hand fly to her mouth to stifle a cry.

'I want to talk to you,' Caroline announced, with no preamble.

'You had better come into my sitting room. Helen, keep an eye on the little ones for me,' she said to Florrie's elder daughter, a sensible girl. She led the way into her immaculately tidy room.

Caroline looked about her disdainfully.

'It suits me,' Fanny said quietly.

'I don't know what you mean.'

'You were looking at my little room and not seeing it as I do.'

Caroline took a handkerchief from her bag, wiped it across a chair, then sat down. Fanny felt anger boil to the surface, but repressed it.

'I know all there is to know about you now.'

'How interesting.' Fanny took a seat opposite her adversary. 'And what have you learned? Do tell.'

'I know why you were dismissed as a governess – you seduced your employer, a vulnerable grieving widower, but you were after his money and his mother dismissed you. And then you threw yourself at Sir Charles, hoping he would come to your rescue and keep you.'

'Then you have been misinformed. I did neither.'

'Don't lie to me.' Caroline, angry and spiteful, was no longer the pretty creature Fanny had thought her. These emotions aged her and made her almost ugly.

'I'm not in the habit of doing so. Why should I begin now?' Fanny spoke calmly but she was seething inside.

'If so, then you are accusing Sir Charles of lying.'

'Sadly that must be the case, *if* he's your informant – which I doubt.' Fanny could not bring herself to believe that he had slandered her in such a way. She had the satisfaction of seeing that at her answer Caroline wavered slightly, as if it were not what she had wanted or hoped to hear.

'I'm here to tell you that you are to leave Charles alone.'

'I've been here a month and I haven't seen him once, so evidently I already am.'

Caroline looked puzzled and paused as if working out what Fanny meant. 'Well, if you contact him, if he knows Augusta is here, I shall remove her from your clutches and I will ruin you into the bargain. Do you understand?'

Fanny's inclination was to throw the woman out and tell her to do her worst, but how could she, with Augusta so desperate to learn and so upset at the prospect that she might not be allowed to? 'Every word,' she said instead, calmly. 'I shan't say a word to a living soul that your daughter is my pupil, if you promise to do the same.'

She realised, as she showed Caroline out, that the woman had not registered that she had referred to Augusta as her daughter. As she finished the lessons for the day, she found herself wondering who the child's father was. She hoped it was Charles – he had no children with his wife, and was good with them. And if she could not see him, she had the next best thing: the privilege of teaching his daughter. That was a comforting thought.

2

In the evening, when Fanny had prepared the lessons for the following day, it had become her habit to change into one of the fine gowns Florrie had given her. Then she read for half an hour before Polly served her dinner. It was always a simple meal, she did not have the money for anything lavish, and anyway she preferred simple food. So she would have soup and a dessert, or fish and a dessert, or occasionally a chop with some vegetables. Polly fretted over this since she enjoyed the cooking more than the housework. After her frugal meal, Fanny would return to her book or sometimes sew. She was never lonely: her reading saw to that. And she became aware that, after years of living in other people's houses and being subjected to their routines and regimes, it was a joy to be her own mistress. If she didn't want to do something, she didn't. If she didn't want to eat, she didn't. And she went to bed when she wanted to, not because it was time for her charge to go.

The more she saw of Florrie and her friends, the more she came to respect them. Theirs was not an easy life, even if the trappings implied that it was. One day Florrie had appeared with a black eye.

'How did that happen?' Fanny was fussing about her, insisting on cold compresses. 'I've heard a crushed rotten apple is a good treatment.' She knelt down beside the chair.

'Steak's better. I should know, I'm the expert.'

'I could send Polly for some.'

'I was only trying to get you to stop fluttering about me. I've already slapped a good two pounds on it.'

'Did you walk into a door?'

'Hell no, it was his nibs. He sometimes likes to knock me about a bit when the drink or the fancy takes him.'

Fanny sat back on her haunches shocked. 'How *dare* he?'

'It's his choice. I'm his, he does what he wants with me.' She shrugged her shoulders.

'It's barbaric.'

'He doesn't do it often. Only when he's had a difficult day.'

'He shouldn't do it at all.'

'You tell him that! He'd lambast you too.' Florrie laughed. 'At least I get paid for it. Think of all those poor wives whose husbands beat them. What do they get out of it? Nothing, and there's nothing they can do about it. I can walk away if I want to. And my man always pays me generously for the privilege. But what happens to them? Their bastards keep their money. So who's better off? I feel sorry for the poor cows.'

'Is that why the girls don't live with you?'

'Partly, but he wouldn't like them there. And I don't want them too aware of what I do for a living – I want them to be proud of me, not ashamed. They'll know in time, and I'd like to keep them innocent for a little bit longer. Still, I didn't come here to talk about my problems and what monsters men can be. I want to know how the school's doing.'

At the mention of her pride and joy, Fanny was easily distracted and chatted away happily about the curriculum, who was progressing, which child needed extra help, the plans she had.

'Some of us were wondering if it might not be a good idea to move the school to the country?' Florrie looked quizzically at Fanny.

'Oh.' Fanny was dejected. She'd imagined herself living and teaching here for ever. It had been foolish of her for she, better than most, should know how insecure any tenure was.

'Only, you see, I'm not alone in wanting to protect my girls from knowing the truth about me. And, of course, I'm not the only one who gets beaten up. Away in the country, they need never know. And they'd have all that fresh air. It would be good for them.'

'I see that. You mean a boarding-school?'

'Exactly. Of course, we'd have to find a property large enough. And there's nothing to stop us expanding. We'd make a proper business of it, and I think, if we started a partnership, it might be a good investment.' Florrie was getting carried away with excitement as the plans evolved and developed. 'I fancy somewhere in Devon, where I come from and where I hope to retire to one day – that is, if I last at this game and don't get bumped off.'

'Florrie, don't say such things.'

'It happens. Only last week a woman on Mulberry Avenue—' She made a chopping motion at her throat.

'Devon is a lovely county.' Fanny preferred to change the subject.

'The best. And London can be such an evil place, especially for young girls.'

'Yes.'

'So you like the idea?'

'For the children, yes. For myself, no. I love teaching them.'

'But you still would, wouldn't you?' Florrie leaned forward anxiously.

'I wasn't sure you were including me in the plan.'

'Why on earth not? You're what makes it a good idea. We trust you. We know you'd fight through thick and thin for our children. We wouldn't countenance it with someone else.'

Later when Fanny was alone, she began to think about Devon, the prospect of going back there and the chance of seeing Eliza. She *would* write again, and again and again, until she knew that Eliza had read what she had to say, that she understood others had lied.

Although initially excited by the thought of this new venture, the more she thought about it the more scared Fanny became. How could she possibly run such a large organisation? She would have responsibility for the teaching, housekeeping, administration and the welfare of the children. Was she up to it? Already she spent many a long hour working into the night, making the books balance for this small school, so afraid was she of losing a penny and having someone – Caroline or Sarah – accuse her of stealing. She'd have more staff, of course, and it would be pleasant to have other teachers to talk to and consult. While she was happy here, she had to admit that now everything was settled she longed sometimes for conversation and to exchange ideas with other adults.

Other teachers . . . It was a pity how adamant Peter was about these ladies of the night. He would never countenance teaching their offspring. It would have been nice for them to be together under one roof. Or perhaps they had been too long apart – certainly they held different views.

For the time being, though, she was in this pleasant suburb and she would stop worrying about something that might never happen. She began to pack away her books.

There was a tap at the front door. So late? She looked at the clock on the mantelpiece – a gift from Florrie. It was past nine. She had already sent Polly to bed so, gingerly, she picked up the oil lamp and ventured to the door.

'Who is it?' she said, before she opened it.

'Me.'

'And who, pray, is that?' But her mind was singing for she had recognised the voice.

'Have you forgotten me so soon?'

She was smiling as she opened the door to see Charles Wickham standing there, swaying ever so slightly on his feet, a wide, cheeky grin on his face.

'How did you know where to find me?'

He tapped the side of his nose with his forefinger. 'Spies.'

'It's late.'

'It's never too late.'

'You put me in a difficult position.' Her instinct was to open the door wide and usher him in, but she controlled it. 'It's not right you should call on me, a woman living alone, at any time let alone so late,' she said instead.

'I thought you'd be pleased to see me.'

'I am, but you know the conventions.' *Oh, I am, I am.*

'Bah! Conventions!' He waved his hand – and almost toppled over.

'Charles, take care! You visit me, unchaperoned, and I am compromised.' She tried to sound severe but it was difficult.

'Who's to know? Who can see us?' He peered into the darkness of the chilly night.

'Oh dear.' She wavered. 'Well, I suppose you had better come in before someone sees you in this state.'

'What state?'

'Slightly intoxicated.'

'Only slightly, though.'

In the small front passage he brushed against her, and she felt the old jolt of excitement.

'You shouldn't be here,' she said, once they were in her sitting room.

'I know, but isn't it nice that I am?' From under his arm he produced a bottle of port. 'Knowing what an abstemious woman you are I thought I should bring my own. I do hope you're not offended.'

She laughed. 'You're right. You would have died of thirst here, if you hadn't.' She went to the cupboard and fetched a glass for him.

'Won't you join me?'

'Just a very small one then,' and she brought another glass.

The drinks poured they sat opposite each other, he on the small sofa, she on a hard chair. 'You'd be more comfortable here.' He patted the seat beside him.

'Thank you, but I'm happy here.'

Now, by the light of two lamps, she could see that he was far more drunk than she had first thought. He was having difficulty in putting the glass to his mouth. She hid a smile.

'How did you find me?' she asked. He shouldn't be here! What if Caroline finds out?

'Augusta told me.'

'I thought she had been told not to . . . by Caroline.'

'She didn't tell me directly, but she never stops talking

about her new school and how happy she is. I knew it must have something to do with you.'

'Why? I could have been back in Devon.'

'I sensed your nearness.'

'Charles, don't be silly.' She hid another smile but this time one of pleasure at his words, even if they couldn't be true.

'But I did. I would sit under the tree, our tree. I could feel you near me, smell you almost. You were in the air, in the breeze . . .'

'How you exaggerate!' She laughed with delight.

'No, it's the truth.' In one smooth movement he slid off the sofa and on to his knees, so that he was in front of her and holding her hand. It had happened so quickly that Fanny was taken unawares. 'I have been so miserable since you left. My life has not been worth living. Come back, my darling. I need you. I know now that I love you.' She shrank back on the chair. Words that she had imagined in her day-dreamings, words that she had never believed she would hear, were frightening her.

'Charles, please!'

'You knew, Fanny, how I felt about you? Tell me you did.'

'But, Charles, I didn't. I would not have presumed.'

'I felt you loved me.'

'No.'

'Don't lie to me. You loved me. At Harcourt Barton, I knew. It was in your eyes, in the way you moved, in the very scent of you . . .' He lunged towards her. His hands seemed to be everywhere.

'Charles! Desist!'

'Why? I want you, you want me. Look how you're dressed, as if you were waiting for me!' He grabbed at her breasts, tearing at the lace she had sewn in to protect her modesty.

'Sir Charles!' she shouted, and with one mighty push sent him sprawling on to his back on the rug. 'How dare you?' She stood over him, flustered, enraged, hurt, but also . . . wildly excited.

He scrambled to his feet. She stepped back warily, looking about her for something, anything, that she might use in her defence. But Charles threw back his head and roared with laughter. 'What a fool I've made of myself! What an idiot I am!' Still he laughed and she joined in, realising that the drink had made him behave in that way.

'I'll make you some tea.'

In the kitchen, while she waited for the kettle to boil, she wrapped her arms round herself. If only he had meant what he said. She was not aware of him entering the kitchen until she felt his arms about her. 'I meant every word I said, Fanny.'

She turned to him. There were tears in her eyes as she looked up at his handsome face. 'But it can never be, Charles. You have a wife, I could never countenance—'

'I have no wife. Not a true wife. She has a lover.'

'Surely not!'

'He has been her lover for three years. She loves him, not me.' He said this with such bitterness that her heart went out to him.

'How could she?' she said, tenderly.

'He was my dear friend, Hedworth, and my wife knew him well too. I see now how easy I made it for them . . .'

'Poor Charles. How dreadful for you.'

'So tell me why I shouldn't try to find happiness too?'

'But it would be wrong. You made your vows.' She could have wailed with misery.

'But I don't believe in God so they are worthless.'

'Then you should never have spoken them.' She stepped away from him. 'It can never be. And, in any case, you have Caroline, don't you?' He hung his head. 'Don't you?' she repeated.

'I do not feel any love for her. She comforts me in my loneliness, that is all.'

'Then that is reprehensible of her too. Now, Charles, I think it would be better if you left.' She led the way purposefully out of the kitchen.

'But, Fanny . . .'

'There is nothing more to be said. There is nothing that we can do.'

'But there is,' he muttered, as he walked through the door.

Fanny watched him climb on to his horse with such a heavy heart.

3

The walk to the Barnards' at Barton Farm was pleasant. First Eliza went through the knot garden, then down the steps lined with statuary to the lake, her presence scattering the ducks but not the swans, who ignored her. She skirted the bank, beyond which was the chapel, and began the climb to the wide rhododendron walk – so lovely in the spring. Then she cut across the beechwood, also known as the bluebell wood, down a steep path to the river. She forded the water, lifting her skirts clear and jumping from one large stepping-stone to the next, all worn smooth through hundreds of years of use. With the oak tree this was one of her favourite places on the estate. She loved to come here in summer and sit in the cool of the trees, watching the sparkling water, delighting in the brown trout skimming through its depths. Next came the arboretum her father was creating. Here, she liked to imagine what it would be like in a hundred years when the saplings would be in their prime. By now she was on the road that led past the estate cottages, on which were carved her family's arms – or rather her grandmother's, since they had none of their own – and the date they had been built, 1835. She went down a lane and there was Barton Farm.

It was not a large farmhouse but it was pretty, a traditional Devon long-house where animals were kept at one end and the family lived at the other. The yard was cobbled and Mrs Barnard had filled old barrels with geraniums that glowed against the whitewashed house. On the far side were the stables from which, at the sound of her light footstep, inquisitive horses' heads appeared. She paused to greet them, then negotiated her way past the chickens, who scampered this way and that, nearly tripping her. Over the door that led into the kitchen a rambler rose was still flowering in a last burst before winter came. There was a front door, but 'It's only used for weddings and funerals. Or when quality like you come and visit. Shall we go in that way?' Ruby had explained on Eliza's first visit, and she had laughingly refused: she preferred the door everyone else used.

Now she knocked on it. 'It's only me,' she called.

'Miss Eliza! Come in!' As she entered Grace Barnard was removing her apron, brushing back her hair, collecting some dirty plates and shooing out the dog. It was amazing how she did so many tasks all at the same time. Ruby's mother was a marvel, always dashing about.

'I hope you don't mind me appearing with no warning but I was on my way . . .' She trailed off. Jerome was sitting at the table. Eliza was glad that the kitchen was so dark for no one could see her blush.

'Miss,' he said, standing up, his chair making such a scraping racket on the kitchen floor that they all laughed.

'Mr Barnard.' She bowed her head in greeting, and resisted the urge to stare at him. Instead she turned shyly to speak to his mother. 'I wonder if you've read this book – *A Tale of Two Cities*. Of course it's been published several years now, but I so enjoyed it and I hoped you would like it too.' She knew she was babbling but whichever way she looked she was conscious of Jerome. He seemed to fill the room and even though she spoke to his mother it was as if he were the only person there.

'No, I haven't. Of course I've heard about it. How very kind of you to bring it.'

'No Ruby?' Jerome looked behind her.

'She didn't want to come. But I wanted you to have the book. I hope you don't mind, Mrs Barnard?'

'Of course not, miss.'

'Didn't want to come or couldn't?'

'I beg your pardon?' She looked at Jerome, puzzled.

'Too much work is more likely to be the reason.'

'She had some duties to attend to, yes.'

'I'm sure she did.' He looked away but glanced back at her again, almost as shyly as she.

'Jerome!' his mother said, warningly.

'It was only the truth, Mother. Nothing wrong with that, is there?'

'I'm sure that Miss Eliza is fully aware of how hard Ruby works.'

'Oh, I am . . .' she said.

'Unlikely . . .' Jerome said simultaneously. She laughed nervously, he didn't.

'But I am, Mr Barnard. Why, I don't know how I'd manage without Ruby.'

'So you like the works of Mr Dickens. Wasn't it sad him dying with work unfinished?' Grace manoeuvred the conversation on to safer ground.

Jerome had sat down again. At first he looked steadfastly at his hands, occasionally glancing at her as she and Grace continued to talk. But then, abruptly, he picked up a pamphlet that was lying on the table and began to read. How rude, thought Eliza.

Grace and she chatted about the books they liked and Eliza, to her shame, was astonished at how well read the older woman was. Why, she'd read far more than Eliza had, and *she* read all the time.

The door opened. 'Miss Eliza!' It was Ivy who

bobbed to her. Eliza couldn't be sure but she thought Jerome had laughed, though at what she could not imagine.

'Ivy, how lovely to see you, and how's your poor ankle?'

'It'll never be the same again, miss,' she said, putting a package on the table for Mrs Barnard.

'Poor you, and you've been all the way to the lodge?'

'It's good for me to walk else my ankle stiffens and then it hurts worse.'

'I am sorry. So you won't be coming back to us? That's sad.'

'No, miss.'

'Your family wouldn't want her back, couldn't get enough work out of her, that's why. Where's the justice in that when it wasn't her fault?'

'Jerome, stop it!' his mother ordered.

'I'm sorry, I don't understand that either. You must think me very stupid today.' Eliza smiled somewhat crookedly. The atmosphere had become unpleasant.

'Didn't you know? You mean no one told you?'

'No.'

'They wouldn't be bothering Miss Eliza about such matters, Jerome.'

Ivy looked from one to the other, a smirk on her face.

'Well, then, perhaps someone should tell you. She fell on a dangerous staircase that the maids had asked to be repaired for months and it wasn't. Now that she limps she can't get work.'

'But she works here.'

'Only because my mother has a kind heart.'

'Is this so, Mrs Barnard?' Eliza swivelled in the chair to face Grace, who was busying herself folding linen, then refolding it, looking distressed.

'In a way, yes, but it's no hardship to me.'

'It's another mouth to feed.'

'Jerome! Stop this rudeness. What *is* the matter with you?' Grace snapped.

But Jerome was in no mood to listen to his mother. 'And one we can ill afford.'

'Please!' Ivy wailed.

'If this is the case then of course my father will want to make restitution to you, Mrs Barnard. He obviously doesn't know—'

Jerome snorted explosively.

'Ivy, I think I hear Alex crying, would you attend to her for me?' Grace said.

Meanwhile, Eliza was fumbling in her pocket for the small purse she carried. 'It's not much I know . . .' She tipped the coins on to the table.

'No, Miss Eliza, that isn't necessary.' Grace pushed the money back towards her.

'We don't need charity.'

'Jerome! You anger me.' Grace glared at him and he picked up the pamphlet again.

Eliza wished he'd never put it down. 'I don't understand you, Mr Barnard,' she said. 'Just a moment ago you said you could ill afford Ivy and I'm only trying to help. I suggest you make your mind up what you want.' She had gone a deep shade of pink that even the gloom could not hide. She was mortified and miserable to be speaking to him in this way, but why should he be so cross with her?

Ivy had reappeared. 'I meant for you to see to Alex upstairs in her room.' Grace sounded exasperated.

'But she asked for you, Mrs Barnard.' She handed the baby to Grace.

'What a lovely child!' Eliza exclaimed.

'And I suppose you are going to say that you know nothing about this child either.' The pamphlet was lowered. 'And please, Miss Eliza, don't tell me you don't understand *again*.'

'But I don't.' Eliza looked flustered.

'This has nothing to do with Miss Eliza,' Grace began.

'But it has, Mother. It has everything to do with her

209

family.' Jerome had stood up and towered over the table. Eliza felt herself shrink back in the chair to get away from his anger.

'She's but a child herself. She knows naught about these matters.'

'Then perhaps it's time she learnt.'

'I don't—'

'If you are about to say *understand* one more time, I swear—' Jerome's fist crashed down on the table.

Eliza was on her feet now, tears pricking the back of her eyes. 'I think I should be going, Mrs Barnard. I'm sorry . . .' And, not waiting to hear her response, she rushed from the kitchen, faltering as she reached the yard, momentarily dazzled by the bright sunshine after the darkness of the kitchen.

She had sauntered here, enjoying the walk, the scenery, but going back she raced past the trees, the river, slipped on the stones and wet the hem of her skirt. She ran up the path, past the rhododendrons, the lake, across the knot garden, as if demons were after her.

Ruby, who had seen her from the window, was in the hall waiting for her.

'Miss, what's happened? What's the matter?'

Eliza fell headlong into her maid's arms. 'I'm sorry!'

'What on earth have you got to be sorry about?'

'Everything! Oh, Ruby, he hates me.'

'Who hates you? No one does.'

'Jerome does. Oh, Ruby, what am I to do? What have I done? He loathes me.'

4

Ruby was exasperated. She could not persuade Eliza to tell her what was upsetting her so. All the girl would say was 'Nothing,' which, given the torrent of tears, was unlikely to be true. What if this made her go silent again? Ruby didn't think she could stand that.

In the kitchen she was having a late supper – it had taken all this time to calm Eliza down and to get her to sleep. Maggie hadn't minded her missing the main sitting. 'There's plenty left over, I'll heat it up for you.'

'I can do that.'

'You sit down. This is my job and my kitchen.' Maggie beamed with pride, as she dished up a plate of beef stew.

'You're so proud of it, aren't you? And so you should be. You are doing so well. Everyone loves your cooking.'

'Have they said so?'

'Lots of them.'

'I wish they'd say it to me. No one even says thank you and they used to with Mrs Satterly.'

'They were all scared of Mrs S!'

'It won't last,' Maggie said mournfully. 'Once the family come they won't want me. I'm not good enough for them.'

'What are you going on about? Mr Didier will be coming and he'll still need help, won't he?'

'Yes.' Maggie looked dubious. 'But he's a chef, he'll want a professional cook with him.'

'But you helped him before, didn't you?'

'I was just doing what I always used to do, peeling the vegetables, looking after the stockpot, washing up. I shan't want to go back to that.'

Ruby leant across the large pine table. 'Nor you will. Now please, I've had enough of people being miserable tonight to last me for months. Not you too.'

'And who's been miserable?' Mrs King had swept in. She usually came at this time to discuss the staff menus with Maggie. She placed her pad and pencil on the table and took a seat. 'Any tea in that pot?'

'It's a bit stewed. Shall I make another?'

'If it's not too much bother. So, Ruby, who's miserable?'

'It was nothing.'

'Whenever anybody says that it always means it was something.'

Ruby wiped the gravy from her plate with a piece of bread.

'Miss Eliza, is it?' Mrs King asked.

'She's asleep.'

'I thought it would end in tears.'

'What?'

'A visit to your family home.'

'Eliza decided for herself she wanted to go. I can't stop her, can I?'

'So you'd let her put her hand in the fire if she wanted to?'

'No, Mrs King,' Ruby said wearily. 'She's not a child and she's not likely to do such a thing, is she? That was what I was trying to say, that she's almost grown up and she is beginning to make her own decisions.'

'And wrong ones they are. I shall be glad when the family returns. This responsibility is too much.' She stood up, muttering to herself, and bustled out of the kitchen.

'Do you think she's going mad?' Maggie asked, arriving with an apple pie and a bowl of clotted cream. 'She's always talking to herself.' She cut them both a slice of pie.

'I don't know why but she disapproves of my family. What have we ever done to her?'

'It's your dad.'

'My *dad*?'

'Your mother got him and she wanted him. She's never forgiven your mother.'

'Mrs King? It can't be true.'

'Ask your mum. I overheard Mrs Satterly and Merry talking about it one day. Quite rude they were too. Oh, not about your parents, about Mrs King. Merry said she'd set her cap too high – she was a still-room maid in those days, apparently, and your mother was a senior housemaid. No comparison, was there?'

Ruby began to laugh. 'Heavens above! She could have been my mother!'

'She would never have had anyone as nice as you,' Maggie said shyly.

'But I was pleased when Eliza wanted to come to my home. I thought it would help her, make her think of other things – and it's done *that*,' she said, with irony.

'Mrs King doesn't want her getting too close to you and your family. Jealousy is what *that*'s all about. More pie?'

'Ruby, do you feel hard done by?'

Ruby had brought Eliza's morning tea and was pulling back the curtains.

'No. What a strange question.'

'Please, be honest with me. I don't expect you to do too much?'

'Well, there are days when I seem to be chasing my tail, and never catching up – yesterday was one like that. But, no, I think I have a good position here.'

'You are sure?'

'Miss Eliza, why are you asking me these questions? Is it something my brother said to you? Is that why you were so upset?'

Eliza shook her head. 'No, of course not. It looks as if it's going to be a lovely day. Would you mind taking Bumble out for me? Thank you so much.'

Ruby called the dog. She did this every morning, wet or fine, and yet every morning Eliza always asked her politely. It was charming, yet silly too. Did she feel hard done by, she wondered, as she stood on the back steps waiting for Bumble. No, she had spoken the truth. She worked hard, they all did, but she no longer worked as hard as she once had.

That afternoon, without asking Eliza or Mrs King, she put on her bonnet and cloak, and sped towards her home. Hers was a longer route than Eliza had taken since servants were not allowed to walk in the front gardens.

As she entered the kitchen, she said, without preamble, 'Mum, is Jerome around?'

'And hello to you too, Ruby. It's nice to see you.' Her mother smiled.

'Sorry, I'm in a hurry. No one knows I'm here.'

'What do you want to see him about?'

'If you don't mind, Mum, it's private.'

'About Miss Eliza, is it? Upset, wasn't she?'

'Do you know what happened?'

'Jerome was speaking without thinking. I feared something like this. It was so silly . . .'

By the time Jerome appeared, looking for his tea. Ruby knew exactly what had taken place. 'How dare you speak to her like that? Who are you to know what my duties are and what they're not, and if I feel overworked? Have I ever discussed it with you?'

Jerome looked shamefaced.

'I've never heard anything so preposterous in my life,' Ruby went on. 'She's kind and considerate, not like some of them. She'd help me herself rather than overwork me.'

'You think so?' Jerome gave a cynical snort.

'I know so. She even suggested yesterday that I come too. It was me who decided not to. You shouldn't jump to conclusions. And why blame her over Maud's baby? She didn't know. No, you don't, you're not going anywhere.' And, moving faster than Jerome, she placed herself between him and the door. 'You're going to listen to me. How could she have done anything? She doesn't even know where babies come from. If she wants to help Mother with the expenses who are you to refuse her kind offer? An offer, I'll have you know, that would have been made in the best Christian tradition.'

'We don't want charity.'

'But it wouldn't have been that. It would have been her doing her family duty to an employee. With your stupid pride, you've stopped Mother getting help that she needs.'

'Have you finished?'

'No, I have not. You broke her heart yesterday with your nastiness. She cried and cried for hours. You, Jerome, are going to call on Miss Eliza, and you are going to apologise.'

'I'll do no such thing.'

'Yes, you will. If you don't I'll never speak to you again.'

Jerome moved towards her, picked her up effortlessly and placed her back by the table. 'Now, you listen to me. No one tells me what and what not to do.' He put on his cap and strode out, the door slamming behind him.

'He'll apologise.' Grace nodded.

'He didn't look as if he would.'

'Oh, yes, he will. He likes her. But he doesn't know he does – yet.'

5

'You have a visitor, Miss Eliza.'

'Who is it? Show them in here, Ruby.' Eliza was in the library where she had begun the immense task of cataloguing her father's books. He had so many that she wondered when – if – she would finish. However, it had been a good decision to do so since it was taking her mind off recent events. And she was enjoying it.

'I'd rather not, miss.'

'Why? Do I look too untidy?' Eliza laughed, pushing back her hair. Moving books was hot work. She looked down at the dust on her apron, which she had sensibly put on over her dress. 'I know the maids work hard but I think we're going to have to ask them to take all these books down and give them a thorough cleaning.'

'Yes, miss.'

'So, show the visitor in. They'll just have to take me as I am.'

'It's better I don't.'

'Then I must look dreadful.'

'No, it's not that. And, in any case, you don't.'

'Such a mystery. Well, if they won't come here then I can't see whoever it is. I'm far too busy.'

'I've sent him to the summer-house.'

'Him?' Eliza paused at the top of the library steps. 'Who?' She felt a flutter of excitement in her chest.

'Jerome. He wants to talk to you.'

'Then why can't he come here?' It was difficult to speak in a normal tone since the feeling of agitation had transferred from her heart to her throat.

'It wouldn't be proper and Mrs King wouldn't like it.'

'I don't care about Mrs King.' She descended the steps. 'What if he's angry with me again? I couldn't bear that, Ruby.'

'He won't be. There's a bit of a drizzle, so I've got your cape.'

Eliza found herself fumbling with the catch so that it slipped off her shoulders and fell to the floor. Both women bent to retrieve it, almost crashed into each other and laughed. 'He will wait, you know,' Ruby said kindly.

In the hall, just as they were opening the inner door, Mrs King appeared, followed by a maid carrying a pile of linen that threatened to unbalance her. 'Surely you're not going out in this damp, Miss Eliza? It's most unpleasant.'

'I need some fresh air.'

'It isn't particularly invigorating today.'

'It's the dust from the books.' She sneezed.

'I think what you're doing with them is not a good idea. I don't know what your father will say.'

'He'll be pleased,' Eliza called over her shoulder, as she and Ruby swept out of the door.

By the time they had reached the rhododendron walk,

it was raining quite hard so they broke into a run. They could see the summer-house now: it was a thatched cottage, which from one side looked like a complete house with a front door and windows but on the other was open, furnished with benches and a table.

'You go in first, see if he's there.' Eliza pushed Ruby forward.

'Jerome,' she whispered but she had no idea why she did since there was no one about, not even a gardener.

'Ruby,' he whispered back.

'He's there,' she said unnecessarily to Eliza.

'I heard him.'

The cottage's front door swung open and Eliza turned away to look out over the garden. She was afraid to meet his eyes, afraid he might see the confusion she was feeling.

'Miss Eliza,' she heard him say quietly, 'I need to talk to you.'

Slowly she turned to face him. 'What about?'

'I would rather speak to you alone.'

'Ruby, don't go,' she said, panic in her voice.

'As if I would! I'll sit over here. You two talk on the other side.' She crossed to the bench on the far side and dusted it with her hands.

'If you'd do me the honour.' Jerome bowed to her, holding his arm out towards a wicker chair beside a table. 'May I?' He indicated the other chair and she nodded. He took his seat and they sat in silence.

'When I was a child we often had picnics here, Merry and I. I liked to pretend it was my house,' she said, to fill the silence. But she could not bring herself to look at him.

'I'm glad you came,' he eventually said.

'Ruby made me.'

'You didn't want to?' He frowned.

'No, no, I was joking.' She looked at her gloved hands. 'It's difficult . . .' Silence descended.

'What is?'

Ruby interrupted. 'Miss Eliza, I'm embarrassing Jerome, by being here. It's stopped raining now so I'll wait outside.'

'I'm not sure . . .' she began, remembering how she had been lectured never to be alone with a man lest she was compromised – oh, that dreadful fate! This was the first time she had been put in such a position. She risked a glance at him. He looked as worried as she was sure she did. 'You wanted to say something to me?'

He cleared his throat. 'Yes. I wish to apologise.'

'What for?'

'I was rude to you the other afternoon.'

'Were you? I can't say I noticed.' What a lovely voice he had, low and husky as if he spoke through chocolate. What a fanciful thing to think!

'You are amused by me?'

'No, Mr Barnard. What makes you say that?'

'You appeared to be smiling to yourself.'

'I wasn't aware of it. I was listening to you.'

He looked confused. 'But it doesn't alter the fact that I was impolite and I had no right to be. I'm truly sorry. Ruby told me the truth.'

'And what's that?'

'That you are kind to her. That you did not know about the problem with Maud . . . The baby and everything . . .' He was playing with his cap, which he had put on the table.

Eliza blushed furiously at the reference to Maud and the baby! Now, that was improper. On his cap she saw a long blond hair – his. How she would love to own it! And she noticed his hands. He had well-kept nails, despite the hard work he did, and his fingers were long and artistic-looking, yet capable and strong-looking too.

'I'm glad you spoke to me as you did. I've been thinking of what you said. You were right. I do take Ruby for granted. I don't notice how hard she works for me. I am grateful for what she does but I have resolved to be less demanding in future. And I intend to let her know how much I appreciate all she does.'

Jerome looked astonished.

'And to an extent you were right about Maud and her ... problem.' This was difficult. 'We should have known of her plight. Of course, there may be people in the house who do know, but they would not have told me, would they?' She looked at him for assent, praying he had understood. He nodded. 'But she had worked for us for some years and should have been given help – financial, perhaps. I know nothing of these matters.' She wished she had a fan: she felt so hot, she must look like a beetroot by now. It seemed unreal to be speaking of such things to a man! But, then, perhaps it was a dream and she was going to wake up at any moment. She hoped not, she liked sitting here with him, even if they were talking about such unseemly things. She glanced at him again, and was glad to see that he looked discomfited too. 'You understand, Mr Barnard, I could never condone what has happened. But ... she must have been so afraid. It must have been dreadful for her.' Tears welled in her eyes.

'Please don't upset yourself, Miss Eliza. I don't think she was very afraid, and my mother came to her rescue.'

'Oh, I see.' Could he be speaking the truth? What had happened to Maud was worse than death – Merry had said so often enough. 'Your mother is another matter. I am mortified that I offended you with what you called charity. I did not mean it to be. I felt it was my family's obligation to yours, that is all. I know you would never in a million years accept *charity*.'

'You've shamed me,' Jerome muttered, 'and I feel I shall never be able to make amends to you. I misunderstood, and all I can do is apologise and say that now I feel privileged to have the honour of knowing you.'

'Oh.' She sighed. What a beautiful speech! 'So I may visit again without being growled at?' she asked, lightheaded with happiness that all appeared to be resolved.

'Will you ever forgive me?'

'I've forgiven you already, Mr Barnard. So, are we to be friends?'

'I should like that.' He took the hand she proffered and as she did so she realised she had forgotten her gloves. But she was glad she had, for she was able to touch his skin, which was warm but rough, a strong hand. A strange sensation raced through her, wonderful, but a shock too. She did not know what it was or how to describe it – like a bolt of lightning was the best she could do. She could not know that he had felt exactly the same.

6

Eliza lived in a dream. She meant to finish in the library, continue with her sampler, read and generally improve her mind, but she did none of these. Most of the time she sat staring into space, invariably with a secret smile playing about her lips. She spent a lot of time hanging aimlessly out of windows, letting in the cold October air to which she seemed oblivious.

Maggie was in despair: no matter what she prepared, Eliza's tray came back with the food untouched. 'Is she ill?' she asked Ruby.

'I suppose you could say she is – of a sort.'

'What's that mean?' Maggie was scraping the cheese soufflé into the pigs' bin.

'*Love!* That's what I mean.'

Maggie dropped the plate. 'Bloody hell! That was your fault. See? A bit of best Derby gone to waste. Now what's going to happen?'

'Nothing. Remember, you're in charge. Just report it to Mrs King, and don't put up with any nonsense from her either.'

'I am, aren't I?' Maggie collected the broken pieces and put them into a box, in case the plate could be mended. 'But in love with who? How can she be? She never goes anywhere, never sees anyone, only us.'

'She does go out. Often.'

'Where?'

'Around the place. Different spots. Including my house.'

Maggie's eyes were two perfect circles of astonishment. 'You mean she meets *him* there? Now you've *got* to tell. I'll only give you scrag end and fat if you don't.'

'Promise not to tell.'

'Cross my heart and hope to die.'

'My brother,' Ruby whispered.

'Your brother!' Maggie yelled.

'Shush!'

'What's she doing with him?' Maggie squeaked.

'Spooning, I guess, I don't spy on them. I try to be as discreet as possible. I leave them to themselves – though she is always chaperoned,' she added hurriedly.

'How long?'

'About a month. Not that they see each other every day. I can't get away as often as Miss Eliza likes, but it can't be helped.'

'Does anyone else know? Mrs King?'

'Not likely! No, we say we're going visiting or shopping and take the governess cart. Mrs King is pleased. She thinks Miss Eliza is now fully recovered and getting back on her feet. Little does she know!'

'Just think, if she married Jerome, you wouldn't have to call her Miss Eliza any more.'

'And Mrs King couldn't bully me.'

'Oh, Ruby, it's so romantic.' Maggie sighed.

It would be difficult to know who spent the most time thinking about the romance – Eliza or Ruby. While Eliza mooned over Jerome, Ruby planned the great changes that such a relationship would mean to them. Already there were signs. Jerome had accepted Eliza's help with the expense of Ivy and little Alex, and they had tea in the caddy again, coffee too, neither of which they could afford before. Her mother's small library of books was growing by the week. Alex was showered with new clothes.

Where to meet was a problem. Eliza and Jerome's favourite place was the thatched cottage, but they also went to a disused keeper's hut. They had even met in the chapel on a couple of occasions. But these places were getting colder, and they had to be careful about going to the farm. When they did Grace was agitated and none of them trusted Ivy, who wanted Jerome for herself.

Grace fretted that the news would leak out and that there would be trouble.

'Who from, Mother? Who would want to hurt them? Just look at them – they make such a pretty picture. How could anyone wish them ill?' Through the kitchen and parlour doors, both left open for propriety's sake, they could see Eliza and Jerome, sitting side by side, looking at some books Eliza had brought with her, laughing, almost touching – but not quite.

'I should think there'd be a queue of people wishing to put a stop to it.' Grace and Ruby were huddled over the large open fire in the kitchen. Ivy had gone into Exeter for Grace so the coast was clear.

'Well, maybe her father won't be pleased.'

'He's more likely to get his shotgun out, I'd have thought. And then there's Lady Gwendoline and Lady Wickham. I can just see them killing the fatted calf for my son.' Grace's laugh was mirthless. 'I can't sleep worrying about them. It will end in sadness, I'm sure.'

'Lady Gwendoline won't mind. Her bark's worse than her bite. She's very fond of Eliza and she'll want her to be happy.'

'You're wrong, Ruby. Like should marry like, and that sort have made a religion of it. If they were Catholics they'd be sending her to a nunnery, you mark my words.' She threw another log on to the fire. 'By the way, Ruby, you never returned my book. I hope you haven't forgotten. *Ruby*, you're blushing! Don't tell me you've lost it. You know what store I set by my books *and* that one was a present.'

'I'd best tell you . . .' Ruby relayed her ploy.

'*If* Miss Chester received it,' Grace said.

'When I didn't hear I asked Mrs King if she had sent it and she had.'

'Then perhaps she didn't understand.'

'I'm sure she would have.'

'Then the only conclusion is that she has returned it and someone else has taken it.'

'But who?'

'Why, Ivy, of course.'

'She wouldn't!'

'Wouldn't she? She thinks she's in love with Jerome and I think she'd do anything to put a stop to what's happening. Ruby, for your own sake, you mustn't interfere any more in Miss Eliza's affairs. At this rate you'll lose your position and then what would you do? And if Mr Forester found out about those two . . .' She shuddered. 'We could have the tenancy taken from us, just like that.' She snapped her fingers in the air.

'But we have an agreement with Mr Forester.'

'Agreements can be broken.'

On Eliza's next visit, they were in the big barn. Ruby was at the far end, wrapped in a blanket, pretending to read and hoping to hide from them that she was frozen. Jerome had brought in a brazier he had made from an old bucket. 'Can't have you catching cold, can we?' He looked at Eliza as he tended the coals.

'You think of everything.' She put out her hand to touch him then realised what she was doing. She longed to, but she must not appear forward.

'It's not what you're used to.'

'I think it's wonderful.'

'No one will guess we're here. Not in this temperature.' The fire was glowing bright red. 'There, that's better. Ruby, do you want to join us? You must be cold.'

'No, thanks,' Ruby called back, to Eliza's relief.

He sat down on the bale of hay beside hers.

'Hay is comfortable to sit on, isn't it? Quite surprising,' she remarked.

'Have you never sat on it before? Built a playhouse of straw? Climbed in the ricks?'

'No, but it sounds fun.'

'Ruby and I used to play house together in the straw.'

'I wish I'd been there.'

He looked at her so penetratingly that, although she enjoyed the attention, she felt nervous. 'I wonder what other things there are that I've done and you haven't and the other way round,' he said.

'Lots, I expect. I've never milked a cow or fed pigs.'

'Then you wouldn't make a farmer's wife.'

'I could learn,' she said, without thinking, then realised what she'd said and hurried on. 'But, then, I know how to decant wine. And the best vintages. Do you?'

'No, I don't.' He laughed. 'There's not much call for that at our house.'

'Not when you have a dinner or luncheon party?'

He laughed even louder. 'We never have guests.'

'Never?'

'Only you.'

'That's nice.'

'Tell me, Eliza, do you make your own bed?'

'Whatever for?' It was her turn to laugh but on seeing his expression she stopped abruptly. 'There's no need.' She thought that sounded better.

'You've never had to do a thing for yourself, have you?'

Eliza did not like this conversation. She felt that Jerome, in a roundabout way, was trying to say something to her, and she wasn't sure if she would like what it was. 'I've been privileged, yes, but if I stopped

being cared for, people would lose their employment.'
That, she decided, was a good answer.

'We don't have much in common, do we?'

'Of course we do. We love the same poetry, books – we talk a lot about them – and the countryside. I could never live in a town and neither could you. We love Harcourt Barton – I never expected anyone to feel as strongly for the estate as me.' Her face was animated, her pulse racing. Was he trying to say she bored him?

'I love the place. I'm not sure I like my position in it.'

'I don't understand.'

'It doesn't matter.' He looked away.

'But it does. Please explain.'

'I'm tired of being poor.'

'Poor? How can you say that? You have a wonderful family, a mother who adores you. Work you love . . . I envy you.'

'Only someone who was rich could say that.'

'Money is not important to me.' Was he bothered that he was wrong for her because he had none? She had to reassure him.

This amused him. 'Eliza, you're adorable!'

'I like the time we spend together.'

'Me too.'

'Honestly?'

'There's no one else in the world I'd rather be with.'

She smiled. What a stupid old worrier she was.

Eliza was waiting in the hall, just as she had in Miss Chester's time, to welcome her grandmother, who was coming for Christmas. She hoped that Lady Gwendoline's arrival would not make it difficult for her to slip away and see Jerome. The days when she could not go to him were long and dull. She seemed alive only when she was with him. Lady Gwendoline was normally here long before this, but she had been delayed in London, struck down by a fearsome cold that she could not shake off.

Her grandmother alighted from her coach, Benson circling her like an attendant whale – how fat she had got! But at the sight of her grandmother Eliza's hand shot to her mouth. She was half her normal size, bent and gaunt, needing both Mr Densham and Benson to support her.

'Grandmama, you look so pale.' Eliza bent to kiss her cheek.

'What sort of welcome is that, pray?'

'But you don't look well.'

'Don't state the obvious, child. Of course I don't. I'm ill.'

'I'm sorry.'

'Why are you apologising? You didn't make me ill.'

'No, but . . . The sorry was meant for the illness, not as an apology.'

'For an intelligent person you can sometimes be quite stupid, Eliza. Get me that bag.' She pointed imperiously with her cane towards the pile of baggage that the footmen were beginning to take upstairs to her suite of rooms. Eliza did as she was bidden. 'Why are you limping?'

'I hurt my leg. It's nothing serious.' She had been running down a hill, chased by Jerome, and had fallen. He'd made such a fuss of her afterwards that it had almost been worth the pain in her ankle.

'Take that silly smile off your face. And in my day no self-respecting woman had legs.'

'How did she walk, then?' Eliza giggled.

'Don't be so impertinent. Really, girls these days! How standards are slipping. Now someone, anyone, get me upstairs to my rooms.'

Two Jameses lifted her effortlessly and carried her up the long staircase.

'Benson, she's so thin, half her normal size.'

'It's difficult to get her to eat anything. She's a bit better now, though. It's been a very worrying time, Miss Eliza.'

'I wish someone had told me. I'd have gone to London immediately.'

'She didn't want to worry you.' Benson patted her arm. 'The doctors say there's nothing to worry about but I don't think they know what they're saying.'

A loud shriek, '*Benson*,' wafted down to them.

'I'd best go and settle her.'

A little later Eliza was summoned to her grandmother's boudoir. 'So, tell me everything you've been doing.'

'Not much, Grandmama, I'm ashamed to admit.'

'Well, at least you didn't lie. Why not?'

'I couldn't seem to find anything to interest me.'

'Not still fussing over that governess woman? Forgotten her name.'

'Miss Chester? No, not any more,' she could answer, in total honesty.

'Dismissed any more servants?' Lady Gwendoline looked fierce, but Eliza saw the twinkle in her eye.

'No, Grandmama.' She chuckled.

'I feared we would arrive and find that Benson and I were doing the cooking and making the beds.' She lifted her lorgnette on its pearl and diamond chain and peered at Eliza. 'You look different. What is it?'

'Nothing, Grandmama.' She smiled.

'No, there's something distinctly different about you. You haven't been up to anything?'

'I don't know what you mean, Grandmama.'

'I remember that look. Young gentlemen, that's what I'm talking about.' The cane was pointing at her accusingly. Eliza could feel a blush rising. 'Who?'

'I don't know what you're talking about. There is no one,' she lied.

'Then why are you blushing?'

'Because it is such an embarrassing question.' And to cover any further confusion, Eliza bent down and made a fuss of one of the King Charles spaniels – she could never remember their names.

'Hm!' muttered Lady Gwendoline. 'Read to me,' she ordered.

Eliza did as she was told. Every so often her grandmother fell asleep and she stopped, but when she woke up and asked Eliza what she thought she was doing, she continued. Finally the old woman was deeply asleep. Eliza didn't dare leave but sat and worried.

Her grandmother was ill and she would have to be in attendance, fetching things, reading to her. To her horror she found she was panicking. How could she see Jerome? She resented the intrusion into her life. And the minute she thought that she was racked with guilt that she could even think it. She sighed deeply.

She put her finger to her lips as Densham, silver salver in his hand, entered the room. She indicated the small tea-table.

'What is it, Densham?' Lady Gwendoline's crackly voice made both of them jump.

'Callers, milady. They left their cards.' He proffered the tray.

Lady Gwendoline's claw-like hand whipped out and took the cards. 'Mrs Gilpin and Miss Jonquil. What sort of name is Jonquil? I've never heard of them. Who are they?'

'I gather, milady, that Mr Gilpin is the new owner of General Fothergill's estate.'

'You didn't tell me this, Eliza.'

'I didn't know, Grandmama.'

'Do we know anything about them, Densham?'

'I gather that Mr Gilpin is . . .' Densham paused here and coughed discreetly behind his gloved hand. '. . . a manufacturer.'

'Ah, trade. Then it's just as well I can't return the call. I wonder . . . Perhaps it would be a good idea if you went in my place, Eliza.'

'Must I?'

'Indeed. Times are changing. Perhaps we shouldn't reject people out of hand. After all, the Prince of Wales sees fit to dine with grocers. Go, see what they are like and report back to me.'

'Yes, Grandmama,' she said, heart sinking. She hated calling at the best of times and to visit strangers would be even worse.

'And you'll have to arrange the estate Christmas party.'

'Isn't Aunt Minnie coming? She usually does that.'

'She's gone to Italy with your father. He wanted to go on his own but your aunt insisted, and she always wins. He's too kindhearted for his own good. He gets it from me, to be sure. However, she won't be back until just before Christmas. No concern for me at all from either of my ungrateful children.'

'I'm sorry, Grandmama.'

'Stop apologising when it isn't your fault. It irritates me.'

'Yes, Grandmama.'

'And why were you sighing?'

Eliza blushed yet again.

7

She handed her card to the butler, who bore it away ceremoniously. Eliza waited, hoping he would return with a message that the ladies of the house were not receiving today. She looked about the hall of Plumpton Manor. It was a lovely house, not as large as theirs but unaltered from the original. She had often visited when the old general was alive. Then it had been musty and far too full of furniture, most of which needed renovation, but the general had not been interested in such matters. Today, however, it smelt sweet and was furnished with lovely antiques and some new pieces too. All the carpets and curtains had been replaced. On the wall hung a plethora of portraits, all of which looked recently painted since the colours were bright and the fashions recent. She heard the ponderous step of the butler returning. She left Ruby in the hall, sitting on a hard chair, and was shown into the drawing room.

'Miss Forester, what an honour. May I introduce my daughters, Miss Gilpin, Miss Jonquil, and my son, Mr Henry?' As she spoke the last name Mrs Gilpin's voice dripped with pride like an over-buttered muffin. Eliza dropped the small curtsy required of her. Miss Gilpin was fat with pale, rather cloudy eyes, as if too much white pigment had been mixed in with the blue. But her face was pleasant and good-natured. She beamed at Eliza, who was fascinated by her double chin and her enormous breasts, which strained to be free of her tight corset. Mr Henry was tall and willowy as if his backbone had been stripped out of him and when he bowed to her a shower of dandruff fluttered, like white midges, about his head. Jonquil was tiny, in cruel contrast to her sister, her movements graceful, and seemed to float over the carpet to welcome her enthusiastically. She had an enviable mass of dark hair, with huge brown eyes, and an amused expression.

'Please, will you take tea with us?'

'You are most kind, Mrs Gilpin. My maid is in the hall.'

'Yes?' Mrs Gilpin looked puzzled.

'If, perhaps . . .' Eliza was unsure how to continue.

'Mama, I think Miss Eliza is concerned for her maid's comfort,' Jonquil explained.

'Oh, I see, yes, well . . .' Mrs Gilpin spoke as one who could not understand the necessity but was happy to oblige. 'Then she shall take tea in the servants' hall. Henry . . .'

Her son rose languidly and tugged at the tapestry bell-pull as if the effort was more than his frame could bear, an expression of suffering on his face.

'My grandmother sends her apologies . . .' The next few minutes were easy for her since she could discuss Lady Gwendoline's health. Mrs Gilpin had heard what a wonderful woman Lady Gwendoline was, her good works, her vivacity, her generosity of spirit ... She spoke of the journey from London and how arduous it must have been for one of Lady Gwendoline's age. The weather, that faithful standby, took up a few more minutes.

These subjects spent, they perched on their chairs, not quite sure how to proceed or what could possibly be of interest since they had no knowledge of each other. The arrival of the butler and four maids with the tea gave them momentary respite. Eliza memorised the contents of the tea-table, the china, the napkins, all of which would interest Lady Gwendoline. She was certain it was silver not plate, but it was difficult to tell these days.

Mrs Gilpin, her daughters and the maids all bothered themselves with the tea and a fine old mess they made as they wove about and got into each other's way. While they were thus involved, and a conversation with Henry had got her nowhere, Eliza took an inventory of the room. At least she'd have something to talk about this evening when she got home.

'And how do you occupy your time here?' Mrs Gilpin asked.

'I read, sketch, go for walks, and of course I ride. But not with the hunt, my grandmother won't allow it. She blames her rheumatism on the falls she had when she was young and out with the Berkshire.'

The mention of aches and pains was providential: Mrs Gilpin was blissfully happy to discuss her own sufferings.

'Is that all?' Jonquil's voice was laden with disappointment.

'It sounds dull, doesn't it? But the time flies past. I never seem to have time to do all I want.' And then there's my visits to Jerome, she thought. She couldn't suppress a secret smile.

'Do you go to Exeter?'

'Infrequently. Sometimes to shop, of course, and to

the cathedral, but I prefer the peace and tranquillity here.' Henry attempted to stifle a yawn. Mrs Gilpin glared at him, but Eliza couldn't blame him – she knew she was being boring but there was little she could do about it.

'You have family here?'

'Only at Harcourt Barton.' Really, if she thought about it, her life did sound intolerably tedious, except it wasn't. Another tiny smile escaped. 'My father is in Italy, but will be returning for Christmas.'

'Your family, I presume, have lived at Harcourt for centuries.'

'My grandfather was the first Forester to live here.'

'Really?' Mrs Gilpin smiled broadly.

'Do you have family locally?'

'Bless you, no. We're from Burnley – born and bred – but I always wanted to move south, more agreeable in every way. So much better for my husband's gout and so much more to do.'

'That's what you promised, but it doesn't appear there will be.' Jonquil looked sulky.

'I think it sounds lovely here.' Miss Gilpin smiled.

Eliza saw the look of fury that passed between Mrs Gilpin and Jonquil and searched frantically for something to say, but the silence descended again, only broken by Miss Gilpin's wheezing and the ticking of the clock.

'Visitors! Splendid, splendid!' A large, red-faced man bounded into the room, his hands held out in expansive welcome.

Mr Gilpin filled the room with bonhomie and noise as he welcomed Eliza not once but several times to his 'humble abode'. He strode about the room, resting for a second in front of the fire, coat-tails lifted to the warmth, then marching to the window to check the weather, moving a book, straightening a picture, inspecting an ornament. He exuded energy, in striking contrast to his son.

'What a pretty young woman you are, to be sure! And how old are you?'

'Sixteen,' she said, confused by the compliment.

'The same as Jonquil. You shall be friends.'

'Daddy, perhaps Miss Eliza doesn't want to be my friend. Don't embarrass her.'

'Of course she'll want to be your friend. It would be a privilege for her.'

'More for Jonquil, surely,' his wife fluttered.

'Why?'

'Because, well, because . . .' Mrs Gilpin began feebly.

'Because she's better than us? Is that what you're trying to say, woman?'

Mrs Gilpin looked close to tears.

'I don't wish to sound rude, Miss Eliza, but you can't expect a father to think that anyone is "better" than his own princess, can you? I expect your father would agree with me.'

Eliza smiled sadly at his optimism. 'I should love to be Miss Jonquil's friend. You're perfectly correct, it would be a great privilege for me.' She said it dutifully but thought she might be speaking the truth. She liked Jonquil's expression, she was in awe of the way she spoke to her father, and it would be nice to have a friend. After all, she had never had one before.

The afternoon wore on. It was evident to Eliza that Mr Gilpin adored both his daughters and had no time for his son. She tried to feel sorry for Henry, knowing how cruel parental rejection could be, but she failed. From his father's barbed remarks, Henry was permanently tired and bored, she decided. She was amazed he had the energy to breathe.

'What did you find out, Ruby?' she asked, once they were back in their carriage and being driven home.

'They're parvenus, that's for sure.'

'You sound like my aunt!'

'They don't know how to handle servants – your grandmother would have a fit if she saw the goings-on in that servants' hall. They were drinking brandy and wine with their tea! Did you notice how long you had to wait for yours? They argued about who was going to serve it. The butler was drunk. Dreadful!' And so was Mrs Satterly, but she thought it politic not to tell Eliza that their former cook had found employment there.

'Oh, the poor Gilpins. They seem such nice people too. Especially Mr Gilpin. He says exactly what he thinks and he adores his girls.'

'But you won't be seeing them again?'

'Yes, I will. I've invited them for dinner when my father comes. And Miss Jonquil is visiting us later this week. Her sister can't – she has an appointment in Exeter.'

'Daft name, if you ask me.'

'I think I might have found a friend, Ruby.'

'I thought you already had one.' Ruby laughed and dug her in the ribs with her elbow, with the easy familiarity into which they fell now when they were alone.

When they returned Ruby was the centre of attention in the servants' hall. New people in the area were always a source of interest. The old general had kept a small retinue of servants, most of whom were nearly as old as he, but a family with young staff, with whom liaisons might be possible, was exciting.

'You would be appalled, Mr Densham.'

'He wouldn't have had anything to do with them – he'd have seen them for what they were when he interviewed them,' Mrs King put in.

'That I would, Mrs King. But, then, what can you expect from the likes of the Gilpins? They know no better, trying to ape their betters – it's inevitable they'll be taken in.'

'They told me that Mr Gilpin had made a fortune from cotton, that he has huge mills and they're so rich they don't know what to do with their money.'

'It sounds as if they should have stayed up north in my opinion.'

'Come, come, Mrs King, it was only a couple of generations back that the Foresters were money-lenders,' said Benson, who had always regretted that her mistress had married beneath her.

'They couldn't stay in Burnley,' Ruby said. 'Their son, Henry, ravished a farmer's daughter and there was trouble. The old man had to pay them off.' Ruby giggled. 'Anyway, Mrs Gilpin was worried for the marriage prospects of her daughters – though one is so fat it's doubtful if anyone would ever want her.'

'If the bank balance is large enough you will be amazed at how slender she will be in the eyes of her suitors.' Benson laughed.

'They don't sound our sort at all. None of you need to think you are going to fraternise with the likes of them,' Mrs King admonished her young maids.

'And guess who the cook is.'

'Mrs Satterly,' they replied in unison.

'No one said.' Ruby felt quite affronted.

'You never asked.'

'Still, Miss Eliza has made a friend of the younger daughter of the house.'

'Lady Gwendoline will put a stop to that!'

Mrs King was wrong. Eliza reported back faithfully, not just on the contents of the house, or its owners' lack of social grace, but about how pleasant the family had been – with the exception of the son. And Lady Gwendoline, who was not nearly as snobbish as her servants, confirmed that Jonquil's visit later in the week was a splendid idea, and that she would send a note to confirm the dinner invitation.

On the day of Jonquil's visit, Eliza wondered if she'd been right to invite her. She'd been schooled in how to entertain – the way to welcome, to introduce, to say farewell. She knew how to pour tea and pass sandwiches, which subjects of conversation were suitable and which were not. She even knew what to wear. But she had not acquitted herself well on her visit to the Gilpins' so how could she hope to do well today?

Used to being with people older than herself, she was filled with trepidation at entertaining someone of her own age. She knew she could talk to Jerome about any subject under the sun, in fact when they were together they hardly stopped chattering, but that was different: she loved him.

She envied Jonquil her confidence as she alighted from her carriage, walked into the house and greeted Eliza as if they had been friends for years. She was happy to take the conversational lead. 'Your house is so lovely. I envy you.' Jonquil looked about her. 'Especially the conservatory. I will tell Papa, he must have one built immediately.' She continued admiring the palm trees and the orchids.

'Does your father always give you what you want?'

'Mostly. One thing he hasn't but I shall continue to try to persuade him,' she said mysteriously, but didn't elaborate. 'I expect you'll be proposed to in here. What a perfect setting for romance!'

'I'm not sure about that, but Plumpton Manor is lovely too.'

'Yes, but it's not as big as this house. It's not as important. It's rather a poor relation, wouldn't you say?'

'Not at all. I think it perfect.'

'Do you?'

'Your mother has wonderful taste.'

'Oh, that wasn't Mama. She had people in London choose the furnishings. Oops, I shouldn't have said that, should I?' Jonquil clapped her gloved hand over her mouth.

'Probably not.' Eliza laughed, enjoying Jonquil's

frankness – it was so like her father's. 'But I shan't tell a soul. Do you think you will be happy here?'

'No. I loved our old house outside Burnley. It was close to the moors, you know, where *Wuthering Heights* was set. Wild country, not gentle like here.'

'We must take a trip to Dartmoor next summer. That's really wild, sometimes quite frightening, especially when the mist descends without warning and you feel you're on the edge of the world in the swirling clouds.'

'Really? That makes me feel better.'

'But why did you move away?'

'My brother made a fool of himself with a girl. I don't know how he found the energy. And my mother thinks our marriage prospects will be better here.'

'Well, that's honest.' Eliza was astonished.

'Are you to do the season?'

'I fear so, next year probably.'

'You are lucky.'

'I'm not sure I am. I don't really want to leave here.'

'But you'll find a husband.'

'I don't want to find one.' *There's no need, I've found him.*

'Really?' Jonquil's eyes widened. 'Then are you not to be presented at Court?'

'My grandmother and aunt mentioned it.'

'But that's when you'll find him.'

'Not if I'm not looking for him.' She laughed. 'Are you being presented?'

'I can't be. My father's occupation is wrong. And we've no title.'

'Neither has my father.'

'But he's a banker and my mother says that's acceptable.'

'Isn't it silly?'

'That's what I think too.' They had wandered back from the conservatory and were now in the drawing room where tea was to be served. Once the maid had left them, Jonquil leant towards Eliza conspiratorially. 'If I tell you something, will you keep it a secret?'

'I'll try.' Eliza hated to be asked such a question: what if it was something dreadful that she should tell? She hoped the *try* would exonerate her.

'My parents think it's the end of the world, but I don't. I had a beau, you see, at home in Lancashire – I can't think of this as home, you understand. But he wasn't thought suitable. And I miss him so, and I love him so, and if I could talk to you about him it would make it seem as if he were near.' The lovely brown eyes were brimming with tears.

'Why do your parents disapprove?'

'He's a farmer's son, and not what they intended for me. The trouble is, I'm sure I could persuade my father, but my mother has become such a snob. I don't think it matters what a man does, provided he's a good man. He's called John.' She said his name as if she spoke of angels. 'This is for your ears only,' she whispered. 'Never tell a living soul. I intend to elope.'

'Elope!'

'Yes.'

'Will you be disowned?'

'I don't care.'

'When?'

'When the weather gets better.'

'I don't understand what that has to do with it.'

'We shall run away to Scotland and it can get fearfully cold there, and I hate being cold.'

'Ah, I see.' Then it was the most natural thing for Eliza to tell Jonquil all about Jerome. And talking about him to someone else made her love for him seem more real, stronger. She was happy she had found a friend, if this was what they were for.

Although the school cottage was rather damp in the bleakness of November, Fanny was relieved that Florrie hadn't mentioned the boarding-school again. It wasn't that she wouldn't have accepted the post – she had thought about it quite a lot and had decided to regard it as a challenge. She was happy not to go because in her young life – at twenty-nine, despite what others thought, she still regarded herself as young – she had had to pack her possessions too many times. It seemed that whenever she became fond of a place she had to leave. She was settled here and did not want another move. And, she acknowledged, there was Charles.

She had not seen him since the night when he had visited her drunk. Most of the time she managed to persuade herself it was better not to see him. But at other times she regretted having been so stern with him. It was easy enough to be honest with herself in the daytime, but at night, alone in bed, the stupid childish dreams would return and she would lie there weaving fantasies, most of which involved the loss of Minnie, though she was never specific as to what had happened to her. It was a thought too wicked to contemplate.

Though still thinking of herself as young, she knew she cheated. She was also having to accept that the chance of her meeting anyone to marry now was unlikely – she was too old, and apart from the occasional walk in the park, or shopping, she never went anywhere where she might meet someone. She saw her pupils and their mothers, and that was all. As she liked children, this was a source of sadness to her.

Of the mothers she saw regularly, only Sarah was still cold and distant with her. At first this had worried her: what if she fell out with her, or there was a row and she was dismissed? Fanny was worldly enough to know that having associated with these women and their offspring, she would be ostracised now by society, as if she were tainted from contact with them.

That, in her opinion, was injustice. They had the children, the day-to-day worry, society's disapproval, yet the fathers, for the most part, walked away without a backward glance: their lives were not blighted.

Despite teaching them all the skills she had, she worried about the future of the young girls in her care. Life was hard and money difficult to come by. What if they decided that the easier option for them was to find a protector? Fanny did not even want to think about the lot of the girls who worked in the streets. Would her pupils look at their mothers, see the fine dresses, the champagne, the jewels, and choose a gayer life? The responsibility she felt towards them was the hardest part of all and the nagging worry never left her.

'Yes, Polly?' She looked up from the poem she was copying out several times, from her own book, to give to the older children to read tomorrow.

'One of the little girls is here, miss. And in a rare old state too.'

'Which one?' Without waiting for a reply Fanny went into the hall to find a shivering, crying Augusta. She scooped the child into her arms and carried her into her sitting room. 'Let's build up the fire, Polly.'

'You sure, miss?' Polly was surprised because Fanny usually made do with a few lumps of coal in the evenings and wrapped a rug around her legs for warmth.

'Yes, and some hot milk, I think, with plenty of sugar. There, my sweet. You cry, Miss Chester's here.' She held the little girl close to her.

When the milk had been drunk and the weeping had subsided, Fanny ventured to ask what was wrong.

'It's Caroline. She told me to scarper, that she didn't want me any more. That I was to get out of her sight.' She burst into tears again.

'Have you had an argument with her?'

'No, I didn't. I was getting my supper, as I always do since Maud left, and she suddenly appeared and screamed at me. She'd packed my valise, threw it at me and told me to vamoose!'

'Did she tell you to come here?'

'No. But I didn't know where else to go. And it's so cold out there, and my bag was so heavy, and I was frightened and—'

'Now, Augusta, there's no need to cry. You're safe now. You can sleep here – I'm afraid I've only one bed so you'll have to sleep with me, if you don't mind.'

It was a couple of hours before Fanny could persuade the child to go to bed and reassure her she was safe. She sat with Augusta, holding her hand, until she fell asleep, exhausted by the trauma of the preceding hours.

Later, leaving Polly to look after her, Fanny put on a thick felt bonnet and her heaviest cloak, changed from her soft shoes into boots and sallied out into the freezing fog. When she had walked this distance before, it had been in daylight and had taken her no time at all. That night, in thick fog, it was a different matter. She had to walk brushing against walls and hedges or she would not have known where she was. Crossing a road was frightening – with nothing to guide her she had to plunge into the swirling mist and hope she was walking in a straight line to the other side. She feared a horse and carriage might crash into her for the thick fog muffled sound. Several times she stumbled and several times she thought her heart would stop with fear when someone else came towards her out of the murk.

What should have been a ten-minute walk took nearly an hour, for twice she took a wrong turning. But finally she was in the correct street.

The door to Caroline's house was wide open. A horse and cart stood at the pavement and a surly man was loading it with trunks and furniture. 'Excuse me, is Mrs Fraser at home?'

'No idea.'

She knocked on the open door and when no one came she stepped inside. 'Hello! Mrs Fraser?' she called.

She heard a door bang above her, then light footsteps. Caroline appeared on the staircase. 'What are you doing here?'

'I was worried—'

'About me? Don't lie.'

'Please let me finish – about Augusta.'

'What business is she of yours?'

'Very much mine. She came to me and is at this moment asleep in my bed.'

'I thought she might find her way to you.' Caroline's smile was sly.

'Mrs Fraser, there is thick fog out there as well as darkness. It is freezing cold and she is seven years old.'

'Eight.'

'All right, then, eight, but still no age to be wandering the streets on her own.'

'You think not? But you wouldn't, would you? You don't even know what hardship is, do you, Miss Mealy Mouth? I was working in the mills when I was her age. But you wouldn't understand that. I could look after myself, so can she.'

'Whether you managed to look after yourself, as you say, is a matter of opinion judging from your current way of life. I'd have thought a mother would want something better for her daughter than to become a kept woman too.'

'She's my sister!'

'I don't believe you, Mrs Fraser.'

'I don't bloody care if you do or you don't. None of it's any of your business.'

'Augusta has made it my business. She says you don't want her.'

'You're so fond of her, you have her. All she does is talk about you and how bleeding perfect you are. Let her find out for herself what an evil, conniving bitch you are! You caused all this trouble and you can have some of the bleeding problems too.'

Fanny reeled back from the onslaught. She took a deep breath. 'Insulting me isn't going to help.'

'Who was rude about me and what I do?'

'I came to protect your child.'

'Then do it. You're welcome to her. I never wanted her. I tried hard enough not to have her. So get out and stop lecturing me, Miss High and bloody Mighty. Making eyes at my fellow. And don't deny it because I saw you time without number. You're nothing but a cock-chafer, that you are.'

Fanny felt an almost uncontrollable urge to hit Caroline. 'My, when you're angry, have you not noticed, you don't lisp any more?' And so saying she turned and quickly left the house.

That night in bed it was strange to feel another soul lying beside her. She put her arm protectively around the child, who did not stir from her deep sleep. How could anyone not want Augusta?

It had been a pleasant evening. Fanny and Augusta had unpacked her valise. Her numerous clothes – she had far more than Fanny – were neatly stowed away in drawers from which Fanny had removed her own possessions. If she was to stay, Fanny would have to prepare the empty spare bedroom for her but not yet. Next week would be time enough because Augusta had begged to be allowed to sleep with her for a little while yet.

Now the child was in bed and Fanny was finishing the last of her preparation for the morning's lessons.

'You've a visitor, miss.'

Polly was in the doorway and behind her stood Charles, with a large bouquet of flowers and a bottle of champagne.

'It's late, I know, but I was just passing,' he said. 'May I come in?'

'Just passing at this time of night with such a display of flowers? I don't think I believe you, Charles. But come in.'

'Champagne?' He held the bottle aloft.

'Two glasses, please, Polly.'

She waited until the maid had gone. 'And are you sober tonight?

'I am.' He smiled. 'How is the little school?' he asked, as Polly returned with the glasses. He began to uncork the bottle.

'Very well, thank you. The children are dears.'

'And the charming Augusta?' He handed her a glass.

'Well.' She did not know why but she thought it better if she didn't tell him the child was here with her. Nor did she intend to tell him of the appalling scene with Caroline the night before.

'A toast, don't you think, on this auspicious occasion?'

'Of course, but what is particular about it?'

'There is only one toast, isn't there?' He sat down beside her on the sofa. He looked deep into her eyes and she felt quite weak at the intensity of his gaze. 'To us.' They raised their glasses. 'No, like this,' he said. He twined his arm through hers, and they drank. She laughed as she nearly spilt her champagne.

Almost immediately he topped up her glass. 'Not too fast or *I* shall be inebriated!' she protested breathlessly.

'You? Never. But, my darling, I've done it. I'm free, just as I promised you. She's gone.'

At his use of the endearment her heart soared. But then she asked, 'Who?' with a sinking feeling, for she knew what his answer would be.

'Why, Caroline, of course. I sent her packing.'

'Charles, how could you?'

'Because she had become an impediment to us.'

'The poor woman!'

He grinned. 'She hates you.'

'Is it surprising?' She stood up abruptly. 'I fear I must ask you to leave.'

'Not again.' He groaned theatrically.

'I mean it, Charles. I cannot afford to have you here. My reputation is precious to me.'

'Don't you realise, my sweet one, you lost that the first time you let me visit you? The night I disgraced myself and you wouldn't let me disgrace you.' He seemed to find this funny.

It was difficult to remain angry with him but she knew she must. 'I don't want to beg you to go, I hope you will be a gentleman and just do so.' She hoped she sounded firm but dignified.

'Didn't your previous employer tell you that I'm not a gentleman? He thinks me a rogue.'

'He's probably right.' She tried not to smile. 'I have to admit I don't like Caroline very much, but I don't wish her any harm. And to throw her out because of me is a dreadful thing to have done, and for nothing. We can never be, Charles. I explained that to you the other night.'

'I know and it was painful for me to hear. But listen to me, Fanny. Just five minutes, and then I promise I'll leave you and never trouble you again.' He patted the sofa beside him.

She looked at her watch on its small gold chain pinned to her bodice, which rose and fell as she breathed, then sat down. 'Five minutes, then, that's all.'

'Fanny, I mean you no harm. May I?' Gently he picked up her hand. 'Such beautiful, expressive, artistic hands.' He stroked it gently and she knew she should pull it away from him but something stopped her. 'You have every right to abhor me. I am so many bad things – I drink too much, gamble, womanise, I admit to all those sins. But then I met you, my darling Fanny, and I longed to change, to be a good man. Teach me to love, Fanny. Teach me the decent way to be.' He looked at her with pleading eyes. 'I love you, my darling. I would never hurt you, believe me. You are as precious to me as life itself. Trust me . . . ' he whispered, as his mouth grazed her ear. 'What sin is loving?' he asked softly, as his full, warm, moist lips made a pathway of kisses across her cheek.

'Oh, Charles,' she said, before his lips, finding hers, silenced all speech.

9

To be kissed! It was just as she had imagined in her dreams – only better. The feel of his arms about her was even more wonderful. His strength, his firmness, the power of his hold made her dizzy with joy. She could taste him, smell him! A mélange of tobacco, fine brandy, sweat, a hint of cologne and another, new scent, which she presumed was his maleness, hung about him and she inhaled deeply, wanting to remember it always.

To be able to give herself to him. To feel him beside her in the night. To turn to him and know he was there. To wind her limbs around him, to be held in his embrace. That was the ultimate dream. That was her dearest wish. It would be so easy for her to agree to . . .

'Charles, I must beg you, stop!'

But the kissing continued and his hands were fondling her. She wanted him to, she was enjoying the sensation, she knew she shouldn't.

'Charles, I must insist!'

He groaned and nuzzled her neck. Just the feel of his breath on her skin was intoxicating . . . She pushed hard with all her might but could not extricate herself. He was too strong. There was nothing she could do, he held her too tight. That which had been a dream was becoming a nightmare.

'Miss Chester. I had a bad dream . . .'

Augusta stood in the doorway, holding the doll she had brought with her. 'Miss Chester?—'

The sound of the child's voice brought Charles to his senses. He let go of Fanny, straightened his hair and smoothed his clothes. 'Why, Augusta, this is a surprise!' he said.

'Uncle Charles!' Augusta bounded across the room and into his arms. 'I thought I'd never see you again!'

'Not see me? Impossible! I'm always everywhere. But why are you here and not with Caroline?'

'It's best you don't ask her,' Fanny interjected, standing up now and moving as far away from him as the small room would allow.

'I want to know.'

'It will upset her.'

'No, it won't, Miss Chester,' said Augusta. 'I'm not sad any more now that I live here with you and especially now that I know Uncle Charles has come to see me. And you have, haven't you?'

'But of course. You alone,' he lied.

'I don't mind if you kiss Miss Chester, like you used to kiss Caroline.'

'He wasn't. I had dust in my eye . . .' Fanny knew it was a feeble lie but it was the best she could think of in the circumstances. But she need not have bothered since the child was so engrossed in telling Charles of everything that had happened.

'Why didn't you tell me?' he asked Fanny, when the story was told.

'I didn't want to bother you,' she answered, but the truth was that she had feared he might take Augusta from her.

'And Caroline? Did you see her?'

'Yes.'

'And?'

'I would prefer not to say.'

'Rude, was she?'

'You could say so.' Despite her turmoil she smiled wryly.

'I shall speak to her, tell her to leave you alone.'

'Do you know where she is?'

'I shall find out.'

'And Augusta?'

'What about her?'

'Where shall she go?'

'Can't she stay here?'

'Please!' Augusta was bouncing up and down with excitement. 'I want to stay with Miss Chester, please, Uncle Charles.'

'It would seem a good solution. That is, if Miss Chester wants you.'

'Of course she can stay with me.' Her voice brimmed with relief.

'I shall recompense you, of course.'

'That won't be necessary,' she said, harvesting her pride, though a contribution would have been welcome.

'But I shall insist. I feel a responsibility.'

'I would rather not be under an obligation.' She sat upright, desperately trying to regain her dignity.

Charles laughed. 'You are so adorable when you are maintaining your prim decorum.'

She was not sure if it was his use of words or his laughter that made her feel suddenly angry. 'Augusta, I think you should go back to bed. It is late and we have much work to do tomorrow.'

'Yes, Augusta, do as Miss Chester suggests. She and I have much to talk about.' His grin was wide, too wide.

'I fear I have much work to do.' Her equilibrium, she realised, was restored. 'And I am tired.'

He looked at her for what seemed a long time but was only seconds, then got to his feet. He kissed Augusta goodnight, bowed to Fanny and was gone.

That night sleep was a long time coming. Fanny lay in the dark, Augusta's regular breathing a welcome intrusion, and stared unseeing at the dark ceiling. How close she had been to disaster. How nearly she had let him have his way. She was shocked by herself. After all the years she had spent denying her emotions, her knowledge of right and wrong had almost deserted her. She had made a fool of herself and doubted that she would ever forgive herself. Certainly she would never forget. But her thoughts, in their treacherous way, dwelled dangerously on the sensations she had experienced that evening. The lustful feelings returned and sleep would not rescue her.

'You do look tired, Fanny? I hope you are not ailing.'

'I couldn't sleep, Florrie. I'm not ill,' she said hurriedly, for it was all too common in her profession that dismissal quickly followed illness.

'Worrying?'

'Yes.'

'Anything to do with the school? Do you want to talk about it?'

'No, thank you. Really, there's nothing wrong. I can resolve this problem. I can.'

'A man?'

'What on earth makes you ask that?' She laughed, hoping she sounded as if she hadn't a care in the world.

'Because you're blushing. And that would imply, to me . . .' She arched her eyebrows.

'I never heard such rubbish!' And to her own and the children's consternation, she promptly burst into tears.

'Polly,' Florrie yelled, 'come and look after the children.'

'I don't know how, Mrs Paddington.'

'Just watch them, you don't have to teach them.' She ushered Fanny towards her sitting room. 'How can such a stupid girl survive?' she muttered to herself. She closed the door against the children's excited chattering: their teacher's distress was a source of profound interest. 'What you need is to put your feet up and have a calming drink.'

Fanny allowed herself to be led to the sofa and wondered how on earth resting her feet might mend the pain in her heart.

In the kitchen Fanny kept a small bottle of brandy for medicinal purposes. Florrie had found it quickly and now handed her a small glass. 'There, that will help.' Despite her distress Fanny was amused to see that Florrie had poured herself some too, but a much larger measure. 'Warms the cockles, doesn't it?' She smiled kindly. 'Now, you tell Florrie, and I won't tell a living soul.'

'Last night, someone betrayed my trust. There isn't much to tell you. I shall come to terms with it, in my own good time, I expect.'

'You *hope*, more like. Did he ravish you?'

'No! What a thing to ask!'

'Um,' was all Florrie said.

'Nothing like that. I managed to keep my dignity.'

'It's not your dignity you should be concerned about but your honour. Hard won is that. Who was it?'

'I'd rather not say.'

'Sir Charles Wickham?'

'Really! That's ludicrous.' Fanny tried to laugh at the proposition but failed miserably and the laugh issued more like a sob.

'Not so ludicrous. I heard from two sources that you were moving into his little love nest.'

'And who, pray, has slandered me in this way?' Her heart was thudding painfully.

'The first was Caroline Fraser – a bitter enemy you've made there, to be sure.'

'I've done nothing.'

'She thinks otherwise.'

'You said two sources?'

'My gentleman friend overheard him talking in the club.'

'And you chose to listen to tittle-tattle? I'm disappointed in you, Florrie.'

'No need to get uppity with me, I'm trying to help you. He isn't one for gossip. He told me since he knows how much this school means to me. He thought I should be warned that you were about to scarper. You're not, are you?'

'Of course not.'

'Thanks be!' Florrie rolled her eyes heavenwards in such a comical way that Fanny laughed. 'There, that's better. So, if you are not about to be stupid then why are you so down in the mouth?'

'Oh, Florrie!' The tears welled again and Fanny blew her nose in a less than ladylike manner. 'Florrie, I was awake half the night wondering if I wasn't being a fool. If I had agreed then maybe I would have been happy and secure. I might be able to come to a compromise and accept the sinfulness of it.'

'Oh, my love! Don't even think in that way.' And Florrie was beside her, scooping her into a sweet-smelling, comforting embrace.

'But you see, Florrie, I'd never been in such close proximity to a man. And I'm ashamed to say I liked it, that it was wonderful, and that I wanted it to go on and on.'

'But worth giving up your reputation and standing for? No! What happens when he's tired of you and moves on to the next girl, as surely he will? These men don't stay with the likes of us. If you put on weight, if your looks fade, if you are expecting *their* child, they're off to the next woman. They're like bees with pollen. Take all you want from one flower then on to the next.'

'But it might not be like that.'

'I can guarantee it would be.'

'But I don't want to live all my life alone – and I thought maybe with him . . .'

'You're not alone. You have us and the children.'

'But, Florrie, this could be different. He said he loved me.' She smiled at the memory of his words, the soft way he had spoken to her.

'Fanny, my love, they all say that, it's part of the ritual. You talk of loneliness, I can tell you about that. It's being with someone and liking them and knowing you're only there for one purpose – to gratify their animal lusts. They don't care about us. Empty themselves into us and back to the adoring wife – that's loneliness.'

'Florrie!' Fanny blushed furiously.

'Do you for one moment think that if I was clever like you, if I could teach like you, cook, dress-make or be a milliner, even, that I would be doing what I do? Submitting to a beating when he feels like it. Always ready and available, even when I don't want anyone near me. Pretending he's wonderful when he isn't. And every week of my life wondering if he'll change his mind about me. That's loneliness, that's lack of security.' Florrie, too, was flushed now, from the passion with which she spoke.

'Am I being a fool?'

'Yes, Miss Chester, you most certainly are!' Florrie said gently. 'And I'd come to you with splendid news but maybe you don't want to hear it now.'

'What is it?'

'We've found premises for the bigger school.'

'Where?'

'Near Exeter, large enough for twenty and we could fill it twice over. But, of course, you won't want to go now, will you?'

'Who said I wasn't interested?'

'Splendid!' And Florrie kissed her cheek firmly. 'You'll be out of harm's way there.'

'Yes,' said Fanny, thinking that if she were in Devon, not only might she meet Eliza but perhaps see Charles too.

Jerome's kiss was just as Eliza had imagined in her dreams – only better. The feel of his arms about her was wonderful, made her dizzy with joy. She could taste him. Smell him!

They broke apart as they heard the latch on the kitchen door rattle and Ruby enter. They stood in the little parlour, looking at each other, grinning broadly at this new secret they shared.

'You smell of hay,' she whispered.

'Nothing worse, I trust? I apologise, I shouldn't have kissed you.'

'I wanted you to.'

'So you're not angry with me?'

'Why of course not. It was a wonderful kiss.'

'I've dreamed of it night after night.'

'Me too! When can we do it again?' Eliza clasped her hands together and Jerome laughed with joy.

'You two aren't up to any hanky-panky, are you?' Ruby was in the doorway. 'Only I promised Mother I wouldn't leave you alone for a minute and I did. What a silly question! You both look like the cat that's had the cream.' Ruby turned back to the kitchen.

'Don't tell on us, Ruby, will you?' Eliza begged. She and Jerome had followed her into the kitchen.

Ruby put the basket of eggs she had just collected on to the table. 'As if I would, and get a clip from Mother into the bargain.' She hung a pan of water on the hook above the fire to boil. From the earthenware crock that stood in the corner she took out one of her mother's crusty loaves and began to slice it. 'Have you spoken to her?' Ruby asked Jerome.

'Not yet.' He looked at the floor.

'Spoken to me?' Jerome nodded. 'About what?'

'Something my mother wanted me to say.'

'She's not here?'

'No, she's visiting a sick friend.'

'Avoiding me?' It was a question that she needed to ask since the last few times she had been here Mrs Barnard was absent. 'Why doesn't your mother like me?'

'She does, Miss Eliza.'

'But whenever she's here, she watches me closely and she frowns when she does.'

'She worries about us, Eliza.' Jerome stroked her cheek. That he did it in front of his sister made Eliza even happier.

'Are you sure? It's not me? What is there for her to worry about?'

Jerome pulled out one of the chairs and she sat down. 'She fears that if your father finds out that I love you he will be furious. That's the plain truth of the matter.'

'But why?' Eliza wasn't concentrating: he'd said he *loved* her! And with another person present! Had she been the fainting sort of girl she would have floated clear away. Instead she sat with a dazed smile on her face.

'Miss Eliza, don't pretend you don't know.'

'I don't, Ruby.'

'Jerome won't be good enough for you. Your father will want a fine marriage for you to a man with plenty of money, not one of his tenant farmers.'

'With no money!' Jerome added, with a grin, but it was tinged with sadness.

'Do you really love me?'

'Yes, Eliza, I do. But we have to talk.'

'I love you too.'

'You're not listening, are you?'

'I don't want to hear unpleasant things, only nice ones.'

'I fear there can only be the bad ones for us. My mother can't sleep at night, worrying about us and our feelings for each other. I promised her I would speak to you, so, my sweet Eliza, please listen to me.' He put out his large capable hand and covered her small one. She noticed for the first time that fine blond hair grew on the backs of his fingers as if gold dust had been blown there.

'Yes.' She looked at him with adoration shining in her eyes.

'My mother thinks we should stop seeing each other.'

'No!'

'It's why Ruby went to get the eggs. I was supposed to tell you then, only I kissed you instead.'

'You don't want to see me any more?' She felt her throat constrict.

'How can you ask that? It's not my choice. I have to think of you too. If Mr Forester found out, not only would he be angry with me but you too. I can't risk that. He is your father and you shouldn't argue with him over me. I couldn't have it on my conscience.'

'Why should my father care? I rarely see him. And when he is here he avoids me. You know that's true, Ruby.' But Ruby stood mute.

'That may be the case. I mean, we all know. Everyone on the estate talks about your position and how sad it is. But he will care over something as important as your future husband.'

'I've found the husband I want. No other will do,' she said boldly, surprising herself that she had dared.

'Dear Eliza, there are other considerations. You are a fine lady, I couldn't buy you the things you need and want. Why, we struggle as it is.'

'Money! Is that your worry? Then there is no problem for us.' She laughed. 'I have money – well, not much now, but when I'm eighteen or when I marry I inherit a considerable sum, I don't know how much, from my maternal grandmother. And when my grandmother Forester dies I shall receive money from her too, she told me. So we will have enough.'

'I think you might find that you will not be allowed any of it if you make an unsuitable union. Somehow they will stop you. It will be entailed or some such thing. You must listen to me, Eliza.'

'I'll always listen to you, Jerome. But even if they did that, even if I didn't have a penny, do you think I would care? I would have your love and that would make me the richest woman in the world.'

'Drat! I've hard-boiled the eggs!' Ruby exclaimed.

'And failing everything, we can always elope, have you thought of that, Jerome? How romantic! I have a friend who knows all about what to do. Yes, let us!' She was clapping her hands with innocent excitement, while Jerome looked at his sister helplessly.

Without doubt this was the worst book that her grandmother had ever asked Eliza to read – St Thomas Aquinas. When Lady Gwendoline had first asked her to read aloud it was always a novel, and though it was never one that Eliza would have chosen, it had not been too irksome. But just recently the only things she wanted to hear were religious tracts and extracts from newspapers. And, which was worse, she liked to question Eliza about the reading, so she had to concentrate on the content instead of forgetting it instantly.

'That's enough for today,' Lady Gwendoline said. Eliza closed the book with relief and sat ready to spring up the moment she was told she could go. 'Why is it, child, that you are always in such a hurry to leave me, these days? There was a time when you seemed to enjoy my company.'

'But I do, Grandmama.'

'Then you don't enjoy what you read to me.'

'Sometimes . . .'

'You want to improve your mind, don't you? Miss Chester once lectured me about the need for you to learn.'

'And I want to, Grandmama.'

'It doesn't seem so to me. Why are you spending so much time at Barton Farm?'

'No more than usual, Grandmama.'

'It's been reported to me that you virtually live there. Why?'

'I like the family and there's a child who I think is partly our responsibility and—'

'A child? What child?'

'One of our maids . . . She shouldn't have, of course . . . The scandal . . . But she suffered . . . She's two now and so pretty and—'

'The maid?'

'No, the baby,' she giggled, 'Alex, Mrs Barnard calls her. She's very forward.'

'I'd be most interested to know where you have learnt so much about matters that are not, and never should be, any concern of a young maiden such as yourself. It's quite scandalous!'

'Yes, Grandmama. I understand.'

'I have to confess I am somewhat lost in this narrative. Begin at the beginning.'

Eliza recounted the story. But she had made a valuable discovery: if she talked about the child her grandmother lost interest in the amount of time she spent at the farm.

'Of course it's highly commendable of Mrs Barnard to be so charitable,' Lady Gwendoline said, at the end of the saga, 'but if she felt the need to take on the responsibility then I don't see how it has anything to do with us. Perhaps she should have thought more deeply of what she was doing. A baby is hardly a stray dog, now, is it? They need endless care.'

'But I think it's a beautiful thing to do. And, as I said, Alex is very bright, and I teach her the alphabet . . .' This was almost true: she had looked at a picture book with her once, and she had taken her some of her old toys, so it wasn't too bad a lie.

The 'umph' which issued from her grandmother was

not one to instil confidence, however. 'And your friend Jonquil Gilpin, how is she? Is she not sufficient to amuse you?'

'Oh, yes, we have had great fun and talks together.'

'Though from all I hear, she is not an ideal companion. However, she is slightly more suitable than a tenant farmer's family.'

'Yes, Grandmama.'

'There's talk of her making an unsuitable liaison.'

'Really? She's never said.' Oh dear, how unfortunate that it was so often necessary to lie, Eliza thought.

'I'm relieved to hear it. But you are not to discuss the matter with her. I don't want you getting any stupid romantic notions.'

'Yes, Grandmama.'

'And you have tasks to do for Christmas.'

'Yes, Grandmama.'

'I want you to wrap my gifts for me. Benson is getting too arthritic to do it properly.'

'Yes, Grandmama.'

Jonquil was helping her wrap her grandmother's presents. For every member of staff there was a gift, which they would receive at the Christmas party from the large tree, decorated with candles and sweets, that was always placed in the corner of the great medieval barn at Barton Farm. They were sitting at the large refectory table in the centre of the hall, a huge log fire crackling.

'I love the tree. What a pretty idea.'

'Yes, my grandmother was at Queen Charlotte's court. She always had a tree each Christmas.'

'To belong to a family that moves in *such* circles! You *are* lucky. I suppose the tree is like our evergreens.'

'Just like them.'

'My mother doesn't give presents, she always says the servants prefer money to baubles.'

'The presents are nice, though, don't you think? It's

so sweet of you to help me, I haven't seen' – she put a finger to her lips and winked – 'for nearly a week. My grandmother *will* insist on me reading to her. But my aunt arrives tomorrow and it will be easier for me then – at least I hope it will be.'

'What's it like not having a mother?'

'For me it's normal, since I can't remember having one. It's all I know.'

'Where's she buried? Do you visit her grave?'

'No, she died in Scotland and I've never been there.'

'What did she die of?'

'Having me, I think, but I'm not sure.'

'How awful for you. Does it make you feel guilty?'

'Why should it?'

'Causing her death, of course. How sad, how dreadful for you.'

Eliza looked at the wrapping paper in her hands. Jonquil's words had hit her as hard as if she had struck her. What a monster she must be not to think in that way. It was obvious she should, and yet it had never crossed her mind. Was it surprising, though? Her mother was never mentioned, certainly not since Merry had left, and it was easy for Eliza then to forget. It was a defence of sorts, she decided. But if that was so, and here her spirits lifted, perhaps that was why her father had taken so against her. It was strange how there was so much about her life she didn't know and there was no one she felt she could ask. Maybe Uncle Charles would enlighten her.

'My mother says the way you are neglected is wrong,' Jonquil continued.

'Am I neglected? It doesn't feel as if I am. I've always lived here alone like this with the servants. Apart from nearly two years in London, which I didn't like at all. Too noisy and smelly.'

'But the countryside smells worse!'

'It's nice!' And they argued the merits of country versus town.

Eliza was packing up the wrapping materials when Jonquil said, 'Eliza, there's something I think I should tell you.'

'What's that?'

'My mother knows about you and Jerome.'

Eliza dropped scissors, glue, ribbons and paper, so shocked was she. 'How could she? She doesn't know the Barnards, does she? You've been here no time at all . . .' Though what that had to do with it she wasn't sure: one could find things out in a day as well as a year. But she was cold suddenly with fear.

'Our cook told her. She was doing the menus and mother mentioned inviting your family to dine, and it transpired she used to work here and knows you well.'

'Mrs Satterly?'

'I don't know her name – I don't even know for certain where our kitchens are!' She laughed.

'She doesn't like me.'

'What shall you do?'

'What is there to do? Will your mother say anything?'

'I don't know. I can't promise she won't.'

'Then I shall have to tell my father how I feel.'

'Do you dare?'

'I have no choice. I love Jerome, and my father will have to know sooner or later that I want to marry him.' Brave words, so it was puzzling that she felt sick with nerves.

II

It was to be a small party for Christmas, the family only. When this information filtered down to the servants' hall, it led to much speculation. The servants always took an inordinate interest in the financial status of their masters. Not only was it a matter of pride to work for the rich but it was always advisable to know that all was well and that new positions need not be looked for. They decided that they had no need to worry, that the reason was probably the declining health of Lady Gwendoline, who, despite Maggie Bones's best efforts, was hardly eating at all.

'She won't last long into the New Year at this rate,' was Mrs King's opinion. And most agreed with her, since the old lady now spent most of her time sleeping and seemed unable to find the energy even to complain. Benson, her maid of forty years, was frequently red-eyed with distress.

His not eating might have been a contributory factor but it wasn't the only one. That became evident when Frederick Forester arrived.

'Papa, are you not well?' The words escaped Eliza before she had time to think, for her father looked so ill. He was thin, his complexion was muddy, and there was a look of exhaustion in his eyes that she had never seen before.

'Don't fuss,' he snapped, as he swept past her.

She wouldn't have known where to begin fussing over her father, of all people. One needed to know someone before one could care for them.

Now that she was older she was expected to dine with him. She dreaded this, with no one else present to help her with the conversation. He sat at one end of the table and she sat at his right hand. She had told Densham to lay her place there for it would, she felt, have been presumptuous to sit where her grandmother habitually did, at the other end.

'Did you enjoy Rome, Papa?'

'It was hot.'

'So late in the year?' Evidently the weather was not a subject to pursue. Silence descended, except for the occasional clatter of a dish on the sideboard where Densham and one of the Jameses stood most of the time like waxworks.

'Grandmama is very tired.'

'So she tells me.'

'I read to her.'

'How dutiful of you.'

The fish was served. She noticed how quickly her father ate so that he was finished before she was half-way through hers. And she also observed how rapidly he drank his claret – he never touched white wine – so that the decanter was soon empty. Densham appeared to pour from a second without a word being said.

When her father looked at her plate with annoyance, she laid down her knife and fork as though she had finished. 'I have new friends, the Gilpins. They live at Plumpton Manor.'

'So I was informed.'

'They are very pleasant people.'

The entrée arrived. Nothing she said was of interest to him. She knew he did not care what she did or what she thought and was no longer hurt by this, but she wondered how she would ever introduce the subject of Jerome. Or maybe if she did he would wake up and take notice of her. More likely he would not even register what she was saying.

'The new cook is doing well.'

'Domestic matters are of no interest to me.'

Eliza looked down at her plate. Should she say something?

'I visit the Barnards at Barton Farm quite often.'

'Father's a waster.'

'I never met him.'

'Ill, isn't he?' Good gracious, she thought, a glimmer of interest.

'No, he died. Did you not know?' Her father shrugged but said nothing. 'His son works hard, though.' She couldn't quite bring herself to use his name.

'Have you no conversation other than domestic trivia?'

'Apparently not, sir.'

Eliza's mind was now a complete blank as to what to

say next. Had he always been like this? Had her mother endured such dinners?

'Where's my mother buried, Papa?'

His eyes, which had looked so dull and exhausted, now stared at her intently, black with anger – she knew that look from the past.

'I would like to visit her grave. Put some flowers on it. Talk to her . . .' She trailed off as her father stood up abruptly, pushing back his chair before Densham could do it for him. Without another word he strode from the room.

'Dessert, Miss Eliza?'

'No thank you, Densham.'

Eliza was even looking forward to the arrival of her aunt Minnie – and of course she longed to see her uncle: at least there would be some life in the house. When she was here alone with just the servants she took the silence as normal and it did not bother her. But with people in the house, it seemed unnatural. At last Aunt Minnie and Uncle Charles arrived.

'I'm worried about my father,' she said, as she poured tea for them. 'He's so thin, and his complexion concerns me. We have a new doctor, a Dr Forbes, and I was wondering if I should call him. What do you think, Aunt?' She handed Minnie a teacup and saucer.

'I think your father would consider it none of your business. He's quite capable of calling the doctor for himself.'

'But he says he's not ill.'

'If he says so then evidently he isn't.'

'Minnie, don't be unkind to Eliza.'

'I wasn't aware I was being so. I'm speaking the truth to her. I know Freddie, he won't appreciate anyone fussing over him.'

'That's what he said when he arrived. And I don't. But sometimes in the morning he looks yellow, as if he has jaundice, and that can't be right, can it?'

'A bit liverish, probably. Your father has always enjoyed his wine. But has he told you the momentous news? You are to come to London for the season, I am to be your chaperone, you will be presented at Court and there will be balls, parties . . .' As her aunt listed the delights ahead Eliza, who had known this was to be her fate, felt her spirits plummet with despair. She did not want to go to London, she did not want to be part of society, she wanted to marry Jerome and be a farmer's wife.

'You might show a little more interest. You are such a dour creature, Eliza, no spark in you at all.' Aunt Minnie stood up. 'I must go and see Mama. Are you coming, Charles?'

'No, you go first. I'm going to have another slice of this delicious Dundee cake.'

Eliza passed him the cake and poured him more tea.

'I met a friend of yours the other day.'

'Really, who?'

'Miss Chester.'

'No! How wonderful! How is she? Where did you meet her?'

'In London, she has her own school to run.'

'That *is* good news. But let me know the address . . .' Already she was up and swooping to the desk for paper and pencil.

'I no longer know. She has decamped to the country-side. Larger premises, I was told.'

'Did she mention me?'

'But of course. We talked of nothing else.' He gave his sardonic grin, which Eliza had always thought was the most attractive thing about him.

'I should so love to see her again.'

'I fear that would not be possible, or suitable. She has a protector and your father would never agree.'

'Miss Chester!' Eliza's eyes widened. Jonquil had told her all about such liaisons. 'That is so hard to believe.'

'It happens.' He stood up, crossed to the decanters

and poured himself a large whisky, to which he added no water. Eliza sat watching him. Was this the opportunity she needed? He shouldn't have given her that information. But because he had, maybe . . . He was the one person who was most likely to understand. Should she talk to him, trust him?

'Uncle Charles, may I confide in you?'

'I should regard it as an honour.'

'I have a friend.'

'You mean' – he waved his glass in the air – 'a special sort of friend.'

'Yes, you could call him that.'

'Ah, a *him*. I'm all ears.' He leant towards her, looking over his shoulder as he did so, checking they were still alone. That made her sure she could trust him.

'You promise not to tell?'

'Cross my heart and hope to die!' There was the grin again. He was so understanding!

'He runs Barton Farm now, since his father died. You might know him. Jerome Barnard.' There, she had said his name to someone in authority, to one of her own family.

'Big strapping fellow, blond. Must make a few maidens' pulses race.' He smiled.

'I love him.'

'Does he love you?'

'Yes. We wish to be married.'

Charles put his plate back on the tray. 'This is serious.'

'Very.'

'But you haven't thought about it logically, Eliza. You are allowing your heart to rule your head. And that is always dangerous.'

'I'll never feel like this about anyone else, ever. I just know.'

'I should tell your father.'

'Uncle Charles! No! You promised!'

'It would not be—'

'Please don't say *suitable*, or I shall scream.'

'But, Eliza, what has this man to offer you other than his looks and charm? Has he any money? Any prospects?'

'No, but I have. We shan't starve.'

At this Charles laughed. 'I wouldn't put money on it. If your father knew, he would make certain that this young man never saw a penny of your money.'

'I don't care.'

'You would. When the babies came, and you had nothing and you were worn down with work the resentments would build.'

'They wouldn't.' She looked stubborn.

'Then what about him? Say you do have money, how is he to feel as a kept man? It is not a manly thing. I should know.'

Eliza tossed her head proudly and stared pointedly out of the window. 'But he would have, since any money I have would be his. It's the law.'

'But the law can be avoided. Properties can be entailed, money left in trusts, many ways. It's true. What I tell you is possible. Listen, Eliza, let me tell you about myself. I have nothing, your aunt has all the money – which your father gives her. I have to ask for everything I need. And what has happened to me as a result? I am half the man I was when I married her and had some money of my own – all of which I stupidly lost. My wife despises me. If you love Jerome, think of what it would do to him.'

'But I'm not like my aunt.'

'Bad-tempered and horrible, you mean? Don't look embarrassed, I know exactly what she is like. The point is, Eliza, she wasn't like that when I married her. She was sweet and pretty, much like you. I made her how she is. The responsibility lies with me.'

'Why?'

'Because she cannot respect me.'

He looked so sad that Eliza burst into tears and hurled herself across the room to comfort him.

Now two others knew, her uncle and Mrs Gilpin. In the few days left before Christmas Eliza felt sick with apprehension. She told Ruby, who was aghast that she had mentioned the romance to her uncle.

'He won't tell, I'm sure.'

'You don't know that. What if my family are turned out of the farm and with Christmas coming? What would we do?' Ruby looked as though she was on the point of tears.

'It hasn't happened yet and I won't let them. You've nothing to worry about.'

But Ruby was even more agitated than she: she jumped at the slightest noise and was constantly dropping things. For the first time in their relationship, she began to snap at Eliza, which she would never have dared to do before.

For her part, Eliza watched her uncle like a hawk. He seemed to grin at her more frequently, and wink at her as if he were enjoying the conspiracy. If so, it was cruel of him. Her clothes began to hang loose on her since she could hardly eat a morsel.

The worst ordeal was the dinner arranged for the Gilpin family. Eliza's mouth was so dry she could barely speak, and she knocked over a glass of wine which, from her aunt's reaction, was a serious crime. Jonquil came to her rescue, sparkling for her, and Miss Gilpin was kind and talked to her about the birds that visited her birdbath. Mr Gilpin was in fine form and as he took centre stage with his stories she allowed herself to relax.

They had a new house guest too, a friend of her uncle and aunt, Hedworth Alford. He was extremely handsome, with dark hair and eyes. He was tall and moved with effortless elegance. His clothes were of the best and their fit accentuated his fine figure.

'Miss Forester,' – he bowed over her hand – 'your aunt did not exaggerate.'

'I beg your pardon?' Eliza was flustered by this sophisticated man. As they spoke, he arched his eyebrows quizzically, which, she later learnt, others found attractive. It alarmed her, for she was not sure if he was laughing at her.

'Your beauty.'

Eliza turned scarlet.

'Charming,' he said, then apologised fulsomely for embarrassing her.

'It's the heat in this room,' she explained, and knew that he was not convinced.

'May I?' He indicated the seat beside her. She wished he would go away, but then the strangest thing happened: suddenly, as they spoke, she felt as if she were the only person of importance to him, as if he were interested in everything she had to say. It was a new experience for her.

Mrs Gilpin fluttered over to them and Eliza thought the woman was going to have the vapours when she introduced her to Lord Alford.

Then dinner was announced, and Eliza was flustered all over again when Alford proffered his arm.

'I'm not sure,' Eliza said. 'I did not check the list.'

'You aunt instructed me to escort you.'

She was glad he was not acting from choice. He was charming but far too intimidating for her.

The meal wore on and Eliza persuaded herself that if Mrs Gilpin was going to tell her father about her and Jerome, she would hardly do it at the table. Surely she would speak to him in private. She even managed to eat a little. But she felt all the time as if she were about to cry and that if anyone had said, 'Boo!' to her she would.

Later, in the drawing room, she avoided Mrs Gilpin, who was content to chat with her aunt.

'Isn't your uncle *wonderful*?' Jonquil gushed.

'He's very popular with the ladies.' As soon as she

saw the disappointed expression on Jonquil's face she regretted saying that. 'He liked you, though,' she added. 'It was obvious.'

'You spoilt it!'

'I'm sorry.'

'That Lord Alford is rather divine too.'

'Better than your John?'

'Well . . . he would make a fine catch.'

'Jonquil!'

The gentlemen joined them and the courtly flirting continued, but Eliza kept looking at the clock and wishing the evening would end. At last, Mrs Gilpin stood and began her farewells, a somewhat lengthy process. She finally reached Eliza. She leant forward. 'Miss Forester, certain information has come to my notice. If you desist in such matters, then I shall of course say nothing. I am not one to cause unpleasantness in any form.' She spoke in an undertone, smiling, so that no one could possibly have guessed what she was saying.

'Yes, Mrs Gilpin.' She dropped a small curtsy. In a way she was grateful to the woman. There was nothing for it now but to tell her father of her feelings. All that remained was to decide when.

'What appalling people,' Aunt Minnie said, as the door closed behind them. 'I do hope you don't invite them ever again, Eliza. Not our sort, at all.'

'I rather liked Gilpin. And Miss Jonquil is delicious,' Charles said.

'You are such a poor judge of everything,' his wife admonished.

'But Miss Jonquil was nothing compared with our Miss Eliza,' Lord Alford interjected.

'There's no need to over-egg the pudding, Hedworth,' Minnie snapped.

'Miss Bones, may I speak with you?'

'Of course, Mr Didier.'

Maggie removed her apron. 'A brandy, Mr Didier?'

'That would be most agreeable.'

'So, what can I do for you?' she asked, once they were settled at the kitchen table.

'We work well together, and you are a wonderful cook,' he said. Maggie's smile threatened to split her face in two.

'I have a proposition to put to you. Should you not be interested then I would not be offended.'

'Yes?' She looked at him with curiosity.

'I don't want to remain a chef in service all my life, you understand?'

'I do.'

'I have been saving for many years, and I have found a property that I am in the process of buying. It is a hotel, not a big one, but it is a start.'

'Where is it?'

'In Exeter. It has ten chambers, a smoking room and a tap room, and I hope to open a restaurant – they become so popular – fine food, not a chop house you realise. And I wondered if you would join me.'

'Me?'

'I realise that with your talent you have a fine future here. That your work is secure for the rest of your life, if you wish. But if you could see yourself taking a risk . . .'

'Oh, yes, please!'

'That is wonderful news. And if it works well, and we are content together, then perhaps we could have a partnership?'

'Mr Didier, you've made me a very happy woman.'

'And you, Miss Bones, have made me a happy man!'

Chapter Four
Saturday, 18 December 1875–
Sunday, 19 December 1875

Every year, on the Saturday before Christmas, Frederick Forester held a party for the tenants and staff on his estate. He did this because it was expected of him. He did not enjoy the event but always attended. His sister avoided it if she could for, as she loudly proclaimed, she disliked such close proximity to the *hoipolloi*. His mother, however, enjoyed the party and even this year, poorly as she was, insisted she would go.

As for the tenantry and servants, their feelings about the party were mixed. There were many, mainly the younger ones, who looked forward to it and enjoyed it, but the older people would have preferred to be given money instead. But everyone enjoyed the food and drink.

Planning for the event started weeks before the date, and in the days beforehand, Mr Didier and Maggie worked non-stop to prepare the food. Whole pigs and scores of chickens were roasted, and every oven was in constant use. Even the enormous spit, rarely used, which hung over the range was oiled and set in motion, the cogs and chains clanking as half a bullock rotated over the hot coals. Pasties were prepared, potatoes scrubbed and oiled for baking in their jackets while jellies set and trifles were decorated. Barrels of beer and cider were hauled up from the cellars.

Nearly three hundred people would be coming. The musicians, four fiddlers and an accordionist, were estate workers who had been given a day off to practise – they knew that if they did not perform well their lives would be made miserable by the others.

It had taken a week to decorate the thatched medieval barn at Barton Farm, which was now garlanded with holly and evergreens. Boxes of long gaily coloured ribbons had been unearthed from the attics at Harcourt Barton and tied to the beams so that they wafted and twirled prettily in the draughts from far below. Rushes, candles and dozens of oil lamps lit the scene, but even they were not enough and there were many dark corners for those who might be in search of privacy. The floor, with its uneven cobbles, had been swept, scrubbed and covered with straw, but a few ricked ankles were inevitable. For all the scouring, though, there was still a fine cloud of dust in the air, which would increase a hundredfold before the night was out; the partygoers would cough, wheeze and sneeze for days to come.

Opposite the great double doors large enough, Eliza thought, for a brace of elephants to pass through, six long trestle tables were placed and covered with pristine white cloths, on which the food would be set out. Next to them were the barrels of beer and cider, and tables with rows of tankards and jugs of lemonade for the women. The presents for the staff from Lady Gwendoline and Eliza were piled invitingly beneath a large pine tree – a recent addition to the festivities. And a gaggle of impatient children had been in attendance all day.

All was ready.

This year Eliza was dressing with especial care. She wanted to look pretty for Jerome. 'It feels so silky.' She wriggled as Ruby slipped the new dress over her head. She stood still as Ruby laced the back for her. 'It is pretty, isn't it?' She looked at her image in the long mirror. The dress had been made for her in Exeter and now she smoothed the bodice and her slim waist. 'It fits like a glove, doesn't it?' It was made of white satin trimmed with pink. There had been a lovely green silk too but she felt this fabric was more suitable for one of her age. It would not shock her father and grandmother as the other might have done. 'Do you think it's modest enough?'

'Perfect. And the pearls look just right.'

'Grandmama offered to lend me her rubies but they're too ornate.'

'If you look too grand Jerome will run away.' Ruby giggled.

'I wouldn't blame him.' Eliza turned her head and saw in the mirror the silk roses that cascaded across one shoulder and down the back of her dress – it was as pretty from the back as it was from the front.

'One of the flowers is slipping. Could you sit down a minute, miss?' Ruby rearranged one of the Christmas roses she had pinned in Eliza's hair. Considerately the flowers had bloomed to perfection just in time. 'You look ever so grown-up with your hair in a chignon.'

'I don't feel it.' Eliza liked the image that was reflected back at her. She had never dressed up grandly for the party before, usually wearing the least elaborate of her dresses: anything else seemed like showing off when their guests had so little finery. But tonight was different: tonight she needed to look older, more confident. Ruby dropped the comb. 'Butterfingers!' Eliza said.

'I'm all fingers and thumbs this evening.'

'Henry?' Eliza teased her. Yesterday Ruby had confided in her that the gamekeeper's son appeared, at last, to have noticed her.

'I've liked him for years, but it was as if he didn't see me.'

'Perhaps he's shy?'

'Shy or not, I shall punish him and dance with everyone but him.'

'That would be cruel and it might take him years to pluck up courage to notice you again.'

'True! There, that's all done. You look a treat.'

'You must run along and get yourself ready. Does the dress I gave you fit?'

'It's lovely, miss.'

'Here, wear this too.' And from her jewel case Eliza took her cameo, and a tortoiseshell comb. 'For your hair.'

'You're so kind, miss.'

'We two shall be the belles of the ball. Now, I must go and see my grandmother.'

'Is she coming to the party?'

'No. She'd hoped to, but she's very tired. Benson has persuaded her to have a light supper and go to bed.'

The family congregated in the drawing room.

'It's too far to walk to the barn. I trust you've ordered the carriages, Freddie?' Minnie, resplendent in gold taffeta and diamonds, enquired.

'Don't I always?'

Eliza was sitting by the window. She felt her aunt looked more suitably dressed for a grand London ball than a country barn dance. She would look intimidating and out of place. She admired her father, her uncle and his friend, Hedworth Alford, in their high-collared, diamond-pinned cravats and blindingly white shirts with their black tail-coats. They were so smart, but she wished her father didn't look so tired. And whatever was ailing him was not improving his temper.

The others were chatting while Eliza watched, as always, from the edge of the company. As she observed them she was sure they weren't even aware that she was there, as if she were of no consequence to them. Only her grandmother and her uncle noticed her. But then, she thought, as she hugged herself, not for much longer!

Soon she would belong to a real family. At first she had been surprised at, then envious of, the easy, happy atmosphere she had encountered at the Barnards' and also at the Gilpins'. These families chatted, laughed with and teased each other. If there was a problem then they solved it together, she was sure. She had always accepted the way she had lived as normal, but now she saw it was the other way round. They were not distant and cool with each other as she and her father were. That was the wrong way. She had already resolved that when she and Jerome had a family – ah, such a happy thought – she would make certain that none of their children ever felt left out as she had. And she would tell her children every day of their lives how much she loved them.

'I could quite envy Mama, feeling too fatigued to be present. These events are so dull in their vulgarity.' Aunt Minnie's strident voice reached her.

'Duty, Lady Wickham, can be tedious.'

'How right you are, Lord Alford. And I must have endured twenty-five of these parties now.' She smiled coyly.

That's a lie if ever I heard one, thought Eliza. She knew that her aunt was forty next birthday. She was flirting outrageously with Hedworth Alford and that was surely wrong. She wondered if Uncle Charles minded. She watched them closely for a minute or two, but concluded that he wasn't aware of what his wife was doing. Poor innocent Uncle Charles.

Eliza was thinking of such matters since she was sure that if she concentrated on herself she would have to race from the room to be sick – she felt so nervous. She wished her father was in a better mood. He had so much to be happy about but always looked miserable. Poor Papa, to be grieving still.

'Eliza, if you're going to be unsociable, then at least sit straight. You are slouching.'

'Yes, Aunt.' Why was it that the woman only ever spoke to her to correct her? It was as if she enjoyed humiliating her.

'Aunts can be such dragons, can't they? May I?' Hedworth Alford was standing in front of her, a footman behind him with a tray of glasses. 'I thought you might like some champagne?'

'I may not, thank you.'

'I think that this evening you may, to help you through a function that your aunt thinks will be tedious. May I?' He sat down opposite her.

Eliza glanced across at her father, and he nodded his assent to the drink. 'It won't be tedious. I always enjoy the Christmas party. They have far more fun than we do.'

'Oh dear, I stand corrected. Or, rather, I sit corrected.' He smiled but she didn't bother to respond since she found him rather patronising, as if she were still in the schoolroom rather than about to enter society.

'My aunt was a real dragon. But everything she did was for my benefit, really. She had my interests at heart.'

'I am sure she did, Lord Alford,' she said, convinced that her own aunt did not give a button what happened to her.

'You look very beautiful this evening.'

'Thank you.' She bowed her head in acknowledgement, though she didn't believe he meant it. She wondered if Jerome would find her so and what he would say.

'I hear you play the piano well.'

'I can't imagine who told you that. I play very badly.'

'You are too modest, Miss Forester. I trust you will play for us upon our return?'

'I'm sure I shall be far too tired by then, Lord Alford.'

She wished he would go away. She was quite content to sit here and think her own thoughts rather than making this false, stilted conversation, which, she knew, her aunt regarded as scintillating. In marrying Jerome she would be saved from the tedium of London society.

'The carriages await,' Densham announced, in his normal sombre tone. But, as usual, it was a good five minutes before her aunt was ready, and Eliza was swept away to her destiny.

With no social niceties to impede her, Ruby was already half-way across the park to the party. She'd put on the blue dress Eliza had lent her then taken it off again. It was far too grand: she didn't want to frighten Henry, and she would probably be laughed at in it by some of the others, who'd think she was trying to be a cut above herself. And she would have had to tolerate snide comments from those who were jealous of her having it in the first place. It was best not to antagonise the others when she had to work with them. She hoped Miss Eliza wouldn't be hurt when she saw she was wearing the plaid dress she'd made herself and worn last year.

As she neared the barn she could hear that the musicians had already struck up: they were playing Sir Roger de Coverley, but Ruby's favourite dance was Strip the Willow. They wouldn't have that, though, until after Mr Forester had said a few words. Most of the men, she suspected, would already be a bit tiddly. By the end of the evening few of them would be fit for dancing so the women would partner each other. Ruby had vowed to have just half a glass of cider – any more and she'd be giggly: it was strong stuff. The old crones, retired workers or widows, would be waiting and watching like a row of crows hoping to see one of the girls behaving improperly. By tomorrow any victim they spied would be labelled a hussy and a drunkard, and her marriage prospects would lie in tatters. She'd seen it happen many times in the past. She loved Harcourt Barton and was content to spend the rest of her life there, but there were disadvantages: the number of people required to man the large estate – a couple of hundred, she'd heard, at the last count – meant that they were a complete community, if a small one, so gossip and spite were rife.

As she scurried along she heard bushes rustling.

Someone's early, she thought, and wondered how many babies would be made tonight. Yet more tittle-tattle to amuse those old witches!

'You look nice.'

'Thanks, Maggie. But you look *lovely*! I've never seen you dressed up before.'

'Bet you thought I slept in my overall. I bought it in Tiverton. What do you think? Is it all right?' And Maggie twirled the better to show off the gingham dress she was wearing, but Ruby noted she was still wearing the high-buttoned black boots she wore every day in the kitchen.

'It's perfect. And I love your hair.'

Maggie's hair was curled into ringlets, which bounced as she walked. It was strange how, out of uniform, everyone looked so different. Ruby supposed she did too.

'I handed in my notice today.' Maggie was whispering so that the other girls didn't hear. 'It's silly to try to keep it secret, I know, when the news is probably out already.'

'You're leaving us? You never said.'

'I didn't want to until it was all arranged in case something went wrong.'

'Where will you go?'

Maggie leant forward and murmured, 'Mr Didier has asked me to go into business with him. He's bought a hotel in Exeter and he's asked me to join him.'

'Maggie, that's wonderful. He's such a nice man.'

'I think I can trust him, don't you? Mrs Satterly hated him – I think because he was the better cook.'

'Probably.' Ruby laughed. 'Maybe he's thinking of more than a business partnership.'

'Oh, Ruby, you do say daft things.' And Maggie gave her a push, but not before Ruby saw that she was blushing.

The musicians tuned up again. The dancing was still sedate, and it was mostly the older couples and some children who were circling in what approximated to a waltz. The others were standing or sitting on the bales of hay arranged around the barn. They were watching and waiting, pretending nonchalance while seething inside with nerves.

Ruby was looking out for Henry, and saw him standing, tankard in hand, with a group of other young men, by the drink trestle. Only Jerome, beside him, was taller. Henry's trousers were tight, as if they had shrunk, but they showed off his lovely strong legs to perfection. She knew he'd seen her for he had turned away abruptly, blushing bright red. Should she go up and pretend to greet her brother? No, she'd sit over here with Maggie, let him come to her. No point in seeming forward – men didn't like that.

'There's your mum, Ruby.'

Grace Barnard was standing by the double doors with a group of other outdoor workers' wives. 'Funny, isn't it, how the indoor servants hardly ever talk to the others?' Maggie continued.

'Not all of us,' Ruby said, with a happy smile, glancing secretly at Henry.

'Your mother doesn't look well, Ruby. Is she all right?'

Ruby saw that Grace was clutching a shawl over her coat. 'I'd better go and talk to her.' She wove her way through the throng. 'You look frozen, Mum.'

'Ruby! Thank goodness you're early. I must talk to you.' Grace took her arm and led her outside.

'Should you be out here, Mum? It's so cold – look, it's snowing.'

Fat flakes were falling but her mother propelled her along the wall of the barn far from those who were still arriving. 'I don't want to be overheard. You know what this place is like.'

'What is it? What's happened?'

'Jerome is about to do something stupid. He's going to ask Mr Forester if he can marry Eliza – tonight!'

'But that's wonderful.'

'For God's sake, Ruby, don't be so damned stupid.'

Ruby stopped dead in her tracks. 'Mum!' Grace never swore and could not abide those who did.

'We shall be thrown out, lock, stock and barrel. He's a vicious man, is Forester. He'll ruin us, but most of all Jerome.'

'If he says no, what can they do? She's under twenty-one – they'll have to wait.'

'And in the meantime we lose everything for a stupid romance!'

'He can't help being in love with her. It happened, they didn't mean it to.'

'And how long do you think it will last? They are from different classes, she has money and he has none.'

'They have a lot in common – Jerome reads, he likes poetry. They spend most of their time quoting it at each other . . .'

'Ruby, you're not listening to me.' Again she grabbed her daughter's arm. 'I want you to talk to him, make him see sense.'

'It's too late now, if he intends to speak to Mr Forester tonight.'

'I've been waiting days for you to come. I needed to talk to you.'

'With Lady Gwendoline ill we haven't been able to get away. Eliza's been sitting with her hour after hour.'

'But you haven't. I sent you a note to come urgently, that I had things to discuss with you.'

'I didn't get any note.'

'But you must have. I sent it with Ivy . . .'

'And did you ask her if she'd delivered it? Does she know you're worried about Jerome and Eliza? Of course she does. There's your answer, Mum. She can't be trusted. You know that, after the business over the book. She's caused me enough problems. Mrs King has been distant with me ever since.'

'No, that's not likely. That was because of Miss Chester, nothing else.'

'Oh, Mum!' Ruby sighed. It was then she noticed that her mother was shaking. 'Look, Mum, if you're right, her father will refuse his permission and that will be that.'

'But you don't know the rest of it. If he does refuse, they plan to elope.'

'Elope!' Ruby knew she sounded like an imbecile. 'Where to?'

'He says that if they go to London, join a large parish, who's to know who they are and how old she is? There are always careless priests who for money . . . And then there's Scotland.'

'Scotland!' There she was again.

'And where will that leave all of us, pray? Out in the yard. I know Frederick Forester of old. He's not a man to be crossed.'

'But if that were so, then I'm sure Eliza will buy a farm for us, somewhere far from this. She has money, I know, and she told me that when she marries she inherits a lot. Mind you, it'll break her heart. She loves this place more than anywhere else on earth. So she must really love our Jerome, don't you see?'

'*If* she sees a penny of it. Her father will make sure she doesn't. And I don't know what to do, or where to turn . . .' To Ruby's horror her mother burst into tears, which Ruby had never seen her do, no matter how hard life was, even when her rheumatism was playing her up.

'Oh, Mum, don't cry. Maybe they'll be too afraid to say anything. Maybe it will all blow over. Perhaps he won't punish you for something your son has done.'

'Then you don't know the Foresters!' she sobbed. 'And there's more . . .'

'Cooeee . . .' Mrs King was moving towards them.

'What does she want? I'll tell you the rest later, Ruby.'

*

'How long do we have to endure this?' Minnie asked, as the carriages approached the barn from which they could hear the sound of many people enjoying themselves.

'An hour?' Frederick suggested.

'How about half an hour?'

'It's our duty.'

'Every time you say that I wish I could scream. In any case I don't see that it's tactful of us to stay too long. You know our being there always makes them subdued. Spoils their peasant fun. I'm sure when we depart a great cheer goes up.'

'Three-quarters, then,' Frederick conceded.

'I think I can endure the stench for that amount of time.'

Eliza, squashed in the corner of the carriage, could happily have hit her aunt. She was always talking about how the servants smelt, which was ironic, given that her own armpits often stank, despite the number of sweat guards she wore.

But she no longer cared about her aunt. She was about to see Jerome. Her life was about to be illuminated with his presence, which changed everything about her so that she could see no ugliness and hear nothing discordant.

The carriages halted and Lord Alford, who had ridden over the park, was waiting to help Minnie Wickham out of the carriage. There was much squealing at the sight of the snow on the ground, and laughter at his offer to carry her.

'Just get out, Minnie, and let us get this over with,' her irritated brother snapped at her.

Uncle Charles helped Eliza. 'What a sparkle in your eyes! Am I to understand a certain someone is here?' he whispered.

'Ssh.'

Her father took his sister's arm. Alford offered Eliza

his. She would have preferred to enter on her uncle's arm but courtesy forced her to accept.

Eliza always hated the moment when they entered through the great doors of the barn: the music stopped dead, as did the laughter and conversation. Tonight was no different. Silence, like a giant blanket, descended as the doors were flung back and they stepped inside. Women bobbed and men bowed as they progressed down the centre of the barn to the dais that had been prepared for them. Minnie Wickham nodded graciously and smiled to left and right. Eliza expected her to wave at any minute, as if she were the Queen. All eyes were on them but she dared not look up in case she saw Jerome. Then, she knew, she would smile broadly and blush, and everyone would know.

As they sat on the dais they were served wine by hired servants – Eliza noticed that Mr Densham was watching every move they made with a beady eye.

She was trying hard to find Jerome without making it obvious. She had a fan, which she was able to use to some effect, hiding behind it yet spying over the top. She saw Ruby and her mother across the hall and smiled at them, but was alarmed that they did not smile back. Had something happened to Jerome?

At this point the estate agent got to his feet and made a ponderous speech of welcome to them. Eliza did not listen: he always droned on, saying little of importance but liking the sound of his own voice too much to stop. He did so eventually, but only after two little girls were pushed on to the dais by the gamekeeper and she and Aunt Minnie were given bouquets. Eliza wasn't sure how to respond. Her aunt took them with a frosty smile, but Eliza bent down and kissed the little girl, which was met with a satisfactory murmur of approval from the throng.

Her father rose to make his reply. Would it never end? she thought. She saw Ruby and Grace Barnard sneaking around the back of the crowd. Still she watched for Jerome. Ah, she sighed, with inward relief, there he was, standing by the cider table. She couldn't imagine how she had missed him.

How smart he looked. She'd never seen him in a suit before, and it made him look even more handsome. He had boots on, not shoes, but they twinkled in the rush lighting as he walked. And he had a cravat at his neck. But the way he stood made her think he was not happy dressed up in his finery. It made her love him even more.

She watched as he joined his mother and Ruby. But what were they doing? His mother appeared to be cross with him for she was berating him. It was difficult to see his expression since their heads were bent together. Then Jerome raised his head and looked directly at her. She gave him a secret smile and fluttered her fan flirtatiously, but he did not smile back either.

'A fine specimen,' Uncle Charles whispered in her ear. She decided to ignore him, afraid her emotions would show on her face.

The audience applauded her father and then the music began again, not as loudly as when they had arrived, and few took to the floor. Still she could see Jerome and his mother and sister arguing ... What about? They kept looking at her, and her heart thudded. The others in her party were chattering but she was not aware of what they said. What could be going on? Unable to stand it a moment longer she stood up. 'Excuse me,' she said, to her aunt and her father, and jumped off the platform, landing lightly on her feet. Then, moving swiftly, not giving herself time to think what she was about, she skirted the dance area and arrived beside Jerome.

'Hello,' she said, smiling brightly – which, given her unease, was difficult – and knew that something was afoot. Ruby and her mother couldn't look at her, and although Jerome did it was with such a sad expression that her instinct was to throw herself into his arms and ask him what was worrying him so. But she could not do that here, not with her father present, for she was sure he was watching her every move.

'Ruby, would you do me the honour?'

Henry, unnoticed by the others, was suddenly at Ruby's elbow. Poor Henry, he was as red as a beetroot and he'd got spots, Eliza noticed, not like Jerome.

Ruby looked uncertain. 'It's a bit difficult, just at this moment, Henry.' She looked pointedly at Eliza. Henry went an even deeper red. It had cost him dear to ask, Eliza saw, and Ruby must accept – it would be cruel not to. There was an awkward silence – torture for the shy.

'Jerome, will you honour me?' Eliza decided to rescue the situation and tugged at his sleeve. She heard both Ruby and his mother say, 'Miss Eliza,' in warning tones, but she took no notice. Already she was on the dance floor, or what passed for one, her hand held out to Jerome, her love for him beaming from her face for all to see. 'Please.'

Jerome held her round the waist, his hand in hers. 'One, two, three,' he said, 'I'm not very good at the polka.' He began to twirl her round with such speed that they spun past the more sedate dancers. But they too, upon seeing their young mistress speeding among them, caught the excitement, and everyone moved with more joy and freedom.

Eliza flung back her head and saw the great oak beams swirling above her. Round and round they whirled, and she felt as if she were in the centre, an integral part, of a giant, whirling kaleidoscope. She was laughing, fuelled by the heady combination of Jerome, the heat, the excitement, music, the squeals of the other women, and the intensity of her love.

'Oh, Jerome! Such excitement.' She would have liked to collapse into his arms with exhilaration. But sense prevailed. Instead at the end of the dance she dropped him a graceful curtsy.

'I love you,' he whispered, as he held out his hand and helped her upright. 'Never forget.'

'As I love you,' she whispered back, but she wanted to shout it to the assembled company, longed to stand on the stage and proclaim their love, climb to the rooftop and shout it to the surrounding countryside.

'Shall I take you back to your father or do you want some lemonade?'

Eliza could see her father glaring at her. 'Lemonade, please.' The decision was easy.

Guiding her decorously through the throng towards the back of the barn, as far away from her family as possible, they found a couple of vacant bales. While Jerome went to join the mêlée where the drinks were being served Eliza waited, trying to ignore the curious looks.

'Happy, miss?' Ruby swept up with Henry, who went off to fetch her a drink.

'Oh, Ruby!' She thought she would never be able to speak again without a sigh of happiness.

'You certainly look it, Miss Eliza.'

'You too, Ruby. Henry's very handsome.'

'Do you think so? He's a bit on the thin side, apart from his legs!'

'Then you'll have to feed him up when you marry him.'

'He hasn't even said he likes me, let alone loves me.'

'You just have to see the way he looks at you to know he does.'

'Honestly?' Ruby hugged herself.

'Why were you and your mother so cool with me, just now?' Eliza said.

Ruby looked flustered. 'Were we?'

'You know you were.'

'I wasn't aware.' She glanced about her. 'I think you've made everyone talk, dancing with my brother.'

'I don't care. Let them. Everyone has to know sooner or later about us.' How wonderful her defiance made her feel. But why was Ruby changing the subject?

'Judging by the gossip, I'd make it later if I were you.'

'I didn't think you listened to gossip, Ruby,' she teased.

'Just take a quick look.'

Around the barn she could see huddles of people whispering. Every now and then they glanced in her direction then hunched back and the mumbling began again. It was one thing to say she didn't care what people said. It was entirely different to see them gossiping about her. She looked away. 'Perhaps I should leave.' Just as she began to stand Jerome and Henry returned.

'Lemonade, as requested.' Jerome handed her the glass, making an exaggerated bow. She patted the bale beside her.

'Jerome, what is wrong? Your mother was looking so anxious, and I don't think she wanted to talk to me. I don't think she was happy that I joined you.'

Jerome took a long draught from his tankard of beer. 'She's had a warning about us.'

'What?'

'Henry's father, Luke, came to see her this evening – just as she was about to leave to come here. He wouldn't say who had told him but the message was that you are to stop coming to the farm and stop being my friend. If not, we lose the farm.'

'It's gossip!'

'Luke Morgan isn't a gossip. That's what bothered my mother. Someone has told your father about us.'

'Mrs Gilpin. Her cook spoke to her about us and she threatened to tell my father if I didn't stop seeing you. But I presumed she would warn me, not just act. And in any case we haven't seen her for several weeks.'

'Have you told anyone else?'

'No . . . Well, that's not strictly true. I told my uncle Charles but he would never say anything, he's my friend.'

'He's also your family. Far more likely him, I should think.'

'Impossible. But it doesn't really matter, does it? The deed is done. Jerome, what do we do? I can't not see you.'

'Nor me you.'

'We could pretend not to see each other and be even more careful when we do.'

'But it would only be a matter of time . . .'

'And why should we live a lie?'

From happiness they had been plunged into misery.

'There's only one thing we can do.' She stood up and held out her hand to him. 'Come.' She held his tightly as she led the way down the side of the throng, swooping round the crowds, aware that they were being watched, but having to move swiftly in case her resolve weakened.

'Eliza, is this wise?' She heard Jerome ask, but did not dare to respond. They approached the dais. Was it because they were on the barn floor and looking up that her father, uncle and aunt appeared so much larger, so much more threatening? She was having to drag Jerome now. Why was he so reluctant to do as she wished? She climbed the steps that had been built for them.

'Papa.' Her father had his back to her.

'Eliza?'

'Papa, I would like you to meet my friend, Jerome Barnard. Jerome, this is my father.'

'Good evening, Barnard. I do know your friend, Eliza.' He spoke in a friendly enough manner.

'But I want you to know that Jerome is my *special* friend. That I love him and wish to marry—'

Her head jerked with the force of the blow. She heard herself gasp, was aware that others gasped too. The talking and laughing ceased, the music trailed off in a squawk. Silence filled the barn, silence like a crystal poised in the air. And then the crystal shattered.

'Don't talk such claptrap!'

'Sir!'

'Papa!'

'Freddie!'

'I say, Forester!'

And a groundswell of murmuring from the crowd below them.

'You, Eliza, keep silent.' He stabbed his finger at her. 'Minnie, mind your own business. As for you, Charles, what did you think I was going to do with your information?'

'Uncle Charles!' Eliza looked at her uncle. He had deceived her!

'Barnard, get out.'

'Sir—'

'I do not wish to speak to you, Barnard.'

'But I have to speak to you, sir. My feelings for your daughter are honourable. I would in no way harm her.'

'I have no plans for her to marry a peasant such as yourself.'

'Papa!'

The second slap, oddly, did not hurt as much as the first, though her feelings were as deeply wounded.

'Mr Forester, I beg you—' Jerome lunged forward and caught Frederick's hand as it sliced through the air towards Eliza but, like quicksilver, a figure appeared on the stage with them, grabbed him and pulled him back with all her strength.

'Jerome, please. Don't do anything you'll regret.' Grace held on so tight that Jerome could not move. 'He is not himself, Mr Forester. He's not thinking straight.'

'Evidently.' Frederick straightened the sleeve of his jacket. Then, tidying his cuffs, he turned to Jerome. 'You are a fool. You need a good whipping. You are a presumptuous young cur. You—'

Jerome made a roaring noise, like an animal at bay. He shook himself free of his mother's grasp. He was trembling with rage.

'Mr Forester, Lady Wickham, come quick!' It was Benson, red-faced and wheezing. 'It's your mother, she's dying!'

Eliza ran across the park. She was sobbing and praying. They should never have gone to the party. She should have stayed with her grandmother. God was punishing her. She could hear the jingle of the horses' harness as her father's carriage raced along the pathway, the sound of hoofs deadened by the snow, which now lay thick on the ground. She slipped and stumbled, her dress was soaked and it was freezing, but she did not feel it. Her breath was loud, rasping, laboured, but she did not hear it.

Her grandmother's room was even hotter than normal and there was a sweet, sickly smell that Eliza could not identify. In her four-poster bed Lady Gwendoline appeared to have shrunk, and before she had entered the room, Eliza had heard the stertorous breathing. Now, she sat with the others, as far from them as she could manage. There were agonising moments when Lady Gwendoline's breathing stopped and Eliza thought she was dead, only for it to start again with an abrupt snorting noise. She saw the struggle each breath was for the old lady and wished that death would take her. And then she was overwhelmed with guilt that she could think such a thing – how could she wish for her grandmother to die? How evil she had become.

Minnie sat on one side of the bed, and Eliza wished she had the courage to ask her to move and let her sit in her place. She longed to hold her grandmother's hand for she would have liked to talk to her, tell her how much she loved her, how much she had learnt from her. Her aunt looked bored and once or twice Eliza had even seen her yawn, which shocked her.

Her father and uncle paced the floor, speaking in an undertone. She did not know if they were talking about her or not, and in her misery she did not care – she had been ignored since their return a good three hours ago. Everything would have to be faced later but not tonight.

She was aware of the pain in her cheeks, where he had hit her and, but for Jerome, would have hit her again. The humiliation was hard to bear. How could she continue to live here and face people? Were they all laughing at her and her shattered dreams?

Not now. Don't think about it now. But how she longed for Jerome to be with her, to hold her, to tell her all would be well.

The nurse, who had been hired in the last few days, entered the room. She was a kindly looking soul and Eliza was glad someone so comfortable and nice was caring for her grandmother, like Merry. She wondered where Merry was now, and if the stories about her were true. Would she ever be able to trace her and find out? She wished she was here.

And Miss Chester. Her father had died, she would know about grief, about mourning and sadness . . .

Ten minutes later there was a rustling from the bed and the comatose patient stirred. There was an irritated wave of the thin hand, even more claw-like now it was so emaciated. 'Amelia,' they heard the old woman call. Her father swore softly. 'Amelia, come, talk to me . . .' Again the hand was waved, but this time in Eliza's direction.

'Go to her,' her father ordered, without looking at her, 'and remember she's not herself.'

'Yes, Papa.' Eliza approached the bed, the fusty smell more pronounced the closer she got. 'Grandmama, it's me, Eliza.' She touched the hand, the skin so transparent that she was sure she could see the blood passing through the veins. 'I love you . . .'

'Amelia, listen to me.' To everyone's astonishment, Lady Gwendoline began to haul herself up in the bed. The nurse rushed to her aid. 'Leave me, all of you. I wish to speak with my granddaughter.'

'Mother, it's not wise.'

'Do as I say, Freddie.' Dying she might be but the imperious tone had not left her and her son did what he invariably did when ordered by his mother: he stepped back into the shadow of the room, beckoning his sister to follow him. Eliza was just aware of them huddling together and whispering, constantly glancing in her direction – afraid they might be missing something, she thought.

'It's Eliza, Grandmama.'

'Amelia you were christened and Amelia I shall call you at my end.'

'Yes, Grandmama.' She knew it was her baptismal name, but she was not fond of it – it belonged to another – but if it made the old lady happy . . .

'Come close. I don't want those vultures hearing. Yes, you!' She said, with spirit. 'Be careful, my dear one . . . Remember, it's secured . . .' The effort of talking was taking its toll and she slumped back on the pillows. She beckoned Eliza with a finger more bone than flesh. 'Give your mother the jewellery from the box from Bristow's.'

'Of course, Grandmama,' she said, to placate her. 'Now, don't tire yourself. Try to sleep. You won't get better if you don't rest.'

'Still stupid! What is to happen to you?' And Lady Gwendoline slipped into a deep sleep, a contented expression on her face. They were the last words she was to say.

The window of Lady Gwendoline's room was opened wide to allow her soul to flee. The blinds in the hundreds of other windows at Harcourt Barton were drawn. Every mirror was turned to the wall or covered in crêpe, black was donned. Candles were lit at the four corners of her bed and the vigil began.

Eliza sat beside her grandmother and expected her to breathe at any minute. She did not look dead but deeply asleep, and Eliza could not believe that she was no more. It was a comfort of sorts to see how young she looked with the pain of her struggle to live erased from her face. The odd times when she was alone with her she talked to her, told her her secrets, told her how much she had loved her, regretting now that she had not said it while Lady Gwendoline was alive. But when others were there she refrained, afraid they might think her odd, mad or stupid.

Her sadness weighed heavy but it was not the all-encompassing thing she had expected. She had cried when it had happened but not since, yet she knew she had loved her grandmother. Her aunt Minnie was in a dreadful state and had had to be given laudanum, but, if anyone had asked Eliza, she would have said she had loved the old woman more than her aunt had. But then, she thought, observing the weeping heap in a chair on the other side of the bed, she had been her mother. Was it not uncharitable of her therefore to stand in judgement of her aunt's grieving when she, who had no mother, could not imagine what it would be like to lose one?

What had her grandmother meant, 'Give your mother . . .' She must have been delirious. Did she mean find her grave? There was so much she did not know – yet how could she find out? No one was speaking to her, not even her uncle Charles, and the way the staff scurried away if she approached made her think that they had also been warned to have no contact with her. Of Ruby there was no sign. Twice she had tried asking other maids, and once had even asked if they would convey a note to her, but the blank looks and refusals were so humiliating that she did not try again. She was aware that an interview with her father was inevitable, and not knowing when it would take place was torture. She wondered if he was waiting until after the funeral.

Eliza had already decided what she was going to do. She could not stay here, not with this cloud of disapproval over her, not with the studied silence, which was cruel in the extreme. After the funeral, when she could again venture out of the house, she would see Jonquil, find out all she knew about elopement and go.

No one had told her anything about her grandmother's will. As far as she knew it had not even been read, but if her grandmother had said she was leaving her her money then that was what she would have done. And there was the inheritance from her other grandmother. They would find another farm, they would take his mother, brother and sisters with them. She would miss this house more than she dared contemplate, but the sacrifice would be worthwhile if she could be with Jerome. She had thought about not seeing her family but she had reached the sad conclusion that, now her grandmother was dead, she had no family: her father loathed her, her aunt ignored her and her uncle had betrayed her. With no mother she was alone, and as such she felt she had the right to do what she wanted with her life, not what others deemed appropriate.

Eliza waited in the library for her father. He was already half an hour late, and the wait was nerve-racking. She wondered if he was late on purpose, to make her even more afraid. She could not sit still but wandered around the room picking up books and putting them back. She must finish the cataloguing she had started. She was at the far end of the library when at last he entered so had the uncomfortable experience of having to walk the length of the long room, aware that he was watching her every step, seeing the disapproval etched on his face, knowing that in the dense black of her mourning she looked far from her best.

'Father, I'm so sorry,' she said, when she reached him.

'As you should be. Be seated.' He flicked up his coat-tails as he took a seat behind the large mahogany desk with the intricate carving, which she had so loved as a child. 'But I'm happy you have seen sense enough to apologise. Perhaps we can come to some compromise.'

'I wasn't apologising, Papa. I was commiserating with you over Grandmama. I have not seen you since . . .'

He leant menacingly across the desk. 'I beg your pardon? Did I hear correctly?'

'What compromise?' Don't let him frighten you, her inner voice told her.

'You have made a fool of yourself. You have dishonoured not only yourself but your family. The chances of you making a decent marriage after that public spectacle are remote.'

'I have told you whom I wish to marry. I have not changed my mind.' She sounded and looked defiant but she was quaking inside.

'Does your family mean anything to you?'

'Do I mean anything to you, Papa?'

He avoided her gaze. 'You cannot stay here for the moment.'

'I realise that.'

'Well, I suppose I must be grateful for small mercies. I suggest that for three months—'

'I think it will be longer than that, Papa. If you cannot accept my husband, how can I ever live here?'

Frederick Forester smote his forehead with the palm of his hand. 'There are times, Eliza, when I think you are mad enough to be certified. You cannot marry that unsuitable man. I forbid it. You can plead all you want but my permission will never be granted.'

Eliza concentrated on the bookcase opposite her. She must not allow her anger to get the better of her. If she was too recalcitrant he might learn of her plans and he would move heaven and earth to stop her. She had to control herself; she had to appear more acquiescent than she had managed so far. 'I had hoped that, given time, Papa, you might see what a good man Jerome is.'

'I'm not saying he isn't but he is not the man you will marry.'

'But what am I to do, Papa?' She looked meek. This was the better way.

'It is my plan that you leave here and I have given orders for the house in Exeter to be opened up. You will stay there with a companion until you come to your senses.'

'Grandpapa's old house? The one in Colleton Crescent?'

'It's small but it will be sufficient for you. When you have realised the error of your ways you may return to Harcourt Barton.'

'I trust Ruby will be there for me.'

'You are to have no further contact with that accursed family.'

'She did nothing!'

'No doubt she helped you arrange your assignations.'

It was the expression of disgust on his face as he spoke that made her want to strike him as he had her. But then ... Exeter ... Colleton Crescent. After this interview she would sneak out and go to the farm, she would tell Jerome where she was going and when he was in Exeter ... Her heart sang with the possibilities.

'How exciting, my own establishment.' She was content to see him relax visibly as he explained the financial arrangements he had made for the running of the house. 'When am I to go, Papa?' she asked, with an innocent expression.

'Your possessions are being packed now. You leave in five minutes.'

'No!' She stood up and this time it was she who leant menacingly across the desk.

'Don't take that threatening stance with me.'

'Grandmama's funeral ... Afterwards ...'

'Your help will not be required. Everyone who witnessed your shame will be there. It is not appropriate for you to be seen.'

Slowly she sat down. 'What will people think?'

Her father snorted. 'A fine time to be thinking of that. A pity you did not consider it sooner.'

'You are unjust.'

'Your opinion is irrelevant.'

'Everything about me is irrelevant to you, isn't it? I

am amazed that you are even concerned about my love for Jerome. It must be the first time you've taken notice of me in all my life.'

'Stop this!'

'I will not. I'd always hoped a day would come when you would love me, have regard for me. But this . . . I loved my grandmother as she loved me. She cared about me, and what I was doing, and what I was thinking. But you! All you do is criticise me, make my life a misery. I think you enjoy seeing me sad and take pleasure in thwarting me. Do you do it because I remind you of her? Are you still punishing her through me?' This time when he hit her the force of the blow knocked her sideways on to a chair. 'You've stopped using whips, have you? It's just fists now!' she screamed, and was rewarded with a further blow.

'I am finished! I was willing to compromise with you. I see that you are beyond reason. For speaking to me in that manner I have only one course of action. The Barnard family will be evicted this day.'

'No, please, you can't do that.'

'The point is, Daughter, I can do whatever I like. Give up all ideas of helping them, you have no money. I control your fortune and you will get not one penny if you elope with that man.'

'But to evict them! It is too cruel.'

He stood in front of her now, his legs astride, menace exuding from every pore. 'Yes, it is, isn't it? And you know who can make me change my mind? You.'

'Me?' It was a pointless question. She knew what he wanted.

'Before you leave you will meet this young man. Where was your favourite place?'

'The summer-house.'

'Very well, write him a note to meet you . . .' He dipped a pen into the ink and handed it to her. '. . . at one thirty. We want you in Exeter before dark – the roads can be dangerous otherwise.'

He stood over her as she scribbled the note. He read it, strode to the bell-pull, and handed it to Densham with instructions to deliver it forthwith. 'Now, this is what I want you to say . . .'

It was cold in the summer-house: more snow had fallen and a freezing mist had descended. Through it the great trees appeared only as vague outlines, as if drawn in charcoal. Eliza would not hear anyone approach or see them through the fog. But she was blanketed in a misery more dense than the mist that swirled around her and nothing else existed.

It was but three months since she and Jerome had begun to meet here and had learnt to listen to and tolerate each other. Three months in which her life and longings had changed, and her future had been decided.

Now all lay shattered. The hopelessness of her situation made her want to weep, except that now her tears were locked inside her with her sadness.

'My love . . .'

She swung round to see that Jerome had entered the cottage.

'I didn't hear you.'

'The snow . . .'

He moved closer and took her hand. 'But you are so cold. Let me warm you.' He lifted it to his mouth and blew gently upon it, just the merest whisper of his breath, and she felt her resolve melt. He unbuttoned his coat and, holding it wide, wrapped it round her so that they were both held tight in its folds.

'I was so sorry to hear of your grandmother. You will miss her.'

Eliza nodded mutely.

'I have been in such torment. When your father hit you I wanted to kill him!' She shook her head violently. 'I know, he's your father, I shouldn't have said that – I apologise.' She smiled her understanding. 'Was it dreadful? Did he punish you?'

She shook her head. Jerome must not know.

They stood in silence for a few moments.

'We have decisions to make.'

She was still wordless.

'I've thought. If I leave – since I am his enemy, not my family – they will manage. It will be hard but I doubt your father will harm them. I can always find work on another farm, perhaps a situation with a cottage. Or we could go north. There's work up there a-plenty in the factories. I don't have to be a farmer. We won't be rich, my darling, but we shall have each other.'

Tears began to roll down her cheeks, but she made no attempt to wipe them away.

'It will be hard for you, used as you are to such fine things, but I'll work every hour of the day to buy you things, pretty things . . .'

The sob that escaped, given her previous silence, was all the more shocking.

'Don't cry, my darling.'

She nestled further into his embrace, seeking the warmth of his body. And then, in one violent movement, she pushed him away from her and, clutching her cloak about her, she looked at him with a wildness in her eyes that he'd never seen before.

'I have to go.'

'I understand. When shall we run away? Where shall we meet?'

'I can't do that.'

'Perhaps not immediately but we shall, if we plan . . .'

'I will not live with you.'

'Not until we are married, of course not. I'd never suggest such a thing.'

'Jerome . . . I do not love you.' The words emerged so quietly that he looked quizzically at her.

'What did you say?'

'I do not love you!'

'Eliza!'

'I do not love you! I do not love you!' She shouted it this time.

'But you do.' He stepped towards her, and she took a step back and held up her hands as if pushing him away. 'You've been made to say this.'

'No.'

'You have. You would never say that to me.'

'They are my words.'

'Eliza, please, do not do this, do not destroy the beauty we have, the greater beauty we shall have . . .'

'I do not love you.'

'Stop it! I do not believe you, this is your father.'

'I hate you!'

'From love to hate in five minutes, and I'm to think that is the truth?'

'You cause me too much trouble. It amused me to play with you. How could someone like me live with someone like you?' She made herself laugh, a shrill, hysterical sound.

'Eliza . . .' She had turned away from him, no longer able to look at him. But something in his voice made her turn back. 'Eliza, don't say these things.' To her horror she saw his hands lift towards her in supplication, and then his tears fell. 'Eliza . . .' His voice broke.

'I do not love you.' Tears were streaming down her face. 'I hate you!'

'Then curse you and curse your father!' he roared.

She fled from the cottage, fled from her dreams, fled from his voice calling her name, begging forgiveness. She stumbled as she ran, falling in the snow, twisting her ankle, but not feeling the pain. As she ran tripping, skidding, stumbling, blundering through the mist and the snow, 'I love you,' she sobbed, over and over again.

Chapter Five
1876

I

Fanny was grateful for the lift into Exeter she had been offered. She had learnt in her short time at Cheriton Speke how helpful people in the country were to each other compared with the city – she had not been aware of this before, living in large houses, with all the necessary conveniences to hand. Here, though, it was rare for her neighbours in the village not to tell her when they were going to Exeter or Tiverton and ask if there was anything she would like them to purchase for her. Even better were the times when they invited her to join them: if she could arrange it she never refused for it saved on the train fare.

Her lack of independence was a constant worry for her since, with the children – twenty of them – to be considered, she dare not run out of provisions. At night she would often lie in her bed mentally listing the contents of the store cupboard, worrying if the rice or flour would last until the next trip to the shops and market. Next time she saw Florrie she would have to address the lack of a pony and trap, although neither she nor her two assistants, Mavis and Rosamund, knew anything about the care of horses. It would be something else to learn.

'Are you settling happily, Miss Chester?' Mrs Voysey, the vicar's wife, asked, as they bowled along through the high-hedged lanes in Mrs Voysey's yellow-painted governess cart.

'Thank you, Mrs Voysey, I am. It is such a lovely area of the country.'

'You know Devon well?'

'A little.' She was not about to tell Mrs Voysey of her shock at finding where in Devon the new school was to be. When Florrie had announced they had found a property she was not too concerned, given the size of the county. And she had not been alarmed at the name of the village – Cheriton Speke – since she had never heard of it. But when they had travelled here from the station in Exeter her heart had pounded so hard she feared it would leap right out of her chest. They were a mere eight miles from Harcourt Barton! Worse was to come when Florrie explained the terms of the lease and how very understanding Mr Forester, who owned the property, had been.

That had been a restless night for Fanny, as she wondered whether she should explain everything to Florrie. Finally she decided against confiding in her. If Frederick Forester discovered she was here he would be so angry. The lease had been signed, the upheaval would be enormous and, worst of all, she would be duty-bound to resign to prevent that happening. So she said nothing. When asked about her past she said she had been born in Kent, which was true, that she had been a governess in Hampshire and London, equally true, and left it at that. She prayed that Mr Forester would not take it upon himself to inspect the school and his property.

'And the school? It prospers?'

'Very much so, Mrs Voysey. I was a little afraid of the responsibility when I began, but I'm learning.'

'Such dear little girls. I was only saying to my husband the other day what enchanting creatures they were and all of them so beautifully dressed – evidently they are not orphans.'

'Far from it. They all have doting mothers.'

'And fathers?'

'Sadly they are widows.' She wondered if lying to a vicar's wife was worse then misleading anyone else. But she could not tell her the truth: they would be ostracised, even drummed out of the village.

'Rich widows?'

'Reasonably well-to-do.' At least that was the truth.

'I counted at least twenty-five children. So many, I said to my husband.'

'Then some you counted twice. We've only twenty,' she said politely. She was not too sure of Mrs Voysey, who, while appearing pleasant enough, she sensed was perhaps two-faced and more than a little inquisitive. And there had been an edge to the way she said, '*So many*'. From Fanny's experience the likes of Mrs Voysey should always be treated with circumspection.

'You must need a large staff.'

'No, we all help. Teaching, ironing, washing-up, it's all the same to me.'

'And how many are there to help you?'

'I have one woman who helps me teach the children, and some in the house. But we could do with another pair of hands.'

'And why did you choose Devon?'

'I didn't, the mothers decided the air would be better for their little girls. However, they have all been poorly from one thing or another since we arrived.'

'Nothing serious, I trust?' Mrs Voysey's large face looked concerned.

'No, no. Only minor things, upset tummies, head-aches.'

'Water.' Mrs Voysey's ample lips were drawn in. 'Water,' she repeated for good measure.

'You think so?'

'Undoubtedly. When we go and visit my daughter in Axminster my husband is a martyr to the change in the water. They'll adjust.'

'I do hope so. It becomes expensive constantly having to call the doctor and for the medicine he prescribes.'

'You shouldn't bother with the doctor. Surely the apothecary would do just as well – cheaper too.'

'I don't think the mothers would like me to economise on their children's health,' Fanny said.

Mrs Voysey reined in the pony as they approached a hill. Fanny got down from the trap, carefully closing the little door behind her. Given her size, it might have been kinder to the pony if Mrs Voysey had alighted.

'You know Dr Whitney is retiring?' Mrs Voysey called over her shoulder.

'No!' Fanny quickened her step to catch up. But the day was hot and it was difficult. 'Who will take his place?'

'There's a scandal if ever I heard of one! He *says* no one has come forward to buy his practice . . .' She didn't say he had lied but her sniff implied that that was what she thought. 'The doctor from over Harcourt way is to care for us until a replacement is found. No doubt Dr Whitney is asking too much. And how long will one have to wait in the night if there is an emergency? If a baby comes? It will take him nearly an hour to reach us. It's ridiculous.'

'Surely Harcourt is nearer than an hour's ride away – half an hour perhaps?'

'Depends on the horse, doesn't it?'

'Or if he stays on the roads.' Charles, she thought, would get here in fifteen minutes, she was sure, but he was a fine horseman. To her shame, on those frequent nights when she couldn't sleep she fantasised about him discovering that she was here and riding over to find her.

She trudged on, the trap far ahead of her now as she laboured up the hill. Losing Dr Whitney was a serious blow: she knew she often called the doctor too soon, and sometimes unnecessarily, but she would not take any risks with other women's children.

'Perhaps Dr Whitney would still step in if it was something serious,' she said, when she eventually caught up.

'He's off to Lyme to lodge with his daughter. Inconsiderate man.'

Fanny climbed back into the trap for the last mile into the town.

All was bustle in the city, and the bars of the public houses were full to overflowing. There was the sound of a hurdy-gurdy man further along the street, children playing noisy games, the racket of the horses and carts on the cobbles.

Everyone was in such a good mood, no doubt helped by the sun on this glorious day. Enjoying a sense of well-being, Fanny soon forgot her worries about the doctor. She had arranged to meet Mrs Voysey in three hours, in the cathedral close, since she was going to a luncheon party in the town. Fanny had brought sandwiches with her: a picnic, on a sunny day like this, would be a pleasure. Meanwhile she plunged into the pleasant task of shopping, her list clutched firmly in one hand, her basket over one arm.

She had been directed to Queen Street to the market there. She entered between the noble pillars at the entrance and the shouts of the stall-holders, praising their wares, almost deafened her. This market was a particular bonus for Fanny since the produce she bought from the farmers was cheaper than it was in the shop.

There was a particularly fine display of cheese, and she wondered if she could afford to buy some strawberries, displayed among the dairy produce, as a treat for the children. Next year, she had resolved, they would be growing their own fruit and vegetables, although, she had never worked in a garden. But, yes, the children would appreciate the fruit. Would three pounds be sufficient? No.

'Four pounds of strawberries, a jar of clotted cream and two pounds of that cheese, please.' She was busily pointing out the various objects and not looking at the girl serving her. Then she looked up to smile. 'Ivy! It is

Ivy, isn't it?' She was astonished, although it was likely that she would meet someone she knew. Then her heart sank: surely the news that she was back would spread like wildfire.

Ivy looked at her with a stupid, uncomprehending expression.

'You've forgotten me? Miss Chester.'

'Sorry?'

'I was the governess at Harcourt Barton.'

'I don't work there no more.'

'As I see.' Fanny felt a measure of relief. 'I should think this is more pleasant work for you.' Ivy ignored her and turned to serve another customer. Fanny remembered her as being a quick and jolly girl. Had something happened to her? And there was something else: she had a marked shifty look, which wasn't very pleasant. 'Excuse me, Ivy, have I done something to offend you?'

'No.'

'Then why are you so offhand with me?'

'Because I don't know you.'

'I see. Well, I wonder if you would give Ruby Barnard a message from me? She, I'm sure, *will* remember me.'

'I might.'

'How very gracious of you.'

She had the satisfaction of seeing Ivy look puzzled. From her reticule Fanny took paper and pencil. Quickly she wrote down her message and her address and suggested they meet, then handed it to Ivy. 'I would appreciate it if you remembered to give this to her? Thank you.'

Fanny's basket was heavy with her purchases and she still had to buy smelling-salts, string, and a small present for Augusta whose birthday was next week. Rosamund needed some elastic and she must find a new broom for the yard. She was going to have trouble carrying all of this. She spied a tea shop and entered. Perhaps if she bought a cake and a pot of tea they might agree to guard her basket for her while she finished her shopping.

'You sold a lot of strawberries while I was away,' Ruby said to Ivy, having noted the display. 'When you do that it's best to fill the space with something else.' She sighed as she delved under the cloth with which they had covered their stall and began to pile more cheeses where the strawberries had been. Ivy could be so unhelpful. On the cobbles she noticed a screwed-up piece of paper. Ivy was so untidy too. She picked it up and pocketed it to throw it away later. 'Anything happen while I was taking my break?'

'Nothing.'

2

In the past six months Eliza had not been able to distinguish between her grief for her grandmother and her grief for Jerome. She had lost so much, the two people she had loved.

Her father visited the house in Exeter intermittently – if he was delayed in the city, on business at his bank, or when he had dined too long and well, he stayed overnight. His room was always kept ready for him, and food was always available, and it was why the house, though rarely used, was staffed. His visits, however, were usually late at night and often Eliza did not know he had been there until he had left in the morning.

Although she was saddened by the circumstances of her life, in some ways this enforced isolation was a blessing. She had time to recover, for recover she must – she had decided that when she had left Jerome. If she did not, her father would have won. So although her spirits were low, whenever she saw him she pretended she was not unhappy.

At least there was something she could be thankful for: had her grandmother not died she would now be in London, 'coming out', and no doubt hating it. The strict mourning, which she was observing, restricted her social life to walks and church services, no visiting, no visitors, and that suited her well. She had time to think, plan and recover.

Although all her life she had drawn and painted she began now to do so in earnest. She had always enjoyed it as a pastime, for that was what it had been, but now she worked at it every day and consequently her skills improved. She was never satisfied with her work, but she could see it was getting better. From water-colours she ventured into pastels and was thinking of working in oils but didn't yet have the courage. Of all the subjects she approached, still-life, flowers, landscapes, it was portraiture that attracted her most.

'I never thought that I, of all people, would have my portrait executed,' Beatrice Holland said, from the chair across the studio, where Eliza had placed her, draped with a length of blue silk, holding a large lily.

'It's kind of you to pander to me.' Eliza was rubbing at the colour she was using, trying to match Beatrice's hair – not easy when it was of such an indeterminate colour.

'You are so talented.'

'Thank you.'

'Still, I suppose you would prefer it if I didn't chatter. I know I prattle on, my mother always said . . .'

Eliza made no attempt to stop her because she knew she would not succeed. Morning, noon and night, Beatrice babbled away. When she had first come Eliza had felt guilty when her attention wandered and she did not concentrate on what she was saying. But not any more: it quickly became apparent that Beatrice did not expect any answers – it was the sound of her own voice she enjoyed.

Beatrice was her companion, appointed by her father.

Eliza thought of her more as a gaoler. She was a nice enough woman, friendly and kind, but Eliza knew that everything she did or said was reported back to her father. Had she received letters, she felt that Beatrice would have opened and read them first. Wherever Eliza went her companion trotted along beside her, feet twinkling, hands semaphoring, her mouth, like a fledgling's, constantly open, talking, talking, talking . . .

Eliza was only free when she was in her bedroom or working in her studio, which she had created on the next to top floor in the red-brick house, high on the hill above the River Exe. It was not a large room but spacious enough for her. She had a table on which she placed her paints and pencils, a small easel, a chair for her subjects and one for herself. She had covered the walls with paintings from elsewhere in the house, her own sketches and a lovely tapestry of knights and castles she had found in a chest on the first landing. She had had the curtains removed from the windows so that even more light, for it was not a dark house, flooded in. Often she would sit at the window, looking down at the quay below, feeling like a bird. She spent a lot of time here, not just to get away from her companion but also because there was always something to watch. She had done many sketches of the ships that docked in the port below. She enjoyed watching the people swarming over them, unloading or loading, the horses straining as they pulled across the cobbles the sledges weighed with cargo. There was always bustle, life unfolding, making her feel like a privileged observer.

When her father had first told her that she was to live here – 'Until the dust settles,' he had said, as if her broken heart were of no consequence – she had been appalled: she disliked cities to such a degree that she thought she would never find contentment here. She had been wrong: she found that being an observer suited her.

However, she missed Harcourt Barton in the same

way that she had missed all the people in her life who had left her – Merry, Miss Chester, Ruby, Jerome. It was as if the house were a person too. She longed to be there, dreamt about it constantly, but knew she could not go, not yet, not until she could think of Jerome without wanting to cry.

'When will you return to Harcourt Barton?'

'Not yet, if you don't mind, Father.' She was not aware that she had ceased calling him Papa.

'You're not a very dutiful daughter, are you?'

'I apologise.' She was enduring one of those stilted, difficult, but thankfully rare dinners with her father. They were alone, since Beatrice had a cold and had taken to her bed.

'At least we are spared the inane chatter of your companion.'

'Yes, Father.' She would have loved to point out that it was he who had appointed her in the first place.

'If I insisted on you returning to Harcourt what would be your reaction?'

'I should comply with your wishes.'

'It is difficult now that your grandmother has departed. I have no hostess.'

'But you are still in mourning. Do you have any guests? If so, then it must be – difficult.'

'Are you attempting to be impertinent?'

'No, Father.' But his use of the word made her long for her grandmother – it had been one of her favourites. She often wondered how her grandmother would have reacted to her drama. She had endured in a loveless marriage: would she have been more sympathetic than everyone else?

'We are in half mourning now. Life will begin to return to normal. Don't you see it as your duty to help me?'

'Of course, but on the other hand I don't think I would be very good at it. I assumed Aunt Minnie would be with you.'

'Your aunt and uncle have gone abroad.'

'I didn't know.'

'She said they were going for the art and music, but in my opinion she wanted to get away from this period of mourning she so hates.'

Eliza nearly choked; she'd never heard her father criticise her aunt before, and he'd certainly never confided in her, for that was what it amounted to. But so distant was their relationship that she was unsure how to react. She decided to ignore it.

The meal dragged on, and Harcourt was not mentioned again.

Eliza often thought of trying again to discuss her mother with him. Time had passed since the last time when he had reacted so angrily. But there were so many imponderables. Was she really dead? Or was she alive? And if so why had she never met her? What had her mother done to deserve banishment?

There were days when she was sure that her grandmother, as she was dying, had tried to tell her that her mother was alive, and there were others when she convinced herself that the old woman's mind had been wandering. But she had also to face the fact that sometimes she hoped her mother *was* dead: the anger she would feel at being deceived would end what little relationship she had with her father. Then why, when there was so little between them, did it concern her so? She concluded it was because she hoped that they might eventually become close. She could not risk losing that hope: she knew her father, but her mother would be a stranger if she ever met her. So Eliza did, said and asked nothing.

There was another reason she did not wish to return to Harcourt Barton. A secret reason. Three months ago she had been in the market one morning, with Beatrice, and among the hurly-burly, the clutter of stalls selling every sort of produce, she had spied Ivy selling cheese. Eliza returned, on different days, and discovered that she was there on Thursdays, so every Thursday she made an excuse to go to the market, which was close, fortunately, to the new museum and the library. Then, one glorious day, she saw Jerome. It had been hard to see him and stop herself pushing through the throng to speak to him, kiss him, hold him. He looked thinner and sadder, and knowing that she had put that expression on his face tore her in two. But she told herself that seeing him from a distance was preferable to not seeing him at all.

'To the market again, Miss Eliza?'

'Yes, Beatrice. I've decided I would like to do a large painting of it. It's such a colourful scene with the different stalls and their wares, and the people . . .'

'A painting like dear Mr Frith, is that your aim?'

'Hardly. I have nowhere near his talent – I only wish I had.'

'Will you paint it there? Among all the people?'

'No, I couldn't possibly. I would hate to be noticed. I shall find a quiet little corner and do my sketches as discreetly as I can.'

They had set off and she positioned herself in the same place. She could see the Barton Farm stall but they couldn't see her.

As she had hoped, Beatrice quickly tired of watching her and, content that Eliza was safely occupied, wandered off. And that had been the pattern ever since. She would settle with her sketch-pad and after five minutes Beatrice would make her excuses, leaving Eliza free to concentrate on the stall, willing him to appear. In three months she had seen him three times, but that was enough to keep the flame burning.

She spent hours trying to work out how they could be together. Her father had kept his word, and although she had an adequate allowance, she did not see any of the capital of her grandmothers' legacies to her.

She began to worry about the money after she had been to Bristow's Bank to check for the box her grandmother had told her about. There was a box containing a small leather pouch in which were some unset stones. From what Lady Gwendoline had taught her she recognised them as semi-precious and she doubted if they were valuable. So her grandmother *had* been rambling about them. Had she been confused when she had said she would leave her money to Eliza? But inside was a smaller box and these stones she saw were valuable. Her next visit was to see the family lawyer, who had offices beside the Guildhall. 'Mr Joiner, can you assure me my visit is confidential?'

'Client confidentiality is sacred to me, Miss Forester. Anything you say will remain with me.'

'That is a relief. I know I was left money by both my grandmothers.'

'That is correct.'

'Substantial sums?'

'Very.'

'I've been wondering why it is that I have not been told more about this money.'

'Because we didn't want you to bother your pretty little head with such concerns.'

'It would be no bother to me, Mr Joiner.'

'I have to tell you, Miss Forester, that it is your father's wish that you should not be concerned. Rest assured, the money is safe and well invested. Put in trust for you and' – at which point he gave a discreet cough – 'and any children you might have in the future.'

'Can I have any of it?'

'That is at your father's discretion.'

'Has he the right to do that?'

'By the terms of your grandmothers' wills, yes.'

'May I see them? Their wills?'

'But would you understand them?'

'I can always try, Mr Joiner.' She smiled sweetly enough, but she was seething inside.

'You must realise, Miss Forester, that I do not have them to hand. And I fear . . .' He made a display of taking out his pocket watch and checking the time. '. . . I have a pressing appointment.'

Eliza had not even reached the cathedral close, a mere two minutes' walk from his chambers, before Mr Joiner was sending a message to Mr Forester at his bank in Fore Street.

'Don't bother Joiner. He has more important matters to attend to than you,' her father said to her, passing her on the stairs one morning.

The unfairness of it all made Eliza angry. She was sure she had been left the money so that she would be independent – a stupid dream, she began to realise.

It was not that she lacked money. She had everything she wanted and more: all she had to do was ask and it was provided. But her father saw that she never received enough to enable her to help Jerome and his family, and it would take her years to save enough to buy them a semblance of security.

3

Fanny was excited to receive a letter from Ruby a week after her trip to Exeter. But it was another two weeks before she could go since Rosamund had been ill and she could not leave Mavis to cope on her own.

At last she found herself sitting by the window in Moll's coffee shop, overlooking the close. She was early but it was a pleasure to view the magnificent west front of the cathedral, and to watch the people scurrying by. Now, with her quiet village life, she was always excited by the bustle of the city. She enjoyed watching people, wondering what their occupations were, their station in life, if they were happy or sad . . .

'Ruby!' she called, and waved as the young woman appeared in the doorway. 'I couldn't sleep last night with excitement. I ordered scones and cream – I hope that is all right. How wonderful to see you.' She laughed. 'Just listen to me, I'm not letting you get a word in edgeways.'

'It's lovely to see you, too, miss. And I shall enjoy a scone.'

'I've missed you all so much. Your family, how are they?'

'In good health, thank you.'

'And the farm?'

Ruby laughed. 'I'm sure it's not my family farm but Miss Eliza you want to hear about.'

'Well, I didn't want to offend you . . .' Fanny smiled shyly.

'I'm afraid I have to disappoint you, I have no news of her.'

'Never mind. We shall be able to enjoy a chat anyway.' She hid her disappointment. 'You don't still work at Harcourt Barton?'

'No, I was dismissed at Christmas. You see . . .'

Fanny's facial expressions went through the gamut of emotions – from eagerness at having news to shock. Then she felt concern, anger and sadness, as Ruby related what had happened between Jerome and Eliza, and Frederick Forester's actions.

'And you've no idea where she is?'

'No.'

'But someone must know. She hasn't been done a mischief?' She felt breathless at the idea, but she knew it wasn't impossible for one read such dreadful stories in the newspapers.

'No, nothing like that. Other people know but they've been forbidden to tell any member of my family, we are certain.'

'Then they're not very good friends.'

'We don't blame them. No doubt Mr Forester has told them that if they do he will dismiss them, or evict them from their homes.'

'How wicked of him.'

'He's a bad man.'

'I agree with you,' Fanny said, with marked feeling.

'My mother is ill from the constant worry, and my poor brother is racked with guilt that he is the cause of her anxiety and blaming himself for Eliza being sent away.'

'And poor Eliza must be devastated by the death of her grandmother. Such a sweet child, so determined to be happy, and her destiny appears to be sadness.'

They sat for a few minutes, both lost in thought. Fanny found herself wondering whether if she had still been with Eliza the catastrophe might have been avoided. Would she have been able to persuade her that her liaison with Jerome was likely to lead to trouble? That, romantic as it all was – and, no doubt, true love – it was not a desirable relationship because the differences between them, both social and educational, were too vast.

'And what about you, Miss Chester?'

'Well, I have been more than fortunate . . .' And, as always when she talked of her school and her pupils, her face became animated, her eyes shining with pride.

'It sounds perfect. I'm so happy for you.'

'But I've had an idea! I need a housekeeper – perhaps you'd be interested in such a position?'

'Normally I would have been more than interested, but I'm getting married next year.'

'Ruby! Such exciting news! And who is the lucky man?'

'Henry Morgan, the gamekeeper's eldest son. When his father retires next year Henry hopes to take over.'

'Lucky you. Then you'll never have to leave the estate.'

'You will come to my wedding?'

'There is nothing I would like more, but I fear I must decline. People would recognise me and the last thing I want is for Mr Forester to know I am here. And please, Ruby, don't let anyone know where I am, will you?'

'I promise.'

'I worried about seeing Ivy – do you think she will say anything?'

'Unlikely, for she would have to admit that she had thrown away your note to me. Fortunately I'm a tidy person and I picked it up from the floor, otherwise I wouldn't be here.'

'Why should she do a thing like that?'

'Because she would know I'm going to ask if you received a book from me?'

'Why, yes, Jane Austen. I replied immediately. I was so sad when there was nothing more from either of you.'

'My mother was right then – she said Ivy must have taken the parcel. No doubt she told on both of us. I'm going to insist my mother gets rid of her. She's nothing but trouble to my family.'

During the rest of their tea they concentrated on more pleasant subjects and the news from the estate: who had married whom, the babies born and who had died. When they parted it was with a promise that they would meet again soon and that if either of them acquired any news of Eliza they would let the other know.

Fanny avoided the market and its temptations and instead went to the newly built, in grand Gothic style, Royal Albert Memorial Museum and Free Library to while away the time until she went to the station to catch her train home. One of the problems with returning to this area was the constant reminder of happy times with Eliza. Whenever they went to Exeter they had visited the museum. She wished she had greater funds and could bring her pupils here, but there was little chance of that.

'Fanny Chester! What a wonderful surprise! I feared I should never set eyes on your lovely face again.'

'Charles!' Her heart fluttered with excitement – and then with fear: could she rely on him not to tell anyone that she was here? Hadn't Ruby this very afternoon told her that Charles had betrayed Jerome and Eliza? But that was different: Eliza needed his protection.

'I heard you had moved to the country, but I hadn't realised you had come here.'

'Yes, I'm happy to be back. It's a lovely county.'

'And the school, is it still in existence?'

'But of course.'

'And where is it situated?'

'I have Augusta with me still.' She avoided his question. They fell into step and began to walk around the exhibits, a fine collection of Roman artefacts.

'Is she well?'

'Very.'

'Does she miss me?'

'She doesn't say.'

'Do you miss me?'

'How wonderful the blue is in that glass. How miraculous that it has survived.'

'You didn't answer me, Fanny.'

'I think it must be so exciting to be an archaeologist, don't you?'

'Answer me!' He took hold of her sleeve and turned her to face him.

'No, Sir Charles, I don't miss you. I'm far too busy.'

He laughed so loudly that other people turned to see who was interrupting their peace. 'Ssh!' She put her finger to her lips.

'I don't believe you, Miss Chester.' At which he leant forward and kissed her full on the lips.

'Well, really!' An enraged matron gathered her children to her and bustled them out of the room. Which only made Charles laugh the louder.

'Please, Charles, you put me in an impossible position. People are staring.'

'And do you think I care? I've missed you so deeply.'

His voice was low now, husky with longing, and Fanny's knees felt weak. 'I have to go. I have a train to catch,' she stammered.

'The hill to the station is steep to walk down and I have my carriage outside. Let me drive you there.'

'No, thank you. Really.'

'We must meet again, please.'

'Charles, I don't think that is a good idea.'

'And why not, pray?' He followed her out of the door and back into Queen Street. She turned to the right. 'Let me drive you.'

'No, thank you.'

'How adorably prim you can be.'

She stopped. 'Charles, I can never give you what you desire. I do not wish to see you – in fact, I will go so far as to say I *never* want to see you again.'

'I won't give up.'

'I beg you to cease. If you do not leave me alone then I shall be forced to notify that constable over there that you are harassing me.'

He removed his tall hat and bowed. 'Then I am vanquished.'

Fanny continued walking, conscious that he was watching her, feeling his eyes as if they bored through her back. She held her head high, and strode quickly, despite the heat. She would have loved to fall into his arms, feel his kisses, how much she longed for that . . . But she would never forgive herself and she would be lost to respectable society. Why, if most people knew how she thought she would already be a pariah. It had been hard to resist him but she could be proud of herself, she thought, as she entered the station and purchased her ticket.

4

'You can't spend the rest of your life skulking here.' Minnie Wickham was in an edgy mood, constantly moving about the drawing room, picking up objects and inspecting them. 'You do realise your behaviour is quite ridiculous.'

'I'm not skulking, I was sent here,' Eliza answered calmly, while pouring the tea.

'Your father has requested you return to Harcourt Barton.'

'I am content here.'

'You're being selfish.'

'I'm sorry you think that.' She handed the cup to her aunt, who paused long enough in her pacing to accept it. 'I like your dress.' And she did: it was made of black and white striped satin, for her aunt was now in half mourning, and the skirt was pulled back into a neat bustle decorated with a bow. Eliza wondered how the effect was achieved: was there a pad beneath the skirt or a whalebone cage? She would ask Jonquil when she next saw her.

'I haven't come here to discuss my *toilette*, I've come to tell you that you *must* leave here, that you *must* come to London with me.'

'I thought you said I was to go to Harcourt.'

'Don't be cheeky.'

'Did you enjoy Italy?'

'I wasn't there for enjoyment, I was in mourning – or have you forgotten already?' To Eliza's relief, she had finally sat down.

'No, of course not. There's not a day I don't long for Grandmama.'

'You should be out of black by now.'

'I've been thinking about it.'

'Well, I suppose that's progress of a sort.' She was up again, wafting about the room. 'I met your companion. It doesn't surprise me you're depressed, having to contend with her. She'd drive me to murder.'

'I like her,' Eliza answered loyally.

'You always were perverse in your choice of friends, as your poor father is fully aware.'

Eliza chose to ignore the remark. 'Cake?'

Minnie was still roaming the room.

'Aunt, you seem very tense. Is something wrong?'

'Of course there isn't. I am baffled by your refusal to comply with your father's wishes.'

'But I don't know what he wants, Aunt Minnie. He appeared to accept that I was happy to stay here – he did not object. The less he sees of me the better, as far as he is concerned.'

'So, you're going to become a hermit.'

Eliza laughed. 'No. I have been planning to go to concerts at the Royal Clarence, the theatre. It's silly to live in a city and not do such things. But I'm not ready to return home yet. I fear that without Grandmama the house won't be the same. For that reason I dread going there. And I'm sorry, Aunt Minnie, but London is not attractive to me.'

'How odd you are. Young women love London, the balls, the parties – the young gentlemen. How else are you to meet a suitable husband?' Eliza would have liked to say she had already found him, but common sense prevailed. 'If you are to do the season next year there is much planning to be done. The parties, your ball, your wardrobe ... endless lists of planning.' Her aunt's irritation was mounting, Eliza thought, judging by the increased shrillness in her voice. Suddenly she sat down. 'Dear child, listen to me. Please come to London, not now but in the New Year. I had so looked forward to introducing you to my friends. To present you at Court would have made me so proud.'

Unfortunately for Minnie, the change in her tone, the sudden sweetness, put Eliza immediately on her guard. She knew that if her aunt wanted her in London it was for her own reasons, and she wondered what they were. But, still, if there was something she wanted perhaps Eliza could use that to her own advantage.

'Aunt, may I ask a question?'

'I can't undertake to answer.'

'But you don't know what it is.'

'You may ask, and if I answer, will you come to London?'

'No.'

'Then don't bother.' Minnie was up again, prowling, inspecting a painting on the wall. 'I don't know this work, it's rather fine.' She peered at the still-life in a myopic way, too vain to wear the spectacles she needed. Eliza could not bring herself to admit that the painting was hers; it was only at Beatrice's insistence that she had hung it. But she was pleased by her aunt's reaction – although she couldn't help wondering what she would have said if she had known who the artist was. 'What was it you wanted to know?' Minnie asked, her curiosity getting the better of her.

'Is my mother dead?' Eliza asked, because the night before she had had such a vivid dream, of her grandmother repeating again and again the name Amelia.

Minnie dropped the silver snuff box she was holding, which hit the floor with a clatter. 'What a question! Of course she is.'

'Then where is she buried?'

'I can't remember. London, I suppose. I think that's where she died.'

'Father said Scotland. Did you like her so little that you don't know where she died?'

'Not particularly. She was not a good wife to my brother.'

'In what way?' Eliza could hardly breathe: no one had ever said anything about her mother before.

'I'd rather not say.'

To Eliza's frustration, the maid appeared to announce a caller. Had she been alone she would have refused to receive whoever it was.

'That will be Lord Alford. I arranged for him to collect me from here.'

'Show him up,' Eliza said to the maid, and stood up.

'Miss Forester.' Hedworth Alford bowed low over her hand. 'May I express my condolences.'

'Thank you for your letter, Lord Alford, I appreciated your kindness.' She curtsied. 'We have just had tea, if you would like some? Or perhaps something else.'

'He'd appreciate a whisky, wouldn't you, Hedworth?'

'Very much so.'

Eliza sent the maid to bring the decanter and invited him to be seated. Her aunt monopolised the conversation to the point where Eliza felt she might as well not be there. As she watched and listened she sensed a camaraderie between the two that was deeper than acquaintanceship. It was the way her aunt looked at him, her expression softening as she did so. Which led her to wonder what their relationship was . . .

'But, Lady Wickham, we neglect our charming hostess. We've missed you, Miss Forester.'

'I wouldn't have been very good company.'

'I understand. When my grandmother died I was broken with grief, far more so than when my father died.'

'Really?'

'Oh, yes, she was a wonderful woman. From what I've heard very much like yours . . .'

The next hour passed quickly as Eliza listened with interest to Alford. He was an entertaining guest, while sympathetic and sensitive to her feelings. As the minutes ticked by she relaxed, and by the time they stood up to go she had even been laughing.

'I wonder, would it be presumptuous of me to ask permission to call when I'm next in Exeter?'

'It would be my pleasure.' She swept to the floor gracefully in a deep curtsy, then she glanced up at her aunt nervously. She need not have worried: Minnie was smiling broadly.

Eliza had enjoyed the afternoon but only, she was aware, after Lord Alford had arrived. He was not nearly as slick as she had thought him, nor as bold. He had behaved impeccably. There could be no harm in him calling.

However, there was one matter she had to think about in a more concentrated manner. She could not keep putting it off. Her mother! Last night's dream had bothered her more than she had at first thought. She would have to see Mr Joiner again and this time she would insist he tell her all he knew. He might report her to her father but it was a risk she would have to take. However, she had decided she would let him know that she was aware of his disloyalty last time. She would shame him into keeping her visit a secret. But if he ignored her perhaps it would not be such a bad thing: her father would know then how concerned she was, that she wanted to know – why, that she had a *right* to know.

It was a waste of time. Mr Joiner had the grace to look ashamed when she asked him not to run to her father this time, but he could not help her: he had not been the family lawyer at the time of her mother's death. And, no, he did not know which firm of lawyers had handled the family's affairs. She had to believe him on the first count; she found it difficult to believe him on the second.

In the following weeks it was extraordinary how often she happened to bump into Lord Alford. He was at a concert she attended, she saw him at the museum twice, in the cathedral once and in the close twice.

'Why, Lord Alford, if I didn't know better I might have thought you were following me.' She was amazed at her boldness.

'Would you mind if I did?' When he smiled he looked younger, which he needed to: at thirty, to Eliza, he was aged.

'I hardly think I am important enough for that.'

'A matter of opinion.'

'Then I would have to say that *if* you did, you would be wasting your energy. I'm not worth it.' She laughed and realised she could say this and tease him and, she supposed, flirt with him, because she didn't care.

'Another matter of opinion. But I would be honoured if you two charming ladies would join me for luncheon.'

Eliza wanted to return home to continue with a painting that was evolving well, but seeing the expression of longing on Beatrice's face she hadn't the heart to say no.

They deposited their coats in the cloakroom of the small hotel situated just off the close, in the high street, and a waiter settled them in the dining room. The walls were covered with a pretty red and gold paper, while candles burned in gilt sconces. It was a welcoming room. Eliza looked about her: the tables were full of chattering, animated people, none of whom she knew. It was a new experience for her to eat in public, an exciting adventure, rather a grown-up one, she decided. Her grandmother would have been appalled at the idea of her eating in a popular restaurant and would have declared that no lady should be seen in such an establishment. But that, somehow, made it even more exciting. It was also a novelty to choose from the menu and there was much discussion about what to eat. 'I can't make up my mind. Everything sounds so delicious.'

'May I order for you?'

'That would be perfect, Lord Alford. What about you, Beatrice?'

'I think that might be better.' Beatrice chuckled.

'Wine?'

'Lord Alford! What are you thinking of?'

Once again Eliza found herself enjoying his company.

'If you would forgive me for interrupting, milord?' A small, pretty woman stood at their table. 'Miss Eliza, you don't remember me?'

'I'm sorry?' She looked closely at the woman's face.

'It's Maggie! What are you doing here?' Eliza clapped her hands with pleasure.

'I'm, well, actually, I . . . Well, I'm in partnership with Mr Didier.' She beamed.

'How exciting! Sit down, you must tell us everything.'

'I couldn't possibly, Miss Eliza.'

'I insist. May she, Lord Alford?'

'We would be charmed.'

Maggie was settled, a glass of wine was poured for her, and Eliza noted with approval the kind way in which Alford dealt with her. When talking about her new venture Maggie became animated and even prettier. 'And it's all thanks to you, Miss Eliza.'

'Why? Because I dismissed Mrs Satterly?' And they had to explain to Lord Alford what had happened, and soon they were all laughing.

'And there's something else, Miss Eliza. Hyacinthe and I are to marry next month.'

'That is the most wonderful news.'

'What a fortunate man Mr Didier is,' Lord Alford said.

'Please, may I come to your wedding?' Eliza asked.

'Would you?'

That afternoon, when Eliza returned to her studio it was to find that, for the first time in months, she had enjoyed a truly happy day.

5

Fanny's travel problems had been solved. Every day one of the tradesmen, a baker, called with his cart and she arranged with him that if she needed to go to the railway station he would take her. Although she had offered him a consideration he had been offended and refused. She could now go to Exeter when she wanted but, for economy's sake, she restricted herself to one trip a month. She always went on a Thursday so that she could see Ruby. The vicar visited his aged mother and the Bishop on Thursdays, travelled on the same train and returned her to the school in his horse and trap. It was a perfect arrangement.

She looked forward to these rendezvous: not only was it pleasant to see Ruby, it was a break from the children, the other teachers and the school.

On one particular Thursday in October, she had met Ruby, had been to the library and was about to visit the cathedral where she liked to sit and listen to the organist and choir rehearsing.

She was just about to enter the cathedral when she heard someone call her name. It was a case of *déjà vu*, she thought, and after all this time the sound of his voice lifted her spirits as nothing else could. 'Charles, how very nice.' She hoped she sounded merely polite.

'You always say that and yet we never get past "nice". Such a dismal, disappointing word.' He had doffed his high hat and she knew he was laughing at her. 'May I ask what you are doing this fine day?'

'I was about to go to listen to the choir.'

'Perhaps I could suggest tea and cakes?'

She wavered. 'How kind.'

'There's a fine new restaurant along here. The hotel is run by a former chef of Mr Forester.'

'Not Mr Didier?'

'The very same.' He placed a hand under her elbow to guide her. The intimacy of the action, his touch, excited her.

'In here.' He had to duck to pass through the doorway, which was low for a man of his height. He was so tall, so elegant, she thought. How proud she felt to be with him. He led her into a lounge away from the bars where they found a place to sit and he ordered tea.

'You are not normally in Devon in October, if my memory serves me right,' Fanny said.

'No, we're not. But my brother-in-law is not well. We

came to care for him. My wife was anxious to be with him.'

'Of course. It's nothing serious, I trust?'

'He hasn't been really fit for a couple of years.'

'I'm sorry, I'd no idea.'

'You don't have to say that to me, Fanny. Why should you feel sorry for him, after all the trouble he caused you?'

'Because I never like to hear of anyone being ill.'

'You're too good for your own good! And how is the little school at Cheriton Speke?'

She looked up at him sharply. 'How did you know where the school was? I never told you.'

'I have ways and means.' He grinned at her.

'You haven't told Mr Forester?'

'No, why should I?'

'I'm glad.'

'It might be difficult if he knew you were in one of his properties, you mean.'

'Is there nothing you don't know?' she asked, in as light-hearted a manner as she could muster.

'What's it worth to me not to tell him?'

'Charles!' She couldn't keep the distress she felt out of her voice. He was a danger to her in more ways than one. She must try to resist his blandishments.

'Sir Charles *and* Miss Chester, this is a most pleasant surprise.'

'Mr Didier! Sir Charles was telling me what a great success you are having here. I am so pleased for you.'

'You are most kind. And you, Miss Chester?'

It was Charles who told him about her school. And, thank goodness, he didn't say where it was – Mr Forester might come here and it would be natural for Didier to say he had seen her.

'When did you leave Harcourt Barton?' she asked tentatively.

'March, on Lady Day, when my contract with Mr

Forester terminated. He's been most kind and encouraging, persuading many of the notables of the town to patronise us,' Didier informed her proudly. That wasn't so difficult, she thought. 'But, wait, you must meet with my partner.'

'And who might that be?'

'Why, Maggie Bones, next to me the best cook I have encountered.'

'Of course.' She didn't like to admit that she knew no Maggie Bones, not when Didier was so excited and proud of her. He disappeared, to return a few minutes later with a pretty young woman in a spotless white apron.

'Miss Chester, I'm sorry. I assured Mr Didier you'd never set eyes on me and wouldn't know me from Eve but he would insist. I worked in the kitchens at Harcourt but, of course, our paths never crossed.'

At this point Charles, no doubt bored with their talk, excused himself, having spied an acquaintance across the room. Immediately Maggie leant across the table. 'Do you see Miss Eliza?' she asked, in a low voice.

'Sadly no. I wrote but she never replied.'

'She never got the letters.'

'So Ruby told me.'

'Miss Chester, we are not supposed to tell anyone where she is, I don't know why, but that was Mr Forester's orders. But she has been so sad, even though she pretends she isn't. I'm sure she's lonely living with just her companion – not an easy woman to take to. In my opinion you are the one person who should know where she is. She's here in Exeter.'

'Do give me her address.' She delved into her small drawstring purse in which was a miniature pencil and pad.

'You won't tell anyone I gave it to you?'

'Of course not. But I would be obliged if you didn't tell Mr Forester you'd seen me either.' It was inevitable

that he would find out she was here, but until then . . .
'I'd be so grateful,' she added, for emphasis.

'I can keep a secret, miss.'

Charles wanted to take her home in his carriage but
Fanny steadfastly refused. 'It would cause too much
speculation, and I have already arranged to meet the
vicar.'

'Always so concerned about your standing.' He
laughed, which annoyed her.

'You do not have a problem with society, Charles. It
doesn't matter to you what people think. You are a
baronet but, most importantly, you are a man. I have
nothing, so my reputation is my most important
possession.'

'Do you mean I am never to break down this barrier?
That we are never to be lovers?'

'Charles!' She stopped dead in her tracks, appalled
that he should say such a thing to her. It was not fair of
him and he knew it.

'Don't be shocked, my dear Fanny. It's what you
think.'

'I most certainly do not!'

'Tut, tut – lying to me! That won't do at all!' And
he'd doffed his hat with the sardonic grin she found so
attractive. Today it was almost demonic.

On the train, she was glad that the vicar was intent
on reading some papers so that she could think and not
have to talk to him. How dare Charles speak to her in
such a vulgar fashion! How dare he be so presumptuous!

And yet . . . If she succumbed who would know?

If they were discreet . . .

But what if they had a child? The shame, the
degradation . . .

Would he desert her? Surely not . . . But what about
Caroline and Augusta?

If only he were free, if only they could marry. Instead he was trapped in his bitterly unhappy union . . .

She moved restlessly in her seat, thoughts tumbling about in her head, making her feel physically uncomfortable. She looked out of the train window but it was already dark and all she could see was her own reflection. She saw her worried face, saw the lines that were beginning to appear, saw a dull-looking woman, who was never to know personal happiness, domestic bliss. Surreptitiously she wiped away a tear.

The train began to slow. 'Here we are. On the dot.' The vicar had removed his gold hunter watch from his waistcoat pocket and checked the time, as he always did.

'It's so kind of you, Vicar.' Which was what she always said.

When they got off the train the carriage was waiting and ten minutes later Fanny was home to pandemonium.

'Thank goodness you're back, Fanny. Three of the girls are so poorly I've been at my wit's end what to do.' It was Rosamund who met her at the door, as if she had been waiting for her.

'Which children? What's the matter?' She felt fear clutch her like a vice.

'Mary, Victoria and Augusta.'

Even before she had spoken Fanny had known who she was going to say. She was already half-way up the stairs.

'They've a fever – it began so suddenly, they were right as rain this morning and now they're delirious.' Rosamund pounded up the stairs behind her.

'Have you called the doctor?'

'I didn't like to – I didn't know what to do, what with the expense.'

'Oh, Rosamund! Run to the vicarage – hopefully the horse will still be harnessed – and ask the vicar if he will send his man over to Harcourt village.'

At the door to the sick room, where at least Rosamund had had the sense to isolate them, Fanny paused. She straightened her skirt and took a deep breath before entering the room. Mavis, who was sitting beside the beds, stood up as she entered. 'Thank goodness you're here, Fanny. They are seriously ill.'

Fanny looked down at the little girls: their faces were flushed, and all three were sweating profusely. They had been sick and had complained of bad headaches. As soon as a blanket was pulled over them they kicked it off.

'It's very warm in this room, so I don't think we need worry about keeping them covered. It only makes them more fretful. Have you been sponging them? No? Then get two bowls of water and three flannels.' Fanny took off her cuffs and rolled up her sleeves. 'Augusta, my darling, it's Miss Chester.' She stroked the little girl's forehead, which was frighteningly hot. She opened her eyes and Fanny was shocked to see that she was not focusing. She turned to comfort the other two, aware that she must not favour Augusta over them.

The minute Mavis returned they began to sponge the girls with the cooling water, first their hot little faces, then their arms, torsos and legs. Once the water was changed they began again, calmly, smoothly, talking softly to the children, comforting them.

An hour later Dr Forbes arrived. He looked so young that Fanny cursed the other doctor for leaving them in the lurch. What could this young man know?

As soon as he entered the room he removed his coat, then his jacket. Fanny was shocked – what an unprofessional way to behave! He sat on Augusta's bed and took her pulse. He was explaining to her what he was doing, soothing her with the gentleness of his voice. And how calm Augusta became. How kind he was, she thought.

'You've done well,' he said to Fanny, standing up as he finished examining the third child.

'Do you know what is wrong?'

'We will know for sure tomorrow if a rash appears. But the sudden onset of the fever, their headaches, their reddened throats and rapid pulses indicate that it is probably scarlet fever.'

'Oh, no!' Not Augusta, Fanny wanted to call out. 'What should I do?' she asked, pulling herself together.

'It was a good decision to isolate them from the other children and they should remain so for a fortnight even when they appear better. We should keep an eye on the other children and I should examine them too, tonight, just in case. Meanwhile these three will need careful nursing, a minimum of movement because there is a risk to their hearts.' From his bag he took a bottle of tincture. 'This is willow bark, to help with the fever. And I recommend camomile tea every two hours; boiled water with a little sugar with two drops of the willow bark for the older child, one drop each for the smaller ones.' He handed Fanny a small brown bottle from his bag. 'This will calm them. Watch the fever and sponge them again if they seem too hot. Now, if I might see the other children?'

Fanny led him to the other dormitories, leaving Mavis and Rosamund with the three patients. It was past midnight before they had finished.

'Might I offer you some refreshment or do you want to get straight home?' she asked.

'Some of the camomile tea you have made would be pleasant.'

Fanny showed him into the sitting room that doubled as her office, and went to the kitchen for the tea. When she returned he was looking at her small bookcase.

'You like to read, I see,' he remarked.

'It affords me great pleasure.'

He looked at her, and evidently saw the depth of her concern for the children. 'You must try not to worry or you will become ill, too, and that will not help them.'

'I'm so afraid. They are so precious.'

'Aren't all children? Let us hope it is the simple form.

You see . . .' And he explained to her the different types of fever, the risks, what to look for, especially the rash he feared.

'You are the first doctor I have ever met who did not treat me as an imbecile.'

'I believe that knowledge dispels fear better than anything.' He stood up, collected his bag and put on his heavy coat. 'I shall return first thing in the morning. As I said, try not to worry and try to sleep. They will need you fit and well.' He smiled at her, and his rather plain, ordinary face was transformed.

6

'I do understand, you know,' Hedworth Alford whispered to Eliza since, of necessity, Beatrice was sitting in the room. 'I really do.' Eliza looked at him with a somewhat cynical expression. 'You don't believe me?'

'I find it difficult.'

'I, too, was in love with someone unsuitable.'

'I hate that word!' she said sharply.

'Yes, it's not really *suitable*, is it?' He smiled. Despite herself Eliza found herself smiling back. 'She was my sister's governess, Emily . . .' He said this in such a soft, dreamy manner that Eliza found herself leaning forward with interest. 'I thought my mother would have had a stroke. Unfortunately she disappointed me.'

'Lord Alford! What a dreadful thing to say!'

'I think one should always speak the truth, don't you? I did not like her and she did not like me. It was as simple as that. Sad but true.'

'Did it hurt your feelings?'

'No. Since she had never cared for me I was not aware that I lacked anything. She didn't like any of us.'

'You mean your sister?'

'And my younger brother.'

'I thought I alone had such problems.'

'You felt the same about your mother?'

'No, I never knew her. I meant my father. But it's different in that I want him to love me.'

He leant forward and took her hand. 'How deeply tragic,' he said softly, and squeezed it gently. There was a cough from the other side of the room. 'Come, Miss Holland, I hold Miss Eliza's hand only to comfort her.' He beamed at her and Beatrice blushed with pleasure. He turned his attention back to Eliza. 'Don't you find it grossly unfair that the parent who has no time for you is the one who has forbidden you to find happiness with the one you love?'

'Exactly. Why, Lord Alford, you really do understand.'

'I told you,' he teased. 'And I also said I speak only the truth. But no mother – that makes it doubly tragic. At least my father was my friend.'

'I had hoped my mother was still alive,' she murmured. 'It was something my grandmother said before she died, but she must have been rambling. I asked the family lawyer, who confirmed she had passed away.'

'I would love to take that sadness from your eyes. Do you think there is any hope you might allow me to?' He spoke with a sudden urgency.

'Lord Alford!' She sat back in her chair as far as she could, alarm registering on her face.

'Ignore me! I'm a fool, too romantic for my own good.' He laughed. 'You have a most interesting view from this window. So many ships, and one wonders where they are from and where they are going, what cargo they bring – silks and spices.' They looked down at the bustling scene below.

'Probably coal.' She laughed. 'Sometimes I would love to steal away, hide on one and go wherever it takes me.'

'Maybe we shall one day . . . Oh, Miss Eliza, don't look so startled, I'm joking. That's all. Forgive me. I must learn to stop alarming you so.'

'May I offer you some refreshment, Lord Alford?'

When he left and asked if he might call again, she found herself agreeing, although she couldn't understand why. He was her aunt and uncle's friend, how could he be hers? Yet she enjoyed his company and he made her laugh.

She looked at her watch. It was still only four and it was Thursday: the market would still be open.

'Beatrice, I would like to do some sketching.'

'But it's late and it's getting dark.'

'You need not come, if you don't want.'

'You can't go out alone.' Beatrice began to fold away her embroidery with an injured sigh.

'I'll take the maid. You stay here in the warm.'

'Well, I do wonder if I don't have one of my chests coming on.'

'I shan't be long,' Eliza said quickly, before Beatrice could change her mind.

With a feeling of liberation she ran down the stairs, grabbed her coat, and left the house without bothering to call the maid.

Fanny was tired. She had not slept for two nights now, preferring to sit with the girls but unable to find a comfortable position in which to nod off. True to his promise, the doctor had called the next day. Fanny had been hopeful, since there was no sign of a rash on their faces, that it was not as bad as he had thought. Her hopes were dashed when he explained that the rash did not appear on the face but on the body only. And that the white rim around their mouths was a second confirmation of his fears.

Rosamund was caring for the other children, though judging from the noise issuing from the schoolroom, without much success. She was a good teacher but a little too indulgent.

They were particularly worried about Mary, marginally less about Augusta, and Victoria was improving.

Fanny made the decision she had dreaded and sent telegrams to the mothers. Florrie replied by return that she was travelling on the next available train, but there was nothing from Victoria's mother. What to do about Augusta? She had no idea where Caroline Fraser was, so she must inform Charles. She was surprised to find that she was reluctant to do so. But if he was her father he should be told, and if he wasn't, he might know where her mother was. The doctor undertook to deliver her note since he had to call on Frederick Forester. 'I'd prefer not to explain why but could you give this directly to Sir Charles?'

'Of course.'

'When will you return?'

'This afternoon, I promise.' He took the liberty of patting her hand. 'Don't worry, Miss Chester. I'm sure we shall pull them through. But I really think you should consider employing assistance, a woman to sit through the night, perhaps, to enable you to sleep. If you would permit me to say so, you look very tired. The last thing we need is for you to become ill.'

'I understand, but . . .'

'It's presumptuous of me and I don't wish to pry. No, I shouldn't.' He looked mortified that he had said so much.

'Are we in financial difficulty? Is that what you were going to ask? I do assure you, your account will be met in full.'

'Miss Chester, please, that was the last thing concerning me. I spoke out of turn, but it was my concern for you . . . What can I say?' He pushed his hand through his hair in obvious distress.

'Doctor, forgive my over-sensitivity.'

'It becomes you.' His face reddened.

'I appreciate your solicitude, Doctor. Yes, I am worried. We have only just opened this school, we haven't had a full year to see how well we are doing. We were looking for a housekeeper but I decided against it because of the added expense. So you do understand?'

'I do. But as your doctor I have to advise that you do too much. I have in mind a kindly soul who has just moved into the area and whose fees are modest.'

'Perhaps.'

'I'll ask her to call, a Mrs Denzle.'

Each time Fanny dreaded the moment when the doctor left: she only felt safe when he was here. He had such a calming influence and was always so kind. Now she found herself thinking how glad she was that the other doctor had left since she felt this one really cared about the children.

'Fanny, there's a Mrs Denzle wanting to see you. It's about helping with the nursing.'

'Show her in, will you?' Fanny was changing Augusta's soiled nightdress – and her poor little body was covered in the rash they had all dreaded. It was on Mary too, but as nothing had appeared on Victoria she had been moved out of the sick room into another near by.

She had still not heard from Charles – he had not even acknowledged receipt of her letter. But, then, she reasoned, perhaps he was no longer at Harcourt Barton. Otherwise surely he would have called. 'There, that's better, isn't it?' She tucked the sheet around Augusta.

'Miss Chester?'

Fanny looked up from her task to see a familiar bulk filling the doorway. 'Merry? *Merry!*' She covered Augusta with a blanket.

'I thought it might be you when they said the headmistress was a Miss Chester.'

'I can't believe it's you.' And she wondered how pleased Merry had really been, given their past relationship.

'Mavis, would you finish seeing to Augusta for me while I talk to Merry?' She led her downstairs. 'But they said a Mrs Denzle was going to call.'

'That's right. That's me. I'm married. I'm Mrs Denzle now.' She appeared to double in size with pride. 'You wouldn't have had call to know my Bert – he was a gardener at Harcourt Barton. When we married we thought it best to move away. After the unpleasantness that happened to me we thought it unlikely that Mr Forester would let me, of all people, stay in his cottage. So we went to Kent – that's where I'm from.'

'That's where I was born too, in Rochester.'

'Well I never. I was born in Chattendene, just a few miles away. Snails and snowdrops, and we never knew! That's why we get on so well.'

'I expect it is.' Fanny hid a smile. 'But you've returned to Devon?'

'Bert's parents passed away and he's inherited their smallholding – over Rewe way. So, here I am, and happy to help you out. It'll be like old times.'

'And we are in need of help.' Fanny hoped they would get on better than they had in the past. 'We've been lucky only three of the girls have gone down with the fever. But two of them are very poorly. We could manage but we have eighteen others to care for . . .'

'Ferrets and fogles, don't you fret. I'm here. And my Eliza, how is she?'

'Merry, I don't know. I haven't seen her for such a long time. And getting news of her is difficult. I, too, was dismissed you see, and banned from contacting her.'

'Dismissed? You?'

'It's a long story,' she said, 'but I have just received an address for her. She is living in Exeter. I was going to call but I didn't have the chance to, with the children being so ill.'

'What is she doing there?'

'She fell in love . . .'

'Eliza! My little Eliza! Impossible!'

'Sadly not, Merry. And her father found out . . .' Fanny began to tell Merry all she knew.

'What was she thinking of?' Merry huffed, when the tale was told. 'No wonder her father acted as he did. What was she imagining? It wouldn't have happened if I'd been here. He should never have dismissed me, so he's only himself to blame.'

'But, then, you wouldn't have been happily married.'

'True, but Eliza would be where she should be.'

'Merry, forgive me, but if you are to work for us, I have to ask you a personal question. I was told you had stolen jewellery and Maud was blamed. Is this true?'

'Yes, it is.' Merry spoke with no hesitation. 'Partly,' she added.

'Oh, Merry.' How could she possibly employ a thief? Yet they needed help and Merry would be perfect for the task if she set her mind to it.

'I did and I didn't. I took the jewellery but I gave it to the rightful owner. Is that stealing? I don't think so.' She sat proud and immovable.

'I don't wish to pry but I have to know. You must see that.'

'It belonged to Eliza's mother. I took it to her. And I took Eliza with me. And we were seen with her – that Lady Wickham, I reckon. So I was dismissed.'

Fanny sat back with a shocked expression. 'So she's alive? Who knew?'

'No one but me and him and the family. Everyone else was told she'd died. And, really, she might as well be dead. She's had a dreadful life. What else was she to do?' Merry looked distressed. 'I feel I can't tell you, Miss Chester, you being a respectable woman and all.'

'Is she a fallen woman?'

Merry nodded regretfully.

'Then perhaps I should explain about this school to you. Then you will know that I shall not be shocked by anything you have to say.'

'He's here again.' Beatrice, peering out of the drawing-room window, was panting with excitement. She stood on tiptoe the better to see him on the pavement below. 'I would recognise that elegant walk anywhere.'

'Who?' Eliza asked, although she knew to whom Beatrice referred.

'That will be the second time this week. I really think Lord Alford is courting you, Miss Eliza. How exciting!'

Eliza carried on calmly with her sketch of leaves. She did not find his attentions exciting. It wasn't that she didn't like the man: he was always charming and considerate, and took an interest in those things that interested her. There were times when she found being with him almost comforting – she had thought about this, not sure what she meant, until she realised one day that she felt secure when she was with him.

In different circumstances, perhaps, she would have been complimented, even flattered by him. But how could she be when she still dreamed of Jerome, still missed him? And he was so old!

They heard the bell and waited. Eliza continued to sketch, while Beatrice began to pat her hair and smooth her dress. The tread of the maid on the stairs drew nearer. 'Miss Eliza?'

'Yes, Sarah, I'm receiving. I'll see Lord Alford.'

Now why didn't she take the simple way and send the message back that she was not at home? Was she flattered by his attentions after all? If so, she wasn't very impressed with herself. Perhaps she was bored and his visit amused her. Yes, that was a far more comfortable conclusion.

'Lord Alford.' She dropped a graceful curtsy.

'Miss Forester.' He bowed.

Eliza sank on to the sofa, and Beatrice took up her position in the window. Eliza indicated the chair opposite her. He placed his hat under it – at least he was not staying long. To her astonishment she felt a sliver of disappointment.

'Forgive me for coming so soon after my last visit but I found this book and the minute I saw it I thought of you and had to bring it to you.' He handed her the brown-paper parcel he was carrying.

'Why, thank you.' She undid the string, unwrapped the tissue paper and exposed an expensively tooled and gilded leatherbound folio of plant paintings. 'These are exquisite, so finely executed.' Which was no exaggeration. She looked up. 'It is so kind of you, Lord Alford, but I couldn't possibly accept such a valuable gift.'

'Why not, if you like it?'

'It would embarrass me.' And compromise me, she thought. It was far too costly to be a casual gift.

'And your refusal would offend me.' He smiled to take the sting out of his words. 'I should assure you that it is from my own library. I had been reorganising my books while in Yorkshire. I have another exactly the same. And when I realised that, I knew who should have the duplicate. That is, if I can persuade her to accept it.'

'Well . . .' She stroked the fine binding. She would love to possess it, and if he had not purchased it then perhaps it would be all right to take it. 'Then I accept with pleasure.'

'Such a relief!'

'Refreshments, Lord Alford?'

He took out his pocket watch. 'I fear not, Miss Forester. I have an appointment with your esteemed father that I cannot miss.'

Surely not, she thought. Surely he was not presuming . . . ?

'I have a business matter to discuss with him. It's always better to deal with friends, don't you think?'

'Of course.' Eliza felt light-headed with relief and shame that she should be so presumptuous as to think that Lord Alford might be talking to her father about marriage! How conceited of her. It was Beatrice's fault, she consoled herself, putting silly ideas in her head. 'I thought you were staying at Harcourt Barton with my aunt and uncle.'

'I am. And how I envy you your house.'

'Then . . .' She looked at the book still on her lap.

'I sent for it. Once I had seen your wonderful drawings . . .' He was already on his feet and readying himself to go. 'You know, Miss Forester, your aunt is concerned about your father. He is far from well.'

'He says there is nothing wrong with him. He hates fuss.'

'We wondered, in the circumstances, if you wouldn't return to Harcourt Barton?'

'*We?* Lord Alford, pray, who is "we"?' She set her mouth determinedly. She hadn't wanted to come here, she had been ordered to. If her father wanted her home then he would have to ask her or order her there. And she did not like being coerced in this way.

He looked taken aback by her icy tone. 'Your aunt and uncle.'

'I am comfortable here.' She longed to return, wanted to be in her turret room again. She missed the smell, the warmth, the *security* of the place. But how could she return if she risked seeing Jerome? She feared what she might do if she saw him there, and she loved him too much to put him and his family at risk.

After Lord Alford had left she continued with her sketch. For five minutes she was engrossed, and then her pencil stopped, poised motionless in the air over the paper. How strange. She was certain Lord Alford had never been told the painting in the drawing room was hers.

'Anyone home?' a voice called from the kitchen door.

'Hello?' Grace Barnard left the soup she was preparing and opened the door on to the porch.

'It's me.'

An elegantly dressed woman stood in the doorway. She wore a fine tweed ulster and a tiny, pheasant-feathered hat was perched at a cheeky angle on her head.

'It's me, Maud.' She threw back her head and laughed at the astonishment on Grace's face. 'Changed, haven't I? And for the better.'

'I'm so sorry, Maud, You've changed so much. But you'd best come in.' She opened the door into the kitchen. 'I trust, despite your finery, that you won't mind the kitchen?' She, too, was laughing. 'It's warmer in here.'

'It is nice to be back. I always said I'd come.'

'It's been a long time . . . I mean, time flies.'

'I've been bad, I know. And neglectful. It's been hard, Mrs Barnard, but now I'm in a position.' She sat down at the kitchen table just as the door opened and Ruby entered. 'Hello, Ruby.' She chuckled.

'You took long enough to come, Maud.' Ruby looked across at her. For her mother's sake she hoped Maud hadn't come to reclaim Alexander.

'Ruby!' Grace said warningly.

'I know, and I've felt so guilty, but I was just telling your mother it's been hard for me.'

'And hard for my mother too. Why didn't you write?'

'I did.'

'How often? Once, twice?'

'You know me, Ruby, I hate writing. But I came to make up for it now.' She opened the tiny bag she carried and took out several gold sovereigns, which she tossed on to the table.

'There's no need for that.' Grace pushed the money back to her.

'But I always said—'

'The Foresters give me ten pounds a year for her.'

'The Foresters? Whatever for?'

'There's every need for that.' Ruby scooped the money back to her side of the table.

'Ruby, I don't want it,' said Grace.

'Keep it, Ruby,' Maud said dismissively, as if it were of little importance.

'I intend to.' Ruby stuffed it into her pocket.

'Miss Eliza arranged for her to be cared for,' Grace explained.

'She was always a real toff that one,' Maud said.

'They could have been more generous than they were, in my opinion,' retorted Ruby.

'I am content, Ruby. I wish you would give Maud her money back.'

'No, Mother. You need it. And it is obviously of no importance to Maud,' she said sharply.

'Go on, Mrs Barnard, take it. There's plenty more where that came from. Do you mind if I take my coat off?' And, oblivious to Ruby's resentment, she draped the garment over her chair, fiddled with her corset, loosened the top buttons of her boots and sat down again with a contented sigh. 'That's better. You'll never guess who I bumped into in London? Eliza's governess, Miss Chester, that's who.'

'Miss Eliza to you,' Ruby said.

'She got the push for trying to seduce old Freddie Forester. Can you imagine? Miss Prunes and Prisms!' Maud ignored Ruby. 'She runs a school now for children of the likes of me. What a laugh! Tarred with the same brush, you could say.'

'And what's that, Maud? Likes of what?' Ruby asked ominously.

'You know, Ruby.' Maud winked.

'No, I don't.'

'I don't want to offend your mother.'

'I've lived long enough that you won't upset me, Maud.'

'All right, then. I've a protector.' Maud tossed her head as if she hadn't a care in the world.

'You're a kept woman?'

'If you prefer.'

'A whore?'

'Ruby!'

'She can call it what she wants, Mother, but that's what she is.'

'Why be so horrible to me? What have I ever done to you?' Maud looked tearful. 'It's all right for you, you've a home and your mother. You didn't get caught out. But don't you try and tell me that if you weren't in the same mess you wouldn't have done the same.'

'I wouldn't have got into that mess in the first place.'

'Ruby!' Grace flapped her hands ineffectually, convinced now that Maud would demand the return of Alex.

'I didn't expect you to be so rude,' Maud said.

'You went off promising my mother you'd return and then you didn't. You didn't even write, let alone send her any money.'

'I didn't have any money!' Maud wailed.

'Were you interested in Alex? No. Who got up with her in the night when she had bad dreams? Who comforted her when she was teething? Who has loved her?'

'Your mother volunteered. If she doesn't want to look after her she needn't. I'll have her back, so there!'

'No!' Grace wailed.

'You've been here how long? Half an hour? Have you asked after the child once? No. All you want to talk about is *you*.' Ruby pointed a finger at Maud aggressively. 'Do you think I'd let you walk out of the door with her? You don't care a jot.'

'I often think of her.'

'That doesn't put food in her belly, clothes on her back. You're a thoughtless, selfish woman, Maud.'

'I wish I hadn't come.'

'So do I!'

'You're kidnapping my child.'

'We're doing no such thing. We're caring for a neglected waif. Protecting her from you.'

'I'll tell my gentleman friend.'

'Oh, yes, and what will he do? Does he want you *and* your child? I very much doubt it.'

'He loves me. He said so. He'll help me.'

'How?'

'He'll get you thrown out of here, that's for certain. He's related to the Foresters. So there.' Maud poked out her tongue.

'Who?' Ruby asked, not believing her for one minute.

'Sir Charles Wickham, that's who!'

Grace didn't so much sit down as collapse on to the chair.

8

Florrie Paddington's face was worn with fatigue, her eyes red-rimmed from lack of sleep and, Fanny thought, tears. Not that she had seen her crying, but she was convinced she wept in private. 'You should try to rest, Florrie,' she said. 'You look so tired. And when Mary's better you want to look your usual pretty self, don't you?' Fanny gazed at the figure of Florrie slumped in the chair by the fire in the small, somewhat cluttered sitting room. With her books, her papers and the children's paintings, which she liked to hang on the wall, the room never looked as neat and tidy as she would have liked. Florrie was wearing a plain blue dress and a pinny, no rouge, and her hair was pulled back in a severe bun. Without all the trappings of her profession, Florrie was truly beautiful.

'*If* she recovers.'

'She will. With you and Merry and Dr Forbes, she'll get better. I despaired for Augusta at one time but the danger is past for her. The doctor says we are fortunate that you and the other mothers are so insistent they are fed well. That is what has given them the strength to fight the disease.' Fanny had been doing the accounts, a task she hated since she always feared that either the books wouldn't balance or she would find the school was making a loss. Today she had discovered, to her astonishment, that despite Merry's added wages they were in profit, but it was too early to celebrate. She still had the doctor's fees to pay. She must remember to ask him how much they owed him: it would be unwise to let it mount too steeply. She scribbled a reminder to herself.

'You're always working.'

'There's much to do.'

'You love it, don't you?'

'You know I do, Florrie. I could never go back to being a governess.'

'Do you think you could manage it all yourself?'

'How do you mean?'

'Collecting the fees as well as paying the bills. Dealing with the mothers.'

'But you do that beautifully, Florrie.'

'Not any more. I've decided to give up my life as it is.' Fanny laid down her pencil. 'I couldn't manage without knowing you were there to help me if something went wrong.'

'You would, you know. You're far more capable than I am.'

'Perhaps I give the impression I am, but I'm in a state of panic most of the time.' She laughed but Florrie looked even more serious. 'You mean it. But why?'

'I've made a promise. If Mary recovers then I give up my sinful life.'

'You promised God?'

'Yes. I expect you find that funny.'

'No, I don't. But you never used to think your life was sinful.'

'I do now. I'm being punished for my wickedness. What else can I do, Fanny?' She began to cry. 'I didn't mean to do this in front of you.' She blew her nose and flapped her hands as if by semaphoring she could stop the tears.

'And why not, pray? Am I not your friend?' Fanny crossed to the chair, knelt on the floor and took her hand. 'I understand what you are doing. I am being selfish in wanting you to continue with the school – I fear trying to do it on my own. But the other mothers rely on you too. Will they trust me?'

'Of course they will. The main problem is getting the money out of them – sometimes I have to shout at them. You might find that hard.' She managed to smile. 'But, you see, Fanny, I couldn't go on, could I? Not feeling as I do.'

'No, I see that. I made a promise to God too. I told Him if He spared Augusta that I would cleanse my mind of all thoughts of Charles.'

'And have you?'

'I'm trying, but it's hard.'

'Concentrate on the doctor.'

'I don't understand what you mean.'

'He's in love with you.'

'Florrie! You make me laugh with your romantic imagination.'

'It's not my imagination. I know men – I should do after all these years – and he loves you.'

'For once, my dear friend, I think you are wrong. Why, we haven't even noticed each other.'

'You say?' Florrie arched her brows. 'Speaking of Charles Wickham, he stays near here, Merry was telling me.'

'Yes, he's related to the Foresters of Harcourt Barton.'

'Did he come to see Augusta?'

'No, I was deeply disappointed. Oh, not for myself,' she said hurriedly, 'but I thought he cared for the girl.'

'Only as a possible candidate for his advances.'

'Florrie, no! You can't say that, she's a child.'

'Do you think that stops the likes of him?'

'That is a truly dreadful thing to say. Charles is a kind man.'

'You think so? He spoilt the child then dropped her without a second thought when he tired of her mother. Is that kindness?'

'That was wrong of him. But I cannot believe the rest of what you say about him.'

'Then perhaps it is as well that you *cleanse* your mind of thoughts of him. A good word to choose in the circumstances.'

'No, you are wrong.' Fanny shook her head in disbelief. 'Sometimes I've wondered if she is his daughter.'

'As it happens, I know she isn't. But I doubt if he'd bother to ask. Dear Fanny, even with knowing me and the others, you live in such an innocent world. Children are at a premium for some men.'

Fanny put her hands over her ears. 'I don't want to hear this. I don't understand. Augusta? No. I'd rather die than let that happen to her.' She could not believe this of Charles, she *would not* believe it.

'Fanny, I'm sorry. I shouldn't have told you.'

'I did not know such monsters existed.'

'Fanny come, I apologise for frightening you. Augusta is one of the lucky ones, as are all the children here. They've got you. But promise not to laugh at me, Fanny, if I tell you what I want to do in the future.'

'I promise.'

'I've some money set aside for when I stopped working. I'm going to use it now. I intend to rescue the likes of me, the ones who have fallen on hard times, but especially the young girls and the children.'

Fanny brightened up. 'That is a wonderful thing to do. And because of your experiences in life, they will trust you perhaps more than someone respectable.'

At this Florrie laughed. 'I'll take that as a compliment,' she said.

Fanny was puzzled until she realised what she had

said. Then she blushed. 'I'm sorry, Florrie. How rude of me.'

'It's one of the funniest things I've heard all week. And in any case, it's true.'

'Then I have a candidate for you, a Mrs Amelia Orme – that's what she calls herself. She's fallen on hard times, according to rumour. Merry has the details. If you could find her for me, I would be so grateful. I have some savings and I could help with your expenses.'

'Then I will. But I couldn't take your money.'

'Why not? You would be doing me a favour. There must be so many families who would like to find lost loved ones such as she.'

'A business, you mean? I hadn't seen it in quite that way. More a charity.'

'And why shouldn't a charity make money too?'

A tap on the door made Fanny scramble to her feet.

'May I come in?'

'Dr Forbes. Of course.' She was strangely flustered at the sight of him – it must be because of what Florrie had said, she thought. 'Can I help you?'

'I was looking for Mrs Paddington. I think I can safely say your little girl is out of danger now.'

'Doctor, thank you!' Florrie grabbed his hand and pumped it up and down. 'I must go to her and leave you two in peace. Mrs Orme, you said, Fanny. I shall not rest until I find her, never you fear.'

Sleep was a long time in coming to Fanny. She kept going over Florrie's words time and again. Charles was a ladies' man – she knew that, but the rest? No, it was not possible. He wasn't a corrupter, she was sure.

And then there were the things Florrie had said about the doctor – Jock was his name, one of the cleaning women had told her. He didn't look much like a Jock who, Fanny thought, should be a giant of a man, with fine legs and a kilt. Dr Forbes was slight, with no outstanding features, the sort of man one would pass in the street and not notice.

Charles wasn't like that. She'd seen the sly looks other women gave him when they walked along in Exeter. But, then, she had always found that rather uncomfortable. Perhaps a man whom no one noticed would be ... she wasn't sure what she was thinking. *Reliable*, she supposed, was the word she was looking for. But was there any excitement in that?

What thoughts to be having!

And Jock was one of the kindest people she had ever known. That, above all else, had to be important.

Ruby had requested and been granted an interview with Frederick Forester. She felt sick with apprehension as she crossed the park, skirting the front of the house and making for the back entrance. Her mother had hardly stopped crying since Maud's visit, convinced that she was about to lose Alex. Ruby doubted it: the last thing Maud wanted was to be hampered with a child. But no matter what she said she could not reassure her mother.

'We don't often see you here, Ruby. Are you sure it's wise?' She had met Mrs King in the back hallway. 'I thought you'd been banned from entering the house ever again.'

'Mr Forester is expecting me.'

'Really? He never said.' Mrs King arched her eyebrows. 'Do you know anything about this, Mr Densham?' she asked the butler, who was passing regally.

'Ruby? Yes. You're early.'

'Because I didn't want to be late.' Honestly, she thought, you would have thought she still worked here, the way they spoke to her.

Ruby stood outside the library. Densham had told her pointedly to stand *here*, indicating the very spot on the carpet as if she were a dog. Thinking of dogs, she wondered what had happened to Lady Gwendoline's spaniels. She wouldn't have minded taking one herself.

When she was shown into the library, she was shocked at Mr Forester's appearance. He was badly jaundiced and had dark circles under his eyes as if he hadn't slept in months.

'Yes?' He didn't look up from the papers on his desk.

'You have Lady Gwendoline's dogs?' She couldn't imagine what had made her say that, just as if she were making conversation with a friend.

'What did you expect? That I'd have them shot?'

'No, I was just wondering . . .'

'Sit there,' he said, to her astonishment. She took the chair before he changed his mind. She looked about the once familiar room. Eliza's presence was so strong she half expected her to burst in. She had loved the library.

'You wanted to see me?'

'Yes, sir.'

'About?'

'You kindly pay my mother ten pounds a year for the child of one of your maids that she cares for.'

'An adequate sum I'd have thought.'

'It's not that. The mother has turned up.'

'Commendable of her. Does that mean I no longer have to pay Mrs Barnard?'

'No, sir. She's blackmailing Mother. She says she wants the child back and if she doesn't give her up then she will have us thrown off the farm.'

'Shouldn't the child be with its mother?'

'Normally. Every child needs a mother.' Her hand shot up to her mouth at the realisation of what she had just said – to Frederick Forester, of all people. 'I didn't mean . . . It's just . . .' She took a deep breath and started again. 'She's not a suitable person. It's breaking my mother's heart. She's looked after the little girl so long that she feels she's her own.' All she could hope was that he hadn't noticed what she had just said, for even as they spoke he was continuing to write.

'Not a wise course of action.'

'No.'

'And how can she have you thrown out of the farm?'

'She is going to ask her protector and he will ask you to do so.'

'Really?' He smiled, at least that was what Ruby thought it was. 'And who is this powerful man?'

The walls of the large room seemed to close in on her. She took a deep breath. 'Sir Charles Wickham, sir.' She closed her eyes, said a little prayer and wondered if he could hear the pounding of her heart.

He laughed, loud and long. 'A former housemaid of mine, you said?' This appeared to amuse him even more. Ruby sat waiting for his mirth to subside. It was all right for him to find it so funny but it wasn't funny for her mother, or for her. 'They tell me you're marrying my gamekeeper's son.'

'Yes, sir. In the new year.'

'His father is retiring in January.'

'Yes, sir.'

'And your intended is hoping to obtain the position for himself?'

'Yes, sir.'

'And, I gather, his father is moving back to Scotland to work his croft?'

'So he has said, sir.'

'And you will be living in the cottage he vacates *if* his son is fortunate in his ambitions?'

'Yes, sir.' Ruby felt uneasy. She did not like the way this conversation was going, the way he spoke to her as if he were playing with her.

'Then I have a proposition to put to you, Ruby. Comply with my wishes and the position and cottage are yours. Comply with my wishes and your mother need not make alternative arrangements.'

'Yes, sir . . .' She knew she was not going to like whatever his wishes were.

'You are to visit my daughter in Exeter. In the course of your meeting you are to tell her that your brother Jerome is married. Why, we could even have the young

354

woman – I leave the choice to you of who is the lucky one – with child. Yes, that makes it even better.'

'But he isn't married.'

'Exactly.'

'But I would be lying.'

'You would.'

'But if she came here and asked him she would find it was a falsehood.'

'She wouldn't do that. She is my daughter. She would be too proud even to acknowledge your brother.'

'Sir, I'm sorry, but I couldn't do that – lie.'

'Then I shall leave it to you to tell your mother and Henry the sorry news, shall I?'

9

'Miss Eliza, there's a *person* to see you.'

'Yes, Sarah, and did this *person* give a name?' Eliza hid a smile at her maid's evident disapproval of the visitor.

'Yes, miss. She said she was a Miss Barnard.'

'Ruby!' Eliza shot out of her chair, rushed to the door, yanked it open, hastened out on to the landing and hung over the banister. 'Ruby, up here,' she called.

Ruby sprinted up the stairs with equal speed.

'Oh, Ruby . . .' Eliza stood with her arms held wide in welcome and Ruby darted into them, much to the astonishment and displeasure of her current maid. 'This is a wonderful surprise. Come in.' She hustled Ruby into the drawing room.

'This is nice,' said Ruby, looking about the spacious, airy room, which was filled with winter sunshine, as Eliza fussed over her, helping her take off her coat.

'Tea, please, Sarah. You must be cold, Ruby. Come and sit by the fire.' She continued to bustle about her guest as Beatrice, alerted by the commotion, came into the room to see what the noise was about. 'This is my companion, Miss Holland. Beatrice, this is my dear friend Miss Barnard from Harcourt Barton come, I trust, with much news for me.'

From her expression Beatrice did not approve of Ruby being described as a friend, but she shook hands then made to sit on a chair by the fire.

'Would you mind, Beatrice?' Eliza smiled, not wanting to hurt her feelings.

'Would I mind what?' Beatrice said obtusely.

'I would appreciate you leaving Miss Barnard and myself. We have much news to exchange and it would be tedious for you, since you won't know of whom we speak.' Again she smiled, but Beatrice looked affronted.

'As you wish,' she said, and with head held rigid and indignation in every movement, she made her way to the door.

When she had gone Eliza leant forward and took Ruby's hands. She sat still for a moment just looking at her. 'Dearest Ruby, I can't believe you are here. I've missed you so much and you can't imagine how I have longed for you to come.' She wondered if she should confess that she went often to the market and watched her and her brother, but decided against it. Ruby might be offended that she hadn't let her know she had been there, that she had been spying on her. 'I wrote, you know, but when I received no reply I presumed the mail was being intercepted.'

'Most probably. I've tried to persuade my mother to ask Ivy to leave but she's so soft-hearted she won't, so we are left with a spy in the house.'

'How horrible for you.' Just as well she hadn't said anything about the market. She wished Ruby would mention Jerome. 'And your dear mother, how is she?'

'Very well. Working too hard, of course. Alex is so clever and pretty. Maud came, you know.'

'Never! How did she find the courage?' she said, while wondering if perhaps Ruby had a message for her from Jerome. What bliss that would be.

'Mother was sweet with her. I wasn't.'

'Quite right. And how are you?' They were interrupted by the arrival of the tea, which seemed to take Sarah an unconscionably long time to set out.

'Where were we?' Eliza asked, once the tea was poured and sandwiches dispensed. 'I was asking how you were.' But I want to know . . .

'I'm getting married.'

'Ruby! How exciting. Who is the lucky man? Henry?'

'Yes.'

'When?'

'We had hoped in December but it's more likely to be in the new year now.'

'At Harcourt Barton, of course? And will you remain there?'

'Yes. Henry's father is retiring as gamekeeper and your father has kindly offered the position to him.'

'So you'll be living at Bower Cottage. I always loved it, so pretty. I should, of course, love to come to the ceremony. But you understand . . . I'm not sure of my plans . . . Well . . .'

'Miss Eliza, please, I know it would be difficult for you.'

'But I shall think of you on the great day.'

A silence descended, which eventually Ruby broke. 'Perhaps it's presumptuous of me, Miss Eliza, but I must tell you that I fear your father is not well. And well, in your present position . . .'

'Our barely speaking, you mean? I do see him occasionally, you know. And the last time I mentioned his health he assured me he was well, merely tired.'

'It's not my business but . . . when might that have been?'

Eliza frowned as she worked out dates. 'A month ago, maybe a little bit longer.'

'Then I think you should see him again. He is poorly even if he says he isn't.'

'Thank you for warning me, Ruby. I know you do it

with the best intentions.' Eliza paused. 'Are you all right, Ruby? You look uncomfortable. As if something were bothering you.'

'No, there's nothing. Guess who I met the other day?' She appeared to brighten. 'Miss Chester.'

'Where? She's here? What is she doing?'

'She's the headmistress of a girls' school, and very happy. But I don't know where.' She said this so hurriedly that Eliza was sure she did know and wondered why she wouldn't tell her.

'Did she ask after me?'

'We spoke of little else.' Ruby laughed.

'When can I see her?'

'I couldn't give her your address since I didn't know where you were.'

'But you know now?'

Ruby went red with confusion. 'Yes, but I haven't seen her since I found out. We were not allowed to know, you see, but as soon as I learnt where you were I came rushing round to see you. I said to my mother—'

'Ruby, there *is* something the matter. What is it? Please tell me.' She was concerned for her friend.

'It's just . . . I'm so afraid your father will find out I've been here. He might take a dreadful revenge on my family. You know how he feels about us . . .' She looked miserable.

'Poor Ruby. Why should he know? I'll tell Beatrice that if she tells him I shall send her home immediately. That will frighten her into silence.'

'Oh, Miss Eliza . . .' Ruby burst into tears. 'I don't know how to tell you this. It's so awful. But I have to. It's my duty . . .'

'Yes?' Eliza's heart was thudding suddenly; she knew what Ruby was going to say. She feared it, and wanted to race from the room so as not to hear the words.

'Miss . . .'

'He's getting married, isn't he? Was that what you couldn't bring yourself to say to me?'

Mutely Ruby nodded. Eliza felt the room close in on her. The bright sunshine disappeared and darkness flooded the room. How could she live with this, how could she survive . . . ?

'Poor Ruby, how awful for you, knowing you were going to have to tell me. Who is the bride?' Her voice sounded harsh as she spoke, so she coughed to hide it.

'Ivy.' Ruby snatched the name from the air.

'Just as well you didn't persuade your mother to get rid of her, wasn't it?' Ruby was staring at her lap as if afraid to look at her. 'Ruby, you need not have been so concerned. See? I haven't thrown myself out of the window.'

Ruby looked up slowly.

In fact, the news has come as something of a relief. I wasn't quite sure how I was going to tell you but I, too, have met someone. It must be the season for romance.' She laughed as she said this, as one without a care in the world, whose heart wasn't breaking. And she instilled happiness into her voice, when it was really laden with tears.

'Really? Oh, that is good news,' Ruby said. 'May I ask who?'

'Lord Alford, an old friend of the family,' Eliza said, with all the pride she could muster.

'Imagine that! You'll be Lady Alford!'

'It will please my father.' She heard bitterness in her voice as she said those words, and wondered if Ruby had recognised it.

10

'Father, why didn't you tell me?'

'You said you didn't wish to return to Harcourt Barton. I respected your wishes.'

'When I said that to you, I didn't know you were so ill. But you knew, didn't you? Why not tell me?'

'Because, Eliza, I think we are two stubborn people.' He smiled somewhat bleakly. 'Your aunt tells me she informed you of my condition. I gather Hedworth Alford did too. How many people did you require to tell you before you believed it?' He spoke sharply.

'Just one, Father. You,' Eliza replied simply. 'I apologise. I thought everyone wanted me to return against my will. I wasn't ready to do so.'

'And now?'

'You were right, Father. I should have listened to you.'

'That is most satisfactory.' With a great sigh, he sank back on to his pillows. 'But who did you believe this time, to come so rapidly?'

'I had a visitor who was concerned.'

'And who might that have been?'

'I would rather not say, it might anger you.'

'Did I ban whoever it was from your presence?'

'Yes.'

'How draconian.' He smiled wryly. 'Most satisfactory,' he repeated, and closed his eyes. They were in his bedroom: she had only ever entered it once before and that had not been a happy occasion. It had the now familiar smell of the sick room, the mustiness, the sweet, sickly odour of flesh that was not long for this world. Half an hour ago, when she had entered it, she had nearly run out straight away. It was her grandmother all over again, within less than a year.

He was fast asleep, she saw, in that strange way of the very sick, one moment speaking, the next sleeping as if they had been so for hours. She would have liked to hold his hand as she had her grandmother's when she lay mortally ill, but she couldn't. He might not like it. She watched him, saw the flickers of pain that crossed his face. Still, despite his unhealthy pallor, he was a fine-looking man. His hair was scattered with grey now but that made him even more handsome in her eyes. How she wished he loved her. And now . . . That was just a forlorn hope, which had never, despite Jerome, despite everything, left her.

She jumped as she heard a step behind her. 'I'm sorry, Miss Eliza, but the doctor's here.'

'Thank you, Mrs King. I would like a word with him.' Silently she stood up and left the dimly lit room. 'Dr Forbes, isn't it? I'm Mr Forester's daughter.'

'Miss Forester.' He bowed his head. 'I was hoping you would come. You will be a great comfort to him.' She was concerned to see how young he appeared. She was used to old Dr Whitney.

'I fear my father's very ill.'

'I would have to agree.'

'He seems to be in pain. I don't want him to suffer.'

'I shall attend to it, Miss Forester. His need for larger doses of opiate increases with the progress of his illness.'

'I should have come sooner. I regret that I wasn't here. I didn't realise the urgency.' She was twisting her hands in anguish.

'You must not punish yourself, Miss Forester.'

'That is hard not to do, Doctor. Six months ago he said he was tired. I had no idea . . .'

'It would have made no difference had you known. Your father has been to see many specialists in London, Paris and, no doubt, elsewhere. He is resigned and, I am certain, calm.'

'Then it isn't long?'

'No.'

'How long?'

'I cannot say. That is God's decision.' He looked at her with such tenderness she had to look away for fear she would cry. 'Now, if you will excuse me . . .' he said, in a businesslike manner.

After the doctor had gone to her father, Eliza paced the landing. She should have known, she should have been here . . . These two thoughts went round and round in her head. She could not stop them or the racket they made.

'There you are. At last!'

'Aunt.'

'I'd begun to think the poor man would die before you saw him.'

'I feel guilty.'

'As you should. You should have come weeks ago. Is the doctor still here? I need to talk to him.' Minnie Wickham had joined her in pacing up and down the thickly carpeted landing. The portraits of earlier Foresters and her grandmother's ancestors looked down at their progress. Eliza wondered how many such scenes they had witnessed with their implacable, frozen stares. 'Tell me, Eliza, has your father made a will?'

'I beg your pardon?' Eliza stopped dead, her face etched with astonishment.

'It's essential he has made one.'

'Really, Aunt, this is neither the time nor the place for such a conversation.'

'On the contrary, it is exactly the time and the place. I can assure you that if he hasn't then there will be many complications.'

'Then I'm sure he has.'

'Where is it?'

'I wouldn't know. In the library with his papers, perhaps.'

'No, it isn't. There's nothing there.'

'You looked in his papers?'

'What else was I to do? We need to know.'

'I don't.'

'But it's *you* I'm thinking about, you silly girl.'

'Then please don't concern yourself with my affairs.'

'You have become remarkably forward in the last few months. Or is it because you sense you will soon be your own woman?'

'How could you say such a thing, Aunt?'

'How dare you speak to me in that tone?'

'Because you are so impertinent as to speak to me of such matters at such a time.'

They stood on the landing facing each other, their faces distorted with anger. Eliza would have liked to cry but controlled herself: she would not give this woman the pleasure of seeing how upset she was.

'Do I sense a *frisson* of displeasure?' Hedworth Alford, his footsteps silenced by the carpet, appeared beside them.

'My aunt is concerned that my father has not made a will.'

'Lady Wickham, is that not a little insensitive of you?' He smiled, as if to show her he bore her no ill will.

'I worry about Eliza and her inheritance.'

'Quite properly. But I'm sure, will or no, that Miss Forester's inheritance is certain and safe.'

Eliza could almost swear that she heard amusement in his voice, though what he might find funny at a time like this she could not imagine. She was surprised to find him here at all. And she was even more surprised when she learnt it was at her father's request. She would have thought him far too ill to want visitors. 'Ah, Doctor.' She sprang towards him as he emerged from her father's room.

'I have left instructions with the nurse to increase the doses for him. He will be more comfortable. He has made a request.'

'Yes?' they said in unison, and all leant forward eagerly.

'He wishes to be moved.'

'Has he lost his mind?' Minnie snapped.

'To his wife's room, he said.'

'How lovely.' Eliza sighed.

'What on earth for?' said Minnie.

Fanny felt she could at last travel to Exeter: the children, while still weak, were no longer in danger.

'You go, I'm here, what can go wrong?'

'Merry, don't say such things, you're tempting fate.'

'Get away with you! You need a day away from all these worries and disappointments.'

And there were indeed worries and disappointments, thought Fanny, as the baker's cart rocked her this way and that, in the rutted lanes, on their way to the station. She had been deeply hurt by Charles, who had responded to her third letter, sent at great risk to herself should Frederick Forester find out. He had written to say that Augusta was her responsibility, not his. She had confided in Florrie that perhaps because he was with his wife he had to be careful lest she discover that Fanny was close by, for she would surely tell her brother. Florrie, however, thought it far more likely that he was afraid of catching Augusta's illness – 'Men are cowards like that.'

It was a time of great anxiety: five of the girls had been removed from the school by their worried mothers and had returned to London. She didn't blame them: scarlet fever was a dreadful illness. She had tried to reassure them, as had Florrie and the doctor, but they were adamant: the disease might still be lurking.

Therefore the number of pupils was down to fifteen. While this might not have been such a disaster, it had been complicated by Florrie losing her temper when the five mothers had requested, politely, that the fees for the rest of the term be returned to them. Fanny was ready to persuade them against taking the money, or offer them a compromise, hoping to convince them to return their girls when a little more time had passed. Instead Florrie had flared up in a fine old temper, told them a few unwarranted home truths and ended up throwing the money at them. She had apologised but the damage had been done. They had scooped up the money and swept out for ever. Consequently funds were badly depleted and where would they find replacement pupils? With Christmas coming she had wanted to buy the girls treats but now she could not afford them.

Nights were hard for Fanny: sleep was elusive,' and she spent hours trying to solve the insoluble. And as she climbed down from the baker's cart she found she was weary already, and the day had barely begun. It was only nine o'clock.

'Miss Chester, might I join you?'

'Dr Forbes. Please . . .' The doctor climbed into the carriage of the train and sat opposite her and the only other passenger, an elderly but well-dressed woman.

'How cold it is.'

They took refuge in discussing the weather, then the recovered invalids, the school. When the train stopped, the other passenger alighted and left them alone. The journey continued then suddenly the train juddered to a halt. Dr Forbes looked out of the window to see what the problem might be. 'A herd of cows on the line,' he explained, 'and much confusion. The guard is not a herdsman. The delay might be longer. I will, if you wish, enter another carriage.'

'That won't be necessary, Doctor.' What sensitivity he showed, she thought. And how shocked her brother would be to find her in such a situation, and refusing the solution to it. Once she would have been afraid to be alone with a man in a railway carriage – which was why, if she was not with the vicar, she normally travelled in the Ladies Only compartment. But she felt comfortable with the doctor. And somehow, perhaps because they were alone, or because the trouble with the cattle persisted, she began to confide in him her problems over the loss of students.

'Why not take day pupils?'

'It might be difficult.'

'Of course, the fees would be less.'

'It's not that.'

'If you like I could ask around for you, when I am out on my visits.' He smiled so kindly at her.

'I doubt that any of the local people would like their children to associate with my pupils. You see . . .' She explained who the pupils were and, as delicately as possible, what their mothers did. It wasn't until she reached the end of the tale that she realised what a shock it must be to him and, no doubt, that he would never want to speak to her again. The thought made her feel sad.

'Miss Chester, I beg leave to tell you how very much I admire you and the action you have taken,' he said instead.

'I shouldn't have told you.'

'I feel privileged that you did. These children should be helped. You are a good woman, Miss Chester. I have always respected your devotion to your pupils, but my esteem for you now knows no bounds.'

Fanny blushed at his compliments, at the earnestness of his expression. The train jolted back into motion. They had arrived at Exeter far too soon for Fanny.

Her time with the doctor had been *so* enjoyable, she had found him *so* easy to talk to, he had raised her spirits *so* much, she told herself, as she walked along Colleton Crescent searching for Eliza's house. Her disappointment that she was not there was not nearly as intense as it might have been but for the pleasant journey.

'She's gone to nurse her father at Harcourt Barton, he's seriously ill, not expected to live,' Ruby explained later, over cake and coffee.

'Oh, the poor man. Poor Eliza.'

'I don't see why you should feel sorry for him after what he did to you.'

'It was unfair but I do not bear him such ill will that I cannot feel sadness at your news.'

'You're a better person than me, then, Miss Chester. But there's other news – Eliza's getting married.'

'What wonderful news!' She felt pleased but sad, too, that she would not be there for her on the great day. 'Who is the most fortunate man?'

'A Lord Alford.'

'That's *much* more suitable.' Her gloved hand shot up to her mouth. 'Ruby, I didn't mean ... How dreadfully rude and insensitive of me.'

'It's all right, Miss Chester. Like my mother says, you don't mate a duck with a chicken, do you?'

'Well, no. When is the ceremony to take place?'

'Well ...' Ruby looked doubtful for a moment. 'It's not official yet. Eliza said ... At least, I think that's what she meant.'

'So it hasn't been announced?'

'No.'

'I wonder why.'

'But I've other news. Guess who turned up right out of the blue since I last saw you. Maud.'

'Never!'

'Bold as brass. Dressed up to the nines she was and full of herself.' Ruby looked about her to see if anyone was near, then leant across the table and put her hand up to her mouth so that no one could hear. 'She's a kept woman,' she whispered.

'No!'

'And guess who?'

'Who?'

'Sir Charles Wickham, no less.'

This news had stunned Fanny, but she hoped she had been able to hide her shock. And she had behaved with dignity, she was sure. As soon as she had parted from Ruby she had gone to sit in the cathedral. Once she began to rationalise everything she realised she was being stupid. Why should she have thought he would regard her in a different light from his other women? Why was she shocked when she knew how he had dealt with Caroline Fraser? Florrie had warned her, but she hadn't wanted to believe her friend. He was an unscrupulous man, that was painfully obvious. A bad man! Poor Maud, flighty, empty-headed girl that she was – certainly no match for Charles. What would happen to her when he tired of her, as he no doubt would? She should be grateful to Maud: she had woken Fanny up to her silliness. How easily she could have been in Maud's shoes now.

On arriving at the station she tried not to look for the doctor too obviously. Why, he hadn't even said he was returning this evening, let alone on which train. When she saw him she felt quite light headed and wasn't in the least put out to find that the vicar was not on the train. Even better was when the doctor offered to drive her back to the school after she had told him she would have to walk.

A day that had started so badly had ended most satisfactorily, she thought, as she blew out her candle much later that night. And then she sat bolt upright: what a thing for her to think!

II

The move from his own room to that of his wife had an amazing effect upon Frederick Forester. He appeared to recover. He brightened. He rarely mentioned pain. He ate more. He talked. He was even known to laugh. But, best of all, he was sleeping in a more natural way, which was the largest contributory factor to the improvement.

Why this should be was a constant source of conjecture among the others. The room, which had been left as it was on the day of his wife's departure, had been tidied, not that he had wanted it done but finally even he had accepted that half-packed trunks and female attire littering the floor were not appropriate to a sick room.

'It is totally macabre, and ridiculous,' was Minnie's opinion.

'This room has a better outlook,' was Hedworth's.

'Maybe he was bored where he was,' was Charles's.

Eliza felt love had called him back. A strong smell of

tuberoses still lingered here – evidently it had been Amelia's favoured perfume. Perhaps by smelling it he could conjure the sense of her more easily. She was certain he had wanted to move to be closer to his Amelia. As far as she knew she was the only person who had witnessed his emotional outburst in this room, calling for her. Perhaps, for him, her soul lingered here.

Eliza began to allow herself to hope that he might recover completely.

'I've said all along that it was simply his liver – he's always taken far too much claret and port but he'd never listen to me. Then he's ill and does not drink so he is better,' said Minnie Wickham. A week had passed and he was even talking of Christmas and of going to Rome in the spring.

'Yes, Aunt.'

'Giving us such a fright. And that stupid doctor aiding and abetting him. But this has been a timely warning to us all. It doesn't alter the fact that he should be asked about his will.'

'Yes, Aunt.' Eliza carried on with the sketch she had been working on. She was learning that the best way to deal with her aunt was to agree with everything she said, then ignore her. Otherwise the nagging and bad temper lasted for days.

'You are the obvious person. *You* should broach the subject.'

'Yes, Aunt.'

'So you will?' Minnie crossed to the table and leant on it, pushing her face close to her niece's. 'You're not listening. I thought you weren't.'

'Aunt, I was.'

'What have I just said then?'

'About my father. His liver . . .' Why did her aunt have to be so unpleasant all the time? She was an attractive woman, she had Uncle Charles to love her, and yet . . .

'And? After that?'

369

There was a drawn-out silence as Eliza tried frantically to think of an answer. 'I don't know,' she had to admit.

'You are so insufferably rude!'

'Yes, Aunt.'

Minnie stamped about the room, venting her anger with Eliza on cushions and books. Eliza was trying to work out how she could leave the room without fuelling the fury when the door opened and she was rescued.

'Lord Alford, you were able to come.' Minnie's mood changed in a split second. Now she was all smiles and graciousness, the perfect hostess instead of the virago she had been a minute before. Instantly Eliza felt in the way, as she so often did when these two were together.

'Miss Forester.' He bowed elegantly.

'Lord Alford.' She smiled, and began to collect up her pencils and paper.

'You're not going because of me? Please, I shall leave this instant if that is so.'

She laughed. 'No, Lord Alford.' She shut the sliding lid of her pencil box.

'It was so kind of you to invite me for the weekend.'

She had not known that she *had* invited him, but she was glad to see him anyway: her aunt was always much sweeter-natured when he was here.

'The reports on your father are satisfactory.'

'Aren't they? He is so much better. Now, if you will excuse me . . .'

It was a bitter December day, one of those days that come as such a surprise and blessing in the midst of winter. The air, though cold, was invigorating, the sun shone, and the branches of the leafless trees silhouetted against it appeared to be outlined in gold. Even though it was near midday, frost still decorated the plants, silvering them rigid. Cobwebs looked as if spun from lace. Eliza stood in the doorway, took a deep breath and felt as if she was inhaling a rejuvenating tonic. After the heat in the drawing room, upon which her aunt insisted, it was refreshing. She called Bumble and the other dogs. 'Bumble, a walk will do you good. You're getting too fat,' she chided him. Reluctantly the dog followed her. He was so lazy, these days. Once, he would have rushed out at the chance of a walk.

Eliza cut across the front lawn. As she walked she sensed someone watching her. She turned round and looked up at the house. In a window she saw her father watching her. She waved, he raised a hand in acknowledgement. Someone was with him but she was too far away to make out who it was.

Her father had been kinder, gentler and – dare she think it? – more interested in her since his illness. Sometimes she would look up and find him watching her with such a sweet expression. But when he became aware that she had seen him, the look would change, as if he were embarrassed at her knowing. She was beginning to think he might be fond of her and wondered if some strange shyness prevented him showing it. She wanted him to love her just as much as she always had. She had forgiven him for the way he had treated Jerome. After all, the speed with which Jerome had recovered from losing her and married Ivy showed that perhaps her father had been right all along. Jerome couldn't have loved her as much as he had said.

For those few months she had revelled in Jerome's friendship, in the novelty of having someone who thought as she did, who wanted what she wanted, who had made life appear different and far more worthwhile. Still, it was over, finished with, she told herself. But then ... She turned to encourage Bumble, who was lagging far behind. It might have been for the best but that didn't stop her missing him: she had learnt that love was not like a tap that could be turned off, and she still loved him with the same intensity. She would love him until the day she died.

Ahead was a small wood, which the spaniels particularly enjoyed and she saw them disappear into it. They would be there for ages now, so there was no point in waiting for them, especially if they put up a rabbit. She was about to set off back the way she had come when she saw Jerome, dragging a large log, heading towards her.

'Good morning,' she said politely, her heart pounding.

'Miss Eliza.' He doffed his cap. 'Cold, isn't it?'

'Bitter. Still, you've a fine log there.'

'Yes.'

They both stood in awkward silence. This was the first time they had seen each other for nearly a year.

'The spaniels—'

'Have put up a rabbit—'

'Yes.'

The silence lengthened.

'Your mother?'

'Well. Your father?'

'Much better, thank you.'

'That's good for you.'

The awkward silence returned.

'And Alex?'

'Bonny.'

'Please give all your family my regards.'

'I'll do that.'

'Well . . .' She should turn and go but she was rooted to the spot, wanting to go but not wanting to.

'Miss Eliza—'

'Yes?'

'I—'

'Yes?'

'Jerome!' a voice called. They both turned. Running across the park towards them, waving and laughing, was Ivy.

'I must be going.' She felt cold, as if the frost had touched her, and turned sharply then began to run towards the house, Bumble puffing along behind her.

*

Eliza had got into the habit of sitting with her father before dinner. It enabled the nurse to eat her own supper, and since her aunt always took longer than she to dress they were rarely disturbed. Although he spent a large part of the day in a chair, he was always in bed by six. She began to regard it as her private time with him. He did not like to be read to but he liked someone to be there so that he was never alone.

Over the last few days, since his health had improved, she was not sure if he wanted to continue in this manner. She had thought it best if she waited for him to summon her and when he hadn't she had felt sad. So she was pleased when, that evening, Densham appeared to tell her her father wanted her.

'I missed you the last couple of evenings,' he said, to her astonishment.

'I didn't want to intrude.'

'Why should you think I would mind?'

She did not answer.

'A rather stupid question – I've hardly made you welcome in the past.'

She was not sure if he expected an answer.

'You look so like your mother, sitting there, especially here, in her room.'

'Do I?' She smiled with pleasure.

'She was very beautiful.'

'Then I can't see how I could possibly resemble her.'

'Don't be so modest,' he chided, with a smile. 'Would you mind pouring me a glass of water?' She did as he asked.

'I have not been a good father to you,' he continued. She was so surprised that she sat down rather heavily. 'I would like to apologise for that.'

'Really, Father, there's no need.' What else was she to say?

'Much happened in the past that is too shaming for me to talk of, especially to you. Know, however, that I was hurt in such a way that the pain remains with me to this day.'

'That makes me sad, Papa.'

'There is much I have said which I now realise was nonsense, the product of my temporarily deranged mind. You are so much my daughter.'

'But of course.' She smiled at him, since she was not sure of what he spoke.

'You do realise how much I wish I had time to make amends.'

'You have, already. In these past weeks you have made me happy. There is no need to apologise to me for anything.'

'There's every need.' He held out his hand to her and she took it, feeling his tissue-thin skin, remembering her grandmother's, which had felt so similar. 'I am dying, Eliza. I cannot do so without resolving various matters, as far as I can.'

'No!' She almost shouted the word. 'You can't be!'

'I fear so.'

'I won't let you die.'

'The choice will not be yours.'

'But you are so much better.'

'Dr Forbes tells me that a rally such as this is common, and that it will be short-lived.'

'He'd no right to say that to you.'

'He had. I asked him. He's a good doctor. Had I not enquired he would not have told me.'

'Then he's wrong.'

'I doubt it. I feel it myself.'

'Papa . . .' There was anguish in her voice.

'I don't mind, Eliza. I have been lucky, I have had time to think about death and confront it. And I have found that it is not such a bad thing, after all. We spend all our lives fearing death and, as it approaches, why, it's become almost like a friend to me.'

Eliza fought the tears that were just below the

surface. He wouldn't want her to cry and she feared that if she did she might never stop.

'I apologise for being as I have with you. I should not have blamed you for others' faults. Things were done and said which caused both you and me much unhappiness. I do not regret what I did, but how it affected us. You were a child, my child, and it was wrong of me.'

'But it was your grief made you so, you must not blame yourself.'

'Oh, Daughter, there is so much I want to say to you and so much I can't bring myself to confess, even now. But one day you will know and all I can do is trust that you will understand.'

'Papa, you speak in riddles,' she said, while registering the tone of his voice, the love she was certain she heard in it.

'You're calling me "Papa" again. That's nice. I have been "Father" ever since that young man . . . Have you forgiven me for him?'

'I think there will always be part of me which will be fond of him, but I see now that he wasn't right for me – the differences between us were so great.' But we could have surmounted them, she thought.

'What do you think of Hedworth Alford?'

'He's very charming.'

'Is that all?'

'No, I like him. He's kind and sensitive.'

'He came to see me today. He wanted my permission to ask if he might court you, with the intention of proposing marriage.'

'But I didn't mean it!'

'Mean what?'

'I don't know.' But she did. For a moment then she'd been muddled and had thought the declaration she had made to Ruby about Hedworth had been voiced instead to her father. 'It's nothing. It's the shock.' She laughed nervously.

'So you have no objection to him calling on you in that capacity?'

'I don't think so.' She sounded uncertain. 'What do you think?'

'It would make me happy to know that you would be cared for when I am no longer here. I must say I approve. He tells me he is well set up, and he's a good age for you. You would have a standing in society which I was never able to give you.'

'Then if it's what you want . . .'

'No, Eliza, it must be what *you* want.'

'Which is to make you happy. And I like him.'

'Then that is settled. There's something else, Eliza. Will you send a message to Mr Joiner tomorrow asking him to come and to bring Simpson from the bank? I have business to attend to.'

'Yes, Papa.' She wondered if Aunt Minnie was about to have her way, that the lawyer was being summoned to draft a will.

12

It was a strange time for Eliza. From being ignored by her father she had become important to him. From not being spoken to, she was now sought out. From not being loved she knew now that she was. And it had all happened so suddenly. The newness of it was difficult, at first, for her to adjust to. But she liked it, her dream was fulfilled, and, because of it, she grew in confidence.

The previous evening she had not dined with the others but had had a tray sent to her father's room – it was pleasant to do so now. The news that Lord Alford was interested in her had not really been a shock: when she was in Exeter, she had thought he was flirting with her. However, the confirmation made her shy with him.

The following morning she sent the message to the solicitor to call as soon as possible, not because she thought her father was right and that he was dying but to please her aunt. As she crossed the hall she met Alford. 'I wonder if I might have a word, Miss Forester.'

'I'm afraid I'm terribly busy,' she said, blushing furiously. Then she rushed from the hall, down the back corridor to the boot room to find her galoshes to go for a walk.

She needed fresh air to clear her mind. She was about to open the door to the stableyard when she saw Jerome. As usual, her heart began its pit-a-pat drumming. Then, Ivy came round the corner and, like yesterday, she was laughing as she approached him, hips swaying. On reaching him she stood on tiptoe as if she was about to kiss him. And he made to push her away. Eliza knew what they were doing now – Ivy would run away squealing with pleasure, he would chase her, she would let him catch up, and he'd fold his arms around her, and he'd shower her face with kisses. Oh, yes, Eliza knew very well what they were doing, for she and Jerome had played that game countless times.

Eliza turned away from the door swamped with misery and longing for that which was now so far out of her grasp. She returned to the boot room and took off her galoshes and her coat. She checked herself in the mirror, patted her hair straight, pinched her cheeks to bring back the colour, which had drained away. Then she returned to the main hall where Densham was sorting the newly arrived mail.

'Densham, would you please tell Lord Alford I am in the conservatory?' she asked.

In the heavily heated room, the cloying scent of tuberoses pervaded the air – her mother's favourite, the smell that always made her sad. She sat on a wrought-iron seat beside a pool with a small waterfall. Her shadow on the water made the fish dart hither and thither in panic. She leant forward, seeing her reflection in the water and wondering what she was doing here. Another image appeared over her shoulder.

'Lord Alford,' she said, straightening.

'I hope I didn't startle you.'

'No, not at all.' With a sweep of her hand she motioned to the matching seat opposite.

'You know why I wish to speak to you?'

'No, Lord Alford. I've no idea,' she lied. What a ridiculous convention they were dancing through.

'I do not wish to appear too forward but, in our talks together, was I right in sensing that you liked me?'

'But of course, Lord Alford. You are a friend of my uncle and aunt.'

'I did not mean because of them.'

'In what other way could you possibly mean?' She bowed her head modestly.

'I would like . . .' He stood up, then with one swift, graceful movement knelt on one knee before her. 'I would like, Miss Forester, to hope that . . . Miss Forester, would you do me the great honour of agreeing to be my wife?'

She sat poised and calm, and looked at him thoughtfully. He smiled – nervously, she was sure. He was handsome, he was rich, he was titled and he wasn't *that* old. He was everything that her family constantly told her was right for her. And what else was there for her now? Jerome loved another.

'Yes,' she said.

'Oh, my love!'

'With two conditions.'

'Anything.'

'In fairness to you, I have to tell you that I do not love you.'

'I have enough love for the two of us,' he said, flinging his arms wide. 'And I will teach you to love me. The second?'

'That we live here and not on your estate. I know this is a lot to ask but I could never leave Harcourt. Or perhaps you do not understand?'

'But I do. And I am happy to live where you wish. And so here it shall be.'

'Then that is all right,' she said, so matter-of-factly that he laughed.

'My sweet, darling Eliza.' He pulled her to him and kissed her full on the mouth. He smelt of tobacco and brandy, and a sweet, musky smell that made her head spin – he smelt delicious. His kiss was hard and fierce, which she found exciting. And he prised open her lips with his tongue and explored her mouth, a new experience for her. She thought she was about to faint from the sensation.

'We have to tell the world!' he shouted. And she laughed too. He was so happy, which made her feel less sad. 'You're smiling such a secret little smile, may I share your thoughts?'

'My friend Jonquil teased me that someone would propose to me in here and I disagreed.'

'You were wrong.' He kissed the tip of her nose.

'And I said I would never accept.'

'You were wrong twice!' And he kissed her again.

'I can't tell you how delighted I am for you both.'

'Thank you, sir.'

'Thank you, Papa.'

'I will take great care of her, Mr Forester.'

'I would never have given my permission had I thought you wouldn't. But I would like the ceremony to take place as soon as possible.' He looked pointedly at Alford. 'Time', he added, 'is of the essence.'

'I shall ride into Exeter tomorrow and see the Bishop.'

'A special licence and here in the chapel.'

'But I've no dress!'

'Yes, you have.' There was a tap at the door. 'Come,' Frederick said, and his sister entered.

'We've momentous news, Minnie. Little Eliza has accepted Hedworth's proposal of marriage.'

'Congratulations, Hedworth. How very satisfactory.

As your almost aunt-in-law, might I kiss you, just this once?'

'My infinite pleasure, Lady Wickham.'

'But, please, you must now learn to call me Minnie.'

Eliza thought her smile rather stupid and the kiss unnecessary. But, then, that was her aunt, she supposed.

Early that evening, accepting the congratulations and drinking champagne in her father's room, Eliza felt happy. Maybe being engaged was not such a bad thing after all. Only one person seemed less than pleased.

'Have you thought about what you are doing?'

'Of course, Uncle Charles.' She was sitting apart from the others, on the window-seat, gazing at the sun setting over the park, watching the trees silhouetted black then disappear into the night.

'I don't believe you.'

'Then don't.'

'I think you are still miserable over the boy on the farm and you think he', he nodded towards Alford, 'will help you forget.'

'Not true.'

'But it is, or why won't you look at me?'

'I can if I wish. I don't wish.'

'You know nothing about this man.'

'I like the little I know.'

'I'm trying to warn you.'

'Like you warned my father over me and Jerome?' At this she looked him in the eye.

He had the grace to look away. 'I felt it was my duty.'

'As you see it your duty to spoil my happiness now?'

'Just listen, just for a minute . . .'

'I would rather you tell me nothing about my fiancé. It would, I am sure, be out of spite.' She turned her back on him. 'Papa, does this make me adult enough for a second glass of champagne?' And everyone, except Charles, laughed as it was poured for her.

Densham appeared. 'Mr Joiner and Mr Simpson await below, sir.'

'At this time of the evening?'

'They said your summons was urgent.'

'I did say so in my message, but I didn't mean they should come at this time of the evening. Papa, I'm sorry.'

'Joiner was always a fool, but now that he's here, show him and Simpson up, Densham.'

When the two men appeared, introductions were made and Frederick Forester was left alone with his lawyer and chief clerk.

'Shouldn't we have waited for Mr Joiner and Mr Simpson?' Eliza asked as they sat down for dinner.

'Whatever for?'

'To dine. They must be tired driving all this way so late in the day.'

'Rubbish. It's their work. One doesn't invite lawyers to dine. Joiner smells of dust from all those old ledgers of his. And Simpson sniffs, most unpleasant. And he dislikes me so I could not abide an evening with him.'

'How could he not like you, Minnie, of all people?' Alford smiled at her.

'He thinks she's profligate,' said Charles.

'What would a fusty old banker like him know about spending and pleasure?' Minnie asked. 'But I do trust Joiner has come for the reason I think he has.' She sipped her wine.

'It is surely more likely he's come to arrange the marriage settlement of our dear Eliza and her ecstatic groom,' Charles drawled.

'Already arranged, Charles. Freddie and I discussed it days ago.'

Days ago? thought Eliza. She had only accepted him last night. Had her father been so sure that she would? She did not understand why she found this annoying.

'Sometimes you can be so spiteful, Charles. I have every reason to be concerned. What you don't know is that, since no one else would, I asked Joiner and there is no will.' Minnie sounded triumphant.

'It's more common than you would think, near death and no will. People think that if they make a will they will die.'

'Don't be so ghoulish, Hedworth.'

'I don't know why you are making such a fuss, Minnie,' her husband remarked.

'Because, Charles, if you are so stupid that you can't see the need to look after our prospects, I am not. If he leaves us nothing then what will we do? I told the man he must insist that Freddie rectifies this oversight.'

Eliza stood up abruptly and threw her napkin on to the table. 'Aunt, I find this discussion unseemly.'

'Oh, do you? Well, you'll be all right, won't you? But if your father doesn't do something I shall lose my home.'

'And I shall lose my father.'

Even Minnie was silenced by that.

During the next hours there was much to-ing and fro-ing between Frederick's chamber and the library, which Mr Joiner had been invited to make his temporary office and where he and Mr Simpson laboured over certain calculations and the writing of the will. The tension in the room was rising. Frederick's safe had been opened and certificates of stocks and shares and IOUs littered the long table in the centre of the room. Minnie took it upon herself to keep the men supplied with refreshments. She wouldn't allow the servants to tend them: 'I don't want them snooping into Freddie's affairs.'

'I fancy it is you who wants to do that,' Charles observed.

The look she gave her husband would have withered anyone else to a husk, but he was evidently used to it and not in the least affected.

Eliza went to bed, knowing that the making of this

will was likely to be her father's final act. That night, she sobbed herself to sleep.

Three days later Eliza wore her mother's dress at her wedding in the chapel of Harcourt Barton. The dress, with its cascades of lace and artificial flowers and its full crinoline was old-fashioned but charming.

'You look even more like her,' Frederick told her, when she presented herself for his inspection. He could no longer walk but was carried to the chapel. It was far from the wedding Eliza had imagined for herself. Her uncle and aunt, the Gilpins, and the house servants were the only guests. But it was what her father had wanted and she would not argue with him.

'Are you frightened?' Jonquil asked her, as she sat in Eliza's bedroom, while she collected the possessions she wanted to take with her. She was sad to be leaving this room – the previous night had been the last time that she would sleep there. Tonight she would join her husband in one of the grand main rooms on the large landing.

'Why should I be?'

'The unspeakable things Hedworth will do to you tonight.'

'What things?' She placed her silver-backed brush in the basket she was carrying. Far away downstairs they could hear the laughter of the others, celebrating for her.

'You know.' Jonquil looked slyly at her.

'I don't.'

'I have a friend, she says it's dreadful. That you will be torn to shreds. Especially if he's large.'

'Why?'

'When you make babies.'

'I don't want babies, not yet.'

'I don't think the choice is yours.'

*

Later, with Jonquil's words tumbling about in her head, Eliza sat in her new lace nightdress in the large bed in the unfamiliar room and waited nervously for her husband to join her. What was to happen to her? She had wondered if her mother would have told her. But, then, Jonquil had a mother and she was not clear either as to what was involved.

Her heart jolted as the door opened. Hedworth, in a quilted dressing-gown, approached her. 'You look pretty,' he said.

'Thank you.'

'Don't be frightened.'

'I'm not.'

'That's good.' He slipped off the robe and, in his nightshift, climbed in beside her. It was strange to feel the firmness of a man's body close beside her. Strange yet not unpleasant. She turned to douse the light, but he took her hand. 'No, I want to see your face.' At which he kissed her. She relaxed in his arms, she liked his kisses. But then, without warning, he pulled at the pretty nightdress and, with one great rent, it was ripped off her. With no warning, no tenderness, he climbed upon her, forced her legs apart and tore into her. She screamed from pain and shock. She felt fear which became terror. As the agony intensified she wept. He looked down at her with a look of triumph as if he enjoyed her anguish. She was to learn, during the long night, her misery fuelled his lust as he took her time and time again.

Later, Eliza sat on the far side of the room huddled in a chair, with a blanket around her against the cold, but though it warmed her outside, it could do nothing for the chill within her. Tears were rolling silently down her face. She felt disgusted. She felt dirty. She had washed herself but was convinced she still smelt of him.

She heard a scratching at her door. Gingerly she opened it having hurriedly wiped away the tears with the back of her hand. It was her father's nurse. 'Lady

Alford, it's your father, I'm sorry to tell you but he's nearly gone.'

'Where?' she heard herself say foolishly. Then sense prevailed: she scooped the blanket round her and hurried to her father's room.

'Shall I fetch your aunt?' the nurse called behind her.

'No, no one. Just me.' She did not want the others here, they did not love him, they did not care for him, he was just money to them. And she didn't want her husband anywhere near either of them.

She sat by his bed and took his hand. He was deeply unconscious but it did not stop her telling him how much she loved him, how much she would miss him, how she would never forget him.

Through the long night she sat, never letting go of his hand. Dawn broke. Suddenly across the garden, echoing in the still of the morning, she heard the tolling of the chapel bell, nine for the passing of a man's soul, then forty-nine for every year of his life. She was holding the hand of a dead man.

Chapter Six
1876–7

I

'My love, what can I say to make amends?' Hedworth was on his knees in front of the chair in which she sat. She was unable to believe that her father was dead, incredulous at the cruel way her husband had treated her. She did not answer. Her body ached but it was the damage to her mind that prevented her replying. 'I was inebriated. I know it's no excuse, but it was the reason.' Still she sat mute. 'Answer me! For God's sake, speak to me.' She looked down at his handsome face. His eyes glinted with what looked suspiciously like tears, but what had he cared for her tears?

'You frightened me.'

'I know I did – and on the night your father died. You cannot begin to comprehend my shame. I am no better than a beast. I don't deserve your understanding. But I beg you, please, try to forgive me.'

'I didn't know what to expect . . . but not that!'

'And I destroyed your innocence. Should I leave?'

Did he mean the room or her life? She wanted the latter, she feared he meant the former. Could she forgive him? No. Could she forget? No.

'I promise it will never happen again, but we have made our vows, our lives are intertwined. We must resolve this.'

What choice did she have?

'I will try,' she answered. For the next few days he was kindness itself to her.

*

Eliza grieved. She could not believe her father had left her, not when they had finally found and trusted each other. She spent hours sitting by the bed on which he lay, the air suffused with the scent of tuberoses. He did not look dead, he looked as if he slept. He looked younger with all the pain of his illness gone from his face. He was peaceful and she was happy for him, even if it meant he was no more. She sat, huddled in the light of the candles, expecting him to breathe at any moment, willing him to do so, mourning not for him alone but for what might have been had he lived. Everything had happened too late. Would dealing with his death have been easier if they had not had these past few weeks of closeness, of friendship and, certainly on her part, love? Probably there would have been no difference for hadn't she loved him always? Had she not been waiting and longing for him to be part of her life for as long as she could remember?

'You're still here?' Hedworth had entered the room and was standing on the other side of the bed in which her father lay. She had surrounded him with flowers from the conservatory, but their beauty could not help the reality.

'I feel I can't leave him alone.'

'You're going to have to tomorrow.' She did not notice in the dim light of the candles that he was swaying slightly.

'I know. I dread it.' She began to weep.

'For heaven's sake, stop crying. It becomes tedious.'

'I'm sorry,' she said, then wondered why she should apologise for what, after all, was the most normal thing.

'Why weep for him? He never cared about you.'

'Hedworth, please.'

'It's the truth. Why mourn someone who felt nothing for you?'

'At the end he did!'

'You were a comfort to him, nothing more. A nurse, no more, no less.'

'Don't you understand? I'm mourning my father but also for what now can never be!' She was unaware that she had raised her voice.

'How dare you shout at me?'

'I didn't mean to ... I'm sorry ...' But her apology did not stop her husband. He would make a remark and when she did not respond he became angry, shouting at her across the body of her dead father. She did not want this: it was very wrong with her father lying there. What if part of him remained and heard? She did not want him hurt. She stood up, intending to leave, but her husband ordered her to sit. She agreed with everything he said just to stop his relentless voice, which drilled into her head until she felt it would explode with anguish.

'Please, stop this! Please leave me alone!' She stood up. Quickly he came round the foot of the bed. He grabbed her wrists and dragged her from the room, and she endured a repetition of that first horrific night of marriage.

He apologised the next morning. He was full of remorse. She said she forgave him but instead added that night to the list of grievances she kept in her mind.

Dressed in fine black crêpe, she stood on the steps of the house, her house, under the great stone portico, surrounded by the female servants, and watched her father's ornate lead-lined coffin placed in the hearse, the men straining under its weight. The carriage sagged as the springs took the strain. The magnificent matched pairs of black horses pawed the gravel, and tossed their heads so that the black mourning plumes on their heads swayed and their silver harness jingled. The mutes assembled in line, the wind playing with the long black ribbons attached to their top hats. Her husband and uncle entered the carriage behind. Other male guests climbed into other carriages. The footmen and valets led by Densham clambered into the remaining ones. The cortège moved off and she remembered other times, other carriages, when she had stood on these same steps and had waved to her father and his guests. Of its own volition her hand, clutching a black-bordered handkerchief, lifted and waved goodbye to her father. She turned on her heel, and ran back into the house, her aunt in hot pursuit. She made for the library, her father's favourite room.

'That wasn't very respectful, waving him off in that unseemly way. It was as if you were glad to see him go.'

'Yes, Aunt. I mean no, Aunt.'

'I know you didn't care for him, as he had scant feeling for you. But, well, really . . .'

'Yes, Aunt.'

'You're going to have to change your ways now you're a married woman. Think before you act. Hedworth will expect more circumspection from someone of your position in society.'

'Yes, Aunt.'

'And say something other than, *Yes, Aunt*. Don't you have any opinions?'

Eliza swung round to face her. As usual, Minnie was fussing about the room picking up objects, then putting them down again. 'I have many opinions, Aunt, but there never seems any point in discussing them with you. You are so intolerant and so convinced of your own rightness that I would merely be wasting my breath.'

For a second Minnie was made speechless with astonishment. Then she shouted, 'You ungrateful child! How dare you? Have you no respect?'

'I dare because I am tired of being told what I should do and what I should think. I dare because I resent you telling me my father had no feelings for me when I know otherwise. You have never shown me any respect, and I was always taught respect should be earned – which you have failed to achieve. Now, if you will excuse me . . .' She had the satisfaction of seeing her aunt slack-mouthed with shock.

She went to her room to refresh herself before the funeral party returned. As she walked past her father's room, which had once been her mother's, she stopped at the sound of chatter coming from it. Inside two maids were cleaning. 'Change the linen on the bed and then I want this room left just as it is. Tell Mrs King to lock it up,' she ordered. It was too soon for the room to be cleared; she was convinced her father's spirit lingered there and she didn't want him disturbed.

The reception was an ordeal. Mrs King had suggested, kindly, that she make her excuses. But Eliza felt she had to do this last thing for her father. Many compliments were passed on her dignified behaviour. She did not weep once, which was difficult when people were so kind to her. Hedworth was all solicitude. 'Drink this,' he said, and handed her a glass.

'I don't want it.'

'You look tired, my darling, and it will help you get through this. It's my own special pick-me-up – champagne and peaches.'

He could be so considerate that sometimes it was almost as if she had dreamt the more unpleasant aspect of their relationship.

Two long hours later, most of the guests had departed. Aunt Minnie had not spoken to her once since their scene earlier in the day. Eliza found she was not concerned.

'Eliza, a word?'

'Uncle Charles.' She dropped a small curtsy.

'Still cross with me?' He put his head on one side and smiled the crooked smile she had once found so attractive.

'No.'

'I'm relieved. I thought you would never forgive me.'

'I didn't say I had.'

'Ha, *touché*.' He laughed. 'You never let me explain. I told your father about the young man because I was concerned for you. I was only thinking of your welfare.'

'That's what most busybodies say.' But he had been right about Hedworth. Had Charles known of his cruelty when he had tried to warn her off? She would never tell him, though, never give him the satisfaction.

He laughed again. In the circumstances it made the last of the guests turn and look at him with distaste. 'Minnie said you had changed now that you are a married woman.'

'I haven't. I merely said some things I have been thinking for a long time.'

'It makes you much more interesting.'

'If that was meant as a compliment I do not accept it as such.'

'Dear, dear, we are a sharp little Eliza. Since you are not speaking to Minnie she has sent me to request that we have the meeting with Joiner as soon as the last of these old codgers has left.' He indicated a small cluster of elderly men.

'What for?'

'Dear Eliza. You are so naïve at times. For the reading of the will, of course.'

'Of course,' she said sadly. 'Then I leave it to you to chivvy our guests away.' How distasteful, she thought, all that fuss to ensure her father made a will and now this indecent haste to read it.

'Just one thing, Eliza, before we go. If ever you are in need of a friend or advice . . .'

'I shall know who not to turn to.' And with that she went to the library where, half an hour later, they assembled for the reading of the will. Mr Joiner took a long time to sort his papers and settle himself. No doubt this was his moment of glory, Eliza thought.

'Should the members of staff named be present?' he asked.

'I hardly think that's necessary, Joiner. I'll tell those with legacies.'

'As you wish, Lord Alford.' He picked up the heavy document. 'As you realise, this will was made at the last minute, due to irregular circumstances. We have, I believe, covered all eventualities.' He coughed.

'Just get on with it, man,' Minnie fretted.

He began. Eliza was touched by the number of bequests her father had made, the servants, the estate workers, many were singled out. Clerks in the bank. It was a lengthy document and, though she tried to concentrate, the combination of grief, tiredness and champagne made it increasingly difficult. She did not care either. She heard her name mentioned and Mr Joiner droning on. She knew she was rich, had always known she would be, it did not interest her. She wanted her father back, not his money.

Finally it was over. She invited the lawyer to dine but was not put out when he declined.

When she returned to the library it was to find Minnie on her feet, stomping about the room, and Charles was laughing. Her aunt, dressed in the matt black of bombazine on which not a smidgen of light was reflected, was virtually invisible in the darker parts of the room. She would be mortified if she knew, and Eliza wondered if she should tell her.

'There are times when I could easily hate you, Hedworth. Take that stupid smug expression off your face,' she shouted.

'What has happened?'

'Weren't you listening to the reading of the will?' asked Charles. 'Your father is having a joke from beyond the grave. He's allowed us to remain in the house in London, but it remains your property – Minnie had fondly thought he would leave it to her. He's not left her any money, so she's going to have to rely on Joiner and Simpson for handouts. But . . .' He could barely speak for laughing. '. . . Simpson, of all people.'

'The chief cashier in the bank in Exeter? He's a pleasant man.'

'You might think so but Minnie can't stand him and the feeling is mutual. It's such a jape.'

'It's so typical of you, Charles, to find this amusing. You are incapable of seeing the seriousness of our situation.'

'Well, Minnie, old girl, you have to admit it is a fine joke. And even better because Freddie has made him chairman of the bank as well!'

'I don't see it like that at all. To have to go cap in hand for our needs. If only you hadn't been such a fool, you could have had that position. And . . .' On and on she went, her voice rising with every fresh complaint. Suddenly she swung round to face Eliza. 'This is your doing!'

'What have I done?'

'I had your father just where I wanted him, and then you inveigled your way into his affections at the last minute.'

'Minnie, don't.'

'Don't you Minnie me! I know you too well, Hedworth. Forgotten already, have you? No doubt you'll be feathering your nest before the week is out.'

'Minnie! I suggest you desist or leave.'

'So now that you have acquired what you wanted I'm no longer needed. Use me, abuse me then cast me aside.' Dramatically she smote her breast.

'Yes, Minnie, that was exactly what I was thinking.'

'Hedworth!' Charles exclaimed.

'Charles, this is none of your business.' Minnie glowered.

'As you are both so frequently at pains to tell me.'

'I am betrayed!' Minnie declared.

'Charles, I insist you control your wife.'

'I've just been told to keep out of your affairs.'

'Do as I say. I will not have *my* wife upset. Not today,

of all days. My love, you look so tired. Why don't you retire?'

'Perhaps I will. I don't think I can deal with any arguments.'

'Spoilt child!' Minnie said crossly as she left them.

In her room, Eliza's maid helped her undress and she all but collapsed on the bed. When Hedworth joined her she barely woke, just enough to realise he was making love to her and in the most gentle manner possible.

The next day they left Harcourt Barton.

'We should get away from here. It will help you recover from the loss of your father. And I want to introduce you to my friends and family. Let them meet the sweet woman who has honoured me.'

She was happy to go. He was right: a change was what she needed. Away from the unhappiness here, her spirit might return, and perhaps the dreadful tiredness her grief had caused would be remedied.

They went first to London. They stayed in a hotel rather than the house in Belgrave Square, and thus avoided Minnie and her temper. It was a new experience for her to stay in a hotel and it should have been fun. But it wasn't; she had no interest in anything any more. She began to wonder if she would ever be happy again. But the hotel suited her, for Hedworth was often out, busying himself around London, his clubs, visiting, gambling for all she knew, but she didn't care: she was better on her own.

'My darling, I have a confession to make to you. I hope you will forgive me. If you could find it in your heart?' he said one evening, as they dined in their suite.

'I'll try.' But her heart was pounding. What did he mean?

'I have no money.'

'What do you mean? We have more than enough.'

'You have, I haven't.'

'Have you lost it? Have you had a setback?'

'No. The truth is, I had none. I relied on my friends to

put me up. I lied to your father. I feared if he knew the truth he would never let you marry me. Had he not been ill I'm sure he would have been far more efficient in digging into my affairs and would have found out.'

'Is that all? It doesn't matter, I have money as you say. More than enough.'

'You are so understanding. I've dreaded telling you.'

'You shouldn't have. Money isn't important to me.'

'It is to me. Or, rather, the lack of it is. It hurts my pride to be having this conversation, always to be worried about it.'

'But you have paid all the bills for this trip so far.'

'It was your money I was spending. I prised a sum out of Joiner. It was like getting blood out of a stone. Not something I would like to have to do constantly.'

'Nor should you have to.'

'But that is the whole point, I do have to. As you are aware, your father left it in trust for you – presumably I was not as clever with him as I thought, and he didn't trust me or my intentions.'

'Oh, no, I'm sure it was nothing like that . . .' she said, although she couldn't be sure. She didn't know why her father had made his will in the way he had.

'It hurts me that I do not have control of your income, which is normal for a husband. I would like to take charge of it and care for you. Yet he saw fit, as you know, to make it free of matrimonial control.'

'Yes, I heard Mr Joiner say that, but I wasn't sure what it meant.'

'The income is yours. To do with as you wish. Spend it all on pretty frocks, if that is what you want to do.'

'I'd never do that. But what can I do to make it better for you?'

He smiled. 'I was wondering if you would write to Joiner and instruct him to release funds to me.'

'But of course. Now?'

'At your convenience. And perhaps it would be best if you instructed him in such a way that I don't keep having to ask you. Then I can take full responsibility for all the expenses.'

Eliza's husband confused her. From being so unkind that she wished she had never met him he could show such consideration that she felt she had imagined it. Until the next time.

He would tell her she was beautiful and the next day criticise her for looking dowdy. From being intelligent she was stupid. From being stylish she was a disgrace. He seemed to build her up only to knock her down, and as the days ticked by her confidence in herself began to seep away.

2

'My husband is a fraud. My husband is a liar. My husband is a sadist . . .' Eliza wrote slowly, stabbing each letter into the paper, a couple of times even piercing it. 'I ha—' She laid the pen on the desk beside her and picked up the diary in which she had penned these dreadful words. Holding it close to the oil lamp, she read what she had just written. There was no one to talk to about the nightmare in which she found herself. She thought that if only she had been able to confide her problems to a sympathetic friend she would have felt better, more able to deal with it. But would she? Despite everything, he was her husband. While not overtly religious she believed in God and she had vowed to 'love, honour and obey' in the chapel. And to discuss him with anyone would have been an act of betrayal. Instead, lacking a confidante, she had hoped that writing down her thoughts would help, but it had not.

Inside her the great raft of anger that had grown daily since her marriage, eight months ago, remained the same. She looked at the half-written word. She had wanted to write *hate* but she knew instinctively that if she did it would damage her further. By hating Hedworth she would, in a way, be complimenting him. She picked up the pen and scratched it through.

The words were done, now what to do with the book? It had to be hidden, for what if Hedworth found it? She looked about the library – there were piles of books everywhere. When her father had been enduring his last illness she had once more begun the task of cataloguing and rearranging the thousands of books. In the days after he had died she could find neither the inclination nor the time to carry on with the task. She had given orders for the books to be left as they were for she had intended to finish – but, then, she had had no idea that they would leave the day after the funeral or that they would be away so long. Hedworth, despite his undertaking that they would live here at Harcourt Barton, had been reluctant to return, not that he explained why. Nor had she dared ask: he did not like her to query his decisions. They had returned late this night. Unable to sleep, she had crept downstairs to relieve the burden she felt building in her soul.

Wasn't the library the ideal place to hide a book? Who could find it here? It would be like looking for a blade of straw in a haystack. Still, she was uncomfortable with the idea, strange things happened. Instinct might tell him which book was hers. Instead she left the room, holding the lamp high over her head to light the way. She crossed the hall with Bumble padding along behind her, his claws clicking on the oak-planked floor. The light cast huge shadows on the walls as she passed, creepy shadows that she did not care to look at. She went through the drawing room, the furniture still shrouded in dust sheets since their arrival had not been anticipated. She opened the door into the vestibule and then into the conservatory – her father's pride and joy. She hadn't used, or even thought of, these hidey-holes of her childhood for years. She felt behind the yucca plant for the hidden space in the wall. Something was in there – some secret of hers long hidden and long forgotten, she presumed. She pulled out a tissue-wrapped board, a small snuff box, a fan, a box with stones in it and a couple of feathers. In their place she hid her diary.

She looked at the small pile of articles. When had she put them there? When had she last looked at them? What a strange haul. What had induced her to hide them? They couldn't have been important or surely she would have remembered them. What a secretive child she must have been.

She could understand the silver snuff box and the gaily coloured fan: they were pretty objects likely to attract a child. But the rocks, and the feathers? How curious! However, she remembered what was in the tissue paper – the photograph of a pretty lady she had found in the back of an album belonging to her father. Merry had tried to wrest it from her and she had fled here with it. She wondered why her nursemaid should have made such a rumpus. Could it be . . . ? She unwrapped the tissue paper layer by layer, the face emerging as if from a mist. She saw an attractive young woman with sad eyes, despite the smile on her lips. Was it her mother? It would explain the fuss.

If only her grandmother and father hadn't died. If only Merry hadn't left. As she grew older she was sure she would have found the courage to insist on knowing the whole truth of what had happened and would have cleared up the mysteries.

'What on earth are you doing here? It's the middle of the night?' Hedworth stood in the doorway.

'I couldn't sleep.'

'Why are you looking so guilty?'

'I wasn't aware that I was. You startled me – I didn't hear you over the noise from the fountain.'

'I did not like waking up and finding my *loving* wife not beside me.'

'I thought you would not wake.'

'Well, I did. I would prefer if you did not sneak off like that in future. I like to know where you are and what you are doing. Why the conservatory? What can you possibly want in here at this time of night? Why, you can't even see the plants. Were you remembering the romance of me proposing to you?' He laughed mirthlessly.

'I was remembering my father. He loved this place. He drew the plans, designed the ironwork, the pots, even the seats.' She looked up at the soaring roof, sheathed in darkness, but with the stars just visible outside the glass.

'Really?' Hedworth sounded bored. She had taken herself by surprise, boasting of her father's plans, something to which she had never given a thought while he was alive, but she had been trying to interest her husband, ingratiate herself with him. His moods were unreliable and she had rapidly learnt that her best defence was to distract him.

'And the sound of the water is very soothing.'

'Why do you need soothing?'

'Because I couldn't sleep . . .' She knew she was becoming agitated, which was just what he wanted and which she must not allow to happen. 'But, if you'll excuse me, I'm tired now.'

'No, I won't – excuse you, that is. You've woken me so you can stay with me until I'm ready to go to bed. And get me a brandy.' He slumped on to the white-painted love-seat, his legs stuck out in front of him so that she had to step over them. He tried to trip her and laughed as she stumbled. Really, he could be so childish too, she thought, as she ran from the conservatory in search of his brandy.

When she had found a decanter in the serving room off the dining room, and had placed it with a glass on a tray and returned, Hedworth was fast asleep, snoring loudly. Although she tried to wake him he did not budge. She placed the tray beside him, slipped out of the conservatory and back to their bedroom.

Now she was over-tired and still could not sleep so she lay in the dark looking at the canopy above her. She was relieved that he was asleep yet frightened as to what his reaction would be when he awoke and found she was not there. That was her dilemma: whatever she did, it was always wrong. It seemed to her that she was a constant source of annoyance to him yet she had no way of knowing, since he gave no indication, what it was about her that caused him such exasperation.

What was galling was how neatly and expertly he had fooled everyone. Her father had approved of him, taken him to be what he said he was, that he had estates and money. Yet the truth was that he was a bankrupt. There was no family home in Yorkshire, no family – at least none, it would seem, who wanted to have anything to do with him. He had deceived her into thinking him a sensitive, considerate man. He was, it had to be admitted, a brilliant actor.

It wasn't him alone, though. Life had deceived her too. All she had read in poems, books, in Shakespeare, that was lies too. Where were the gentleness of love, the finesse, the beauty, the glory? Hedworth was brutal with her and she had quickly learnt that he took great pleasure in her tears. And therein lay a conundrum. If she willed herself not to cry, she lengthened her trial at his hands. If she allowed herself to cry and begged him to stop abusing her, she felt he had won, and she hated that and despised herself for letting him.

She was fortunate in one way in that he was only violent in bed. But how sad her life had become that she could see it as an advantage. And she found herself wondering how long it might be before he became violent at other times. She loathed him touching her – she feared him. She could not relax when he was in the room – she feared him. She hated talking with him in case she said the wrong thing – she feared him. The hours of her days were full of fear. She had to do something to save herself. She was twenty and if she lived to seventy . . . She shuddered at the very thought.

Often in the past eight months as they had travelled about the country, staying with friends of his, in hotels, in a rented house, she had worked at plans to run away. The conviction that she must had come to her six weeks into their marriage and in the remote house in Lancashire. Two events had galvanised her.

One night, at dinner, she had drunk three glasses of wine. No doubt it was this that had given her the confidence to question her husband.

'Why do you dislike me so, Hedworth?'

'What gave you such an idea? I don't dislike you.'

'Why did you marry me?'

'I think it is self-evident.'

'But you were so kind and charming . . .' She stopped, she was on dangerous ground.

'And now I'm not? It's quite simple, my dear. One uses a lure to catch a fish – a very rich fish!'

'Is that all I am to you?'

'How I regard you is entirely in your hands.'

'I don't understand. I don't know how to behave for you. Whatever I do you treat me unkindly.' And to make the point she rubbed her wrists, which were marked and sore from the rope with which he had earlier tied her to the bedpost.

'I treat you as my wife.'

'You degrade me.'

'No, I don't. I'm training you in how I wish you to be. Fight me and it will take longer. You would be advised to bend your will to my ways sooner rather than later.'

It was at that point she realised, and wondered why she hadn't understood before, that to him she was like an animal, a horse or a dog that he wished to discipline. He was intent on breaking her spirit, just as a horse is broken in, a dog trained. But there and then, even as he smiled his dark, sardonic smile at her, she determined he never would.

She was surprised to learn that she could become accustomed to humiliation. For now she knew the truth, that she would never care for him, it did not matter to her what he thought. She was glad now that she did not love him for then it would have mattered.

The second incident had made her resolve stronger.

Her aunt had come to stay in the house in Lancashire. It had surprised Eliza that she had, for, after Frederick's funeral, Minnie and Hedworth had not parted the best of friends. Evidently they had made their peace for Hedworth had been in a good mood in anticipation of her arrival.

Eliza, for once, was content for her aunt to be there. She amused Hedworth and thus gave her a small amount of freedom from him. She had time to read and paint instead of being at his beck and call. She could even go for a long walk and not face an inquisition on her return.

The house was situated near the forest of Rossendale, and Eliza enjoyed tramping over the moorland, her spirits lifted by the beauty and the solitude. But these moors were like any others – dangerous – and on one particular walk, without warning, the clouds rolled in black and threatening: a storm of some magnitude was massing. She turned on her heels and returned to the house. By the time she arrived she was soaked.

Leaving her wet coat in the porch and kicking off her boots, she ran barefoot up to her bedroom. She opened the door and stood transfixed.

There, on the bed, her voluptuous body naked, her arms tied to the bedposts, writhing with pleasure as Hedworth violently serviced her, was her aunt. She wanted to go but was rooted to the spot as if her legs had lost all power.

It was Minnie who saw her and gave a little cry of surprise. Hedworth paused in his task and turned. His face was distorted with lust, his eyes blazing. 'Ah, Eliza, do you want to join us?'

Then she was able to move, hearing his laughter as she ran along the corridor, down the stairs and out into the rain. The purifying rain.

She felt disgust, anger. She did not feel humiliation or pain. Instead she felt liberated, free of him. She would leave him: she had no care of what society would think of her. She knew him, they didn't.

Her plan to escape did not get far. They left the house in Lancashire and moved on, never staying anywhere long enough for her to work out something feasible. This constant moving about puzzled her. He said it was because he wanted to show her off to his friends. What friends? There were few. He knew people certainly but there was always a distance – as if they didn't want to be his friends. Sometimes she sensed that they, too, were afraid of him and she would wonder why but could not come to any conclusion because she knew him so little. Often she saw them looking at her with pity in their eyes. No doubt they meant to be kind, but she did not need it: she was going to leave him.

She reached one conclusion: a tiny piece of the puzzle that was her husband fell into place. She became convinced that his restless moving was because he became bored rapidly with any companion and, of course, she bored him most.

She was overjoyed when he announced that they were to return home to Harcourt Barton. It would be easier to run away once she was home: there, she had access to people she knew, to money. Where she would go, and how, she had not yet planned, but she knew that one day soon she would be free of her tormentor.

3

Morning came, and Eliza was woken by a strange maid with a breakfast tray. The girl, Lucy, was pleasant enough, but being back in Harcourt Barton made her think of and long for Ruby. In the almost two years since they had been separated she had learnt what Ruby had really meant to her. She had been more than her maid, she had been her friend, and Eliza missed her desperately. She had tried, for her own sanity, not to think of Jerome but she found it impossible, and now she was home she presumed it would be even harder. She sighed.

'That's a big sigh, milady,' said Lucy, who was folding her clothes.

'Was it? I wasn't aware.' She pushed back the covers and sat on the edge of the bed. 'Have you run my bath?'

'I have, milady.'

'It was kind of you to bring my breakfast but please don't do so tomorrow. I prefer to eat downstairs.'

'Yes, milady.'

'Were you not told?'

'No, milady.'

'Did Mrs King interview you for this position?' She wondered how long it would take her to get used to being called 'milady'. After eight months it still made her want to laugh.

'Mrs King? No, milady.' She looked puzzled.

'The housekeeper. She normally does the interviewing.'

'I haven't met anyone of that name.'

'How strange. I need to see her this morning.'

'Mrs Shaw is the housekeeper here.' The maid was looking at her quizzically.

'Then would you ask Mrs Shaw to come to the library in an hour?'

In her dressing room she found the fire lit, even though it was still summer and unnecessary. There was probably an order, issued by her grandmother, that fires had to be laid in dressing rooms, regardless of the weather. She must check and rescind it. A hip bath stood in front of it, which was strange. 'Lucy,' she called, 'I prefer to use the bathroom along the corridor.'

'No one told me, milady.'

'It's no matter. I'll use this today since you have filled it. We don't want all that effort to go to waste, do we?' She smiled kindly. Thanks to Jerome, she was now fully aware of the exertion required to bring the jugs of water to prepare it.

Sitting in it, with the comfort of the fire beside her, made her remember her baths as a child. Merry would always be on the chair beside her and even when she felt she was old enough to be left Merry had always insisted on waiting, holding the pristine white towel ready to wrap her in the minute she left the water. Dear Merry. She had been gone so long Eliza had virtually forgotten about her – until now. Perhaps because of her circumstances.

An hour later, simply dressed, still in black for her father, she was sorting books. She had resolved during the night that she needed to keep occupied for then she had less time to think and thus less time to feel sorry for herself. And it was essential that she should behave as expected of her and allay any suspicions of her intentions. On the way here she had looked in the conservatory but there was no sign of Hedworth.

'Mrs Shaw?' she asked the tall, white-haired, rather austere-looking woman who appeared punctually in the library.

'It is, milady.'

'Welcome to Harcourt Barton. But what happened to Mrs King?'

'I gather she was dismissed.'

'When?'

'I could not say.'

'When did you start here?'

'January the first.'

'When were you interviewed?'

'In December.'

'Really? Might I ask when?'

'I'm sorry, I can't recall the exact date.'

'Well, the end of December?'

'Oh, no, milady, at the beginning. I was interviewed in London.'

'By whom?' She smiled as she asked, as if it were a question of no importance.

'Lady Wickham.'

As she had thought. 'And my companion, Miss Holland?'

Mrs Shaw looked puzzled. 'I know of no such person.'

'Very well.' Again she spoke as if it were of no consequence. 'Now, to business,' she continued. For the next half-hour she discussed with the housekeeper how she wanted the house to be run. How she wanted the staff to be treated. The wages. How the books were to be kept. The planning of meals. The laundry. She was amazed at how much she had learnt about the running of a large house from her grandmother.

'You'll be wanting to meet Mr Morton?'

'Mr Morton?'

'The butler, milady . . .'

Eliza felt a stab of alarm. No Mr Densham! It would seem that everyone who knew her, and she hoped cared for her, had been removed! It was one explanation for the long delay in returning. With every senior servant gone, others would have had to be found and trained. But by whom? Her aunt? But of course. Not only was she Hedworth's mistress, she no doubt planned to be mistress of Harcourt too! She shuddered at the memory of them together! What a fool they must think her, but she would prove them wrong.

Hedworth was not an early riser and she found him still at breakfast.

'Did you miss me in the night, dear wife?' He looked up from the newspaper he was reading.

'I slept well.' At the sideboard she poured herself a cup of coffee and joined her husband at the table.

'There are not enough blankets in my dressing room. See to it.'

'I will. I shall speak to Mrs Shaw, my *new* housekeeper.' She stirred her coffee but there was no reaction from him. 'Why was Mrs King dismissed, and presumably Densham also? And where is Miss Holland? And how many others have been removed?'

'I decided we should have new servants for our new life together. And you would hardly need a companion when you have me.'

'I would like to have been consulted.'

'What on earth for?'

'Because this is my home.'

'And mine now. I make the decisions, not you.'

'It was a shock. I have known Mrs King and Densham all my life. I shall miss them.'

'It's never a good idea to become too familiar with one's servants.'

'It wasn't that sort of familiarity. They've always been there, that is what I meant. Where are they now?'

'I've no idea.'

'I would like to find out and write to them.'

'That is not a good idea.'

'Why?'

'You ask so many pointless questions. It would not be useful for you to write to them.'

'It would be polite.'

He banged the table, making the cups rattle and Eliza jump. 'I forbid you to have contact with them.'

'Forbid! To write a couple of letters?'

'You will submit all your letters to me before posting them.'

'I didn't even have to do that when my father was alive.'

'Then that was his mistake. Look what happened to you with lack of supervision.'

'Do you not trust me? Is that what this means?'

He looked straight at her. 'No. I don't. You are a woman.'

'I'm confused. You don't trust me because of who I am? Or because I am a woman?'

'I warn you, trying to be clever with me will not endear you to me, Eliza.'

Eliza stood up. Everything made her loathe him more and she dared not even show how hurt and angry she felt. No doubt that was his intention, that was what he would enjoy.

'Where are you going?'

'To take Bumble for a walk.' There was no point in arguing or trying to reason with him. Hedworth had decided and she might just as well save her breath.

'And that's another thing. I don't want that dog brought into the house. It goes into the kennels.'

'But Bumble has always been with me.'

'Not any longer.'

'You do this to hurt me.'

'No, I don't like the dog.' He returned to his newspaper.

As she put on the coat she used for walking and kept in the boot room, she was muttering to herself, an angry frustrated tirade. How she wished she had not married Hedworth. How she wished she could turn him out of the house. How she wished he didn't exist. How she wished she was with . . .

'Jerome.' She said his name aloud, and loved the sound of it, felt gleeful that she had risked saying it. The one thing he could not control, of course, was her mind. She was free to think what she wanted and there was nothing Hedworth could do about it, which was a comfort of sorts.

'Come on, Bumble. We won't go far.' Dear Bumble, what was she to do with him? How was she going to live without her faithful dog? He was fourteen now, he could not have much life left, and how could she abandon him to the kennels? He would think he had done something wrong, that she was punishing him.

When they had gone away she had wanted to take Bumble with her, but she had accepted Hedworth's objection that the dog was too old for travelling. Evidence of his kindness, she had thought. Upon their return, to Bumble's boisterous welcome, she had decided that although the dog had always slept with her in the past she could not expect her husband to tolerate it, so she had made a bed for him in the dressing room. Last night he had whined, but not for long. Had Hedworth heard him?

'Oh, Bumble, what are we to do?' They cut across the knot garden, down the steps that led to the lake. She sat on the bottom step – Bumble needed the odd rest now. This was the route she had taken in other, happier days. If only she had known . . .

Ruby! She'd be married now and in Bramble Cottage. Would she care for Bumble? She would pay her, of course, she knew Ruby liked dogs and, most importantly, she knew Bumble. It would be less confusing for him. 'That's what we'll do, Bumble, my love. We'll find you a lovely new home.' She persuaded the dog to follow her. They crossed the park, cut through Walkers Copse, across a couple of fields and into Great Wood – not that anyone knew why it was so called.

'Nearly there,' she said, as she found the bridle-path through the wood. It was a lovely walk, especially at this time of year with the trees in full-leafed glory. In a clearing was the delightful gamekeeper's cottage. How she envied Ruby her life here! What wouldn't she give to live like this? She tapped on the back door. She heard dogs barking.

'Hello!' she said, laughing. But she spoke to a stranger. 'Oh, I'm so sorry, I expected Ruby Morgan to open the door.'

'The Morgans have gone. I'm Mrs Chapman. And you?'

'Gone? When? Where to?' Eliza did not identify herself.

'I think her husband found work over at Plumpton Manor. January. That was when there were all the changes.'

'What changes?' But even as she asked she knew.

'When everyone was evicted,' the woman explained.

4

'Your dog?'

'In the kennels as you requested.'

'Good. You learn.' He said this with such a smug, unpleasant smirk that she longed to hurl the jug of water at him.

'Nothing, thank you,' she said to the footman, unfamiliar, of course, who offered her food.

'If you don't eat you will become ill.'

'I can't eat if I'm not hungry.'

'Why? I'd have thought your long walk to the gamekeeper's cottage would have made you very hungry.'

She managed to control herself and study her plate: she did not want him to see the fury in her eyes. He would use it against her, she was sure. 'Perhaps a little broth, James,' she said to the footman.

'He's not called James. That was a stupid conceit of your father's.'

She was not prepared to let him know she agreed with anything he had to say. 'I'm sorry. What is your name?'

'Dartagnan, milady.'

'French?' she said, both for something to say and to cover up her own smirk, which threatened to break free. It was odd, she thought, as she spooned her soup, how even now, miserable and furious as she was, she could still find some things funny. She should hold on to that and guard it: it might be her saving grace in an uncertain future.

The lunch was endless as she refused course after course. She was impatient since she was anxious to get away. As to how she would manage it she was not yet sure: circumstances had overtaken her. Hedworth never rested in the afternoon, and her only hope was that he would go out for a ride, or to Exeter or Tiverton. 'Dartagnan is to be your own footman, Eliza.'

'How nice.' She smiled at the handsome young man. 'But I hardly think I need a personal footman here, Hedworth.'

'If you go out you will. I do not want you going anywhere unattended.'

'Thank you, Hedworth,' she said, with a meekness she was far from feeling.

She had had a vague plan that when she had the opportunity she would slip out of the house, round to the stables, harness a trap, take Bumble and hopefully not come back. But now this young man was to guard her, spy on her . . .

'I shall see you at dinner. I ride to Cullompton.'

'Yes, Hedworth.' How easy the meekness was to act.

In her boudoir she rang for Lucy. 'Have you unpacked all my clothes yet?'

'Not all, milady.'

'Then in the large brown trunk you will find my riding habit, and several coats. They all need a good sponging and brushing. Take them to Dartagnan for me, will you? Tell him I need the habit back by this evening.'

Lucy trotted off, weighed down with the heavy clothes. Eliza followed her immediately. She carried a small bag containing a couple of her least favourite rings and a necklace, which she could sell. She raced to the stables. Rodgers appeared at the sound of her. At least one familiar face, she thought. 'Harness the trap for me, Rodgers, please.' She smiled broadly at him. 'I thought everyone I knew had gone.'

'I'm sorry I can't, milady.' He shuffled his boots in embarrassment. 'It's orders.'

'Why? Is Lord Alford afraid I might run away?'

'I couldn't say, milady.'

'I would appreciate you doing so, Rodgers. You won't be blamed. I shall take full responsibility.'

'Milady . . .' He was obviously distressed.

'Be sensible, Rodgers. Look, I have nothing with me. If I was running away, I'd have a bag, wouldn't I?'

'I suppose so.' He still looked doubtful.

'I need to take my dog to a friend to take care of it. Lord Alford wants me to get rid of him.'

'I know. He's given orders for Bumble to be shot.'

The cobbles of the stableyard rushed up towards Eliza and she swayed. 'And has it . . .' It was impossible for her to finish the sentence.

'Not yet, milady.'

'Right. Out of my way, Rodgers.' She pushed past the groom and into the stable. 'If you won't harness the trap I'll have to do it myself.'

'Milady . . .' He trailed along behind her. 'I'll do it. But please don't say I did.'

'Bless you, Rodgers. I won't. I'll go and get Bumble.'

She ran across the yard to where the kennel stood. A disgruntled Bumble was waiting for her and barked his displeasure at her. As she returned with him, Rodgers led a horse, with the trap behind it, into the yard. Without another word Eliza jumped in, Rodgers helped the dog into the back and, with a flick of the whip, Eliza wheeled the trap round and out of the yard.

Shoot Bumble? How could he? And why? She'd done as he wanted. And how ridiculous that she had to steal out of her own stables, beg to use her own pony and trap. She needed to get to Exeter and get money from Mr Joiner. From making sure that Hedworth always had money to save his pride, his so-important pride, she thought bitterly, she had been reduced to having nothing. She never saw money. She signed papers to keep the peace and then she had to ask Hedworth for everything, and invariably endure an inquisition as to why she wanted it. Her own money! She hadn't minded at first, she didn't want to appear to be wanting to control him anyway. But this had all changed. She had been cheated and he was using what was rightfully hers to deprive her of any freedom.

At the Gilpins' the butler was most put out that she was not calling but needed information as to the whereabouts of a Mr and Mrs Morgan in the Gilpins' employ.

'I shall have to ask permission to divulge such information,' he said, in his insufferably pompous manner, and his stately walk as he made his way to seek consent made her want to scream when she was in such a hurry.

'Eliza, what a wonderful surprise.' Jonquil came flying down the stairs. 'I couldn't believe it when the butler said ... But, my dear, you look so ... drawn. Are you well? Is there something I can do?'

'Yes, there is. I'm searching for Ruby, my maid.'

'Jerome's sister?' She looked coy.

'Yes.'

'Papa found her husband work as a farm labourer. On the home farm, I think. I wouldn't know.'

'I must get there. Which way?'

'Take the first turning on the right on the main drive. But won't you take tea?'

'I'll return later, if I may.'

'Eliza, or should I say Lady Alford!' Mrs Gilpin had appeared all a-flutter with Miss Gilpin in tow. 'My dear, you look so flushed ...'

'She's in a dreadful rush, Mama, but she's coming back.'

'If I may?'

'Of course . . .'

Eliza didn't wait for any more pleasantries but was already out of the door, climbing back into her trap.

The cottage to which she was directed was not nearly as pretty as Bramble Cottage. The yard in front was chaotic, full of broken farm implements and so rutted she had to pick her way carefully through the debris. She knocked on the door, Bumble at her side.

'Miss Eliza!'

'Ruby!'

They fell into each other's arms and were not ashamed to cry in their joy at seeing each other. 'It's been so long . . .' They sniffed in unison.

'But, Ruby, what happened?' Eliza looked about the poky, dank room in which they were sitting.

'So much for our dreams. Henry never complains but I know his heart is broken. He's a farm labourer now, and the money is far less than what he earned as a gamekeeper. Mrs Gilpin is very kind but she's fully staffed so there's nothing for me. But she brings me the odd bit of sewing.'

'Oh, Ruby, this is because of me, isn't it?'

Ruby nodded. 'Not that we hold it against you, Miss Eliza.'

'And your mother and Jerome? They were evicted too?'

'He works here.'

'As a labourer?'

'Yes, and he hates it. He's been his own master too long to take orders from others. My mother works in the dairy and that's something. But it's hard times, miss, it really is.'

'Then all my sacrifices were for nothing.' She had thought she was angry before but it was as nothing compared with how she felt now. Had Hedworth walked in at that moment she knew she would have been capable of killing him on the spot. 'When did this happen? In January?'

'We had no warning. Your father's agent came and we had twenty-four hours to vacate the farm. And then, when he'd done all the dirty work, he was dismissed too. Serves him right! We laughed about that.'

'They couldn't do it. I mean, you have some rights.'

'Well, they did. Miss Eliza, when you have nothing how can you fight anything? Who is going to listen? All my brother's work. All the worry and fighting. And now . . .' Ruby rubbed her stomach, which Eliza saw now was slightly swollen.

'Ruby?'

'Yes, I'm four months gone. And I wish I wasn't.'

'Don't say that, please.'

'It'll only make things worse.'

'I'll help, I promise.' Even more need to go and see Mr Joiner now. 'I was going to ask you to have Bumble, but I see now it's impossible.'

'Why? Don't you want the old dog any more?' At the sound of his name Bumble whacked his tail on the floor in a tattoo of delight.

'My husband has ordered that he be shot.'

'Whatever for? Is he ill?'

'No. I don't know why but I begin to wonder if it's because I love Bumble and he loves me. My husband doesn't like that.' The solution had come from the air as easily as that, and once said it seemed obvious. Especially following the dreadful revenge he had wreaked on the Barnard family. He didn't know them so why punish them except because she loved them?

'You're not happy, are you?'

'How can one be happy in hell?' Her eyes filled with tears. She had thought she was learning to endure but by talking about herself to someone who cared for her she knew it was impossible for her to control her emotions. She waved her hands in the air. 'But you don't want to hear about me . . . Jerome!' The joy she felt at seeing him enter the room stopped the tears instantly. 'Oh, Jerome.'

'Eliza! But what has happened to you?'

'Just tired. We've been travelling for a long time.'

'But you said—'

'I didn't mean it, Ruby, I was joking . . .' she said hurriedly.

'Mean what?'

'It was nothing, Jerome. But tell me, how is married life? Any babies yet?' She forced cheerfulness into her voice.

'Married? Me?' He looked at her dumbfounded. 'I'm not married. You're the one who couldn't wait. Not me.'

Eliza looked wildly from Jerome to Ruby, she saw Ruby bite her lip and avoid her stare. 'But . . . Oh, no! Oh, dear God, no!' And then she began to weep.

5

After Ruby had explained what she had done, Jerome's fury with his sister was dreadful to witness. He banged the table, the wall, a cupboard with impotent anger. He stormed about, his bulk menacing, made worse by the smallness of the room. He shouted at Ruby as she cringed by the window. Bumble took refuge under the table and cowered, his head on his paws.

'I did it for us all!' she wailed.

'You had no right!' he bellowed.

'Jerome, please, don't be so angry with Ruby.' Eliza tugged at his sleeve but so blind was he with rage he did not notice. 'Poor Ruby.' She put her hand out to her. 'Jerome, the baby!'

'*Poor Ruby! Poor Ruby!*' he shouted, in a rising crescendo. 'I don't care about her or her baby.'

'Yes, you do,' she said to Jerome. 'He didn't mean that,' she said to a tearful Ruby.

'Did you tell Mother?'

'No, I told no one. Not even Henry. But if I had I know what Mother would have said or done. Exactly the same!' She was shouting now. 'And don't argue with me, you know she would have. You know she thought it was wrong all along, you and Miss Eliza.'

Jerome slumped to the table, he put his hands to his head. 'She's ruined our lives. How could she?'

'She thought it was for the best, that's why. What else was she to do? My father meant it. He'd have ruined you.'

'And what do you think has happened to us now? You call this success?' The vehemence with which he spoke made her recoil from him. 'And what about you? You married quickly enough. You couldn't have been that heartbroken.'

'I was. When Ruby told me, I wanted to die. I was hurt, deeply so. And it was pride made me say it, only pride. Now I know you're not married, I shall be haunted for ever more with the thought that if I hadn't been so stupidly proud maybe Ruby would have told me the truth.'

'I would have, I'm sure I would have!'

'But you were already planning to marry your *lord*,' he sneered.

'I wasn't. It was you I loved. Every Thursday I used to hide myself in the market in case I might see you. It was all I had, a glimpse of you.'

'Then if you did, why didn't you make yourself known? Why did you hide away?'

'Because my father had threatened me too. He warned me he would ruin you, throw out your family, and he would ensure you never worked again. I loved you too much to let that happen.'

'You married, though.'

'But only after I thought *you* were married. Only when my father on his death-bed begged me to. I don't love my husband, I *hate* him!' There, despite all her intentions she had said the word.

'You expect me to believe all this? Well, I don't. Do you know what I really think? I think I was an amusement for you until the right man came along.'

'Jerome, that's not true!'

'Oh, yes, a suitable one. A rich one. Nothing changes – like with like, just as Mother said. But one thing has changed. My family is ruined and it's your husband has done the ruining.'

'Look, take this.' She tipped up her purse and the jewellery she had with her tumbled out on to the tablecloth.

'How like you, *Miss* Eliza. You think money solves everything. You think if you give enough everything will get better. That the problems and the bogeyman will go away. Well, let me tell you, life isn't like that and if you were more intelligent you would know it!' He pushed back his chair with such vehemence that it toppled over.

'Jerome, where are you going?'

'To think! And you can take that with you!' He stabbed at the necklace and rings on the table. 'We want none of your charity.' And with that he left, slamming the door behind him. The tiny cottage reverberated with the noise and a plate on the dresser crashed to the floor.

For a minute or two Eliza and Ruby sat in stunned silence.

'Miss, I'm so sorry.'

'No more than I. Look, Ruby, this isn't charity. You know I have plenty. Take this jewellery, sell it, get some comforts, get clothes for the baby.'

'But what if Jerome found out?'

'Don't tell anyone.'

'What will you do?'

'I can't go back to my husband. He hates me, I don't know why. I am his chattel, nothing more. I've asked the Gilpins if I can go there.'

'Will you be safe?'

'Oh, yes. It's not that my husband is violent . . . .' Only in the bedroom, she thought, but she was not prepared to tell anyone about that side of their life, it was too shaming. 'He likes to control me, unreasonably. And I am not prepared to be treated so. Will you keep Bumble?'

'You need not ask. He'll be safe with me. Shoot you, poor old fellow? Whatever next?' She patted the dog.

Eliza took a tearful farewell of her dog and her friend and returned to the Gilpins'. She was shown into the drawing room. To find Hedworth standing there, a glass of whisky in his hand. 'Ah, there she is. At last – we were getting worried about where you were.'

'I was making arrangements for my dog.'

'Your dog?' Mrs Gilpin fluttered.

'Yes, my husband does not care for my dog.'

'Fie on you, Lord Alford. Not like a dog? Why, I love dogs!'

'As do I, Mrs Gilpin. But not this one.'

'But Bumble is a delightful creature, Lord Alford. Why on earth could you have taken against him?'

'I would prefer not to go into the details, Miss Jonquil.'

'But—'

'Jonquil! Lord Alford is obviously speaking of a delicate matter,' her mother admonished her.

'He was going to have him shot.' Eliza looked across the room at her husband with all the loathing she felt for him in her eyes.

'Who on earth told you that? Would I do such a thing?' He flung his arms wide. 'Someone, my darling, was joking with you.' The charm was oozing out of him. Jonquil and her mother succumbed.

'He's sacked all my servants.' They swung round to look at Eliza.

'All of them?'

'All the ones I knew well.'

'Lord Alford, you do surprise me. I was always saying to Mr Gilpin what a high standard of retainers you had at Harcourt Barton.'

'Drink, Mrs Gilpin. It's a sorry tale.'

'Don't even begin to tell me, Lord Alford, please.' She held up her hand in mock supplication. 'But I shall be checking with you most assiduously in future when I have applicants – just in case they are one of yours! And maybe I should check on one or two who I know worked for you.' She tittered.

'Of course.'

'He does not know any of my father's servants. He dismissed them without knowing anything about any of them,' Eliza protested, but she was aware that Mrs Gilpin wasn't listening to her. 'May I stay here, Mrs Gilpin?' If only the woman would agree, she could counter anything he had to say about the Barnards, for surely if he found out they were here . . .

'Here, Eliza? What for?'

'I don't wish to return home. I'm afr—'

'Mrs Gilpin, let me explain,' Hedworth interrupted. 'Poor Eliza has not been well. She has not fully recovered from her dear father's death. She is at times – well, how shall I put it? Her imagination is a little too active. She says and thinks things that are not strictly true.'

'How did you know I was here? Did you have me followed?'

'You see?' Hedworth looked at them beseechingly. 'Why, my darling, should I do that? That is, unless you have something to hide from me.' He wagged his finger at her jovially. 'I just happened to be passing and thought it would be nice to let Mr and Mrs Gilpin know we had returned and Mrs Gilpin was gracious enough to receive me.'

At this Mrs Gilpin went puce with delight.

'Please, Mrs Gilpin, I beg you, may I stay here? Only temporarily.'

'Dear Eliza, nothing would give us greater pleasure, but you are a married woman now and if your husband wants you to return home with him then return you must.'

'But you don't understand . . .'

'My dear, I do. All marriages have a little upset now and then. We have to weather them and learn to do what our husbands want, take their guidance.'

What was the point of continuing? Eliza thought. No one would believe her, no one would take her word against his. As she climbed into the carriage Hedworth had brought for her, she looked with venom at the smiling face of Dartagnan, as he took control of the pony and trap. So that was how he had known where to find her.

Mrs Gilpin stood on the steps with her daughters waving her guests away. 'Such a charming man. I hope you two are as lucky. And titled too, it's almost too much.'

'I don't like him.'

'Primrose, how can you say such a thing?' she said to her eldest daughter.

'There's something bad about him.'

'I never heard such rot!'

'Then why's Eliza afraid of him?'

At Harcourt Barton Hedworth dragged Eliza from the trap and pushed her in front of him through the front door, across the hall and up the stairs. On the landing he dragged her into their bedroom.

'Hedworth, you're hurting me.'

'I want to talk to you.' He pushed her on to the bed. 'How dare you make a fool of me, in that way? "*Can I stay, Mrs Gilpin?*"' He aped her. '"*Please, Mrs Gilpin.*" You disappoint me, Eliza. Do you know how long that will take to get round the county?'

'You were going to shoot my dog! So how dare *you*?' she shouted at him with spirit. He slapped her hard. 'Oh, yes, Hedworth. What a fine man you are! Shooting dogs and hitting women.' She stood and looked at him defiantly. He lifted his arm, about to strike her again. 'Yes, do it. Show me what a powerful man you are.'

'I warn you, I expect total obedience from you. You need not think you will not obey me, because I shall make you.'

'Why? What have I done?'

'So far, not much. But I intend that you won't do anything further to annoy me. I recognise you, and the sort of woman you may become. You were not taught as a child what was expected of you, to be obedient. Your father was not strict enough with you. I shall be.'

She laughed, a harsh sound. 'Then you haven't got your facts right.'

'Don't argue with me. Your mother was a whore and I have no intention of allowing you to behave in the same way.'

'Do not speak of my mother in that way! You didn't know her, you know nothing about her.'

'I know everything about her. She deceived your father with his best friend, which nearly destroyed him. Behaviour like that might be in your blood and, if so, I shall rid you of it. I am your husband and if that means beating it out of you, so be it.' He grabbed her hair, swung her up from the bed and began to hit her mercilessly. She cried. She tried to defend herself. She begged him to stop. But relentlessly he continued.

Finally she slumped to the floor, her face bloody, her body bruised and battered. 'Change your ways or this treatment will continue.' And for good measure, as he passed her, he kicked her in the stomach. She heard the door slam. She lay there sobbing, not knowing which part of her hurt the most.

'Go away,' she said to a tapping at the door. 'Leave me alone.'

'Milady, it's me, Lucy. Let me help you. Oh, lawks, milady, you look a fright.' She crossed to the dressing room and returned with a bowl of water. Eliza saw the water redden with her blood but she was past caring. Lucy helped her to her feet. As she did so there was a surge of blood that stained the carpet.

'Oh, God, milady. I do believe you're losing a baby!'

6

At great expense, which she could ill afford, Fanny was on the train to Paddington. She smiled at the idea that she was being met by Florrie Paddington – such a sense of humour that woman had. The cost of the fare was worrying because she had lost more pupils. Without Florrie to organise and bully them, a group of the mothers had lost their initial enthusiasm. There had also been many questions about the cost, what she was spending on items such as food, clothes and books. The implication was that she was pocketing money for herself. This had hurt her deeply since she had not yet taken a wage from the school, but used money only for those of her own expenses that she could not avoid, and they were meagre. She had posted copies of her accounts to the ringleader, Sarah; she had known from the start that the woman would be troublesome, and so she had proved to be. By return of post she had had a letter asking how, since she had received a copy of the accounts, she was to know that they were genuine. So, to hurt was added insult.

Fanny had confided in the doctor, who had been a tower of strength and a great comfort to her. It was he who had arranged for her to see a lawyer and an affidavit was sworn that the accounts were genuine. But, of course, all this was added expense.

Sarah continued her vendetta, grudgingly accepting the figures, but removing her child anyway. And, like lemmings, three other mothers had followed suit – they were now down to thirteen pupils, not nearly enough. The losses were mounting and the worry with it.

'It seems to me that this woman dislikes me and I do not understand why. I hardly know her.'

'Perhaps you have done something to annoy her, which you are not aware of,' the doctor counselled. 'There has to be such a reason, for how else could anyone not like you?'

'Dr Forbes, you are too kind.' And she glowed with pleasure at the compliment. 'There are days on which I feel like closing the school. What is the point in struggling on in this way? I shall always be at the mercy of other people.'

'Please, Miss Chester, don't think of it for a minute.' The doctor looked aghast. 'What would we do without you?'

'Oh, Doctor. You embarrass me.' She looked down modestly but was overjoyed at his words.

'I have some savings. Perhaps you would accept them?'

'No, no, I couldn't possibly. It would be too risky for you.'

'I would like to help, if it means you stay.'

'I have to go to London next week to see Mrs Paddington. I'll talk to her about it.' Fanny had thought automatically that he referred to the school, not her.

'The offer will always be there.'

It was the doctor who had driven her to the station. She sat now on the train and kept touching her cheek with her glove. He had lifted her hand and kissed it as he said goodbye. It had excited her so, pleased her so. Dear Jock. But it had been a mortifying moment since her glove had a hole, which she was confident no one would see – how could she have anticipated anyone wanting to kiss her hand? He must have seen it and what must he be thinking of her now?

Florrie was easy to distinguish in the crowds on the station. Her colours were brighter, her feathers higher, her greeting louder. She might have given up her old profession but she looked much the same, thought

Fanny, who, as always in her presence, felt mouse-like in her serviceable navy-blue dress and jacket.

The discrepancy in their appearance made other women stop and stare at them. But so overjoyed was she to see her friend that Fanny didn't notice.

'How's the doctor?' Florrie asked, with false coyness, as they sat in a hansom cab being driven to her new home, a small terraced house in Soho. It was near to Leicester Square, she had explained to Fanny, an area frequented by young girls and their predators.

'He is very well.'

'I presume with no sick pupils that you hardly see him.'

'If Jock is in the neighbourhood he calls.'

'Jock, is it? Things are happening!'

'Don't be silly. He's very solicitous of the little girls.'

'The big one too!' And her joyous bubbling laugh rang out.

'Oh, Florrie!'

'And where will you live when you marry?'

'What makes you think we shall?' It was Fanny's turn to be coy.

'I don't think, I *know*!'

Fortunately for Fanny it was at that moment they arrived at the house. 'How charming.'

'It's small, but it's large enough for Ann and me, and I've two rooms I can use for my girls.'

'You're not thinking of removing them too?' Fanny was aghast.

'No, silly. The girls I find. I bring them here, feed them, talk to them.'

'And then?'

'That's the problem. They go back on the streets. I'm going to have to raise funds to open a home for them, somewhere they are safe and can learn skills.'

'Florrie, you are a wonder. And how will you finance it?'

'I'm persuading some of my friends from the old days

to help. They put the girls there and it seems only fair that they should help them too, don't you think?'

'Of course.'

'And the school?'

'Such problems, Florrie . . .' And she began to explain. 'Why should Sarah be such a bother to me? She dislikes me, I'm sure.'

'Charles Wickham. That's why.'

'Charles?' Her voice echoed her astonishment.

'She wanted him and you got him.'

'I did no such thing!'

'I know, but she doesn't. Like most thwarted women she is beyond reason.'

'But my' – she hesitated – 'muddle happened after the school. She was cool with me from the beginning.'

'But Caroline Fraser is her closest friend.'

'Oh, the tentacles of romantic intrigue.'

'I couldn't have phrased it better myself.' Suddenly Florrie looked serious, which was unusual for her. 'You realise I've found her.'

'The former Mrs Forester? I hoped that was why you had summoned me.'

'She took some finding. At first I employed a man to search for her. Useless, that was. The girls get suspicious, think someone is after money or revenge. So then I decided to snoop. They trusted me more but even then I had to say she was my mother. And that caused a few problems later because she was deeply offended and told them all I was lying. That her daughter was a respectable woman!' This had evidently amused Florrie enormously, judging by the laughter. 'She's in a sorry state, though, and in desperate need of help. She's ill. I fear consumption. Hardly surprising, the way she's been living.'

'Is she here?'

'No, she wouldn't come. She's not the easiest of people.'

'Is she . . . you know . . .'

'A tart? No, she's been lucky, she seems to have avoided that in the sense you are thinking. She's had protectors – goes without saying – but she managed to keep off the streets when she got too old to find a new one after the last one tired of her. As far as I can gather she'd gone down the ranks, from the nobs to the professionals, ending up with trade. Of course, each change of class meant less for her financially.'

'It's so cruel.'

'Fanny, my love, you never spoke a truer word. However, she's been lucky. She was a maid in a brothel for a while – they can make good money. Then she was able to scrape a living together with some sewing and millinery. But I gather her sight is not good – the firewater she drinks, no doubt, you have to be careful with that stuff – and she had to give it up. Then, fortunately, she found work in the kitchens of a hotel in Bloomsbury – not that far from here. Washing up, I gather, for a pittance. That's all there is to tell, really.' Florrie settled back with a glass of champagne. 'I think I did well. This city, talk about Sodom and Gomorrah, every other woman you meet is a whore!'

'You say she's lucky! You speak as if it's a normal way for a woman to live.'

'She is. The competition for any job like that is fierce.'

'Did you find out what happened between her and Mr Forester to make him act as he did?'

'She was a fool, that's what. She had a lover, a great friend of his, and was found out. There was talk of a duel but I don't know if that's true. The silly woman went to meet him in her own carriage, pretended she was going to her dressmaker. Of course, her footman was keeping a diary of her movements, just in case . . .'

'I don't understand?'

'Footmen, maids, they are well advised to keep tabs on their employers, write it all down, dates and all. You never know when it might come in handy, a judicious bit of blackmail, evidence should there be a court case.

It can earn them a handy bob or two. Her footman sold the information to her husband and he wasn't happy. No son, you see.'

'No son?'

'Dear Fanny, you know so little of the ways of the world. In their circles, once a son is born a little hanky-panky is often overlooked. But she'd only got a daughter. Acted a bit too fast, you see.'

'Poor woman.'

'Stupid woman, more like. I have to tell you, Fanny, I don't like her. There's something manipulative about her, false, if you know what I mean. And she's arrogant.'

'Thank you for warning me.' But I'll make up my own mind, she thought. 'If so, why didn't a man as rich as her husband divorce her?'

'Was he religious?' Florrie asked.

'In the years I was employed there I never saw him go to church.'

'Then he wanted a title or something. He couldn't have had the scandal of a divorce, he'd never have got one.'

'And he never did.'

'Said she was dead, didn't he? Then I expect someone in authority rumbled him. Good.'

'But she was wrong to do what she did,' Fanny averred.

'Frederick Forester might have treated her badly.'

'It's possible. Yet two wrongs—'

'Don't make a right. But, Fanny, they often do.'

'I know and understand so little, and you know so much.'

'It's a good job one of us does! Now, dinner. I trust you're hungry – I have food sent in from a restaurant. Ann never got the hang of cooking.'

'Florrie, you are so innovative!'

'What on earth does that mean? You do use long words, Fanny!'

'Mr Potts, this is the friend I was telling you of, Miss Chester. It is she who has been searching for Mrs Orme.'

'How do you do, Miss Chester?' A large, hairy hand was proffered, and Fanny was glad of her gloves. She was also glad of her bonnet, which shaded her face: she was afraid that Mr Potts might recognise her, even though sense told her it was unlikely after all these years. It interested her that the hotel smelt the same as it had then. So much had happened since she had run here from the Foresters'!

'This way.' Mr Potts showed them into the same musty sitting room in which she had fainted and where Charles had rescued her. How simple she had been, how unwise.

'If you'd take a seat. I must say I'm glad someone's come about her. Mrs Orme is becoming a bit of a liability . . .' He made the action of someone drinking. '. . . If you get my drift. And her cough, well, you have to hear it to believe it. In my opinion she's not long for this world. I only took her on as a favour to Mr Densham – and he hasn't had the courtesy to call either. Last good turn I do him.'

Fanny was about to cry out that she knew him, but caught herself in time.

'If you'll just wait a minute,' Mr Potts concluded.

Five minutes later a short, wan-looking woman appeared. She was thin to the point of emaciation. In her pale and pasty face there was a hint of the beauty she had once been, but it was a mere whisper. Instinctively both Florrie and Fanny stood up.

'Pray be seated,' she said, in an educated voice and with dignity. Fanny had to put her hand over her mouth to stop herself crying out with pity at the contrast between the look and the manner of the woman. 'May I ask your business?'

'Don't you remember me? Florrie Paddington?'

'Should I?' There was an arrogant shift of the head.

'No reason why you should,' Florrie said, good-naturedly.

'My name is Chester, Mrs Orme. I was Eliza's governess.'

'I know no one of that name. Pray be swift, I have much to do.'

What next to say? 'I'm a friend of Merry Greensay, though she's Denzle now.'

'Merry – dear, darling Merry. The best friend I ever had. But she's deserted me, she never comes.'

'She lost touch with you. She didn't know where to find you.'

'That's nonsense! She knew my London address. She didn't want to, like everyone else!' She said this in a far more excited tone, which made her cough, and Fanny began to worry for her, but Mr Potts sighed and looked heavenward, and Florrie didn't seem too put out.

'Mrs Orme,' Fanny ventured, once the attack had ceased, 'I've come to take you home, if you like.'

'Home?' She looked at Fanny with more interest.

'To your daughter, Eliza.'

'My daughter is called Amelia, like me. I'm Amelia Victoria, she's Amelia Eliza. You should get your names right, Miss Chester.'

'So silly of me. Now I remember. I gather her father preferred her to be called Eliza. If you wish, if you like . . .' Fanny's original plan had been to find Amelia, then alert Eliza and leave her to decide what she wanted to do, though she felt she knew what that would be. But not having seen her, and not liking to call when she was still mourning her father, she had delayed, and events had overtaken her.

'Why isn't she here? I suppose her father forbade it.'

'No, unfortunately he passed away. Eliza is in mourning.'

'Dead!' She clapped her hands together. 'How wonderful! Such good news you bring, Miss Chester!' She laughed, a dreadful sound since it brought on the coughing again. They all waited patiently for it to cease. 'And my daughter, she is well?'

'As far as I know, yes. She has just returned from her honeymoon.'

'Married, and I wasn't there!' She struck her chest. 'Who has she married?'

'Lord Alford'

'How wonderful. You see, you pathetic little man?' She pointed at Potts. 'You never believed a word I told you. I suspect you're sorry now. Come, Miss Chester, we must depart immediately.'

'But your packing—'

'I have nothing to take.' And with one graceful motion, reminiscent of the woman she had once been, she was on her feet and making for the door. 'Come, hurry up, Chester.'

'See? Arrogant. What did I tell you?' Florrie whispered. 'I'm sorry, Mrs Orme,' she continued, 'there will be no more trains to the West Country today. You will have to stay at my house tonight.'

'And where do you live?' was the haughty reply.

'Soho, Mrs Orme,' said Florrie.

'Dear God, how dreadful,' groaned Amelia. 'However, if I must . . .'

7

The journey was a nightmare. Florrie's maid, Ann, had packed them a picnic basket but upon asking what it contained, Amelia announced she did not like ham, could not abide beef, loathed hard-boiled eggs, disliked *all* cakes and would not countenance lemonade. Instead she demanded salmon, quail's eggs, dry biscuits, pineapple and champagne. This necessitated Ann rushing out to buy the ingredients and repack the basket, by which time they were late and it was a flustered Fanny who arrived at the station, where the departure of the train was imminent. She was already edgy since Amelia hadn't stopped complaining for one minute that Ann had not been able to purchase the pineapple.

At the station, worse was to come when Amelia refused point-blank to get into a second-class carriage. Leaving her on the platform with the basket, Fanny had to rush to the ticket office, weaving her way through the dense crowds to change to first class. She reeled at the added expense.

The other occupants of the Ladies Only carriage did not look kindly on Amelia and Fanny could not blame them: her dress was grubby, her hair dirty, her hands rough, her nails non-existent. A motherly looking matron moved along the seat so that no part of her ample form touched Amelia. Fanny smiled apologetically at the other occupants but none of them reacted. She and Florrie had tried to make Amelia look smarter but it was her size that was the problem. Fanny only had the clothes she wore and a change of underclothes so she had nothing to loan her, and Florrie was so statuesque that anything she had swamped the woman.

Once the train started on its long journey, Amelia began to talk. How she talked. Fanny feared she would never stop. Then she coughed and, to Fanny's mortification, began to scratch. The motherly matron muttered to her companion that servants should be travelling in third. Unfortunately, or maybe on purpose, she did not speak quietly enough.

'I beg your pardon, madam, but Miss Chester is a governess, hardly a *servant*!'

The woman looked scathingly at Amelia. 'Miss Chester looks a perfectly respectable travelling companion.'

'I should think so.' Amelia looked smug. 'Then you should apologise to her.'

'I have nothing to apologise to her for. It was *you* to whom I was referring.'

432

Amelia spluttered and Fanny closed her eyes. 'How dare you? I'm no servant.'

'You are unkempt, and it is wrong that respectable people should be forced to travel with you.'

'I'll have you know my daughter is Lady Alford.'

'And I'll have *you* know I don't believe you.'

'You are rude.'

'And you, madam, are dirty! I doubt you have the correct ticket.'

'Miss Chester, show this woman our tickets.' Fanny demurred. The matron bristled with indignation. 'Show her.' Amelia prodded Fanny with her elbow.

'I apologise, madam, but Mrs Orme is not well. As I think is self-evident.'

'If that is the case, Miss Chester, then you should have taken her by carriage. It is intolerable that such behaviour should be inflicted on us.'

'I can only apologise.'

'No, you can do more than that. You can get out at the next station.'

'It would make our journey more difficult.'

'Miss Chester, I have no concern about your journey, it is my own that bothers me. As if travelling at these appalling speeds is not enough anxiety without one being assailed by such a person.'

Amelia swore. Not one word but a string of invective. 'Please, Mrs Orme,' Fanny begged, 'I must ask you to cease this intolerable behaviour.'

'You turncoat, you sneak, you bitch!' And Fanny received a tongue-lashing from her ungrateful companion.

Fanny could not blame the woman who, as the train shuddered to a halt, hung out of the door, waving her umbrella and demanding the guard. Fanny and a complaining Amelia were moved to another carriage. The same thing happened there but this time, instead of complaining, the other passengers alighted at the next station. This happened several times.

Finally Amelia fell asleep, exhausted, it seemed, by her constant tirades and chatter. Fanny could have wept with relief. Peace at last. However, she found she could not concentrate on the book she had brought with her. She was too agitated and too upset, and not just by Amelia.

Late last night, once Amelia had been put to bed, Florrie had taken Fanny out to the streets around Leicester Square. She had warned her of what she was about to see, but nothing could have prepared her for the reality. Everywhere she looked young women were selling themselves. The theatres had just emptied and the streets were packed; the presence of respectable women was no brake on their behaviour. Instead the street girls resented them and were abusive. Fanny was sworn at – at least, she presumed she was, since words she had never before heard were yelled at her.

The women importuned men relentlessly. Some wore short skirts showing their ankles, which shocked Fanny rigid. She was even more appalled when they flicked them up coquettishly, exposing knees and in one case a flash of thigh. Many wore small feathered red hats that sat at a rakish angle on their heads, like a badge of office. Some wore rouge and their lips were unnaturally red, and the atmosphere reeked of cheap scent mixed with sweat. Most were drunk and all were loud.

Fanny saw pretty young women, old crones and, most upsetting, children, some as young, she estimated, as ten or eleven. There were women to satisfy all tastes, all pockets. There were girls who were obviously ill and could barely stand, there were many with sickening sores on their faces, others with black eyes and scars. She felt sick, violated, and as if she had stepped into hell.

'Florrie, this is dreadful.'

'Not pleasant, is it? You should see some of the back-streets, and down by the docks, it's even worse there.'

'Do you think many of these women have been cared for like you and have still ended up here?'

'Some. The less pretty ones will have gone straight on the streets. Others, yes, just like me. This was what I risked becoming.'

By this time Fanny was nearly in tears: she had just seen a child walk away with a gross man who must have been fifty if he was a day. Florrie had to restrain her from rushing forward to rescue her. 'Do that and you'll get yourself beaten up or arrested. Come on, let's go home. You've seen enough.'

Florrie's house was a sanctuary. But Fanny knew she would never sleep, not when torment was outside.

'What haunts me, Florrie, is that the girls in our little school might be those women in a few years.' Her face was creased with worry.

'I knew you'd want to do something,' Florrie said, once they were settled in her pretty little sitting room. 'It's why I thought you should see things as they are.'

'But what on earth can we – women ourselves – do to help these poor creatures?'

'Work is the solution. If they could find employment they wouldn't be selling themselves. You can take my word for that.'

'They have to be taught skills, that is imperative.'

'Yes, but with no criticism of what they've been doing. That's what too many of those trying to help them do. It's acceptance they need. I've seen well-meaning people fail time after time. It's no good telling girls like that that God will provide when He hasn't put Himself out until now – must be deaf.'

'Oh, Florrie! You are wicked.' Fanny laughed.

They had debated, planned and plotted deep into the night.

Now, on the train, Fanny wondered again what to do. They had to find a refuge for these girls, somewhere for them to recover, to learn new skills – sewing, cleaning, cooking. Health was another issue. Florrie had told her of the fearful diseases they risked catching, which she had never heard of and would rather not think about. But that would be no solution: if she buried her head the suffering would continue. But she was aware that whatever she and Florrie managed to do would be little in view of the magnitude of the problem.

Amelia was muttering in her sleep. Fanny studied her, but could see nothing of Eliza in her face or demeanour. It was a spiteful face, but now Fanny had an idea of what her life must have been like: who was she to judge the damage caused to Amelia's expression by hardship? She had already begun to wish she had not got involved with her. But now that she'd found her she had to accept responsibility for her. Was it wicked of her to wish, a little, that she hadn't? At least, as she'd heard, Eliza was at home now. Fanny could take Amelia to her and leave her to deal with the woman. She might be better in that environment – at least Fanny hoped so.

Now that her father was dead, Eliza would be a wealthy woman. Given her mother's history, would she be the person to approach about money for the plan? And how could she broach the subject with a young woman as innocent and respectable as she? But, then, it was only after meeting Florrie that she herself had learnt of such problems, and what some of her sex were forced to do because of poverty and hopelessness. And how could she tell Eliza of such things? The shock might make her shy away from the project. Perhaps it would be better to talk to her husband.

Dr Forbes was at the railway station to meet them, as he had promised he would be. If he was taken aback by the sorry state of Amelia he hid it well.

'I know it's an inconvenience but if we could go first to Harcourt Barton? You see, Mrs Orme is really Mrs Forester, Eliza's mother,' she explained. She was sitting beside the doctor on the driving seat of the trap, Amelia more comfortable on the seat behind.

'Dear Miss Chester, I fear that would not be a good idea. Lady Alford is not well.'

'What's wrong with her?'

'You could not expect me to tell you, Miss Chester. She's my patient.'

Fanny blushed furiously. 'How stupid of me, of course you can't. I wasn't thinking.'

He leant towards her. 'She doesn't look like her mother,' he whispered, and Fanny felt dizzy at his close proximity.

'It's a tragic story.'

'So it would appear.'

On arrival at the school Amelia made a scene because she had not been taken direct to Harcourt Barton. Her tantrum was upsetting to witness, let alone to hear. 'But the shock to Eliza—'

'She's called Amelia!' Amelia shouted.

'Very well. As I've tried to explain it is not possible to take you to *Amelia* tonight. Perhaps tomorrow.'

'Not "perhaps", definitely!'

'I can't promise.'

'You don't have to, I shall go myself. You can't keep me a prisoner.'

'I'm not trying to.'

'I don't like you.'

'Mrs Orme, I'm not sure that I like you either so please don't let it concern you.' And Fanny swept out of the room, afraid that if she stayed longer she might say something worse.

Amelia's health came to the rescue. Late that evening she was coughing up globules of blood. Dr Forbes came, Fanny apologising that she had to call him so late.

'Coming here is never a trial, Miss Chester, but your problem is solved. This poor woman must not get out of her bed for at least a week.'

'Oh, no . . .' She felt herself blush. 'I mean, poor

woman, not that I didn't want her here!' she said hurriedly.

Dr Forbes chuckled.

'Would it be possible for me to visit Miss Eliza, and explain to her, give her time to become used to the idea that her mother is back from the dead?'

'Provided you will permit me to be with you.'

'I should feel far happier if you were.' She had to look away to hide her smile, for he could have no idea of the real meaning behind her words. In turning from him she missed the similar smile on his face.

8

'Come, Jonquil, we're going calling.' Primrose Gilpin was tying the ribbon of her bonnet under her chin.

'But it's going to rain.'

'No, it's not. The sun is shining and I've ordered the jaunting cart.'

'You're such a bully.'

'We have to call on your friend Eliza.'

'But is she receiving? She was still in black when she called the other day.'

'We're going. As she called then it follows that she is receiving. If she's not, then at least she will be told we were there.' She held open the door for her sister.

'You're not still thinking she's unhappy and afraid of the DL?'

'DL? What does that stand for?'

'Divine Lord, of course.'

'You are such a child, Jonquil.'

'And you're such a miserable spinster,' Jonquil spat, as she climbed into the jaunting cart. 'And I hate calling in this thing. What will people think? We should be in the barouche. Mother will be furious.'

'I prefer this, it's quicker, and you can't drive – well, not safely – so be quiet.'

'Mama says you exaggerate. And Papa says it's none of our business. They're married and that's that.'

'I like Eliza, and I think it *is* our business. If I was in trouble, as I'm sure she is, I'd hope someone would care enough about me.'

'You're such a busybody, Prim.'

The rest of the drive to Harcourt Barton passed in silence. The sisters had never got on: they had little in common.

'Lady Alford is not at home,' the butler informed them.

'Then may we speak to Lord Alford?' Primrose persisted.

'I shall ascertain . . .'

They stood waiting.

'This way, Miss Gilpin, Miss Jonquil.' The butler had returned and led them along the corridor to the drawing room.

'The Misses Gilpin, welcome.' Hedworth Alford walked forward in greeting.

'We would like to see Eliza,' Primrose said, without preamble. Jonquil simply looked starry-eyed.

'I am afraid that won't be possible. My wife is indisposed.'

'What ails her?'

'Really, Miss Gilpin!' He seemed shocked at her presumption.

'She seemed in perfect health, yesterday.'

Alford laughed. 'What is your meaning, Miss Gilpin? You think I have done my wife a mischief?'

'Primrose!' Jonquil winced.

'She wanted to see us. She asked my mother if she could stay with us. She was agitated. That is my concern.'

'So, you are concerned? We make progress. As I explained, my wife is under a lot of strain and was exhausted. She is resting and will soon be fully recovered.'

'Then there is something wrong? You admit it?'

'Miss Gilpin, I find this conversation somewhat wearying. I don't intend to say anything further.'

'Primrose! Stop it!' Jonquil pulled at her sleeve.

Miss Gilpin yanked her arm free. 'It's just—'

'I am sorry, Miss Gilpin, I have pressing matters.' He crossed to the bell-pull. 'Morton will see you out. Good day to you both.' He bowed, smiling charmingly and left the room.

'Well!'

'What did you expect? You were impossible. You discomfited me! I shall never be able to face Lord Alford again!'

Fanny sat on the edge of a chair in the drawing room at Harcourt Barton. She was tense with excitement. To be here again, after all this time, in this lovely room! So close to Eliza and soon to see her! These last few minutes after five years were almost too much for her.

'I'm so sorry to have kept you waiting, Miss Chester.'

'I was content to sit here in surroundings that bring me such happy memories.' So this was Eliza's husband, and what a charming, handsome man he was. Eliza must be madly in love with him – what young woman wouldn't be?

'You know Harcourt?'

'I do. I was your wife's governess for three happy years.'

'Were you?' There was no interest in his voice. 'She has never mentioned you.'

'Oh.' Had it been necessary for him to say that? Was he just thoughtless?

'Ah, Dr Forbes, I didn't see you skulking there.'

'My apologies, Lord Alford, I did not intend to be furtive.'

What an odd word to use, skulking, thought Fanny,

so unfriendly. Perhaps her first impression of Lord Alford had been wrong.

'I was hoping to see Lady Alford,' she said.

'My wife is indisposed.'

'I had hoped she would be able to see me,' Fanny persisted.

'That will not be possible . . . I fear.' The last sounded like an afterthought.

'Perhaps a visit from an old friend might be just the thing to cheer her?'

'I don't think that is a good idea.'

'As her doctor, I beg to disagree.'

'But you are no longer her doctor.' Alford looked at him coolly.

'I beg your pardon?' Dr Forbes looked astonished. 'But I've been treating her.'

'That was an oversight. It was her maid who had you notified. I was not here, you understand.'

'Are you not satisfied with my treatment of your wife?'

'You have done well. But you must understand, Doctor, I would not have consulted with a village practitioner in the first place. My wife is an important person.'

'All my patients are important.'

'You make a mistake if you do not realise that some are more so than others, Doctor. However, I have my own excellent medical adviser, who has now attended her, and he recommends quiet and rest. I shall abide by his knowledge and instructions.'

Fanny wanted to run across the room, take Jock in her arms and comfort him: he looked devastated. He had been made to look a fool, a person of no consequence. How dare this man treat him thus?

'Dr Forbes is an excellent doctor. The best.' Fanny kept her voice calm and even, when she wanted to shout at him.

'I'm sure he is. But not for my wife, Miss Chester. So,

you see, I must listen to her doctor. A visit is out of the question.'

'But I have momentous news for her. News that will no doubt make her much better immediately.'

'And what news can that be, Miss Chester?'

'Her mother is staying with me. She will be astonished by the good news.'

'More than astonished, I should imagine. Her mother is dead.'

'She isn't! She's alive! Isn't it wonderful? I found her. In London.'

'You may have found someone, but not Lady Alford's mother, I can assure you.'

'I was told she was dead too, most people were—'

'I am hardly *most* people. I am somewhat more important to my wife than *most* people.'

'It was an unfortunate expression to use. I'm sorry. But I must insist. You have only to talk to her to know that she is who she says she is. Why, she knows things I had never heard before.'

'Then you wouldn't know if they were true or not, would you?'

'No . . . I admit, I would not. But on top of the facts I knew, which I could and did check with her, there were so many other things she knew.' Fanny was becoming flustered.

'I repeat, I forbid a visit today. It would distress my wife too much.'

'Today, you say? Then we could come another day?' She was almost begging and despised herself. 'That would be much better for everyone since Eliza's mother is ill at the moment.'

'Lady Alford has no mother, Miss Chester. Must I keep pointing this out to you? But how fortunate, then, that this person has such an excellent doctor on hand to care for her. No doubt she can look forward to a rapid recovery.' The way he smiled charmingly while being so rude was chilling. 'Will that be all?' He was already crossing the room to the bell-pull.

'Come, Miss Chester, we are not welcome here.'

Fanny got hurriedly to her feet. 'If I wrote a note, would you give it to her?'

'Provided you don't mention this nonsense about her mother.'

'Then I won't. Thank you for receiving us.' She wanted to be gone now, as quickly as possible, and in her haste she tripped. The doctor saved her from tumbling to the floor. She was aware as they crossed the hall that she had hurt her ankle, but she ignored the pain. They went past the stairs, where, so long ago it seemed now, she had sat and comforted that sweet child. There was something very wrong here – she felt an atmosphere that, if she didn't think it was fanciful, she would have described as evil.

Once outside she took deep breaths of the fresh air. She swayed, feeling faint. Jock Forbes took hold of her arm again to steady her. 'Are you ill, Miss Chester?'

'I don't think so. I feel . . . I'm not sure what I feel.' She laughed nervously. 'Emotional,' she said finally, aware that it was an inadequate explanation.

'Understandable. You were so excited at the thought of seeing your friend.' He helped her into the trap.

'Too excited, probably, and coming here, remembering how it was, how she was . . .' She looked up at the great house, which she knew had once been Eliza's refuge. Had it now become her prison? She shook her head. What a ridiculous notion. She looked up at Eliza's tower. No doubt she did not sleep there now that she was married, but she had loved it. Perhaps she still used it when she felt in need of quiet moments. They were on their way now, half-way along the drive. Did Eliza think of her? She hoped so. She could not believe that she had forgotten her already – Lord Alford had said that to hurt her. But why? They were turning out of the main gate now. She looked back: from here, if one knew where to look, there was a point at which one could just see a wing of the house, hidden among the trees. 'Dr Forbes, do tell me if am being fanciful, but I fear all is not well there.'

Jock Forbes drove the trap into a small clearing and drew the pony to a halt. He sat for a minute, the reins in his hand, looking down at the worn leather straps, deep in thought. She decided not to interrupt whatever he was thinking.

'She is no longer my patient,' he said eventually.

'That was so rude of Lord Alford.'

'That does not concern me. It is she who worries me.'

'You know something?'

'Since I am not her doctor, I feel I can confide in you. But this must go no further, Miss Chester.'

'Of course.'

'When I was called to her it was very late at night. In my opinion she had been at great risk for some time before I was contacted. I did not see her husband. She had suffered a . . . She had lost a baby.'

'My poor Eliza!'

'But she was not as a woman who has lost a baby normally is. Fretful, tearful. I fear she was glad. But also I fear she had been badly beaten.'

'Did she tell you?'

'No, she said very little. But her maid told me she had fallen down the stairs, and I am always doubtful when that is said.'

'So that was why he didn't want me to see her?'

'Perhaps. Or perhaps he has other motives.'

'But what?'

'I don't know. But when a rich woman is married to a poor husband, sometimes things are not as they appear.'

'How do you know he has no money?'

'Having such little regard for village doctors, he has forgotten me. I attended him three years ago after a hunting accident. I was working with my father on

444

Exmoor. Everyone there knew Lord Alford was insolvent and had debts. And, to add insult to injury, he never paid my bill!' He laughed. 'And today he's insulting me!' He laughed even louder, and Fanny joined in.

'But what do we do?' she asked anxiously, once they had calmed down.

'There is little we *can* do. She is his wife and what happens in their marriage is his business. Has she family?'

'An aunt.'

'Then perhaps we should tell her. Would she be sympathetic? Would she act?'

'I'm not sure. She's not a very pleasant woman. And I know one should never listen to gossip, or think it true, but . . . Well, I was led to believe that she was Lord Alford's mistress, but when I heard that he had married Eliza I presumed that that was all it was, a wicked rumour.' For a split second she thought of Charles and, as bad as she now thought him, she could not believe that he would not have warned Eliza or her father if he had known such things about Alford. Or would he?

'Maybe the aunt made sure she married him, then.'

'Oh, Jock, no – forgive me, I forgot myself!'

'I would be honoured if you called me by my name.' Gently he took hold of her hand. 'In return, might I call you Fanny?'

'Oh, please do!' she said and wondered if she should have demurred a little.

'Thank you, Fanny.' He smiled at her and she thought how beautiful her name sounded when he said it. And she was aware that her responding smile was particularly dreamy . . .

'This does not solve the problem with Eliza.'

He frowned. 'If the aunt is in league with Alford . . . Perhaps her lawyer. Do you know who he is?'

'He's in Exeter. I had occasion to go there once with Eliza.'

'Then that is to whom we must talk.' He shook the reins and turned the horse in the direction of Exeter. How decisive he was, how safe she felt with him.

He pulled up again, so abruptly that she rocketed forward in her seat. 'What am I thinking of? How stupid can I be? You haven't seen Miss Eliza for years.'

'That is correct, more's the pity.'

'And you were not permitted to see her this afternoon.'

'I understand – then how would I know there was anything wrong with her? But there's still your professional knowledge.'

'Exactly, *professional*. It was highly unprofessional to tell you what I feared . . .'

'I would never breathe a word.'

'Which is why I felt I could confide in you, but I can hardly tell her lawyer the same thing, now, can I?'

'What do we do?'

'The aunt. It will have to be her despite your reservations. We shall telegraph her this very afternoon.' He turned the horse to face the other way and they began the journey back to Cheriton Speke. As they drove along she looked sideways at him. How odd that she had once thought him plain-looking. Today he looked most handsome, and what fine, virile sideburns he had.

9

Eliza was attempting to read in her room, but she could not concentrate. Her mind kept wandering, she kept falling asleep. When the doctor had called this morning, she had asked him why she felt like this. He had reassured her that it was normal, that she was exhausted. That she was to stay calm, in bed, and to keep taking the medicine. She was far from calm, she had got up, and she had decided today that she was not going to take any more of the medicine. It was that, she was convinced, which was making her tired.

She still ached but she was feeling better for, with the resilience of the young, her body was healing fast. But her spirit was a different matter. She had such anger and loathing within her. At first she had tried to control it, to change it, but then felt she should nurture it, that her rage could help her escape this nightmare. Again instinct told her she must not become acquiescent for then she risked becoming weak. Somehow she had to remain strong.

'Lucy, I want you to take this letter to Miss Jonquil Gilpin for me.'

'Yes, milady.' Lucy bobbed.

'I mean take it yourself, walk there, put it into her hand, tell no one.'

'Why, yes, milady.' It was the simple acceptance of her request that proved to Eliza she had no intention of doing any such thing.

'Then I want you to wait for a reply, to prove you have done as I asked, and have not given the note to anyone else.'

'Milady! As if I would!'

'If you do that, then this is yours.' On the table beside her she placed a guinea. 'But if the note is intercepted you will get nothing.'

'Why, yes, milady.' Her eyes had narrowed at the sight of the coin. 'Your medicine, milady.' On the same table she placed the silver salver with the measured glass, the dropper and the dark brown bottle.

'I'm feeling so much better, I've decided not to take it.'

'Yes, milady.' Lucy bobbed again and made for the door.

'There's just one thing, Lucy. You must know that I am familiar with Miss Jonquil's handwriting, so there's no need to cheat and say you have delivered it when you haven't.'

447

The maid giggled but Eliza wasn't taken in. Now she had to hope that the amount of money on the table was greater than any inducement her husband had paid the maid to spy and report on her. For she was sure that that was what the girl was doing.

Hedworth's motives still puzzled her. Did he resent her inheritance? Would it have been different if her father hadn't protected it by creating the trust? It was common for an estate such as this to be entailed to secure it for further generations. He had acted as many fathers would. Or . . . Involuntarily her hand shot to her mouth at a thought so awful, so frightening, too terrible to contemplate. Did Hedworth want her dead?

That could not be: if she died without children the trust would go to a distant cousin, as would the right to live here. He needed her alive. So why? *Why?*

'Your maid says you have refused your medicine.' Without knocking Hedworth had entered the room. 'And what on earth are you doing out of bed? You know what the doctor said. You must rest.'

'I feel much better.' She could not look at him: then he might read the thoughts uppermost in her mind. That was illogical but fear was stalking her.

'If you take no notice of the doctor's advice you will be a long time recovering.' He spoke so kindly, with such concern, that it would have been easy to relax, but she knew she must not.

She longed to ask if he wanted her better so that he could hit her again. But she knew him now, knew what he was capable of.

'I am very sorry you lost the child.'

Silence persisted.

'You should have told me you were with child.'

Silence.

'Had I known . . .'

'You wouldn't have beaten me?' That was too much. She couldn't remain quiet any longer. Was he trying to blame her for his own actions?

'I regret . . . I was drunk. Will you forgive me?'

Silence.

'You have to take this medicine. I insist.'

'Who called yesterday?'

'Yesterday?' He paused as if trying to remember, which was ridiculous, she thought, since they did not have many visitors.

'The doctor. But I sent him away since you have a new one.'

'I like Forbes.'

'He lacks the experience of Dr Talbot.'

'I'd rather have the doctor I prefer.'

'You will have the one I decide.'

'Who else came?'

'No one.'

'I heard another carriage.'

'You must have been dreaming.'

'I was wide awake.'

'Don't argue with me. There was no other carriage.' He spoke in an exaggerated, slow manner, she saw him clenching his hands, relaxing them, then forming fists again. She must be careful: he was angrier than he appeared. She was in danger.

'I must have dreamt I was wide awake.'

'Exactly.' She saw the fist unbunch.

'Have there been any letters for me?'

'None.'

'I must write to my aunt.'

'Whatever for? Neither of you likes the other.'

'I want to reassure her about money.'

'She's adequately cared for.'

'I thought you were great friends.'

From the corner of her eye she saw a fist forming.

'We were friends. No more. She bores me. My loyalty is to you, not her, and she never said anything good about you. Now. This medicine . . .' He began to measure the drops. 'Here.' He handed her the glass.

'I'll take it in a minute.' Even as she said this she knew it was a forlorn hope.

'Now.'

His tone told her not to argue. She took the glass, looked at the pink fluid, and swallowed it, closing her eyes as she did so. She shuddered, it was bitter. He handed her a chocolate. 'There, this will take away the nasty taste.' He spoke now as if she were a child he loved, he was playing games with her ... 'I have business to attend to.' He walked sharply out of the room. He could not have reached the head of the stairs before Eliza had stuck a finger down her throat and was retching into her wash bowl.

Vomiting exhausted her. She sat in a chair looking out of the window. She had to get away from here. He was going to kill her if she stayed, she was sure. She must conserve her energy, rest, just as he said, but to recover a little more so that she could plan what to do, where to go and finally to be free.

Jonquil and Primrose presented themselves at four, as they had said they would in the note with which Lucy had returned. Just as before, the butler informed them Eliza was not receiving.

'I think you will find we are expected.'

But the butler would not budge, his instructions were that her ladyship was asleep, she was not to be disturbed. But Primrose would not take no for an answer, and insisted he ask Lord Alford to reconsider. He returned with the same message. 'Very well, our father is away at the moment, but you may tell Lord Alford we shall come back with him the minute he returns. And we shall *demand* to see his wife.' And with a walk that declared her indignation, Primrose ushered her sister out of the door.

'Do you think Papa will come with us? You know what he said.'

'Yes, but now we have Eliza's note – *please rescue*

me. He can't ignore that and say it's none of our business, can he?'

'I wish he was here. What about showing Mama the letter?'

'What would be the point? If the devil was a peer, Mama would say what a charming man he was!'

Hedworth Alford was none too pleased to receive a letter in the last post of the day from Minnie Wickham. 'What are you doing to my niece? I have been warned. And I am warning you, should any mischief occur to her then I shall hold you responsible . . .' Three pages of similar interfering hysterics followed. Who had told her? How had she known? That governess bitch, no doubt.

He sat in the library, brooding. That damn governess, the doctor and those stupid simpering Gilpin women! He was going to have to move, and sooner than he had planned.

Fanny was having a difficult time with Amelia. She was not an easy patient. If she asked for tea, by the time it was made she wanted coffee. She ordered fish then rejected it for meat. Six pillows were too many, she needed two, but then, resettled, she asked why Fanny was so mean with the pillows when she needed at least six. The nightdress Fanny gave her was not fine enough, she could only wear Swiss lawn; anything else irritated her skin. Fanny's cologne was vulgar. She needed her own maid.

'Where is my daughter?'

'Why hasn't she called?'

'Why are you caring for me? Why not my child?'

In spite of the difficulties there were times when Fanny felt sympathy for the woman. She could not tell her Eliza was ill, that they were worried about her, for Jock had pointed out that it was likely to distress her too much. So Fanny had to lie and say that Eliza was away but, of course, Amelia had insisted she have an address to write to. And then Fanny had to compound the lie and say she did not know where she was.

'You're keeping me from her. You want me to yourself. You're no better than a gaoler.'

Then Fanny's sympathy disappeared in a puff and she found herself wishing she had never become involved with this demanding, petulant woman. And she was beginning to think that she was doing Eliza no favours in having found her mother.

Until Amelia had another coughing fit, or the fever, which appeared each evening, was higher than before, and she would lie sweating and mewing like a sick animal, and Fanny felt nothing but pity for her.

'Have you heard from Eliza's aunt?' Jock asked, as they dined together. He had arrived to check his patient later than he had intended, looking so tired that Fanny had invited him to dine with her. She was touched by the swiftness with which he accepted.

'Nothing.'

'How strange. I know we were discreet in the telegram but we did say you were *concerned*. I'd have thought that word would be strong enough to alert someone.'

'She probably thinks it is none of my business. Or that there is no need to reply to someone as lowly as I.' She laughed at the very idea. She had always thought Minnie a silly woman – even without the complication of Charles. *No!* her mind screeched at her. You don't want to think about *him*.

'You are far from lowly. You are the most exalted woman I have ever met.'

'I meant it as a joke.'

'I could never make light of your position in life. You are a woman of such dignity, goodness, intelligence that it is a privilege for me to know you.'

'Jock!'

Suddenly Jock flung his napkin on the table. He stood

up, then sank on to one knee. Fanny felt sure her heart would leap from her breast, it was so fast beating. 'Fanny, forgive me.' He looked up at her, with his fine brown eyes. 'May I presume to beg that you would consider making me the happiest man on this planet?'

There was an awkward pause. 'Jock,' she said finally, to fill the uncomfortable silence.

'I understand.' Disconsolately he began to stand.

'What do you understand?'

'That you don't wish to marry me.'

'But you haven't asked me?'

'Have I not?'

'No.'

'So?'

'You would have to say it . . .'

'Fanny, will you marry me?'

'Oh, yes,' she replied, and immediately wondered if she should have spoken so quickly.

10

For two days Eliza had pretended to be sleepy. She took the medicine from Lucy and would either hold it in her mouth if she was watching, or deposit it in the bowl of flowers beside her if her back was turned. Twice Hedworth had been with her and had stood over her while she swallowed it so that twice she had had to force herself to vomit.

Dr Talbot called, morning and evening. He was dour, short with her, and lacked charm. When he examined her she felt like a specimen, not a human being. Once or twice she had toyed with the idea of confiding in him her fears but his steely stare had put her off – just as well when she overheard him and her husband whispering, late one evening, on the other side of her room. Eliza had always had sharp hearing.

'It would be better if we had a second opinion,' she

heard the doctor say, quite distinctly.

'Aren't you competent to decide?'

She could not catch the doctor's response.

'Do you know of anyone amenable?'

The doctor had evidently turned away from her for she could not make out a word of what he was saying.

'She's always . . .' Now Hedworth was moving about the room and she only caught snatches. 'Hysteria . . .' she heard and then, 'mute . . .'

She hadn't heard everything, but she had heard enough: she had kept thinking of going, making plans, but that time was over. Now she should act and as soon as possible. The main hurdle was her health – she was still weak and listless. She had to find strength from somewhere.

They left her room. *Amenable* – she hadn't liked the sound of that. But, then, if another doctor was coming, perhaps she could talk to him, make him understand her predicament. Those two men tonight had been conspiring, she was sure. A plan was afoot and the animal instinct that, until now, she had not known she possessed told her it was unlikely to be to her advantage. She rang for her maid.

'So sleepy . . .' She stretched her arms over her head and spoke in the thick voice she had mastered to fool everyone. 'Early night . . .'

'Very wise. Shall I do your pillows? Anything I can fetch you?'

'Tell my husband I am settling, will you?'

To be on the safe side she waited another hour then lit one candle only. From a basket under her bed she took her sewing-box and from it the nightdress she had been working on for the last couple of nights, in just such a poor light as this. She had inherited the loose gems from her grandmother. With meticulous care she was sewing them into the inside of the nightdress. She had reasoned that if she ran away in a day dress its weight and tightness would hamper her progress. The light night clothes would make movement easier. She must complete the task tonight. Then it would be ready for the first opportunity she had.

Dr Forbes was a kind man and this new instinct told her he would not betray her. She would go to him, beg him to hide her until she could get right away. France, she had thought, might be a good place – she spoke good French, thanks to Miss Chester. Dear woman, if only she were here, if only . . .

The next day dawned extremely hot. 'I think I would like to sit in the garden for a little while,' she said, in her slurred voice to her husband.

'Just for a short time. It's so good to see you improving, isn't it, Lucy?'

'Yes, milord,' said Lucy.

Such a lot of paraphernalia to get her to the garden! A bamboo *chaise-longue* was placed in the small rose garden, a large parasol above it. Hedworth had wanted her on the terrace but she had asked to be here, claiming she wanted to see the roses. The truth was that it was the only part of the garden near to the house that could not be seen from it. A procession of footmen brought her pillows and blankets, underneath which she was certain she would expire from heat stroke. Lemonade, books, her sewing materials. 'We can't take any chances, can we?' her oh-so-solicitous husband said, patting another blanket on to her, ensuring that Lucy and the footmen heard him. 'Shall I stay with you, my love?'

'No, it will be dull for you, I'm such poor company.' Once alone she kicked off the covers. That was better. She was worried about the strength in her legs. She had been in bed for over a week now and was, she knew, still weak from loss of blood and inactivity. She had been walking in her room at dead of night, trying to regain some strength, but today she wanted to walk a little in this garden, convinced that the exercise combined with fresh air would strengthen her.

Her day in the garden had invigorated her – a few more days like that and she would be so much fitter. But events conspired against her. This evening Hedworth had hit her. She was still not sure why: she had been acting as though she was drugged, and perhaps had overplayed her hand.

'Did you contact your aunt?'

'I beg your pardon?' She looked at him as if trying to focus when she could see him perfectly well.

'Your aunt?'

'Which aunt?'

'You have only one aunt as far as I'm aware. Did you?'

'What?'

'Contact her?'

'How?'

And that was when he had hit her, right across her face. His signet ring cut her lip and blood dripped on to the sheet. She sat with a stupid expression and watched the droplets. 'Pretty . . .' she slurred.

'Oh, what's the deuced point?' He stormed out of the room. Eliza held a handkerchief to her torn lip and sank back on her pillows, safe for the time being now that he had gone. But the fear crept back and her skin crawled. She felt sick and knew she was about to retch. So she acted instead.

At any minute Lucy would be here. She whipped off the sheet and turned the top to the bottom – she didn't want the maid to know that anything further was amiss. Quickly she changed into her jewelled nightdress, stuffing the one she had been wearing back into her sewing-box, hiding the dressing-gown under her pillow. She unclipped her hair and turned her face into it so that Lucy could not see the cut on her lip or the bruising that was forming. Then she pretended sleep.

The maid was taken in: she pottered about the bedroom and dressing room for five minutes, tidying up, then quietly left the room.

Eliza lay awake until after one in the morning, listening to the creaking of the house, the owls hooting, all the dear familiar sounds of her home, which she had hoped never to leave, but now knew she must if she was to survive. By two she decided that Hedworth, if not in bed and asleep, would be drunk and as insensible as she had pretended to be.

She slipped on a pair of stockings, holding them in place with her garters – that was silly of her: she could have sewn gems into them too. She put on boots – they would look odd but, hopefully, no one would see her. She intended to escape through the Great Wood and slippers would be torn to shreds in there.

In her dressing-gown, she turned the door handle with bated breath. The lamps on the landing had been extinguished, a sign that Hedworth was in bed. Like a wraith she glided along the landing. At the door to her mother's room she stopped. Her heart leapt to her mouth. Was it her imagination or had she heard a woman scream? A whiplash through the air. Full of fear she began to run down the main stairs. At the foot of the great staircase, memory, no doubt triggered by her fear, cruelly returned. She knew why the stairs made her sad. She was her mother, fleeing in the night. She put her hand to her mouth to stop herself crying out. Nothing stirred, the whole house was sleeping. Her mother had left to her cries, but there was no one to regret Eliza's leaving. In a strange way this galvanised her: her mother had got away, and so could she.

She scurried across the hall to the doors. The glass-panelled inner ones opened easily, but the large outer door with the great brass lock was difficult. But at last she was outside. Here she could have wished she had on her slippers for her boots made a dreadful crunching noise on the gravel. But so far, so good. She raced across the knot garden. In a strange way she was enjoying herself: she was afraid, yes, but exhilarated too. At last she was doing something to help herself. At last she was about to be free of him.

She skimmed down the stone steps to the lake. Her presence alerted a couple of ducks, who called out in alarm at her arrival and took noisy flight. She ran round the lake. At the point where she had once taken the path to Jerome, she paused momentarily. To get her breath back, she pretended to herself. She wished he was not so angry with her, and she regretted that she had never been able to make amends to him and his family. Once away she could write to him and hopefully explain herself. What a curse they must think she was.

The hand on her shoulder made her scream with fright.

'And where do you think you are going?'

'Hedworth!'

'Were you running away from your husband?'

'No, Hedworth. It was so hot and I couldn't sleep, I needed some fresh air. I needed to walk . . .'

'As if all the furies were chasing you?' He sounded amused but she was not fooled: she had heard that voice before. 'You do realise, Eliza, my love, that you've forgotten your play-acting. You are speaking in a very normal voice. Now how can that be?' He lunged towards her but she sidestepped and ran as fast as she could around the edge of the lake, the reeds tearing at her clothes, stumbling as she did so. 'Stop! This instant!' He was catching her up, she could hear the thudding of his feet over the pounding of the blood in her ears. If she could get to the jetty. If only the little boat was there . . . She reached it and ran along it to the end, her steps making it rattle, the noise reverberating across the still waters of the lake putting more birds to flight. She could just make out the wooden ladder that led to where the boat should be moored. Frantically she felt in the dark for the mooring rope. She found it just as Hedworth reached her and grabbed hold of her. 'Oh, no, you don't!' She pummelled him with her fists but his strength was too much for her and she could feel herself weakening. She kicked him hard in the shins with her leather boots and, for good measure, bit his hand. He reeled about the jetty, swearing with pain, pulling her with him, right to the edge. She pushed and pulled, he tugged and threatened. Together they toppled over into the deep, black water.

The weight of her waterlogged clothes and her heavy boots dragged her down into the water. It was as if she were being pulled into the depths. In a way, it was a pleasant feeling. And then she felt the reeds on the bottom curl sensuously around her legs. With one mighty kick, she freed herself, and shot to the surface.

She looked about her, there was no sign of him. Had he climbed out? She trod water peering into the gloom for a sign of him. Which bank was he on? She was becoming cold. Eliza set out for the edge of the lake. She had not swum since she was a child, and was hampered by her trailing night-clothes, the weight of the jewels she had sewn into them. With difficulty she reached the shore, pulled herself out and sat for a second in the reeds at the edge, getting her breath. She had to run. She had to find the strength. She stood up, wavering slightly.

'Help me!'

She looked out into the lake to see Hedworth floundering. He waved then sank under the water only to rise again. 'Help! I can't swim!' she heard him call. She stood there in the darkness, shivering with cold, exhausted, then plunged back in and swam towards her drowning husband.

11

Cold, she felt so cold. Her body shook violently. Her teeth were chattering. She could not remember where she was and she could not concentrate further, to work out why she was in water. Instead she tried to address the bone-chilling cold and how to combat it. She felt such tiredness and longed to rest, to close her eyes and dream. Eventually the tiredness won and conquered the shivering and she lapsed into sleep, except it was not true slumber, more that narrow state between sleep and unconsciousness.

'I've found her!' The voice had shouted so loudly that she stirred.

'Here, over here, she's here!' another voice yelled.

Eliza felt herself being lifted, heard voices shouting, was aware of lanterns held aloft. 'Oh, thank God, oh, my poor darling!' It was Hedworth. She wanted to shout, to warn, to explain, but she couldn't find the words. She seemed to have forgotten how to form them, how to speak. She felt herself being grabbed from the arms of the man who had lifted her out of the lake. Hedworth held her tightly to him. 'Sweet one, speak to me.' And he covered her face with kisses.

'Is she alive?' another voice asked.

'Get the doctor! Send someone to get him here fast. Use my horse. Go!' Hedworth was shouting hysterically.

'Which doctor?'

'Forbes.' She was not sure if she had spoken the word or merely thought it. And when she tried again the effort was too much for her.

'Talbot. He's staying at the inn in Cheriton Speke. Go, man, for God's sake go.'

'I've a blanket here, milord.' She recognised the voice of her maid and tried to move her head to see her, but she couldn't.

'We must get her into the warm. Light a fire. Hot drinks.'

'Milord, look at her head, there's blood – there's a big bump.'

'Lucy, do as I say!'

She fell against her husband as she was carried up the

steps from the lake, she couldn't help it, though she loathed being close to him, touched by him. She knew they had reached the knot garden for she could smell thyme ... Then the sound of gravel ... She began to struggle ... No! Stop! She was going the wrong way ... She didn't want to go into the house ...

'My sweet one, calm yourself. You're safe now. We're nearly there.' Evidently they were not alone since Hedworth was speaking as if soothing her kindly. But his voice made hysteria build inside her.

The portraits on the staircase looked down on her with their implacable stares as they passed by. They were moving slowly now for the flight of stairs was long and her husband, judging by his laboured breath, was tiring.

'I ordered a fire!' he shouted.

'I'm lighting it now, milord. I'm sorry, milord. I was putting a warming pan in her bed.' Lucy sounded close to tears.

'Get another blanket, she's wet.' There was a pause, Eliza found herself wafting in and out of consciousness. Each time she was aware for a little longer, but she was not about to let him know that. Scenes were flooding back, bad scenes, frightening ones. Eventually she was laid on the bed.

'Will she wake up?'

'Of course she will, stupid girl! Undress her. Bathe her with hot water.' She heard his footsteps, heard the bedroom door close. She was going to have to marshal her thoughts, she was going to have to concentrate ... It was so difficult ... Think!

Poor Lucy. He never said please or thank you to the servants, she'd noticed that before. Her grandmother would not have approved of him from the start, behaving in such a way. 'Treat your servants and anyone who serves you in the way you would wish to be treated yourself. They'll stay loyal to you then,' Lady Gwendoline had advised. Why should she remember that now? Because it had stopped her thinking of what had happened down at the lake.

'There, milady. Let me take these wet clothes off you. There. Arm up, I'll help you . . .' Lucy chatted away as she undressed her. She was probably scared and finding it a comfort, Eliza decided. She would have liked to reassure her, tell her she would be all right, but she could not form the words. It was probably for the best – she could not be sure of Lucy. 'Well, this is a ruined nightdress and no mistake. And what a weight! Anything in the pockets?' There went her jewels, her hidden cache. Would Lucy keep them or return them to Hedworth?

There was a tap on the door. 'I've got the hot milk you wanted, Lucy. And Cook said to lace it with brandy.'

'Thanks, Sally. The cook's up?'

'The whole house is. What a night! There's no point in going back to bed, is there?'

'What's the time?'

'Half five.'

'Already!'

So, thought Eliza, she had been down by the lake for four hours. No wonder she had been so cold. But why?

'I don't know how I'm to get this drink down her, she's fast asleep – or worse.'

'Cor, look at that bump on her forehead! Looks like someone whopped her one.'

'Or she hit it on . . . I don't know, something, poor woman.'

Suddenly Eliza remembered and almost cried out. They had been standing on the bank of the lake, she exhausted to the point of collapse after having dragged her panicking husband, who was fighting and clawing at her every inch of the way, out of the dangerous water. And Hedworth's fist, with no warning, arcing through the air at her face. 'Don't you dare leave me!' he screamed, as she had crumpled on the ground.

'Here, I think she stirred – least, her face went all screwed up,' Sally whispered urgently.

Lucy bent over her. 'Milady, it's Lucy. Can you hear me?' She spoke loudly. 'Nah, she's gone peepy-by. Let's hope she stays that way awhile. He's less likely to hit her if she's asleep.'

'Does he?'

'He's a right bastard.'

'Not fair, is it, when she's such a lovely lady?'

'Goes to show, though, don't it? It don't matter if you're rich or poor if you've married a swiper. The bruises hurt just the same.'

'This nightdress and dressing-gown don't half pong. Got slimy weed on it, look. Do you want me to take it and give it to the laundry-maid?'

'No, leave it there. She's very fond of that one, she likes me to wash it myself for her. Here, give me a hand getting this clean one over her head. She's a dead weight.'

Goodbye, jewels, Eliza thought.

'Nice smell you've put on her.'

'Jasmine, it's her favourite. What was that?' Lucy stopped in her task.

'Cover her up, neat, like. I'll see who it is.' Eliza heard the rustle of Lucy's dress as she moved to open the door.

'You can go,' Hedworth ordered.

'Yes, milord. I'll just . . .' She could hear Lucy moving by the bed, collecting her sodden linen.

'You can imagine my shock, Talbot.'

'The lake, you say?'

'Yes . . . I told you maids to go, now!' There was silence until the door closed again. 'They all gossip and I'd rather speak to you in private.'

'But of course.'

'Is she unconscious still?'

Eliza felt Dr Talbot take hold of her wrist. Then he

opened her eye and she forced herself to stare unseeingly. 'Her pulse is fast. She's deeply unconscious. We shan't be disturbing her, if that's what was worrying you.' What an incompetent man, she thought. What now?

'I wouldn't want her to hear the sorry tale, she might have forgotten all about it when she awakens. She will, won't she?'

'Don't fret, Lord Alford. She's young and strong.'

'You see, I checked her when I went to bed. I always do before retiring. It must have been two at least. She was gone – the bed empty. That's when I woke the staff and we fanned out over the estate. Luckily my footman found her.'

'It was a chill night. You're fortunate she's alive.'

'It wasn't that cold.'

'No, but having been in the lake, which, no doubt, was at a very low temperature – even on the hottest day lake water is cold. And this bump and graze here on her forehead! Tut tut! It could have been much worse. How did she come by that? It looks as if she was hit by something.'

'There's a jetty and a boat.'

'Was she near them when she was found?'

'I'm not sure. Yes, I think so.'

Liar! I had managed to stumble to the far side of the lake after saving *your* life!

'She seemed to be much better.'

'She was not taking the medicine you left her, I discovered. I shall, of course, dismiss the maid. She had strict instructions to watch her take it.'

'Why did Lady Alford refuse it?'

'She said it made her feel drowsy, worse.'

'So, she couldn't have gone for a walk and simply fallen into the lake?'

'There's no doubt. She left a note. Here . . . You see, it states quite clearly that she could not go on. That her

464

sadness . . .' Hedworth had injected a fine waver into his voice as if fighting tears.

Liar!

'You did warn me of her mental instability. The loss of the child perhaps made her like this. It's common. A month or two with me and she will recover.'

'And what if she does not?'

'Well, then, Lord Alford, I would suggest she remains with me. I have a high reputation for the treatment of the insane.'

'No!' Eliza shouted, before she could stop herself. Insane! She sat up in bed but winced at the pain in her head when she did so. Her astonished husband and doctor stared at her.

'He's lying.' She pointed at Hedworth.

'She's play-acting again, pretending to be asleep, to be unconscious. Is that normal, I ask you?'

'Don't listen to him, Doctor. Don't you see? He wants me locked away. He wants me certified insane. That way he can get control of my money.'

'She's obsessed with her money, fears she will lose it.'

'There, there, Lady Alford. You've had a shock, a nasty accident to your head.'

'It was not an accident, that was my husband's work. He hit me. He was angry with me and I had just risked my life rescuing him. And this is the gratitude he shows me.'

'But he says—'

'Why should I kill myself?'

'This letter—'

'He wrote it, not I. I was not trying to die.' She was sobbing. 'You must believe me.'

'Calm yourself, Lady Alford. I fear for your health. Here, take this, it will help you—' With one swift movement she hit the glass out of his hand. It flew over the carpet.

'You see, Doctor? You see how wild she is? What an

imagination she has? Listen to him, my darling. Listen to him, for both our sakes.'

'You liar! Get out! Get out of my room – get out of my life!' She was pounding the bed-covers with her fists. 'He's wicked. He's evil! He's . . .' But she did not finish the sentence for the doctor clamped a foul-smelling cloth over her face, and although she struggled, although she held her breath as long as she could, she had to inhale, then felt the dark clouds pile in on top of her.

12

Eliza woke in the morning feeling as if her head had swollen to twice its normal size. She lifted it cautiously from the pillow. The light from the window pierced her eyes as if it were needles.

'So, we've decided to wake, have we?' A motherly looking woman was sitting beside her, dressed in navy-blue cotton, her full-skirted dress many years out of date, a starched apron wound round her ample waist.

'Where am I?'

'Safe. Now, let's have a sip of water. You must be thirsty.'

Eliza was grateful for the water for she was parched and there was a horrible taste in her mouth. She drank deeply but it did not help for it had a strange metallic taste – or was that because of her mouth?

The room was white. She lay quietly, collecting herself. The walls, the curtains, the rug on the floor, the bed, the flowers in the white china vase, even the bars at the window. Her stomach lurched. They were real, not a dream. She was locked up. It didn't take her long to realise where. She put her hands over her eyes.

The woman laughed. 'Everyone does that when they see those bars. Nothing to be afraid of, my dear. They're to keep the nasties out, not you in.'

Despite her fear she went to sleep again. And woke and slept. She had no way of knowing for how long.

Eliza pushed back the bed-covers and swung her legs over the side of the bed.

'Now, you've had a nice long sleep but there's no point in rushing things. I don't think that's a good idea. You might be a bit wobbly on your legs. Best stay there awhile.' The woman had a distinct West Country accent, which was a comfort of sorts since it meant she was still near home. Eliza chose to ignore the suggestion and stood up. The world tilted for a second, but she held on to the end of the bed until it righted itself. 'Now where are you going?'

'I want to look out of the window.'

'Shall I help you? Not much of a view there, to be sure.'

'I can manage.' She was not sure why but it seemed imperative that she relied on this woman for nothing. She peered out. In front was a large and pleasant-looking garden. There was a red-brick wall on top of which she could see shards of glass embedded. But they were on a hill and a steep one at that for over the top of the wall, in the distance, she could just make out the tops of two towers. 'Is that to keep the nasties out too?' She pointed at the wall.

'Well, you're a card and no mistake.' The woman laughed.

'Is that the cathedral I can just spy?' The dizziness had passed and she was feeling much better.

'Bless you, it is, and a finer you'll never find.'

'I like to go and listen to the music.'

'A better choir doesn't exist.'

'You're obviously an Exonian?'

'Born and bred.' The woman beamed with pride. Eliza felt her body sag with the release of tension. At least that was one good thing: she was even nearer to Harcourt Barton than she had dared hope.

'And you are?'

'Eglantyne Smith.'

'What a beautiful name.'

'You think so?'

'The name for the sweet briar, isn't it?'

'Well I never did. How did you know that?'

'I can't remember.' She turned from the window. 'I'm hungry.'

'That's a good Lady Alford. That's what Eglantyne likes to hear.' She crossed the room and rang a bell set in the side of the fireplace. Eliza was disappointed: she had hoped the nurse would go to fetch her food and then she could have run for it. But it was not to be.

'This is Dr Talbot's establishment?'

'And a better doctor you'd travel far to find. He works miracles. I've seen raving lunatics wheeled in here and walk out sane as me after a year or two.'

'I'm not a raving lunatic, though.'

'No, of course you're not. Just a little bit muddled. The good doctor will set you to rights before you know where you are. Now, that'll be your tea, dinner, breakfast . . . I'm not sure what to call it since you've been asleep that long.' She bustled to the door and returned with a tray of tea and sandwiches. White china, of course, Eliza noticed.

'How long?'

'You were brought in Tuesday morning early and it's now mid-morning Thursday – I was never any good at sums. But a long sleep whichever way you look at it.'

Over forty-eight hours! Dear God!

'When shall I see the doctor?'

'He's not here today. He's at his other asylum.'

'Where's that?'

'Up Somerset way. But don't you worry, you won't be moved there and leave Eglantyne. Only his worst cases go there, and you're not going to be one of them, are you?'

Eliza began to eat the sandwich. How was she to get out of here? Did this woman stay with her all the time?

Certainly whenever Eliza drifted out of sleep she was always there, pleasant enough, but her presence was threatening in itself. She took a sip of tea. She would wait and see what the night brought. As she munched the food she noticed that her vision was playing tricks. Eglantyne looked as if the edges of her had been erased. And the window was receding. There must have been something . . .

'There, my lovely, that's nice, isn't it? That old medicine keeping you nice and quiet for Eglantyne . . .'

Panic was forming but the will to do anything was deserting her fast . . .

'What is my treatment to be, Dr Talbot?' Eliza was not sure how many days she had been here: one muddled into the next.

'Peace and calm to balance the brain, rid you of your wild dreams.'

'They've stopped.' It was best to agree with everything he said.

'Precisely as I planned. The cure works.'

'But I'm not sure there's anything wrong with me.' Oh dear, she hadn't meant to disagree.

'Everyone says that when they first come here.' When he smiled his lips, which she did not normally notice, appeared rose red in the nest of his beard, as if he had scarlet worms for a mouth. 'And do you think it was normal to throw yourself into a deep lake in the middle of the night?'

'To escape my husband, yes. He beats me.'

'He said you often accused him of this. He seems a remarkably placid man to me.'

'He did this and this.' She pointed angrily at her lip and forehead.

'He says the injuries were self-inflicted, that you have done this in the past. But you are not going to do so in the future, for I shall make sure you don't.'

She was on dangerous ground here. The key to

getting out was to agree to everything he said, she was sure. But on the other hand she did not want to spend any more time in that room, whose whiteness would surely drive her mad faster than anything. 'Do I have to sleep so much? Can I not leave my room for a little while? You see, I like to come here to this lovely room with books and pictures and colour. My room is so white.' She laughed apologetically, not wishing to upset the man who had her freedom in his hands.

'Progress!' The doctor rubbed his hands together with satisfaction. 'Not yet. I don't think you are ready. No excitement.' He wagged his finger at her.

'And the sleeping? I do realise I am being given medicine in my water.' She said this in a tone of reason, as if she were not in the least bit offended at being dosed without her knowledge, and smiled sweetly.

'You see, Lady Alford . . .' He stood now and, with his thumbs in his waistcoat, began to rock back and forth. 'I have a theory that when things go wrong in life then the brain becomes unbalanced. That too many electrical charges have entered the head and are rushing about, which confuses the patient. So you are not ill, as many would say you are, merely inharmonious.'

'That's good to hear.'

'And the white room and sleep are my balm to your poor head. Nothing discordant, no shocks to the system and, hey presto, the balance restores and order is resumed. Colour is introduced gradually. First pastels then stronger colours, until finally you could be in a red room and remain in equilibrium.'

'How interesting. And how long, might I ask, does this treatment take?' she said, while thinking what balderdash it sounded.

'After this first course we take the minerals, the hydrotherapy. I think you are going to be a good subject . . .' He studied her, stroking his beard. 'Now, this is only a "perhaps", nothing more. It might take much longer . . . but, say, two years.'

At this news the Turkey rug appeared to spring up and almost hit her. 'Such a short time!' Her voice was high with tension. She hoped he didn't notice.

Two days later, on her next visit to his room, although she had intended to say nothing critical, she said, 'It's the whiteness, I need colour. I need people.'

'Are you questioning my expertise?'

'No, of course not. I have every faith in you as my doctor.'

'I think you lie. Come with me.'

She followed him out. His room was only a few steps from hers so she was pleased when they turned in the opposite direction. A change of scenery, a chance to get an idea of the plan of the place. They went out of a door across a pretty courtyard, through a building and out the other side. It was wonderful to be in the sun, and she grabbed the opportunity to take huge breaths of fresh air – Eglantyne did not like the window open: evil spirits, she said. The doctor pushed open another door. Inside there was a woman dressed like Eglantyne. She bobbed to the doctor, then picked up a bunch of keys and opened a gate in the wall. They went down some steps and through another gate. Finally they came to a door.

'Enter, Lady Alford, and see the alternative to your little white room.'

Eliza stepped on to what amounted to a balcony. The stench assailed her before the noise. She did not want to look down for she knew what she was about to see.

'This is where my guests come to view the patients. Look, Lady Alford. Such interesting specimens.'

The large room was crowded with an endless moving group of women. Some were respectably dressed, most were not. They all talked but not, it seemed, to each other. Some had sores, others were covered in deep scratches. 'Self-inflicted, for the most part,' the doctor told her. Two sat on the floor and rocked back and forth, like the metronome she had used to learn to play the piano. Another banged her head incessantly against the wall. Several were sobbing, ugly, rasping noises, saliva dribbling from their mouths. Spying her, they rushed across the room to plead for her help.

'An interesting case, the one on the right. Her child died. She became *difficult*. She accused her husband of many dreadful crimes, then tried to hang herself – you can still see the marks on her neck.' He pointed. 'Mad, you see, the balance irreparably damaged.'

'I want to go.'

'I thought you might. Back to the little white room?'

'Yes, please.' She looked at the floor.

'Good. For, you see, if you are not content in that room then this is the alternative. You should be grateful your husband is willing to pay for the extra comfort and care you enjoy. A considerable sum, I hasten to add.'

At that she screamed, swore and ranted, vowing revenge. Round and round the shrieking echoed in her head. Not that the doctor heard. She reserved her despair for herself.

Chapter Seven
2 September – October 1877

In the weeks Eliza had been in the hospital she had learnt several things. The first was that Eglantyne was not to be trusted: anything she said to her was repeated to the doctor. When she had first arrived she had concluded that it was wisest not to argue with him or query anything, but to be acquiescent in all matters. Then he would see she was not mad and she would be quickly released. But, to her horror, she discovered that he regarded this as suspect too. She no longer knew how to behave, for whatever she did was twisted and used as further proof of her mental instability.

Added to this equation was the realisation that the deeper she became involved in this confusing situation, the more she wondered how long she would be able to maintain her own sanity.

Hedworth's motives were obvious now and she berated herself for not having seen more clearly what he was about. She had worried, at one point, that he wanted her dead. He hadn't, he needed her alive. She had to be declared of unsound mind, then he would have legal access to her money and could do as he wished with it. And if this doctor discharged her, it would be only a matter of time until her husband found another.

Her hopes had been raised when she was told that another doctor would examine her, to give another opinion. She supposed this was necessary legally if she was to be kept locked up. Surely a doctor not involved with her and her husband would see that she was sane.

She was convinced now that Hedworth had bribed Dr Talbot.

When the second physician came she could smell the fumes of whisky on him before he had crossed the room. Then she knew that all was lost.

Except it mustn't be, she told herself.

Having decided that her husband needed her alive, she had less fear of being consigned to the terrible wing of madness. There, Eglantyne had told her, illness was rife, death was common, attacks and fights frequent. She was to be kept in ease, safe and protected, but no amount of comfort could make this white room anything but a prison.

But now it wasn't all white. Eliza was being rewarded. Every other day another colour was added. First there had been a pink bowl, then a picture in pastels of a still-life, and a silver box. She gushed her pleasure, hoping it was right to do so, but she was rapidly reaching the conclusion that while she did not need to be committed the doctor did.

Committed: a terrifying word, yet once it had been innocent of trauma to her: She was committed to Harcourt, to Bumble – she had been committed to Jerome. *No!* Don't think of him . . . But how difficult it was.

She must stop feeling sorry for herself. She must begin to work on a plan.

'Eglantyne, do you think it would be possible for me to have some clothes? I feel so old being dressed in night attire all the time.'

'Old! Well, there's a thing. I'll ask the doctor.'

Two days later some of her clothes appeared.

'Eglantyne, do you think it would ever be possible for me to walk in the garden? I'm a country woman, I need fresh air.'

'I'll ask the doctor.'

That day she was allowed out for fifteen minutes in the sun. Long enough for her to see that in the wall of the garden was a gate, and long enough to see that it was of wood, with a ledge across it, and wire on the top but . . . She was tall. If she ran . . .

'Jock, my dear, I cannot sleep with worry.'

'I think she's in Exeter at the Cedars.'

'But I didn't say what concerned me.'

'I know, but I knew.'

What a comfort he was, how sensitive to her.

'I'm afraid I don't know the city well enough . . .'

'Brace yourself, Fanny, my love, it's a lunatic asylum.'

Fanny thought she would faint. As it was she had to sit down. 'How do you know?' she asked, pulling herself together. This was no time for feminine vapours.

'The brother of one of my patients is Dr Talbot's coachman. I had cause to treat him today. He happened to mention there had been a drama up at the big house a few weeks ago and his brother had been called out at dead of night.'

'What had happened?'

'I don't think I should tell you.'

'I have to know.'

He took her hand. 'Eliza tried to drown herself.'

'That is absolute rubbish!' Fanny sat bolt upright with indignation.

'I understand. It must be hard for you to believe.'

'Because it cannot be. Eliza would never try to kill herself. She's a happy person, optimistic . . .'

'She was when you knew her, but maybe she has changed. It is often the least likely ones who do.'

'But she's a strong swimmer and she wouldn't have chosen drowning.'

'Is she? You've seen her swim?'

'No, but she told me. There's a lake there that her father built and as a child she could swim back and forth for hours with no fear, just pleasure. When she, well,' Fanny waved her hand at the delicacy of the information, 'when she reached a certain age, it was thought unwise that she should continue.'

'Dr Whitney, my predecessor, was convinced that swimming damaged a woman so that she could not bear children.' His tone was dismissive – plainly he did not share this opinion, Fanny thought. 'However, my love, there is worse. She didn't just try to kill herself. I was told she had attacked her husband with a duelling sword and, thinking she had killed him, mad with grief, she had jumped into the lake.'

'Eliza could not harm another of God's creatures and I would stake my life on that.' Surely he did not believe this gossip. Fanny was appalled. She had to make him see. 'Jock, if she was unbalanced I would be the first person to say she must be locked up for her own protection. But *if* she was, isn't her house large enough to keep her there? She could have nurses day and night. *If* that was the case she'd be happier at Harcourt, I know. And money would not be a problem: she could live to a hundred and still afford care. Why remove her?'

He was frowning as he mulled over this information. 'You have a point, Fanny. We must act.'

'We have to go and see Lord Alford again, unpleasant as that may be. If we get nowhere with him, we must go to this place and ask to see Eliza. I think we should visit the family lawyer too. And, lastly, even if her aunt didn't see fit to reply to my letter, I think we must tell her family she has been incarcerated.'

'*If* she has. At the moment it is only a rumour.'

'So many ifs. It's so worrying and confusing.' She put her head on one side. 'Listen – Amelia is calling. I must go to her. She is fractious today, accusing me of keeping her from her daughter. Who can blame her?'

'If Eliza isn't released soon, I fear that she may never meet her mother.'

'How sad,' said Fanny, while thinking how lucky it might be for Eliza – not that she would dream of saying this to Jock: he saw only good in people and might look at her differently if he knew how she could sometimes shock herself with the wicked ideas she had.

'Don't you think you have interfered in my affairs enough, Miss Chester? You caused much dismay and concern in the family by sending an unconstrained letter to my wife's aunt.'

'I was worried and you were obstructive to my concerns, Lord Alford.' Fanny was not going to be intimidated even if her innards felt as if they had melted.

'Obstructive?'

'You wouldn't let me see her.'

'On her doctor's instructions. What is obstructive about that, pray?'

'But we were such old friends, and—'

Alford held up his hand to stop her. 'No more about this so-called mother.'

'I was about to say I was concerned. I had heard—'

'Fanny!' Jock spoke sharply, evidently aware that she was on the point of mentioning the beating. He was right, of course, he always was.

Alford looked from one to the other. 'Surely you haven't been gossiping, Doctor? About my wife?'

'No, he has not. I was about to say—' she blustered.

'Yes?'

'I can't remember.'

'How strange. Is that all?'

'Will you confirm where she is, Lord Alford?'

'No.'

'Then there is nothing more to say.' She felt down-hearted, as if she had betrayed Eliza, but for the life of her she could not think what else to say to this obdurate man.

'Evidently not.'

Fanny and Jock had just reached the drawing-room door when he called after them, 'I should appreciate it if you did not gossip to my neighbours either. Good day.'

Once they were outside, they agreed that they felt like naughty schoolchildren who had been reprimanded by their teacher.

'Wouldn't you think if he cared about her he would be pleased that people were concerned?'

'You would, Fanny, but perhaps he does not care. I think Lord Alford believes he is a lot cleverer than he really is. These neighbours we are supposed to have talked to, he must mean the Gilpin family – they are the nearest. Perhaps they have called and are worried too. Should we visit them?'

'Why not? What else can happen? We can only be thrown out a second time.' It was so much easier to be brave with Jock at her side.

But they weren't. Mrs Gilpin was pleased to see them. It took some time to get to the subject of Eliza but when it was broached she said, 'I'm sure Lord Alford is quite capable of looking after his wife as he sees fit. My girls have called countless times, haven't you, Primrose?'

'Yes, but he wouldn't let either Jonquil or me see her, yet she and Jonquil were friends.'

'Primrose, what have I told you?' Mrs Gilpin looked as cross as her pleasant face would allow. 'I prevailed on Mr Gilpin himself to go, since Primrose made such a fuss. And he did. He had a most pleasant evening with dear Lord Alford.'

'He came back inebriated.'

'Primrose! There's no need for such talk. What will our guests think?' Mrs Gilpin rearranged her cuffs in agitation.

'But there is, Mama. My father never drinks to excess, Miss Chester, Doctor. He has little time for those who do. He claims his drink was interfered with.'

'He never said any such thing to me,' Mrs Gilpin said indignantly.

'He didn't want you upset.'

'But *you* do. Well, I really—'

'Whatever for?' asked Fanny quickly, hoping to forestall a mother-and-daughter argument.

'To make him more amenable of course. Papa was not satisfied so he went to the Cedars and spoke to the doctor there, who confirmed she was a patient. He told him she was deranged.' At this Jonquil burst into tears. 'Oh, Jonquil, do stop. You're not helping.'

'But he never told me he'd been!' Mrs Gilpin waited.

'Again, Mama, he didn't want you worrying. He said it was none of our business and we must not involve ourselves.'

'And he was right. Lord Alford is our neighbour. He needs our sympathy, not suspicion.'

'And what about poor Eliza? She is as sane as any of us.'

'There was that unfortunate business with the farm labourer. That was hardly sane of her but everything was all right in the end.'

'Jerome is a farmer, not a labourer.' Fanny felt quite protective towards the Barnards.

'He might have been once but he's a labourer now.' Mrs Gilpin looked triumphant to have won a point at last. 'Lord Alford threw him off the estate, you know. He works for my husband now. A pleasant enough young man but hardly suitable.'

'This story gets worse and worse. The poor Barnards.'

They took the tea offered, although Fanny really wanted to leave. It was another half-hour before they could decently be on their way.

'Amazing, isn't it? If you've a title it seems you can get away with murder.'

'Jock, don't even say that word! But, yes, it would appear so. Except for Primrose. A sensible girl, wouldn't you say? So, what about the asylum?' Fanny shuddered at the thought of her Eliza locked up in such a place, seeing and hearing sights and sounds that no young woman should ever have to witness.

'I feel that as a doctor I cannot go.'

'Why? Just because he's another doctor? What if he is a bad one? What then?'

'No, it's because he will probably know that I was once Eliza's doctor and if I query him he will put it down to professional jealousy. And will tell us even less.' He did not add that from all he had heard the so-called Dr Talbot was a charlatan. Fanny had enough to worry about.

So Fanny went alone and was not in the least surprised when she was refused admittance. It seemed that nothing could be done. As a last resort she again wrote to Minnie Wickham. Surely she would intercede.

'I've a visitor, Lady Alford. Would you mind if I received her in here? It's just that I'm not supposed to leave you alone, as you must have realised.'

'I understand, Eglantyne. What a trial I must be to you.'

'You're one of the nicest patients I've ever had to sit with.'

'Why, thank you, Eglantyne.' And you are the nicest gaoler I've ever had, she thought to herself. 'It will be pleasant to see a new face.'

But that afternoon when the visitor was shown in the face was familiar. 'Lady Alford, this is my niece.'

'Lucy!'

'I thought I'd be a surprise. I'd have come sooner but things have been difficult.' Finding a new position with no references had taken time.

'You two know each other?' Eglantyne looked frightened.

'Yes, Lucy was my maid, and a good one too.' She must forget the tale-telling, she needed friends now, and Lucy, perhaps, might be a friend, or was she yet another spy? Whom could she trust?

'But you're not allowed visitors. What if it was found out?'

'Lucy is your visitor, not mine. Am I going to tell?'

'Well, no. And I did ask the head nurse if my niece could call.'

'So there you are.'

'What about some tea, Aunt Eg?'

'Well, it's not the time . . . And I shouldn't really . . .'

'I'll look after Lady Alford. We're not going anywhere, Aunt Eg!' She grinned.

'Oh, very well, but don't you try nothing, either of you. And I'd best warn you all the doors are locked.'

Lucy waited until her aunt had left to get the tea. 'Have you somewhere you can hide things?'

'Not really. Why?'

'I've these for you.' Lucy poked into her pocket and produced a large man's handkerchief, which sagged with the weight of whatever was inside it.

'Oh, Lucy.' Eliza's eyes filled with tears for there lay the jewels she had sewn into her nightdress. She felt ashamed that she had thought Lucy might steal them. She looked wildly about the room. There was nowhere suitable. 'Give me a couple, that's all I need.' She sorted through them quickly, took two of the most valuable and slipped them into her skirt pocket. 'You take the rest – I have nowhere to hide them.'

'I'll keep them safe until you need them. You've got to get out of here, milady. It's not right.'

'It's so good of you, Lucy, to help me.'

'Well, it's wrong what went on. I *know*, milady. I know he's lied. I know you were running away and not trying to kill yourself. It's got to be put right—'

'What's got to be put right?' asked Eglantyne, as she bustled back in.

'The old crow I work for. She's no idea how to treat servants. Trade, that's what they are.'

Eliza marvelled at how smoothly Lucy had answered the question. She slipped her hand into her pocket and clutched the diamond and the emerald. All those years ago her grandmother had made her learn about gems –

she could not have known how useful the information would be one day. Now Eliza had the wherewithal for an immediate escape. And then she could collect the rest from Lucy . . . But she didn't know where she worked. How could she find her? And already Lucy was getting up to go.

'So, back to my attic room in Mont Le Grand.' Lucy was putting on her shawl. 'I tell you, number seven is a right come-down after Harcourt Barton!'

'Another walk in the garden, Lady Alford? But we had one this morning.'

'Please, Eglantyne, I've such a headache. It must have been the excitement of meeting Lucy again. What a sweet girl she is. Does she take after her mother?'

Eglantyne was always content to talk about her family, and Eliza knew much about the third generation by the time she had put on the jacket of her walking suit and they were in the garden. 'What a lovely evening. You were saying, Eglantyne? Your third cousin twice removed on your mother's side?'

'Yes, well, a right little hussy . . .' They strolled to the far side of the garden. 'And as I say . . .'

'Sorry about this, Aunt Eg.' With one mighty shove, Eliza pushed the older woman to the ground and on to her back, where she lay arms and legs flailing like an overturned tortoise. But Eliza did not see this for she had looped her skirt over her arm, thanking her lucky stars that this one was of a simple cut, and with hardly a bustle to it. She was running across the grass getting as much momentum as she could to leap for the narrow bracing strut positioned half-way up the wooden gate. The wire pierced her gloves but she wasn't aware of that as she hauled herself on to the wall. For a second she was silhouetted against the setting sun then jumped down lightly and was running up the street before the winded Eglantyne had caught her breath sufficiently to shout for help.

At first she ran down towards the city, fear fuelling her speed. She was moving so fast and the hill was so steep that her body acquired its own momentum. People were staring at her – she was hatless, and her skirt was ripped. On their faces she could see their curiosity – it would not be long before someone realised the asylum was up the hill. With difficulty, she slowed and forced herself to walk at a more dignified pace. At least it was dusk now and fewer people were around than there would have been an hour ago. There was an early autumn chill in the air, which was keeping others at home.

She would need to go up the Heavitree Road to reach Mont Le Grand. She walked quickly down Pennsylvania Road. People were still staring, so she lowered her head and scurried along as fast as she could.

Then she slowed for a moment. At this time of the evening, Lucy would be busy with her duties. If she knocked at the door and asked to see the maid she would arouse suspicion. She should find a room, write her a note and post it to her.

There were far more people in the high street, and thus far more to notice her. She turned off it and began to walk through the labyrinth of tiny streets, past St Catherine's almshouse. She entered the cathedral close as the bell for evensong was ringing. Where was she going?

Maggie Bones! She continued walking, keeping close to the wall of the hotel building, up Martin's Lane and back into the high street.

Light was streaming out of Maggie's hotel and she could hear a fine hubbub. At first she held back, then reason told her that one of the best places to hide would be in a crowd. But, as a woman alone in such a place, wouldn't she be more noticeable? What choice had she? The hue and cry must have begun.

She slipped into the hotel, feeling like a criminal. A

maid was walking down the stairs with a tray. 'Excuse me.' Eliza stepped forward. 'Could you tell Maggie Bones a friend is calling?'

'There's no Maggie Bones here.'

Panic rose in Eliza like bile in an upset stomach. 'Then . . .' The maid moved away from her. Eliza grabbed her arm. 'Please, don't go, let me think. Of course . . .' At that moment there was a loud burst of laughter from a room opening on to the hall. They both looked towards the source of the noise. Eliza nearly fainted. She could see not only Dr Talbot, but her husband. Her legs began to buckle.

'You all right, madam? You've gone deathly pale.'

'Mrs Didier, that's who I meant. Quickly. Leave that!' She grabbed the tray from the startled maid. 'I'll look after this, you go and get her – tell her it's urgent.'

How could time move so slowly? she thought. How much longer could she stand here with her tormentors only feet away?

'Miss Eliza!'

The world darkened and Eliza slumped into Maggie's arms. 'Cherry, here, help me.' At the sound of laughter, Maggie turned and saw Lord Alford in the function room. 'Get her into my parlour.' She took a step towards the room but abruptly swung on her heel and followed her maid. 'Cherry, fetch two brandies. Shut the door. Tell *no one* she's here. No one. Understand?'

Maggie began to remove Eliza's torn and blood-stained gloves. 'Blimey, what have you been up to?'

'Don't tell my husband,' Eliza whispered frantically.

'I've already twigged that. I reckoned that if you'd wanted him you'd have called him when you saw him just then. But you had a narrow escape.'

'Will he stay long?'

'Usually.'

'Oh, my God, Maggie, what am I to do?'

'Well, you'd better start by telling me what's going on. Hang on, here's Cherry with our drinks. This'll warm your cockles.' When Cherry had left them, she got up and locked the door. 'Now, tell me the whole story.'

An hour later Eliza was being smuggled out of the hotel by Maggie and Didier. They went through the hot, steamy kitchens, past the cooks' curious eyes, past the sinks of washing-up and the kitchen-maids, through the yard past sacks of vegetables, to the stable where they found Didier's barouche. It was his pride and joy, Maggie told her, as she got into it. Chump, the tap-man, was waiting to drive her away.

'I'm sorry I can't come with you.'

'Mr Didier, you've been kindness itself. And I've got Maggie with me.'

'I'm sorry, Miss Eliza. I never want to see that man again on my premises.'

'No, Mr Didier, please serve him or he will know you're involved and then he'll know where to look.'

Soon they were driving quickly through the streets of Exeter and out on to the Tiverton Road. She understood why Didier was so proud of this vehicle: it went like the wind. Thankfully when they arrived at the village of Harcourt it was dark.

'Don't worry, no one will recognise our carriage. We never come this way. And this is the last place he'll think to look. Here it is. This is the doctor's. You wait here, Miss Eliza. I'll go first,' Maggie said.

Two minutes later she was back. 'He's not there. He's out at the school.'

'What school?'

'The one at Cheriton Speke.'

'I didn't know there was a school there.'

'Of course you don't. It opened when you were still living in Exeter. But I gave her your address. Didn't she call?'

'Who?'

Maggie hugged herself with pleasure. 'Then I'm not

going to say. But it'll be a lovely surprise.' And Eliza could not get another word out of her as to who they were visiting for the whole twenty-minute journey to the neighbouring village.

The house was in the centre of the main street, a fine Georgian building, which she thought she probably owned. Her father had bought most of the property in this area.

'Come on.' Maggie beckoned. 'You follow me.' The door opened to their knock. 'Hello, Rosamund,' said Maggie. 'Is she home? Good. Hide there, Miss Eliza.' She did as she was told. Maggie knocked on a double door in the hall. At a summons she opened it.

'Why, Maggie, what a lovely surprise!'

'But I've got a bigger one!' And Maggie, with a huge grin on her face, jumped to one side and shrieked with laughter.

Eliza and Fanny were speechless until Fanny collected herself. 'Darling Eliza,' she said, and held out her hands.

Eliza ran to her and they fell into each other's arms, both talking at the same time, both laughing, both crying, stepping back to look at each other.

'Oh, my dear, I've been so worried,' Fanny said.

'Dr Forbes, you're here too. How I've longed to see you,' Eliza exclaimed.

'Lady Alford!' He bowed over her hand.

She shuddered at the name.

'There's something else,' Fanny began.

'Not yet,' Jock ordered. 'I suggest we eat first – in fact, as your doctor, I prescribe food.' He looked pointedly at Fanny.

'I must say now I'm safe I do feel hungry.'

'Fanny, my love, let me assist you . . .'

In the sitting room Eliza turned to Maggie. 'Did I hear correctly, did I hear the doctor call her *my love*?'

'You did. They are engaged.'

'How perfect!'

*

Over dinner after Eliza had explained her circumstances, they discussed her plans. 'I'm far from penniless. I smuggled out some jewellery so I've money enough to go abroad, to France, I think, and I will live there. You can come and visit me, Fanny, and you too, of course, Maggie. In fact, I shall insist you come.'

'It's hardly fair, though, is it? You lose everything for doing nothing.' Fanny had seen the unshed tears sparkling in Eliza's eyes as she talked of her impending exile from Harcourt Barton.

'Harcourt is just a house.'

'Harcourt is you, Eliza.'

'I know. But needs must . . .'

'Jock?'

'Very well, Fanny, surprise number one.' He smiled indulgently at her.

There was much whispering and shuffling at the door. 'Close your eyes,' Fanny called out.

'I think she means you, Miss Eliza.'

Eliza covered her face with her hands as Fanny led Merry, her eyes covered too, into the room.

'You can both look now.'

If Eliza and Fanny's reunion had been emotional it was as nothing to what happened now. So excited and affected was Merry that Jock went to fetch the hartshorn. She went red, she went purple, then white and grey but finally the pink was restored.

'Well, whelks and whispers, whatever next?'

'You're just the same!' Eliza exclaimed, and Merry burst into tears that, it seemed, would never cease.

Maggie had left for Exeter, but Fanny, Jock, Merry and Eliza were still in the sitting room. 'There's something else, isn't there?' Eliza looked concerned. For two hours she had been happy – she had forgotten what happiness felt like. Now she sensed that all was not well and that the happiness was about to disappear again.

'You tell her, Merry.'

'No, it's best coming from you, Miss Chester.'

'Eliza, this will come as a big shock . . . but we have found your mother.'

There was no sound but the ticking of the clock on the mantelshelf. A coal hissed in the grate and Merry's stomach rumbled, but none of them was aware of it.

'My mother?'

'It's a long story and—'

'My mother?'

'Yes, my darling. But she's not well—'

'My mother? She was alive?'

'She's had a hard life and Jock says—'

'Who could have done that to me?' Her voice rose.

'Eliza. Listen. She's very ill—'

'Where is she?'

'Upstairs.'

'Upstairs! Here!' Eliza stood up. And then she sat down. And then she was on her feet again. 'Here?'

'Would you like to see her?'

'No.' She sat down. 'How can I?'

'She longs to see you.'

'Why, if she was alive, did she never contact me?'

'Eliza, she couldn't—'

'I don't believe it. It's not true. She could have, somehow, if she had really wanted to.'

'It was hard for her,' Fanny said ineffectually. This was the one question that had bothered her.

'I can understand that my father might have stopped her, held back letters she wrote to me, my grandmother, too, and my aunt. But there would have been someone surely . . . Merry, perhaps.'

'Once I took you to see her.'

'So that was why you were dismissed?'

'Yes, it was. And then . . . But never you mind.'

'Never mind what, Merry.'

'I don't want you more upset than you are. It's not nice.'

'She told you to go away?'

488

'Now, how did you know that? Yes, it's the truth, once I had lost my employment and was not in contact with the family. And then . . .' She started to say something but evidently changed her mind: her mouth shut tight, like an oyster.

'Poor Merry.' Eliza and Fanny spoke together.

'How deeply hurt you must have been.'

'Treacle and Toby jugs . . . I had to soldier on. But before then, over the years, I kept trying to get her to contact you through me.'

'Then why didn't she?'

Merry took a deep breath. 'I don't want to be saying this, and maybe I shouldn't. But, spotted Dick and spangles, she should know. Then, whatever happens, my Eliza won't be as hurt. Because . . . Eliza . . . your mother was a very selfish woman and thought only of herself,' Merry finished, in a mighty rush.

'Merry!' Fanny said in horror. It was the last thing she'd have expected Merry, of all people, to say.

'But you were loyal to her and helped her?' Eliza asked.

'I was and I did. But, you see, I loved her. I couldn't help myself. There are people like that, you know.' Fanny had to look down at her hands: she knew how true *that* was. 'I did things for her, stole for her, made sure she didn't starve. But she always refused to let me help over you, Miss Eliza.'

'But when you took me to see her . . . I remember her – she was all over me, sweet to me . . .'

'She liked a bit of drama, did your mother.'

'So why has she suddenly appeared, and now?'

'You've Miss Chester to thank for that.'

'You found her?'

'Yes. It seemed wrong to me that someone should be punished for so long. I am not clear about what she did, I'm aware it was wrong. But time should heal wounds, and people should try to forgive.'

Eliza stood up. 'I think I should like to meet her, but I don't want to go alone.'

'Lady Alford, I should warn you, she is gravely ill. I fear she has not long to live.'

'Thank you, Dr Forbes . . . and I'd be happier if you called me Eliza.'

Fanny volunteered to escort Eliza, for Merry was in tears again and said it had all been too much for her. It was then that Fanny noticed how flushed she was and wondered if the cider had caused her to speak her mind.

As they climbed the stairs Eliza could feel her heart racing. She was almost afraid, but of what? She paused at the turn of the stairs. She was entering the unknown. A few more steps and she would be with the woman she had grieved for, dreamt about, longed to be with all her life.

They entered the sick room and stood by the bed. Eliza forced herself to look down. 'Hello,' she said, to the shadow of a woman lying in the bed, her eyes sparkling like black jet, her complexion rosy red as if with health instead of death.

'Who are you?' A thin hand waved at her.

'I'm Eliza.'

'I don't know anyone of that name.'

'Then I'm Amelia. Your daughter.'

'No, you're not. You're not pretty enough to be my daughter.'

'As you wish,' Eliza said, turned from the bed, walked out of the room and down the stairs. Fanny flew after her.

'Eliza, I'm so sorry, she doesn't know what she's saying.'

'It's all right. I'm not insulted. I must look a mess anyway.' She smiled and brushed her hair off her forehead. 'For so many years I thought that to meet her was all I ever wanted. That then life would be perfect. But it has come too late. I had presumed that once I saw her I would love her but when I stood there, I felt nothing. Am I a monster? Unnatural?'

'Dearest, it's the shock. Perhaps I should have waited and discussed it with you. But, believe me, I did it with the best intentions.'

'Oh, Fanny, could you have done it in any other way? I think not. I know you thought of me.'

'Once you have had a good night's sleep you will feel differently.'

'I don't think I will.'

'She can stay here. Perhaps it would be better in the circumstances.'

'No, once I have found somewhere safe to live I shall send for her. She is my mother, after all, and so my responsibility. But, you see, I learnt to love my father, and he had been so hurt by her. His life was ruined and his affection for me too. He could not forgive her so how could I? And how could we know each other now? How could we love each other? Perhaps it would have been better if she had stayed a dream . . .'

The following morning Hedworth Alford had a visitor. He was not in the best of moods. He had been searching all night for his errant wife, with no success, had had too much to drink and now had a bad headache. 'Yes?' he snapped at the butler.

'Mr Joiner, milord.'

'You're early,' he said, when the lawyer had been shown in.

'I felt I should see you as soon as possible. I have heard the somewhat disturbing news. I thought I should warn you that I cannot cooperate with your schemes while your wife is missing. I have, you understand, to ensure my own security. As her trustee, I shall not be paying you any further monies.'

'Don't I give you enough commission on every transaction?'

'I was never happy with that arrangement. I regarded

it as a consideration, not a commission. I begin to find it irregular.'

'Balderdash! You *"begin"*! You knew all along what you were doing. You had nothing to lose. The letters were all above board.'

'She can't sign the letters that allow me to give her money to you if we can't find her.'

'But you didn't need the signature when she was in the asylum!'

'No, but Dr Talbot is now saying she was not insane, that he was about to discharge her and that he has no idea why she ran away as she did.'

'The deuce he did! And you came all this way to tell me that?'

'I never put certain things on paper, Lord Alford. It's safer that way.'

'I agree. So it would be a shame if I put down certain matters in writing, wouldn't you say?'

'What matters?' Joiner was looking uneasy.

'A little matter of clients' funds – your clients. Such a small town, Exeter, why I should think everyone of note knows everyone else, wouldn't you say?'

'What are you talking about?'

'Apart from Eliza – don't deny it. Since her father died a considerable sum has gone missing – but since you were so helpful, I decided to overlook it. But if I should just whisper in one person's ear . . .'

'You're blackmailing me.'

'Why, Joiner, I believe I am!'

'I can show the money went to you,' he blustered, not convincingly.

'But there's also the matter of dear Lady Willoughby's will . . .'

'I know nothing—'

'Oh, yes, you do. You are no more than an embezzler, as you know quite well.' He wagged a finger in admonition. 'And there's a matter I want to discuss with you about the Wickhams.'

Two days later, his mood had not improved. He had still not found Eliza. In the intervening time he had checked all the hotels in the area, the lodging-houses, even the hospitals, to no avail.

That afternoon he wondered if he should check those with whom she had had dealings here – her maid, that oaf Barnard and the simpering governess. He thought it would be a fool's errand, for he was certain she would not have been foolish enough to come to Harcourt. She would want to get as far away from him as possible.

He'd find the bitch if it was the last thing he did, and he took pleasure in contemplating what he would do to her when he did.

'Sir Charles Wickham, milord.'

He had not heard the butler come in and turned sharply. 'What the hell are you doing here?'

'What a charming welcome. A drink, perhaps? Have you had a bad day?' Charles grinned.

'Whisky?' Alford handed him a glass ungraciously. 'So, what can I do for you, Charles?'

'Disconcerting news, old chap. Minnie is a little . . . over-excited, shall we say? We had a letter from Joiner saying you had given instructions that her allowance was to be halved.'

'That's correct, Charles.'

'Might I enquire why?'

'Because I think you receive too much.'

'But Joiner is the trustee, not you.'

'Ah, yes, but I know one or two things about him so he does as I tell him.'

'Not exactly friendly of you, old chap. And what does Eliza have to say about this?'

'She does not know. I wouldn't consult her.'

'No, I don't suppose you would.'

Alford had to admire the way, in the midst of all this bad news, Charles retained his affability, and his delightful smile. 'You take it well.'

'Well, if you've made your mind up, shouting and yelling à la Minnie isn't going to do any good, is it?'

'Well put.'

'There is another matter. We've had a letter from Fanny Chester, making some quite unpleasant accusations about you.'

'Such as?'

'That you beat poor little Eliza and that she is locked up in a lunatic asylum. Presumably so that you can get your hands on her money.'

'I shall sue the miserable bitch for libel.'

'Not much point if she has nothing, is there? I've never heard of a rich governess, have you?'

'No, but it will frighten her witless. And it'll stop her interfering.'

'Even less point. She's harmless.'

'I note you call her Fanny. Know her, do you?'

'You could say so.'

'One of your conquests, is she? Is that why you're concerned?'

'Sadly, no. She's the one who got away.'

'So she's fairly amenable? Maybe I should try my luck there.' He was satisfied to see that at last he had made Charles react – just a small twitch of his mouth, but he'd noted it.

'You'd be wasting your time. She's too principled and, it has to be said, too good a woman for the likes of us. I've always regretted her. I think with her I was the closest I ever came to falling in love.'

'You astound me! I should think your wife would be interested in this information.'

'Don't bother yourself, Hedworth. My wife knows. Tell me, is it true about Eliza?'

'Eliza has had a breakdown, yes. She had a miscarriage, the doctor is concerned for her peace of mind. A temporary measure only.'

'Oh, come, Hedworth. It's me you're talking to. I can

quite see the temptation – I can see myself doing exactly the same.' He waved his glass in the air.

'You're drinking rather fast these days.'

'Needs must.' Charles grinned.

'Very well, you'll find out anyway. The trouble is our Eliza has run away. We can't find her. So, the golden egg has temporarily cracked.'

'That's inconvenient for you. Should I tell you where to look for her? If I did, would there be any chance of my wife's allowance being restored?'

Without reacting with so much as a blink, Hedworth poured him another large whisky. 'I am sure it would be automatic.'

'Then if you could write a note, saying as much, for me.'

'Now?'

'Now, or I shall have forgotten where she is.'

He was smiling as he waited while Alford did his bidding. He checked the note and slipped it into his pocket. 'Try our Miss Chester at Cheriton Speke. I'll bet you a thousand guineas that's where you'll find her.'

'She wouldn't come back here.'

'It's the obvious place to come – if you're intelligent, and she is. Go where you're least expected.'

Alford watched an unsteady Charles mount his horse. If he fell off, which looked likely, he'd come to no harm: he'd be protected by the amount of whisky he'd had. He arranged for his own horse to be saddled.

He was still not sure of his way around the estate, but the groom assured him that the fastest way to Cheriton Speke was through the Great Wood. It was rather pleasant to ride through it in the clear September sunshine, with just a hint of autumn in the air. It was well managed, he noticed with satisfaction, as his horse's hoofs scuffed through the fallen leaves. A wonderful time of year . . .

'Whoa!' he exclaimed, as his horse reared. A shadowy

figure moved from behind a tree. 'Charles! What the hell – what are you playing at? Fool!'

'Get down,' Charles ordered.

'Get out of my way.'

Charles grabbed at the horse's bridle. The animal reared again as he twisted the leather.

'Stop it, you bloody fool, you'll have me off.'

'That was my intention.'

'Very well.' Alford slid out of the saddle. 'What tomfoolery is this? What do you want? More money? Then you'll be disappointed.'

'To kill you,' Charles said quietly, so that at first Alford was not sure he had heard correctly. But when he saw the revolver, which Charles took from the pocket of his ulster, he started with fear. 'Didn't want to make a mistake and shoot the horse,' Charles said casually. 'I like them too much.'

'You're drunk. Is that thing loaded? Put it away before you do any damage.'

'But that is the point of the exercise. And I'm not drunk. I thought I'd fool you into thinking I was.' He cocked the gun. 'No, Alford, I want you dead.' The bang echoed through the woods as he shot Alford in the ankle. He crumpled to the leafy ground, screaming with pain. 'I want you dead for hurting my Eliza, for stealing from her . . .'

'You're mad!'

'Yes, with anger.' And, calmly, Charles shot him in the other foot and smiled as Alford writhed in agony. 'That's for Minnie, whom you ill used and, God help her, she loved you. And for threatening Fanny . . .'

'You'll hang,' Alford gasped.

'No, I won't, because you and I are going together. I want my last action in this life to be a decent one and to rid the world and my niece of parasites like you.'

Two more shots rang out. Two bodies lay in the glade. Two horses bolted.

*

At the funeral Eliza played her role as the woman who had lost her husband and her uncle in tragic circumstances. A terrible accident, it had been decided, though how that explained the damage to Alford she did not ask and she did not care. She could see no point in behaving in any other way. She was dignified and polite, if distant, and everyone commented on her composure.

What none of them knew was that she had looked down into her husband's coffin and had felt no emotion. She had expected to feel relief, if not joy. Instead there was a void.

The guests were puzzled that not one of them had been invited to the interment. 'Close family only,' they had been told. So none knew that the undertakers were waiting with a hearse and a team of four horses to transport the coffin of Lord Alford elsewhere. Eliza did not care where they took it: she had resolved merely that he was never to lie on her land.

'I loved him, you know.' Minnie was weeping uncontrollably. The two women were in the drawing room, the guests long gone.

'Which one?'

'My, but you are a cold one! Just like your father.'

'I will take that as a compliment. He was a man of principle.'

'Your uncle, of course. Life without Charles will be unbearable.'

'You surprise me. I presumed it was Hedworth you loved.'

'When you surprised us that day in Lancashire, he had coerced me, ravished me!'

'I don't believe you, Aunt Minnie. But don't concern yourself. You were welcome to him for I certainly didn't love him.'

'I don't know why he was so cruel to you. I begged him not to be.'

'Money, Aunt. He needed to break me to control me.

And speaking of which, I never want to see you again. I shall abide by my father's wishes. You may remain in the London house and I shall pay you your allowance, but I do not wish any further contact between us.' She stood up to leave the room.

Minnie sat, pale with shock. 'But we are of the same blood!'

'Unfortunately. Good day, Aunt.'

She could hear her aunt screaming abuse as she crossed the hall and climbed the stairs. She knocked on the door of her mother's room: she had thought it right that she should be brought there. Merry looked up from her chair and pressed her finger to her lips.

Every day when Eliza visited her mother she hoped her feelings might have changed, but they hadn't. She began to wonder if Alford had hurt her so deeply that now she was incapable of love. She stood by the bed. Nothing.

Not that her mother was an easy person to feel anything for: she was endlessly demanding and bad-tempered, so that no matter how sorry Eliza felt for her state of health, for the life she had evidently led, her patience was wearing thin.

Still, as she had told Fanny, Amelia was her mother, she would care for her to the end.

As always, Harcourt Barton had taken hold of her, and once more she felt secure and content. It was almost as if she had never known her husband, had never been married.

One of her first tasks had been to recall her old servants and give them their positions back. With her agent, Mr Colley, newly restored in his work, she had begun to work on plans for improving the estate. They had made a list of all the properties she owned and what should be done.

Eliza sat at the large rent table in the library, Mr Colley on one side of her, Mr Simpson from the bank on the other. One by one her tenants were ushered in by Densham. She knew now how the Queen must have felt when she first succeeded to the throne, as she explained their tenancies, what rent adjustments were to be made, and reassured them that nothing was to change.

There was no particular order so she had no idea when his name would be called. But finally she heard Densham call, 'Jerome Barnard.' She did not dare to look up as she heard him cross the room. 'Please sit down,' she said, still not looking at him.

'I'd rather stand.'

'Please don't . . .' Then she looked up at him and all the emotions she had feared she no longer possessed came flooding back. Nothing had changed. 'Really, it's uncomfortable for me to look up at you.' But wonderful, she thought.

He sat.

'Barton Farm, Mr Barnard.' She tried to sound businesslike.

'Yes.'

'I presume you would like to return to it. It is empty, I believe.'

'We should be pleased to.' He wasn't looking at her, she realised.

'We have decided that it would be best if water was pumped into the house. A new kitchen range.'

'That won't be necessary.' He sounded gruff.

'But I'm sure your mother would appreciate it.'

'I said to you once before, Miss Eliza, we don't need charity.'

'This is not charity, Mr Barnard. I'm improving all my properties – for my own benefit.'

'That is different.'

'I'm glad. That will be all, Mr Barnard.'

Why had she been so cold with him, so sharp? She watched sadly as he walked out of the room without a backward glance. She wanted to run after him, call him back, tell him she loved him, that nothing had changed.

But how could she? He did not care for her, that was obvious. He disliked her now and she was to blame. 'Who's next, Densham?' She had better get on – she'd begin to cry if she thought too long about him.

Eliza's life settled back into a routine with only two events of note. Fanny was married in the chapel at Harcourt Barton, and Eliza had enjoyed helping to organise the wedding and the reception afterwards. All the children from the school were there, and Florrie Paddington was the guest of honour. Eliza came quickly to admire her and insisted on hearing all her plans, then offered to finance her houses for the street women, which were to be called the Amelia Homes. She did not tell her mother – she doubted that she would appreciate it.

Two weeks later, Fanny told her that Miss Gilpin had eloped.

'Jonquil always said she would.'

'No, no, Eliza, it's *Primrose*. She's run away with the groom!'

Dear staid Primrose had surprised them all. And it was the one thing that made Eliza laugh, for she hadn't since her return. And all those who loved her relaxed.

Ruby pushed open the back door of Barton Farm. 'Anyone home? Mum?' she called. No one responded. She hoped she hadn't trudged over from her own cottage, in the rain, for nothing. She entered the kitchen. 'Why didn't you answer me?' she asked her brother, who was slumped at the table. He shrugged. 'Cat got your tongue?' Ruby crossed the kitchen to inspect the new cooking range, which had recently been installed. 'That's better. I reckon Mum's pleased with it. We're getting a new copper next week.' She took off her coat and hung on the back of a chair facing the range to dry. 'Where is she?'

'Who?'

'Mum, of course.'

'She's gone to the village with Alex and Ivy.'

'No!' Ruby sat down opposite him. 'I told her I'd try to get over today to help her whitewash the back bedroom.'

'She must have forgot.'

'Any tea in that pot?'

'I don't know.'

'For heaven's sake . . .' Irritated, she lifted the lid and peered inside. 'Stewed by the look of it. I'll make some more.' While she busied herself with the tea, she continued to chatter but, getting no response, she glanced at her brother. He sat like a rock, staring at the blank wall. 'Are you all right?'

'Yes.'

'You don't look it. You look as miserable as sin.'

'Sorry.'

'What is it? Tell me?' She poured the tea. 'Here.' She pushed a cup across to him. 'Honest, Jerome, you can't go on like this.'

'Like what?'

'Mum says you're not working, won't go out and won't talk to her either. She's worried.'

Jerome scowled.

'There's no point in pulling faces like that. We want to help. Is it because of Miss Eliza? Is it because she's back? Have you had a falling out?'

'No.'

'Then *what* is it? Talking will make it better.'

'Sometimes you sound such a fool!'

'I'm only trying to help.'

'Then don't!'

'All right, I won't!' She poured herself some tea, ladling far more sugar than normal into it. He'd have to stew – she'd things to do and couldn't spend all day—

'Trouble is . . .'

'Yes?' She was holding her breath, waiting for him to continue.

'Trouble is I'm afraid of seeing her when I'm out and about. What if I bumped into her?'

'You'd say, "Hello, Miss Eliza," just like everyone else.'

'But it wouldn't be that easy . . . I love her, Ruby. I can't stop loving her and I don't know what to do.'

'Try telling her.'

'What good would that do?'

'She might like to hear you say it.'

'She told me she didn't love me.'

'She was *made* to tell you that! I *told* you.'

'How can I be sure?'

'If you don't ask you'll never know.'

'But even if I did, what good would it do? There's nothing to be done. I've been thinking I'd be better off moving away – Mother could get help on the farm. I could arrange that for her.'

'Move away and ruin two lives for the sake of your stupid pride?'

'Pride's got nothing to do with it.'

'It has *everything* to do with it. Because she's who she is and rich – even if she wants you – you're afraid of what people will say. That's what's stopping you.'

'I'm not!'

'I don't believe you. In a way you're right – I can imagine the gossip in the pub, saying you're after her money, and who does Jerome Barnard think he is?'

'I don't care what folks say of me.' He sat upright for the first time since she'd entered the room.

'Then what's stopping you talking to her?'

'She was very cold when I went to the tenants' meeting, very grand.'

'And how friendly were you?'

'I was polite.'

'I heard you were as stiff as a poker, clod that you are.' She smiled at him but he did not respond.

'But what if she turned me down, Ruby?'

'So says the man who has no pride! You'd weather it, like you've done many things in your life.'

'No, it's no good.' He slumped back in his chair. 'She's not for the likes of me. It wouldn't be right. I can give her nothing. I might make her unhappy, she might come to regret being with me.'

Ruby leant forward. 'Rubbish. Think, Jerome. You can offer her so much. You're a good, honest man. A kind one. You're sensitive and considerate and you can give her all the love you have in your soul.'

'No, it wouldn't be right . . .' he repeated.

'Then don't, you lumpen muffin, you! And I've better things to do then waste the day listening to you whining.'

In the evenings, if it wasn't raining, she liked to go for walks on her own. Sometimes Bumble condescended to come with her, sometimes not. She enjoyed a short spell away from the house, for it and the estate took so much of her time. She spent her days with ledgers and figures, and Mr Bramble, her new lawyer – Joiner had simply disappeared on the day of the 'accident'.

The walk never varied. She went right round the lake, which was two miles. She was surprised she didn't mind the lake after what had happened there, but it felt as if Hedworth had never been there. It was doubtful, though, that she would ever go into the Great Wood again.

Through the knot garden, down by the lake and at the path to Barton Farm she always paused, looked along the path and remembered other days and other innocence.

That evening her heart leapt for someone was there in the shadows. She called out in alarm.

'I'm sorry if I startled you. I didn't mean . . .'

'Jerome? Is it you?'

'I knew you came this way each evening.'

'It's refreshing.' She didn't know what else to say.

'Perhaps I should go.'

'No, stay. You wanted to see me?'

They stood on the path and looked at each other, neither knowing what to say, how to react.

'Jerome—'

'Eliza—' They spoke in unison.

'You first.'

'Eliza. Forgive me.'

'What is there to forgive?'

'For making you jump. I don't know if I should tell you this but I watch you every night – just to make sure you're safe, you understand.'

'But you didn't let me know?'

'I wasn't sure you'd want to know.'

'I would have ... Jerome, why have you stayed away?'

'I couldn't come. I couldn't be a hypocrite and say I'm sorry and give you my condolences ...'

'There is nothing to be consoled about.'

'Then ...' He looked at her long and hard, as if marshalling his thoughts or perhaps his courage. 'I've been a fool, Eliza.'

'Me too.'

'Never. You were always thinking of others. It's my pride.'

'I admire your pride.'

'Is it too late? Should I be saying this?' He looked down at his feet, his cap in his hand. She longed to put out her hand and touch him, hold him. The silence seemed to go on for ever. 'But I was wondering, Eliza, if you would take it amiss if I called on you.'

She looked at him, a sweet smile playing about her lips. 'I can't think of anything I would like more, Jerome.' Shyly, she held out her hand and, equally shyly, he took it.

All Orion/Phoenix titles are available at your local bookshop or from the following address:

Mail Order Department
Littlehampton Book Services
FREEPOST BR535
Worthing, West Sussex, BN13 3BR
telephone 01903 828503, *facsimile* 91903 828802
e-mail MailOrders@lbsltd.co.uk
(Please ensure that you include full postal address details)

Payment can be made either by credit/debit card (Visa, Mastercard, Access and Switch accepted) or by sending a £ Sterling cheque or postal order made payable to *Littlehampton Book Services*.
DO NOT SEND CASH OR CURRENCY.

Please add the following to cover postage and packing

UK and BFPO:
£1.50 for the first book, and 50p for each additional book to a maximum of £3.50

Overseas and Eire:
£2.50 for the first book plus £1.00 for the second book and 50p for each additional book ordered

---

BLOCK CAPITALS PLEASE

name of cardholder ....

address of cardholder ....

postcode ....

delivery address
(if different from cardholder)
....
....
....

postcode ....

☐ I enclose my remittance for £............................

☐ please debit my Mastercard/Visa/Access/Switch (delete as appropriate)

card number ☐☐☐☐☐☐☐☐☐☐☐☐☐☐☐☐☐☐

expiry date ☐☐☐☐   Switch issue no. ☐☐

signature ....

prices and availability are subject to change without notice